ALSO BY LINDA NAGATA

THE RED: FIRST LIGHT

THE TRIALS

THE RED

TRILOGY

BOOK THREE
GOING DARK

LINDA NAGATA

SAGA PRESS

LONDON SYDNEY **NEW YORK** TORONTO NEW DELHI

SAGA PRESS
AN IMPRINT OF SIMON & SCHUSTER, INC.

1230 AVENUE OF THE AMERICAS, NEW YORK, NEW YORK 10020

SAGA PRESS and colophon are trademarks of Simon & Schuster, Inc.
For information about special discounts for bulk purchases, please contact Simon & Schuster Special Sales at 1-866-506-1949 or business@simonandschuster.com.
The Simon & Schuster Speakers Bureau can bring authors to your live event. For more information or to book an event, contact the Simon & Schuster Speakers Bureau at 1-866-248-3049 or visit our website at www.simonspeakers.com.
Also available in a Saga Press paperback edition
The text for this book is set in Adobe Garamond Pro.
Manufactured in the United States of America
First Edition
2 4 6 8 10 9 7 5 3 1
CIP data is available from the Library of Congress.
ISBN 978-1-4814-4659-4 (hardcover)
ISBN 978-1-4814-4097-4 (mass market pbk)
ISBN 978-1-4814-4098-1 (eBook)

GOING DARK

AFTERLIFE

"WE ARE ENGAGED IN A NONLINEAR WAR. THAT MEANS there are no 'sides.' There are no real allies, no fixed enemies, no certain battlefield. Conflict occurs across financial, communications, propaganda, terroristic, and military channels in a continuously shifting matrix that can destroy a culture, crash an economy, or ignite combat depending on the weight and direction of competing interests—"

"Including *our* interests," Lieutenant Logan interjects, like this is some kind of valid counterpoint to my argument.

It's not.

"Including our interests," I acknowledge. "Whatever the fuck those are."

I'm James Shelley, captain of ETM Strike Squad 7-1—a linked combat squad that doesn't exist in any official US Army record. Ray Logan is my lieutenant. Our low-voiced conversation is taking place a few steps away from the six soldiers assigned to ETM 7-1.

We occupy a temporary berth set up in the torpedo room of a US Navy *Virginia*-class fast-attack submarine that is presently passing beneath the Arctic Ocean's winter ice pack. The remainder of the squad is asleep in tempo-rary bunks, stacked two high and set up side by side in a long row between the green tubes of racked torpedoes. The squad is mostly out of sight, at rest in the lower bunks, with their gear stored in good order on top. Only me and Logan are up, conferencing at one end of a narrow passage that runs between the foot of the bunks and one of the torpedo racks.

"The point," I go on, "is that the identities of the good guys and bad guys *will* change; they have to change, as circumstances change. So you never know who the enemy will be next year, or in the next engagement."

Ray Logan is twenty-four, making him a year younger than me. At five-ten, he's not a tall man, but his lean build and chiseled Caucasian features could have gotten him cast as an extra if he'd tried Hollywood instead of the army. He's a hell of a fighter who likes to be at the front of any assault, so it's almost surreal to see him cast an uneasy glance over his shoulder, as if he's worried about someone in the squad listening in. I follow his gaze, but all I see is Carl Escamilla's big, ugly bare foot sticking out from the last bunk.

Logan lowers his voice even further. "Jesus, Shelley, I just never thought the fucking Canadians would turn out to be the bad guys. I mean, my *mom* is Canadian."

"Nonlinear war," I remind him. "Shifting alliances. The target is Canadian. If it makes you feel any better, what's going on within the target might have nothing to do with the Canadian government or even a Canadian corporation."

Our present mission is codenamed Palehorse Keep, and like every mission we undertake, it's been assigned to us by the Red. Our target is an exploratory oil-drilling plat-form named *Deep Winter Sigil*. It's overwintering in con-tested marine territory that Canada wants to claim for its own—but we're not out to referee a territorial dispute. The intelligence we've received indicates something unusual is going on in laboratories aboard the platform, evidenced by security so tight, even the Red can't penetrate it.

When a secret is that well kept, we assume it's dangerous, possibly an existential threat.

So our mission is to approach in stealth, kick in the doors, take command of the facility, and determine what is being hidden there. We call this kind of assignment a look-and-see mission. We've done two others in recent months. Both turned out to be illicit drug labs, which is not something we'd ordinarily go after, but that's the risk of a look-and-see.

I think we're being sent out repeatedly because the Red is searching for a specific operation. What that operation might be, I don't know. We're told to go look, and until we do, we don't know what we'll find. It could be anything, from an insurmountable defense to an innocent operation.

Logan gets a sour look. Like me—like all of us—he used to be regular army. Nine months ago he was part of a US training force in Bolivia. His CO ordered the squad to accompany a local unit on an interdiction, which is just a kind of look-and-see. Logan had a bad feeling; he argued the intelligence was faulty. He was right. When the local unit kicked in the door, there were kids inside; no bad guys. They lit up the place anyway.

"I fucking hate look-and-see missions," he says with bitter sincerity.

I want to tell him I hate them too, but what I say instead is, "I'm going to wake the squad. Be ready to take them through the mission plan one more time before we go."

Our chain of command is simple. We have officers because someone has to be in charge, but we don't use designated ranks among our regular soldiers. It isn't necessary. None of them are here for the pay or the promotional opportunities.

My focus shifts, picking out a half-seen, translucent icon floating at the bottom of my field of view. It's the command node for gen-com. My attention causes it to brighten, making it stand out from the icons around it— all of them part of the display projected by the optical overlay that I wear like contact lenses in my eyes.

The icon offers me a menu but I ignore it, muttering, "Send a wakeup call." My command initiates a signal that's relayed point to point to my soldiers.

Every soldier in my LCS has an ocular overlay like mine, and every one of us also has a skullnet: a mesh of fine wires implanted beneath the scalp that monitors and regulates brain activity. Each overlay receives my command and relays it to the soldier's skullnet; the simple AI that oversees the skullnet responds, triggering a waking routine.

There is no moment of transition, no confusion, no sluggishness. My soldiers awaken simultaneously, with machine precision. Some stretch, some cough, but within ten seconds every one of them appears—sitting at the end of the bunks or standing in the passage—but all looking at me with an alert gaze, eager to learn our status.

Logan takes over. "Piss and wash up. You've got five minutes, and then we're going to review roles and rules one more time."

All of my soldiers in ETM 7-1 were officially "killed in action" or "died of wounds," but death grants them no reprieve from the endless training and mission prep inherent to the army, because their best chance of surviving a mission is to understand it all the way down to their bones.

Seventy minutes later, the sub's commander calls down from the control room to let us know we are ten minutes from our designated drop.

"Holiday's over!" Logan barks. "And goddamn about time. Suit up!"

"Hoo-yah!" Alex Tran proclaims, exchanging a fist bump with Thomas Dunahee.

And then everyone moves at once. Our packs, our weapons, and our equipment are all ready. The only prep work remaining is to get into our thermal gear.

Crammed shoulder to shoulder in the tight passage, we wriggle into thermal skins, pulling them on over the silky, high-tech shorts and T-shirts that are our standard-issue under-gear.

The skins are 1.5 centimeters of supple insulation that will ensure we don't die of hypothermia—although we might die of heat exhaustion if our exit from the sub is delayed.

I wear full leggings like everyone else, pulling them on over my prosthetic legs. The robot legs don't need to be warm to work, but they are a heat sink. If I don't insulate, they'll drain the warmth from my body.

A gray, tight-fitting thermal hood with a full-face mask goes on next. I fit it carefully. There won't be a chance to adjust it after we launch, so I make sure it's comfortable, and that it's positioned so it won't obscure my vision or obstruct my breathing.

Already I'm starting to sweat, but I add another layer: an insulated combat uniform printed in gray-white arctic camo. It's identical to the uniform I wore on the First Light mission, lacking insignia or identifying marks, making no claim that we are part of the United States military— because we are not part of it. We only pretend to be.

It helps in getting around.

I pull on my boots, and then strap on a thigh holster holding a 9-millimeter SIG Sauer. A pair of thin shooting gloves, heated with embedded wires, protects my hands.

My armored vest goes on last, and then I cast my gaze back along the line.

Boots stomp the deck as the squad finishes their prep. Hunched shoulders straighten. Gray-hooded heads turn toward me. Only their eyes are visible, pleading to be released into the cold.

"Sweet Jesus," Dunahee mutters. "Another minute in this heat and I'm going to puke."

He's crammed into the middle of the passage. Behind him is Fadul, who has zero tolerance for griping. "Puke on me and I'll stuff you under the ice," she advises him in her quiet, dangerous tone.

"Fadul, you're supposed to terrify the enemy," I remind her as I get my pack off the top bunk closest to me. "Not your brothers and sisters in arms."

Her lips quirk in a ghost smile as she catches my eye. "I can do both, Captain Shelley."

Dunahee mutters, "That's for damn sure."

Pia Fadul is tall and lean, with black hair shaved to a stubble and wide, dark eyes. After the Coma Day nuclear strike, her unit, stationed in the Sahel, went without resupply or reinforcements for nine days, burning up their ammunition defending against an all-out assault. Her post was eventually overrun by a vengeful insurgent army. I've seen some of the video recorded by her helmet cam. Not something you'd want to see twice. There were no survivors. Officially, not even Fadul.

Thomas Dunahee is Fadul's physical opposite: short, stocky, and fair-haired. He's a college graduate who was working in banking when Coma Day took down the economy, along with his parents and sisters who lived in Seattle. He enlisted as soon as the recruiter's office reopened. Fourteen months later, he was recruited by the Red.

"Dunahee, you're on drone duty. Logan, pass him the angel."

"Yes, sir."

The angel we brought with us is a different model than the one I used when I was regular army. It's smaller, with less range, and no satellite uplink capabilities. But with its wings folded against the blade of its fuselage, it's easy to carry on stealth missions. Logan retrieves it from an upper bunk and hands it off to Julian, who's behind him. "Pass this down."

Bradley Julian is a Somali veteran. Tall and slender, with deep-black skin and dark eyes, he's our quiet intellectual who tends to overthink things. Right now, he's looking anxious behind his mask—something Tran notices when Julian turns to hand off the angel.

"Shit, Julian," Tran says. "You're not worried, are you?" Tran's white teeth flash in a predatory grin as he takes the folded drone. "We got no need to worry. With the Red on our side, we are fucking superheroes. No way we can lose."

"What the *fuck* did you just say?" I ask him.

The whole line freezes.

Tran looks at me, confused, concerned, as he realizes he's in deep shit.

"Do you imagine yourself to be a superhero, Tran?"

"It was only a joke, Captain Shelley. I was joking with Julian."

Alex Tran is skinny and dark-skinned, his African ancestry dominant over the Vietnamese. He's got three years of combat experience in the regular army, a bona fide war hero whose vigilance saved the lives of every soldier in his platoon when a suicide bomber targeted their operation in the Sahel. But in our outfit Tran is a rookie, the newest recruit to sign on for ETM. That's *Existential Threat Management* if anyone bothers to ask, which they

don't, because everything that concerns our identities or
our activities is classified. This mission is Tran's first as part
of Strike Squad 7-1. He's still learning to live in our peculiar,
parallel world, part of a ghost squad so secret even the army
doesn't know we exist.

Tran's gaze shifts uncertainly to Julian, before returning
to me. "Sir—"

"*Never* fucking trust the Red," I warn him.

No one moves, no one speaks. All eyes are on me, everyone aware that the outcome of this confrontation will
directly affect the mission—and I am furious. At Tran, at
myself. Five minutes from our designated drop is a hell of
a time to discover that I have failed to instill in my new
recruit a clear picture of our situation.

"Operating on the wrong assumptions will get you killed
fast, Tran. Just because the Red sent us here, because it
assigned us this mission, that does not mean it's on our
side or that it shares our interests. That does not mean it
will aid us." I hesitate. I don't say it aloud, but I've started
to think the Red might not be a single entity, that instead it
has multiple aspects, not all of them in sync. I'm speaking
to myself as much as to Tran when I say, "We are on our
own. Assume otherwise, and you put us all at risk."

This lecture should induce a simple "yes, sir" and a
humble apology, but what I get is an argument.

"Sir, I *do* understand. We operate on our own. We don't
expect help. We don't ask for it. But we wouldn't be here,
we wouldn't be able to operate at all, without oversight
from the Red."

One thing I've noticed in the eighteen months since I
fell back to Earth: It's not the recruits with a religious background who have a hard time wrapping their heads around
the limited nature of the Red. "You're a fan of comics, aren't
you, Tran? Of superhero movies?"

He wants to deny it. I see it in the shift of his eyes. But lies don't work in our company because we all run FaceValue, an emotional analysis app that uses tone and facial expression to interpret mood and separate truth from lies. Tran remembers this and concedes the truth. "Yes, sir. I am a fan."

"I thought so. From now on, you will forget every depiction you've ever seen of all-powerful, world-eating AIs. We are not operating within comic book rules. The Red is not infallible. It is not all-knowing. Both its reach and its ability to react are limited. Its concern for our welfare is limited—*never* forget that—and it is not on the side of the angels which means that neither are we. We all have our reasons for being here, Tran. Just make sure your reasons are grounded in reality. We are not superheroes. We are not God's angels armed with flaming swords. We are just soldiers."

Tran is still rebellious. "But sir, LT told me that on your last mission—"

"That the Red came through for us?" I spare a brief glare for Logan, who looks at me, teeth gritted, eyes angry behind his mask. "It happens," I affirm. "We *do not* count on it. We do not expect assistance—because most of the time we won't get it. Think about it. If the Red could control the situation, why send us in at all?"

Tran does as ordered, his brows knitting as he puzzles over my question. "You're saying if we get into trouble, we have to get ourselves out."

"Can you operate under that knowledge? Under the certain knowledge that if we fuck up, no one—nothing—is going to save us? Because if you cannot, I invite you to stay behind."

Tran is shocked at my offer. Insulted. Infused with an anger that stiffens his spine so that I swear he grows a quarter inch taller. "No, *sir*. I am part of this squad. Maybe I don't understand yet how the whole thing works, but we are fighting against fucking Armageddon. I know that much. I don't give a shit if we're on our own or not. I intend to be part of ETM for the duration."

I nod, relax my shoulders, lower my voice. "That's good to know. Now pass that fucking drone to Dunahee and make sure you are organized and ready to go."

"We are two minutes behind schedule," Logan warns.

I nod. "Helmets on."

We become anonymous behind our opaque-black, full-face visors. Tiny fans kick on, but my thermal hood negates any cooling effect. I retrieve my M-CL1a HITR from my bunk and then check the icons lined up at the bottom of my visor's display, one for every soldier in my squad: Logan, Roman, Fadul, Escamilla, Dunahee, Julian, and Tran. All of them green—nominal. I want to see them green when this mission is done.

Logan gets his own weapon and then squeezes past me to the front of the line, hauling his folded exoskeleton with him. Our dead sisters are too bulky to wear in the sub's narrow passages, so we'll rig up outside—if heat stroke doesn't kill us first. We need to move out.

Logan is standing ready beside the torpedo room door. "Initiate the operation, Lieutenant."

"Roger that, Captain Shelley."

He cautiously opens the door into the passage beyond and steps out. I'm right behind him, my dead sister in one hand and my weapon in the other. Our sudden appearance startles two sailors. They disappear up a ladder into the control room, leaving us to make our own way through the sub.

We move quickly.

A navy lieutenant dressed in Arctic gear waits for us at

the foot of the ladder that climbs to the hatch. "Cameras and sensors pick up nothing outside," she informs us, her restless gaze shifting from one faceless visor to the next. "Not even a polar bear."

"Conditions?" I ask her.

She turns to me in relief. Mine is a familiar voice, one she's heard on a popular show that played a couple of years ago called *Linked Combat Squad*. She knows who I am; she might have figured out names for all of us. It doesn't matter. At this point in the voyage, the crew will have developed a shared story explaining how we are a black-ops operation staffed by soldiers all reported to be dead—patriots, every one of us—and nearly everything about the story they tell one another will be true.

"Conditions are as forecast, sir. The ice pack at this location is estimated at thirteen centimeters, enough to support your weight, with gear. Temperature is minus thirty-nine degrees Fahrenheit, wind speed between forty-six and fifty knots, heavily overcast, with wind-driven snow flurries."

We are not going to be hot much longer.

I feel the deck tilt and gently rock under me, then a shattering crackle as we break through the crust.

My helmet picks up and enhances the faint voice of the sub's commander speaking to the lieutenant through her headset as he gives her clearance to open the hatch. She scrambles up the ladder, works the mechanism, and then shoves the hatch open, bracing it against the wind before sliding back down. I glance up at a circle as black as our visors. It is 1400 UTC. The date is December 23. The sun won't look on this latitude again for months to come, and at this moment in the long winter night, storm clouds have smothered even the starlight.

I focus my mind on a well-rehearsed command: *Move out*. My skullnet is trained to recognize neural patterns associated with common words and commands. It picks up the thought, translating it to a flat, synthesized version of my voice so that I hear myself say the words over gencom. "Move out."

Lieutenant Logan takes the lead. Leaving the folded frame of his dead sister, he is first up the ladder. Escamilla follows. Dunahee and Tran work together to hand up the dead sisters and then a telescoping gangplank provided by the navy lieutenant. They follow the gear out to the hull. Julian, Roman, and Fadul go after them. I'm next, with the navy lieutenant coming last.

The wind hits with vicious force as I reach the top of the ladder. It's like a negative pressure, emptying my lungs. I have to force myself to breathe as the ferocious cold ignites a searing pain in my throat.

My helmet adjusts faster than I do. My visor shifts to night vision, while the audio system filters out the wind's roar, allowing me to hear the crunch of boots and a glassy clinking as the sub drifts against shards of broken ice.

I climb out, joining my squad on the narrow dorsal hull. A few steps away, the fin-shaped sail, studded with masts housing communications and surveillance systems, stands tall against a stormy sky.

My own communications system wakes up. The satellite relay in my pack links automatically to our secure channel and a new icon flares on my display. "Confirm contact established," the rich, soft-edged voice of my commanding officer instructs. Major William Kanoa used to be squad CO, but our physician refused to recertify him for field duty after a spinal injury. Now he's my remote handler.

"Contact confirmed," I respond as I watch Logan and Escamilla deploy the gangplank—a twenty-centimeter-wide bridge to the unbroken floe. "We are on schedule and transitioning to the ice." But then, because missions sometimes get scrubbed at the last minute, I ask, "We holding steady with the mission plan?"

"Roger that. *Sigil* remains the target. We need to know what's going on inside its labs—"

I flinch hard as the hatch bangs shut behind me. PTSD. My heart rate spikes and I have to fight the urge to swing around with my HITR raised and ready to fire. I don't want to scare the navy lieutenant as she steps past me to check the gangplank.

In the corner of my vision, an icon brightens. It's an intricate red mesh glowing against a black circle—my skullnet icon—its glow indicating a burst of activity in the mesh of wires in my head, signals sent to my brain to trigger neurochemicals that push me back toward a calm emotional center.

I rarely see the skullnet icon anymore and it irritates me to see it now. I don't need a cerebral nanny always watching over me anymore. I've learned to handle my own emotions.

After a second, it goes away.

"There is a problem," Kanoa says. His tone has changed; it's become softer, more soothing. That tells me he noticed my emotional spike, and that irritates me too.

"What problem?" I ask as Fadul moves first across the bridge.

"Oscar-1 is behind schedule. Fuel issues. There's going to be a delay in your extraction."

Oscar-1 is Jason Okamoto, an ex–air force pilot who has pulled us out of a couple of nasty situations. He's scheduled to pick us up in ETM 7-1's little nine-passenger tiltrotor when we're ready to withdraw.

"How far behind schedule?" I ask. Fadul reaches solid ice without incident. She unhooks from her safety line. Logan hooks the other end to one of the dead sisters. "Is he out of the game?"

"Undetermined, but we're looking at alternate means if he can't get through."

"Roger that."

I don't like it, but extraction was always going to be the hardest part of Palehorse Keep, and I trust Kanoa to find a way to get us out.

I watch the folded dead sister slide down the gangplank, secured between two lines. When it's safely across, Logan hauls the lines back and with the navy lieutenant's help, he sets up to send another.

While they get our gear transferred, I make a slow turn, letting my helmet cams record a night vision perspective of the surrounding ice field.

We are four hundred kilometers north of Canada's Ellesmere Island and only three hundred seventy kilometers from the North Pole. Immediately around us, green-tinted flurries of wind-driven snow skitter across a channel of smooth ice. But half a klick out, the floe becomes a badland of broken blocks heaved up and tumbled together.

Kanoa says, "The ice has been shifting. I'm sending a revised map."

"Roger that. Any additional intelligence on the target?"

"Negative. No electronic traffic."

Kanoa saved my life the night I returned to Earth. He pulled me out of the cold water of the Pacific and when I stopped shivering, he offered me a chance to make a difference, to be part of the ETM strike force, a ghost unit that executes missions determined by the Red. Sometimes it's hard to forgive him for that—for giving me that choice.

The dead sisters have all been moved to the ice. The squad crosses next, each soldier hooking up to the safety lines before transiting the bobbing gangplank. By the time I cross, the surface has refrozen. It looks solid, though I

know it's not. I walk quickly but carefully across the little
bridge, relying on the lieutenant to pull me out if I slip.

I don't slip.

I reach the floe and unhook. The safety line snakes back,
and then the lieutenant works to pull back the gangplank,
one segment at a time. Around me, backpacks drop to the
ice, and the dead sisters get unfolded.

I expand the new map in my visor's display. It shows
our target to the south-southeast, only five kilometers away.
The sub's sensors picked up no sign of enemy forces close
at hand, but we are not safe. Even in this wind, a skilled
sniper could hit us from five hundred meters out. Maybe
farther. As I turn my head, the gale claws past the edge of
my helmet in a skin-crawling key.

"Dunahee! Get the angel in the air." I need to see farther.
I need a real-time view of what's out there. "And make goddamn sure you keep the angel on a tether."

"Roger that, sir!"

Dunahee is already halfway into his rig, an operation
made faster by Roman, who is helping him secure the
cinches.

Rosanna Roman is our designated marksman. She's
as tall as Fadul but more willowy. Behind her visor, her
eagle eyes are blue, her hair light brown. On Coma Day,
Roman's unit was on the Korean Peninsula, hunkered
down at ground zero under the artillery barrage of a flash
war that the diplomats later excused as a "miscommuni-
cation"—meaning that the United States wasn't quite as
dead as some had hoped. Kanoa believes the incident was
only a few minutes from going nuclear when a cease-fire
was achieved four point five hours after the start of hostilities. That was too late for Roman. She spent the next seven
months in a hospital in Honolulu, where she eventually
"died" of her injuries.

I unfold my dead sister. The wind nearly blows it over. Escamilla is already rigged, so he comes over and holds it upright for me as I step onto the footplates. "First time I've ever rigged up in a gale," I tell him.

"Yeah, always a new thrill with this job."

Carl Escamilla is tall and broad-shouldered. There's no softness at all in his sharp-featured face; there isn't any in his outlook. He's seen too much. He was a nine-year combat veteran recently home from the Sahel when the nukes went off. He got put on emergency duty, assigned to guard a military facility when riots erupted in the surrounding community. Families panicked. I've heard his former CO is up on charges for a massacre in which twenty-seven civilians who'd been seeking refuge behind the wire were gunned down.

Like all of us, he's driven by what he's seen, what he's done. The cold fact is our world is seriously fucked up. Maybe ETM can help unwind some of that. Maybe if we do, the death, the suffering we've witnessed might be made worthwhile.

But who the hell knows?

With Escamilla helping, I cinch the titanium struts to my legs and then my arms. I swing my pack onto the back frame. My HITR I carry in my hands. "You're clear," he says.

There is a soft, ritualized chatter over gen-com as the squad runs through the standard safety checks, confirming that each rig is properly cinched, with full power. I leave Logan to supervise, while I join Dunahee and Roman.

They're crouched on the ice, Roman helping to hold the blade-shaped fuselage of the angel against the tearing wind, while Dunahee pulls a titanium clip from the angel's belly compartment. A tendril of synthetic, woven spider silk pays out behind the clip; another half-kilometer is wound around a spindle in the angel's belly. Dunahee hooks the clip to a loop on his chest armor. When it's secure, Roman unfolds the angel's narrow wings. Their upswept winglets are separated by a one-meter span.

I watch my display as the angel's AI links in, its icon showing green, nominal. "Angel online," I tell Kanoa.

"Confirmed. Angel online."

A menu slides open in response to my gaze. I call up the angel's video feed and get a night vision perspective of the trampled snow around Fadul's pack. "Angel eyes open."

"Confirmed."

Dunahee takes the angel from Roman. I step out of the way as he angles the nose upward. "Launching drone," he says over gen-com.

"Roger that."

He lets the gale seize it. The angel shoots away, the thread of spider silk paying out behind it—or at least I hope it is. The thread is so fine that even with night vision I can't see it against the ice.

Within seconds, I can't see the angel either. It's lost to my sight against the low, fast-running clouds. But its eyes are open, looking down on the tossed and broken ice floes, and looking ahead to our destination.

"And there it is," Kanoa says.

Deep Winter Sigil, rigged with high-efficiency lights, is kept lit like a downtown skyscraper on New Year's Eve. What the angel sees are the reflections cast by those lights against the racing clouds.

The controversial platform was towed into place last summer when the ice was in retreat. Its presence is an opening shot in a still-incubating territorial war.

Sigil is a spar platform. It floats on the ocean's surface, its superstructure rising above a huge, hollow cylinder that extends seven hundred feet into the deep to keep the platform stabilized. Underwater cables, attached to the bottom of the cylinder, drop down another three thousand feet to an oceanic ridge, anchoring *Sigil* even against the pressure of the ice—so far, anyway.

Whether there's oil in that ridge, no one really knows. Initial drilling on the first exploratory well stopped at the onset of winter. But a small crew of technicians and scientists remained aboard—until mid-October when the staff of technicians was reduced by half, electronic communications went on lockdown, and a private security company was hired to protect the facility and the staff, ostensibly from potential piracy and sabotage.

If our intelligence is accurate, the drilling platform now hosts a force of ten experienced mercenaries. Maybe those mercs are the good guys in this coming conflict and maybe we're the bad guys. Maybe the scientists aboard *Deep Winter Sigil* really are there to study the dynamics of the polar ice pack and the winter habits of passing polar bears.

But I fucking doubt it.

We wait while the angel's tether spins out. I still can't see the line of spider silk, but I can hear it hum with tension. The hum shifts in tone as the angel initiates a turn across the wind, obeying a standard instruction set that directs it to fly in a quartering pattern that will let it survey a wide swath of terrain. But that's not going to work in this weather.

Sigil can generate energy to keep the lights on, but our own power supplies are time-limited. The power packs that supply our dead sisters can hold out for twelve to fourteen hours of use; the angel has a shorter lifespan.

"Kanoa, the angel doesn't have the power reserves to sustain a standard search pattern against this wind."

"Roger that. Canceling the algorithm. I'll try to reinitiate the standard search pattern as you approach the
target."

Until then, we'll have only a narrow view of the terrain
ahead, and we're lucky to have that. If the wind was blowing in the opposite direction, the angel would be blown
behind us, instead of ahead.

Dunahee grunts and staggers a step as the angel hits the
end of its tether.

"You doing okay, Dunahee?" I ask over gen-com.

"Roger that, sir."

It's a shit assignment to be tethered to the angel, but in
this wind the angel would be gone over the horizon and
useless to us in minutes if it wasn't tied down.

My gaze sweeps the squad icons. All remain green. We
should be ready. I confirm it with my lieutenant. "Logan,
status?"

"Squad is rigged and ready, Captain Shelley."

That's it, then.

I turn to the sub. The lieutenant is no longer in sight.
The hatch is closed. I hold my right arm straight out from
my shoulder and give a thumbs-up. Seconds later, the sub
drops away beneath the ice, and we are on our own.

"Logan, I want Dunahee on point so no one gets tangled
in the tether."

"Roger that, Captain."

"Dunahee, you should see a designated path displayed
on your visor."

"I've got it, sir."

The path is a blue line drawn on the map, but it's also
projected on our heads-up displays, where it looks like a
faintly luminous trail laid out on the ice. "Follow it, but
use your judgment. The angel will red-alert if it detects
the thermal signature of thin ice or open water, but angel

sight is going to be limited, so proceed with caution. If you break through, it's a fucking long way to the bottom."

A fully rigged light infantry soldier will sink like a stone. That's not theory. I've seen it happen.

Dunahee moves out. Logan falls in behind and one by one the others follow: Fadul, Escamilla, Tran, Julian, Roman, and then me.

The footplates of our exoskeletons are fitted with tiny triangular teeth that bite the ice, reducing slippage. We go in single file across terrain that Dunahee has already proven safe, separated from one another by a standard interval of thirty meters to reduce casualties in the event of an RPG attack.

Soon, the smooth ice of the freshly frozen channel is behind us. Chaos lies ahead.

Last summer's fractured ice floes froze together in a tumult of autumn storms, leaving a jagged surface of broken blocks and pinnacles, some rising two meters into the air. It's challenging terrain, but we make steady progress because Dunahee leads us on a path of least resistance plotted from satellite imagery by the battle AI that coordinates the squad's activities—and because the powered leg struts of our dead sisters reduce the work load while propelling us over the uneven ice in long, efficient strides.

No snow is actually falling, but visibility is limited anyway because the gale is keeping loose snow aloft, whirling it through the air in a veil that blocks the ambient light used by night vision. The angel sees in night vision, but it's equipped with a near-infrared camera too, and IR wavelengths easily penetrate snow. So my first look at *Deep Winter Sigil*'s glittering superstructure comes via a crisp, digitally translated black-and-white video feed.

The platform is a stack of three decks perched on a round pedestal surrounded by ice. The first two levels hold a maze of pipes and cylindrical tanks lit by bright lights and caged by cross-struts. The third deck is uncovered. The north side—the side we're approaching—supports a tangle of industrial equipment, along with a crane. A drilling gantry rises from the center of the deck. The angel is viewing it from a low angle that doesn't let me see the two-story complex of offices, labs, and dormitory rooms I know is on the southern side, but I can see lights from those facilities shining on the ice and reflected in the swirling, wind-blown snow. More lights stud the gantry, some of them aimed down at a helicopter pad built on top of the living quarters and extending out over the ice.

To my surprise, there's a wind tent erected on the pad. Most of the tent is hidden by *Sigil*'s superstructure. Only its rounded peak is visible, but that's enough to tell me there's a helicopter in residence.

"Kanoa, what's a helicopter doing here? Have additional personnel been brought in?"

"Intelligence is looking into it."

We continue to advance. I'm not ready to suggest that we call off the mission, but the anomaly of the helicopter bothers me even more than Oscar-1's delay. Our intelligence team should not have missed something so obvious. The Red should not have missed it.

Seven minutes later Kanoa comes back with an answer. "We've found a flight plan indicating a supply run only. No additional personnel. Given the distance back to civilization, the pilot probably decided to wait out the weather."

We advance without incident until we're just over two klicks from the target, and then the angel red-alerts. It marks an electromagnetic source point on the map—a potential enemy—one hundred thirty meters south and east of Dunahee. We all drop into a crouch. This puts a low ridge of ice between me and the source point, eliminating any line-of-sight visibility. So I look through the angel's eyes—but nothing is out there. Night vision and thermal both fail to reveal an enemy.

"We just crashed a sensor field," I conclude. "Assume the enemy knows we're coming."

Roman's whispered answer comes through first. *"Fuck."*

"Roger that," I growl. From this point forward there is an excellent chance the mission will degrade into a slugfest on the ice. If it does, I don't want the enemy to be able to harvest our position data from a constellation of motion sensors spread across the battlefield.

"Fadul, go after the device. Destroy it. Then sweep west. Look for more."

"Roger that, Captain."

She's a hundred fifty meters ahead of me. I glimpse her as she departs our line, bent low, her weight and the weight of her pack supported by the struts of her dead sister.

"Julian, you sweep farther east. See what you can find."

"Yes, sir."

"Dunahee, I need the angel forward."

"I understand, sir."

"Stick to the plotted path. I'll be following behind you. The rest of you spread out. Pick your own paths. Move with speed. We need to close with the target as soon as we can—and for fuck's sake, watch the map for thin ice. *Go.*"

Dunahee moves out at almost double his prior pace, scrambling and slipping, his dead sister powering him around the blocks and over the ridges. Behind him, Logan and Tran take off, angling west, while Escamilla moves east after Fadul. Roman stays close to Dunahee.

"Kanoa, you got anything?"

"Negative, Shelley."

The angel red alerts twice more as we set off two more sensors.

"Closest personnel, go after them!"

The enemy has marked our positions, but the locations of their sensors are revealed to us by their EM transmissions.

Kanoa is still analyzing the angel's video feed. "No external activity on the platform," he reports with unflappable calm. "No indication of live enemy on the ice. Satellite surveillance does not indicate gun emplacements—"

"RPG!" I shout over gen-com, reacting to the small, explosive flash of a rocket launch, five hundred meters east of the platform. It's a useless warning. The rocket moves so fast it finds its target before I get the last syllable out. I drop to my belly while my visor goes briefly black, shielding my eyes from the glare of an aerial fireball. The thunder of the concussion booms through the air and vibrates in the ice.

My visor clears. I scan my squad icons. All green, thank God. No alerts, no injuries . . . no angel sight.

"Angel down," Kanoa informs us.

Fuck.

I get my feet under me, jam the teeth of my footplates into the ice, and get up again. I think, *map*, and the skull-net picks up the request. The map's faded icon brightens and expands. Normally it's updated by data from the angel, but it works on line of sight too—and it shows most of my soldiers hunkered down. Only Fadul and Escamilla are moving.

"Roman!" I need my best shooter active in this game. "Try to get a couple meters of elevation. We've got a merc on the ice. I want you to find that fucker and take him out."

"Roger that."

The map shows Roman seventy meters to the south. I make sure there is no thin ice between us. Then I sprint to catch up with her, running in a bounding stride, hammering my footplates down to keep from slipping.

Fadul speaks over gen-com, her tone matter-of-fact. "Grenade."

Boom!

Despite her warning, I flinch. That puts me into a skid and I almost go down.

"One sensor out of the way, Captain," Fadul reports.

I see the flash of another RPG launch. *"Fadul—"*

I want to tell her to take cover, but it's already too late. The concussion shakes the ice. I don't take time to see if she's been hit. Instead, I take off again, running. The best thing I can do now is to help Roman take down the enemy.

Roman, at least, is still alive. I see her ahead of me, using the arm hooks of her dead sister to try to scramble up an angled block of ice that's leaning two meters into the air. "Behind you," I warn her.

"I'm losing my grip. I'm going to slide backward!"

"No you're not." I crouch under her footplates and boost her up, guiding her feet to rest on my shoulder struts. "Steady?"

"It'll do."

Belly down on the jagged surface of the block, she lines up her weapon. I tap into her visor's display to see what she sees.

Kanoa is there ahead of me. "Mark," he says, as a targeting circle appears in her field of view. The AI labels it as seven hundred meters out. Roman has the wind behind her. She lines up, takes three quick shots. All three hit a ridge of ice no more than a foot high. Something moves behind that ridge: a tiny figure wearing white camo, rigged in a dead sister, and equipped with night vision goggles. It jerks into sight and then falls back down.

"Target down," Roman whispers.

"Confirmed," Kanoa says.

Holding my breath, I scan my squad icons, trying to see who got hit by the RPG—but everything is green. "Confirm. No casualties?"

After a second, Kanoa echoes, "No casualties."

I step out of the way to let Roman slide down. An RPG is damned intimidating ordnance, but it has lousy accuracy at a distance.

Dunahee is outraged all the same. "Fucker was shooting at me! Blew a black hole in the ice."

"Fucker was already out on the ice before we got here," I point out, "patrolling with an RPG launcher as a sidearm. Whatever they're protecting in there, they are serious. So we move in and we move fast. *Go!*"

Hit hard before the enemy can fully prepare: That's still our best option. So I run, closing the distance between me and the bright, cheery lights of *Deep Winter Sigil*. Partway to those lights is a massive block of ice looking like the remnant of an iceberg, with a sheer face rising four meters above the surrounding floe. I run toward it, using it for cover. We cannot afford to get bogged down in an extended firefight. Here, on our own, in the dark of the polar night, we have no means to recharge our dead sisters once their power packs run down. We have to withdraw before that happens, or we have to take control of the platform and tap into *Sigil's* power grid. Otherwise, we lose.

As I run, I ask myself: *What would I do if I were in command of the mercenaries aboard* Deep Winter Sigil?

An oil-drilling platform is an amazing piece of technology, but it is not a fortress. It's not designed to withstand an assault team armed with grenades and automatic weapons. If I commanded the defense, I would not risk my clients by hunkering down inside. I would not stage a battle that was certain to destroy what I'd been hired to protect. Instead, I would deploy my soldiers from the south side of the platform, out of sight of the enemy. I would divide them in two groups, sending one east and one west, instructing them to use the jagged ice as cover while they get into position to trap their assailants in crossfire.

If we still had angel sight, we could see them coming. We don't.

A knob of ice explodes in front of me. Out of instinct I dive sideways, land on my arm strut, and roll, trying to make sense of an ominous blur of red and yellow icons flaring in my visor's display. I come up on my belly to a fusillade of automatic-weapons fire, each shot a sharp, hard crack against the suppressed audio of the roaring gale. I squint at the squad icons, but they're faded, translucent, hard to see—because our battle AI wants me to focus on the firefight—but I can see enough to know that we have wounded, with one critical red.

"Kanoa, injury report!" I could pull up the data, but it's faster to ask.

"Julian's down and critical. Dunahee and Fadul are mobile wounded."

"Estimate of enemy numbers?"

"At least six on the ice."

I look around. A meter away, there's a low ridge. It's only eighteen inches high and not thick enough to stop a round, but it offers line-of-sight cover and that's better than nothing. I belly-crawl to it, turn onto my back, and then poke the muzzle of my HITR over the top, using the muzzle cams to look around.

I can't see much, because the iceberg is only thirty meters away and it's blocking my view of the platform.

Frustration kicks in. *I am fucking blind.* I have no visual contact with the enemy, with the target, or with my own soldiers. If Delphi was still my handler, she would know what I need. She would have already expanded the map and given me a verbal summary of everyone's position—but I left Delphi behind. I left everything.

Map! I think—and if a thought can have a bitter tone, this one does.

The AI picks it up anyway and expands the map. It shows my location still a half-klick north of *Sigil*. Fadul is farthest out on my east. Escamilla is with Julian, getting him stabilized. Roman is behind me, but moving up fast. Everyone else is spread out to the west. Logan and Tran are in a fircfight with at least three enemy soldiers. Three more enemy positions on the eastern side of the platform are marked with fuzzy icons to indicate uncertainty.

"Kanoa, do I have a target?"

"Negative. No line of sight and out of range for grenades. You have to move in."

"Roman, come behind me!"

"Roger that."

I want the high ground, so I sprint for the iceberg. The map shows it as twenty meters long, four wide, angled from northeast to southwest. Smooth, open ice lies beyond it.

I loop my HITR over my shoulder and skip-jump, using all the power of my leg struts to launch myself at the top of the wall.

I don't make it to the top—but I get close.

I jam my arm hooks in and try to get a toehold using the teeth of my footplates—but the ice is so goddamned hard, I barely nick it.

Roman is right behind me. She gets under me, gets her arm struts under my footplates. "Got you, Shelley! Now go, go, *go.*"

I'm levitating, enough to get my arm hooks over the top, and then my elbows. After that, it's easy to scramble onto the slanting, wind-swept surface.

I look around, realizing what an exposed position I'm in, no cover at all, but what the fuck. I can see everything on this side of the platform.

HITR in hand, I belly-crawl to the south edge. Check the map again. But I still don't have a target. The smooth ice between me and *Sigil* is patterned in geometric panes of light and shadow cast by the glittering superstructure rising against the night sky just half a klick away.

"Kanoa—"

A gold targeting point pops up on my display. I can't see anything in the indicated position. "You're close enough," Kanoa says. "Lob a grenade."

There are two triggers on my weapon. I curl my finger around the second one, the one that controls the grenade launcher while I correct my aim, bringing a targeting circle into line with the target point. I squeeze the trigger, launching a grenade from the tube mounted under the rifle barrel.

The firefight to my east heats up, shots popping off one after another as the grenade rockets away. It explodes with a flash that dims my visor and tosses up a spray of ice crystals that briefly map the wind's fierce currents as they're whipped away. No fucking idea if I hit the enemy. Kanoa puts up another target point. I cover it and shoot again.

This time, when the wind carries away the cloud of smoke and ice splinters, I see a body wearing white camo and a dead sister, just like the soldier Roman dropped.

I glance at the map. "You got another target for me?"

"Roman, cover it!" Kanoa barks.

Bam! My vision goes bright white as something kicks me in the side of my helmet, hard enough that despite the weight of my pack and my rig, I go briefly airborne, dropping back a second later to land on my side. I want to curl up to reduce my exposure. I want to crawl for shelter—but I know I'll be dead if I do. *"Target,"* I growl at Kanoa. The only chance I have is to lay down enough return fire to keep the shooter from shooting me again.

I roll back to my belly, returning to shooting position—but I'm not fast enough. A rifle speaks, fiercely loud even muffled by my helmet. Three slow shots. To my astonishment, none of them hit me.

"Target!" I scream at Kanoa.

"Negative. Nothing left. Roman's cleared the eastern field."

I shift focus from my visor's display to the wider terrain. Roman is standing below on the ice, looking up at me as she cradles her HITR in her arms. The three shots I heard were hers. "Your head okay, Shelley?" she asks.

Fuck if I know.

I check the map. It's been updated with the locations of four bodies, three of them on the eastern side of the platform, one to the west where Logan and Tran are still dueling with two live mercs. I want to get over there, help them finish things, but not until this side is fully secure. "Roman, I need you to make sure those dead mercs don't do a zombie. Fadul—"

Boom!

I look up, startled by the sound of an explosion on the platform. The distant bleat of a fire alarm follows. The alarm and the muted roar of the wind are the only sounds I hear, because the shooting to the west has stopped.

I scan the squad icons—no changes. No one else is hit. "Logan—"

I want to ask him for his status, but a new sound intrudes: one of the surviving mercs, shouting, pleading for backup. My helmet audio boosts the volume of his panicked voice so that each word is clear: "Glover! Glover, where the fuck are you? Get out here! Get out here or we're dead!"

Vincent Glover. It's a name familiar from the mission briefing. "Glover's the CO," I remind the squad. "Watch for movement on the platform, because he's going to be bringing out the big guns."

"Don't think so," Fadul counters. "Looks like we got no heroes on deck today. Motherfuckers are rolling back the canvas hangar on the landing pad. They're bugging out."

I can't see the landing pad from my position. It's hidden behind the platform's massive superstructure. But Fadul is wide east. I look through her helmet cam to see the wind tent sliding open on motorized tracks, folds of loose canvas shivering in the gale as the hemispherical struts collapse on each other. The tent's retreat reveals a midsize civilian helicopter that my overlay identifies as an Agusta Westland. The blades are loose and starting to spin up.

"It's not just the pilot pulling out," Fadul says. "I make out at least one, maybe two in the backseat. Fucking Vincent Glover is abandoning his soldiers."

I can hardly believe it. Mercenaries work for the money, but they're still loyal to one another—or I used to think so. But I abandon the question of mercenary ethics when my skullnet icon lights up, indicating sudden and significant interference in my headspace. Not that I need the hint. An awareness comes over me, a certainty that I need to prevent that helicopter from leaving. I don't want to destroy it, but I need to know what's on board.

"Fadul, can you hit the pilot?"

"Pilot's a civilian," Kanoa reminds me. "Passengers might be civilians too."

"Out of my range anyway," Fadul adds. "And I'd be shooting across the wind."

I'm closer than Fadul, I'd be shooting down the wind, and it doesn't matter if I can't see the helicopter now, because I'll be able to see it when it takes off. "Cover me, Roman." She's a better shooter than I am, but I have the high ground. "I am not letting that helicopter go."

I stand up on the iceberg, brace my feet against the blast of the wind, and bring my weapon to my shoulder.

"You operating, Shelley?" Kanoa wants to know.

"Roger that."

Operating. That's what we call it when the Red gets inside our heads, pushing its agenda so we feel it, so we know what needs to be done. The skullnet icon is glowing and I have no doubt at all that I am operating on a program written by the Red.

"More figures on the landing pad," Fadul reports as the volume of engine noise climbs. And then her tone shifts. *"Incoming!"*

I don't flinch, even when an RPG explodes to the east, a last rogue shot as the helicopter goes airborne. I see the blur of its rotors through the platform's superstructure. Confidence floods me. I know I'll be able to hit it.

I wait for a better angle. Two seconds, three, the wind steady against me. I think the pilot wants to stay low, keep the platform behind him, but the wind catches his ship, lofts it up. A targeting point pops up in my field of view, sighted on the engine block. I fire a three-round burst.

And I hit it.

I know I do.

But nothing happens. Tracking its flight with the muzzle of my weapon, I shoot three more bursts—but the helicopter keeps going, accelerating southeast across the wind like it's heading for Greenland.

"Nice shooting, sir," Roman says.

She's fucking with me. I expect that from Fadul, but not

from Roman. I scowl down at her—but then I remember the RPG. "Fadul! Status?"

I check her icon—it's gone yellow—but Fadul sounds fine when she says, "Motherfucker missed me."

I look again at Roman. She's standing with her head cocked, watching the retreating helicopter. "The wind's pulling a streamer of black smoke out of the engine block," she reports. "I don't think they're getting far."

My skullnet icon fades from sight. The unearthly confidence I felt goes with it and I'm suddenly conscious of my exposed position atop the highest point anywhere on this ice field. *"Jesus,"* I whisper, looking up warily at *Sigil*'s decks.

Kanoa knows exactly what I'm thinking. "No activity on the platform," he assures me. "And Logan's got an offer of surrender from the two remaining enemy on the ice—though you might want to move to a less exposed position anyway."

"Yeah."

I jump down, managing not to land on my ass, but my hands are shaking—and not from the cold. The Red wanted me to take that shot, wanted it enough to risk making me an easy target. I'd like to believe it ran a calculation first, that it plotted the positions and status of every enemy soldier remaining and determined my exposure was minimal—but I don't believe it.

The Red wanted me to take that shot. That was the priority.

I head toward Logan's position, checking in with my wounded on the way.

"Fadul, you sound functional but you're showing yellow. What's your status?"

"Fucking ice splinter went through my left bicep. But I can walk and I can shoot."

"Roger that. Dunahee, you?"

"Shoulder's broken," he whispers between clenched teeth. "I can walk."

Julian is not ambulatory. He's got a hole blasted in his gut. Escamilla has stuffed the wound with putty and stopped the bleeding, but it's a bad wound, he's losing heat fast, and we need to evacuate him ASAP.

I don't know yet how we're going to do that. This mission now qualifies as thoroughly fucked, and if we're going to unfuck it, we have to move fast. Both logic and instinct tell me that whatever it is we're looking for, it left on the bird—and I'm going to believe that Roman is right. Damaged and fighting the storm, the helicopter won't be able to stay in the air for more than a few minutes. So we need to go after it. We need to reach it as soon as we can after it goes down—but with three wounded soldiers, two prisoners, and an oil-drilling platform that still needs to be inspected, it's going to be some time before we can leave.

"Fadul, I know you're hurting, but I need you to help Escamilla get Julian to the platform."

"Shelley," she points out, "we don't control the platform."

"We will by the time you get there."

Prisoners are a burden and now we've got two.

Logan has got them stripped of their gear. Tossed alongside their neatly folded exoskeletons is a collection of pistols, knives, Tasers, communications gear, and night vision goggles. They're kneeling on the ice, still wearing their white parkas. Their thermal hoods, like ours, hide their faces. One's a big man, his skin black behind the frost collected on his lips and eyelashes. The other has a slight build; the skin around his eyes is pale.

I turn the anonymous dark shield of my visor on them and ask, "Who's left aboard *Sigil?*"

"Just the civilians," the big guy says. He's so cold, his teeth are actually chattering. "We were hired to protect the civilians. But Glover ran out on us! Took Morris and Chan with him. Left us here to die."

Working off of voice and biometrics, the battle AI tags him with an identity: *Darian Wilcox, 26, former US Army.*

"What were the civilians up to, Wilcox?"

He cocks his head, eyeing me for a few seconds, like he thinks I should already know this. "Lab work, sir. That's all I know. Important enough to bring us in. Important enough for someone to hire you."

"How many civilians?"

"Twelve."

The number confirms our background intelligence.

Wilcox adds, "None of them are going to put up a fight, sir. You can take what you need. No need to hurt anyone."

"Nice and friendly?"

"Yes, sir."

"Wilcox, did your friends booby trap the place for us?"

His answer is an emphatic "*Fuck, no!* We're a business. We're not suicide fanatics."

"Dumping you was a business decision?"

He glares up at me, his breath steaming. He's reading a lot into my words. "You don't need to kill us, sir. We don't know who you are. We haven't seen your faces."

"I'll keep that in mind. But right now I don't know what Glover left for us, so I'm going to let you go in first—just in case."

No one with any knowledge has argued there isn't an ocean of oil at the bottom of the Arctic Sea, or that it can't be extracted, but there has been a decades-long debate on whether it makes sense to try. The petroleum industry has a bigger R&D budget than the gross national product of most countries, but even for them, the cost of infrastructure for offshore oil production is staggering. A failed well could bankrupt a company—but the risk isn't limited to capital investment. It's certain that along the way, there will be well-head blowouts along with oil tanker wrecks, and of course there will be more carbon poured into the atmosphere to accelerate the chaos of heat and storm and polar melt that's been fucking over the globe in worse ways every year.

And still, there's a shitload of money on the table. The developmental phase alone provides an opportunity for subcontracting companies to bleed their senior partners for billions in support, supplies, communication, and construction. It's hard for any government to say no to that.

Only five hundred meters of smooth ice separate us from the platform. I want to cross that distance quickly, but our prisoners are clumsy without their dead sisters. They slip on the ice and they slow us down. But our slow pace lets Fadul and Escamilla keep up as they drag Julian across the ice, wrapped up in an inflated emergency cocoon.

As we advance, I keep a close watch on *Sigil*'s decks, but there's no activity, no sign of any defense. I hope that means the twelve civilians are on lockdown, huddled in designated security zones, waiting on rescue. Despite Wilcox's assurances, I'm worried they're armed, that they'll put up a resistance. I don't want any more casualties.

"Kanoa."

"Here."

"You got a status update on Oscar-1?"

"He's still tied up, waiting for fuel—"

"Waiting? I thought he had a fuel problem—contamination or something?"

"Negative. He's having a problem with the facility superintendent at the last refueling stop, north end of Ellesmere."

That doesn't make sense. Infiltrating phony orders into military networks is a specialty of our intelligence team. I'm not going to pretend to understand how the system works. Insofar as I can tell, our ETM strike squad uses bureaucracy as camouflage. A charade of hacked orders, false identities, and compartmentalized oversight lets us operate with the appearance of an officially sanctioned force attached to the United States Army. It's a position reinforced by a black-ops budget and need-to-know security that ensures no auditor ever compiles enough information to prove that we are not who we claim to be.

So far anyway.

And compared to engineering an authorization for transport aboard a nuclear submarine, convincing the superintendent of a remote listening station to refuel Oscar-1 should be easy.

"Kanoa, just get Intelligence to push an order through. I need to get Julian evacuated. It's a two-hour flight just to get here, and if he's not even in the air yet—"

"We're working on it, Shelley."

"Or you could write an order for a military flight. There's got to be buzz on the network anyway. Glover must have put an emergency call through, and if not him, than the civilians—"

"No. The network's quiet. I think *Sigil*'s communications have been suppressed."

"Suppressed? How? I thought we couldn't access their system."

"Look, even if I can get a military flight, it's going to leave a footprint that's hard to erase, and it could have political repercussions. Oscar-1 is still our best option. And you need time to run down that helicopter anyway."

"It's Julian I'm worried about."

"Roger that. We're doing what we can."

The closer we get to the platform, the harder it's going to be for us to return fire if someone does decide to shoot at us from the decks, so I call a halt when we're still a hundred meters out. "Logan, I want you to take Fadul and Tran. Get in position to provide covering fire if we need it."

"What about the prisoners, Shelley?"

"Dunahee! How are you holding up?"

"I'll do what I need to do, sir."

"I know you will. I need you to babysit a prisoner. The small guy. Shoot him if he gives you any trouble."

"Happy to, sir."

"And stay close to Julian."

"Yes, sir."

"Escamilla and Roman, you're with me. You too, Wilcox. Let's find out what Glover left behind."

The platform becomes an ugly industrial roof as we approach the pedestal that supports *Deep Winter Sigil* and houses the pipes and drill. That pedestal descends seven hundred feet into the deeps below us, but I'm only concerned with climbing its upper twenty feet to the first deck. Fortunately, there's a caged stairway to make it easy.

I follow through on my threat and send Wilcox up the stairs first, with Escamilla right behind him. They find no activity, no evidence of booby traps, so Roman and I go next.

We clear the first two decks. Kanoa checks in as we climb to the platform's third level. "We've got a thermal image just in from a survey satellite. Low-res, but it shows a hotspot fourteen kilometers northeast. Probably the helicopter."

"Stationary?"

"Heat profile indicates it—but the ice is rough the whole way. It could take you ninety minutes to reach it."

"Survivors?"

"Can't tell—and it'll be over two hours before we have access to another satellite over the area."

"We'll be there by then."

"Roger that. You need to go after it."

Running down a helicopter: a little task to keep us busy after we secure *Sigil*.

A quick inspection of the third deck reveals no one outside, so we turn our attention to the living quarters.

Though the two-story building has multiple entrances, all but one are sealed with ice. Wilcox gestures toward that one. "Main entrance, sir." It's a glass-paned door spilling bright light out onto the platform, where footprints shadow the frost.

"Move in slowly," I tell him, gripping my HITR in two hands. "I'll be right behind you."

Wilcox turns to look at me. "It's a double door, sir. Outer door has to close before the inner door opens."

I gaze past him. Both the inner and outer doors are glass, which makes it easy to see into the brightly lit, industrial-looking lobby beyond. It's an ugly room: flat-white walls, gray vinyl floor, black lockers, steel benches. Two bodies are sprawled on the vinyl floor. Both are lying faceup in wide, shallow pools of blood, bullet holes drilled in their chests.

Wilcox turns around, sees what I see. *"Holy fuck."*

He falls back a few steps.

"What the hell was going on in there?" I ask him.

"Like I said, sir, lab work. Industrial shit. Some microbiology. I don't know. Those people in there, they were good people. Geeky scientist types, you know? Interested in everything. And polite."

I nudge him forward again. "Open the door."

"Yes, sir."

He punches a fist-sized button to the left of the door-frame. I stay behind him, intending to use him as a human shield if a bomb goes off, but the only thing that happens is the buzz-and-click of an electronic lock. He opens the door manually. I follow him through.

"Roman, come with me. Escamilla, you stay outside."

"Roger that, Captain."

The outer door closes automatically behind us. I hear it lock. The next door opens and we are washed in a billow of hot air, reeking of blood and shit. I push Wilcox ahead of me. No bombs go off. No one shoots at us. One of the bodies is that of a woman, the other a man. My overlay tags them with names. Two of the staff scientists.

We stand there for thirty seconds, just listening. I hear my prisoner's ragged breathing and the soft hum of the ventilation system. Nothing else.

"Quiet as death," Roman says.

I send Escamilla to check out the industrial shops while Roman and I search the labs and the dormitories, our prisoner in tow. Escamilla finds two more bodies. We find seven more, for a total of eleven. All shot multiple times. Kanoa identifies the dead as scientists, engineers, technicians. "The only one missing is Dr. Toni Parris, a microbiologist. American."

We record everything, with portrait shots of every corpse.

My prisoner looks on it all in shocked disbelief. He can't come up with an explanation, but he does point out a lab that was off-limits to everyone except Dr. Parris and two of the other researchers. It's not off-limits now. Its steel door is blown, hanging on its hinges.

I look past the door at two lab benches, numerous shelves, a ventilation hood, a desk, instruments I can't identify—but what draws my gaze is a stainless steel refrigerator. It looks inflated, the sides puffed out and warped, the door hanging open, the interior empty, the walls charred—like someone set a grenade off inside it.

"Stay out of there," Kanoa warns me.

I'm already sweating beneath my thermal gear; fear makes it worse. "You think it's biowarfare?"

I back away from the open door, imagining my skin itching, my lungs filling with fluid.

"We're missing a microbiologist, so that's my guess. She helped them collect the payload from the fridge and then they blew it to wipe any traces."

I think about it, imagining some kind of plague so dangerous it had to be brewed in an isolated Arctic outpost. And I wonder: *Have we found the objective of our recent look-and-see missions?*

I turn to Wilcox. He gets defensive: "I didn't know it was biowarfare, Captain. The people who worked here, they didn't seem like that kind."

We all imagine we can recognize evil.

I gesture with my weapon. "Move." He doesn't need any more encouragement. I suspect we're all quietly hoping that Dr. Parris managed her cultures in a professional manner, because if anything escaped into the air system, we are screwed.

We hustle back to the lobby, where the air stinks worse than before. "Wilcox, I want you to get these bodies outside. Let them freeze. Roman, you watch him. Shoot him if he gives you any trouble."

"Yes, sir."

"You got no worries with me, sir," Wilcox says. "Glover fucked me over. I'm never pulling a trigger for him again. But if you're hiring . . ."

I scowl and walk outside. "Kanoa."

"Here."

"What does Intelligence say about the risk of contamination?"

"Minimal. Glover would have secured the payload. He's not going to profit if he's dead."

"Okay. Then I want to leave the wounded here. Julian is not going to make it if he has to wait out in the cold."

"Roger that."

Escamilla returns from his inspection of the industrial shops. "Found two snowmobiles. They're both shot up. Couldn't get them started."

"Okay."

I walk to the edge of the platform and look down. The rest of the squad is below, anonymous in their black visors, but an overlay identifies who's who: Tran and Fadul, farthest out, watching the lower decks in case we missed a threat; Logan, crouched by Julian; Dunahee nearby, a pistol in his left hand, loosely trained on the second prisoner, and his right arm bound against his chest.

"Fadul," I say over gen-com. "Relieve Dunahee. Bring the prisoner up."

"Aren't we heading out?" she asks suspiciously.

"Roger that—but we're not taking the prisoners with us."

"No, shit, sir. Just wondering why Dunahee can't do the escort."

"Dunahee can barely hold his weapon. Now *move*."

Logan stands and turns around, his black visor angled to look up at me. He opens a private channel: "Why do you need Fadul? You're not planning to shoot the prisoners?"

I ponder this question, wondering why Logan would ask it, wondering what he's heard about my past. I don't think he knows about Carl Vanda, a man I kidnapped, who never again saw the light of day. He does know about Eduard

Semak. I told him that story myself—how I visited the old dragon in his private space habitat and dropped him back to Earth inside an emergency escape capsule, knowing he wouldn't survive the rough reentry.

I guess that makes me a stone-cold killer—so I play along. "I could order Fadul to shoot them, Logan. She'd probably do it. Do you think I should?"

"Fuck, *no*. Shelley, they were just doing their job."

"Yeah, that's how I see it. And that's why I'm going to let them sit in a nice warm room for a few hours, until we're out of here. That okay with you?"

"Of course! Yes. Sorry, sir. I should have known."

Yeah, you fucking should have. Even Wilcox thought better of me than that.

"Get Julian and Dunahee up here. The wounded are staying behind."

I'm waiting at the top of the stairway when Fadul brings the prisoner. His eyes are wide and wary, framed by his thermal hood. It's easy to see he's scared, but I don't think too much about it because I'm already engaged in a low-voiced argument with Fadul on a private channel. "You're going to stay here—"

"No way, Shelley."

She's wearing a brace on her arm where she got hit by shrapnel. The wound beneath will have been glued shut, but that doesn't mean she's ready for a run across the ice.

"You'll keep an eye on the two mercs and take care of Julian." Our prisoner crab-walks in front of us, trying to keep us both in sight as we herd him across the icy deck.

"Dunahee can do guard duty. Medical cleared me to continue the mission."

"Dunahee has a broken shoulder."

"Then leave Tran."

"Tran's green. Your icon is yellow. You're staying." By this time, we've reached the glass door to the lobby. I punch the button to unlock the door and then kick it open. We all stare for a second at the two corpses dumped into the vestibule between the double doors. Wilcox is standing over them with bloodstains on the cuffs of his white parka and more red smears on his boots and his thighs. Roman has her back to the inner door, her weapon loosely aimed at Wilcox. Prisoner number two misreads the situation.

He turns, kicks Fadul hard in the gut, and then makes a grab for the pistol in my thigh holster. I hit him in the face with my arm strut. I don't even think about it. It's instinct. The back of his head hits the doorframe and he drops with his nose a crushed, pulpy, bloody mess. I'm not sure he's breathing.

Shit.

Inside the cramped vestibule, Roman has shifted her aim so that her HITR is now firmly trained on Wilcox. "Don't make a move."

"No problem." He looks at me, his steady gaze communicating that he's a professional. "I got no idea who you are," he assures me in a calm voice. "No idea what you look like. So you got no reason to kill me."

"Get these bodies out of here," I tell him. Then I turn a guilty eye on the merc I just slammed. One more sin I didn't need. "Fadul, check his vitals."

She's still hunched over her bruised belly. "Can I kill him if he's still alive?"

Wilcox intercedes. "Let me look at him."

I step out of the way. Wilcox checks his breathing. "Still with us." Then he takes a moment to share a little personal history. "My people didn't want me to come out here.

They said the fucking Arctic is cursed. Nothing works right. People go crazy."

"You should have listened."

"Wish I did."

Wilcox is right. Most Arctic operations are plagued with issues: failed software, defective equipment, undelivered equipment, piracy, terrorism. The one exception? When a wellhead blew out last summer, personnel and equipment arrived without delay, and the well was sealed within seventy-two hours. It was an anomalous demonstration of competence and efficiency—and strong evidence that preserving the Arctic and discouraging development is part of the Red's agenda.

But the dragons still smell money, and they keep trying.

"We'll be back in a few hours," I tell Fadul.

"I've heard promises like that before."

Julian is resting on a scavenged mattress in an office just off the lobby. I crouch beside him, but he's so high on pain meds he doesn't know I'm there. "Hold on," I tell him anyway. Then I nod to Dunahee, who's sitting on the floor beside him.

"Don't worry, sir. We'll be okay."

"Don't let Fadul kill the prisoners."

"Yes, sir."

We set out after the downed helicopter. Logan takes point, running hard. The rest of us follow in a single-file line: Escamilla, Tran, Roman, and then me.

The dead sisters augment our muscle power, but they

don't replace it. Sensors set into the joints measure the force of our strides. The harder we work, the harder the bones work. That means we can go a hell of a lot faster and farther wearing a dead sister than we could without one, but our bodies are still working, and it's fucking exhausting to run kilometer after kilometer across terrain as rough as the ice floe. But we do it, with the wind blowing harder and fresh snow starting to shake loose from the sky.

There's no sign of life when we finally sight the helicopter—no movement and no lights, not even chem sticks—but the ship is intact, sitting upright on the ice and facing the wind, showing no obvious damage. The pilot must have been able to guide it to a soft landing, which means Glover and his remaining crew could still be aboard, waiting for the weather to clear.

Logan scans the ship with an infrared scope, putting an end to that speculation. "We've got a body in the pilot's seat. It's above ambient, still chilling. Everything else is one temperature—damned cold."

"They're long gone," Tran concludes.

I take him with me to check it out.

No one shoots as we approach. I wipe the frost off a window and peer inside at the pilot, bulky in parka and hood, head bowed, still strapped into the seat. "Check the back," I tell Tran as I open the pilot's door.

It's a woman. There's a bullet hole that goes through the hood of her parka, into the right side of her head. Everyone else is gone.

"What the *hell*?" I demand. "Glover didn't have to kill her. He didn't have to kill all those people back on the platform."

"He's looking for a big payday," Kanoa says. "And he's not taking any chances."

I wonder who he's really working for. I hope I get a chance to ask him.

It takes less than a minute for me and Tran to search the interior. We don't find anything you wouldn't expect to find on a helicopter working in the Arctic. There are parkas, blankets, first aid supplies, chem lights, batteries . . . but no weapons and no biowarfare cultures.

Logan has been conducting a hunt for footprints, but the gale and the now-steady snowfall are against him. "Wind has wiped this place clean."

Tran slams the helicopter door shut. "Or maybe Santa swooped in and scooped them up. We've got no way to tell if another helicopter set down here."

"No, they're on foot," I say. "Even assuming Glover knew another pilot willing to fly in this weather, there's no way a second ship could have already come and gone."

"They're going to be rigged," Escamilla points out. "So they'll make good time."

Logan shakes his head. "They have a civilian with them. Dr. Parris isn't going to know how to use a rig. That'll slow them down."

Tran uses his HITR to gesture toward the dead pilot inside the helicopter. "Until they decide to shoot her like they shot everyone else."

"They took Parris for a reason," Logan insists.

I'm inclined to agree, but that still leaves the central question. "Where did they go?"

Our intelligence team comes through with an answer, relayed by Kanoa: "There's a private research station twenty-nine kilometers to the northeast. It looks like they changed course, tried to reach it after they knew they were hit."

"Private?" I ask. "Like for tourists?"

"Private, like dragon-funded. Mars research. If they prove they can live in extreme conditions, then maybe they can figure out Mars."

I don't give a fuck about dragon hobbies. There's only one thing I want to know. "Have these assholes got a helicopter that Glover can steal?"

"The data I'm looking at indicates they do."

"You think he can make it there on foot? Because that's like running a North Pole marathon."

"Until he can arrange another ride out of here, he doesn't have a choice."

I expand the map on my display and then zoom out until I see a tag: *Tuvalu Station.* The tag marks a cluster of three buildings erected side by side and linked by covered passages. I cannot let Glover get there, get that helicopter, get away. I don't know yet who was paying Dr. Parris for the work she was doing in her lab; I don't know who's paying Glover to recover that work. But I am not going to let this plague escape. The reason I'm here, the reason ETM exists, is to hunt down and slam any asshole who thinks it's a good idea to brew up an apocalypse.

I intend to see that we get the job done.

My guess is the enemy will move with all possible speed toward Tuvalu Station, but I could be wrong. If they believe there's a chance they're being followed, then they might be waiting along the way to ambush us. Without angel sight or good satellite coverage, we can't know. So I instruct the squad to move out in parallel, keeping thirty meters between each soldier so we'll have eyes on a wide swath of ice. We hope to sight our quarry somewhere along that corridor—preferably before they see us.

   Kanoa provides each of us a blue-line path to follow,
warning us not to trust it too far. "Your path is just a best
guess based on limited data. The ice is shifting, so remain
vigilant and use good judgment."

   The paths are mapped by our intelligence team: two
civilian analysts, each backed by a powerful AI that can
access surveillance resources provided by the Red. That's
how we obtained the low-res infrared image that gave us
the helicopter's location. We're still waiting for a high-res
update.

   There are constellations of communications satellites in
polar orbits, so voice and data coverage at this latitude
is solid, but we need an observational satellite. The one
we're waiting for provides coverage in a surveillance corridor that continuously shifts west as the Earth rotates
beneath it. We're waiting for it to make a sweep of our
position. Until it does, we have only our own eyes to rely
on, with our night vision capacity reduced by the falling
snow.

   Glover will be in the same situation. It's possible he has
a drone, but the wind is so fierce he won't be able to control it.

"We've got the image," Kanoa says.

   "Hold up!"

   The squad halts. I crouch to reduce the impact of the
wind, and then tell Kanoa, "Let me see it."

   The detail is excellent. Tagged on the image are seven
distinctly warm objects between us and Tuvalu Station.
Three of those are scattered and solitary. "Intelligence
thinks those are seals or polar bears," Kanoa says. "The
other four—that's your quarry."

   He avoids pointing out the obvious problem: Our

squad appears in the image too, as five hotspots spread out in an east-west line. "Why didn't we get scrubbed?" I ask him. I'm used to spontaneous digital processing erasing our presence from general surveillance, but it didn't happen this time.

"Unknown. Resources may be focused elsewhere."

Right. Didn't I warn Tran just a few hours ago not to count on the Red to back us up? Good advice, that. "If Glover has access to this image, he'll know we're coming. He could set up an ambush."

"You assume that anyway," Kanoa tells me. "And note the distance. They're only nine kilometers ahead of you."

"Yeah, closer than expected."

"A lot closer. They might have an injury, or the civilian is slowing them down."

Either way, it's good news. We're running a marathon, but so are they and I want to catch them before they make Tuvalu Station. "Move out!"

Soon, we reach a plain of smooth ice that allows us to run at a steady pace, one I'd normally be able to maintain for miles—but the wind has turned every step into a struggle, the constant inrush of freezing air is eating at my lungs, and my thighs ache where the cold titanium of my prosthetics meets living bone. In the corner of my vision, I see the skullnet icon flicker. I don't have to wonder what's going on because I can feel it: The pain recedes as a rush of endorphins floods my brain.

Palehorse Keep was supposed to be a short mission: Hit hard and fast with Oscar-1 waiting over the horizon to pull us out. Now it's an endurance race, and we still don't know how we're getting home.

I call another halt as we near the last known location of our quarry. Leaving the squad to hunker down, I send Logan to circle west, while I scout east, looking for signs of a potential ambush. All we find are scuff marks and a single boot print preserved in a thin carpet of snow sheltered in the lee of an ice ridge—but the boot print is an encouraging sign. It's solid evidence that at least one individual in Glover's party is not using a dead sister, and that means they're moving slowly.

We spread out again and resume the hunt. There's so much snow, falling fresh from the sky or being swept up by the wind, that even with night vision, we can't see far. It's disorienting. Feels like running on a treadmill, getting nowhere. But conditions are forecast to change. "There's an upcoming break in the cloud cover," Kanoa says. "You should have clear skies in under an hour."

A tube hooked to a bladder in my pack brings me a swallow of fortified water that's gone slushy. It chills my teeth and my skull and I don't want to drink anymore, but I make myself drink it anyway. I remind my squad to do the same. We're running across the surface of an ocean, but dehydration is a hazard we can't overlook.

I check the time in my overlay. It feels like hours since Kanoa predicted clear skies, but it's been only fifty-four minutes. I want to be able to see where we're going, to see our enemy. I sure as fuck hope we don't run right past them.

"Pull up, pull up!"

It's Tran, whispering over gen-com.

"*Shit.* They're like fifty meters away from me."

I drop into a crouch, breathing hard and relieved to take a break. "Have they seen you?"

"No. No, they're walking away from me."

"Keep them in sight."

"Sighting confirmed," Kanoa says. He pops an image onto my display. It shows me a vague cluster of figures, details lost to snow and night vision, but one at least is rigged—and one isn't. The other two, I can't be sure.

"Automatic weapons," Kanoa says. "And that looks like an RPG launcher."

"I guess they wanted the option of blasting their way into Tuvalu Station." I delete the image and then expand the map. "Kanoa, are we still due for clear skies?"

"Roger that. Latest report gives you another fifteen minutes."

"Okay, this is what we're going to do. Logan, you and Escamilla move in behind them, just close enough to keep them in sight. Roman and Tran are with me. We're going to move around, wide to the east. It'll be a sprint, but I want to get ahead of them while the weather covers us. We're going to stop them now. We will not let them go on to Tuvalu Station. There will be no repeat of what happened at *Deep Winter Sigil*. Clear?"

I wait for the round of acknowledgments. And then I add, "If it comes to shooting, wait for a designated target. We don't want to shoot each other."

I start east, with Roman and Tran running behind me in single file. It's a damn good thing the wind is blowing hard. It covers the harsh rasp of my breathing. The cold sears my throat and I half expect my lungs to shatter, but I keep going until Kanoa says, "Turn west now. Cut them off."

He uses GPS to position us in the path of our quarry.

The swirling snow thins, revealing an expanse of ice as smooth as a frozen pond, with no cover in any direction. "Standard interval," I whisper, gesturing to Roman and Tran to take up positions on either side of me. They spread out, so that we stand thirty meters apart.

The wind slows. Night vision shows me a handful of stars overhead. I brace my feet, bring my HITR to my shoulder, and will myself to see past the lingering scatter of wind-driven snow.

"There," Roman whispers. "Seventy meters."

I see them: three soldiers rigged in dead sisters and night vision goggles. The one in front carries an RPG launcher; the other two are assisting the civilian, half-carrying Dr. Parris as they support her by her arms.

"Drop your weapons!" I bellow, not really expecting them to.

And they don't. They don't even take time to process my request. I might as well have yelled *Game on!*

My tactical AI puts up a target. I cover it and fire a three-round burst, dropping the merc with the RPG launcher as he heaves it to his shoulder. There's a spray of panicked gunfire from one of the other mercs—shots fired without taking the time to aim. Tran hits him twice. Blood flies on the second shot, proving that at least one bullet got past armor, into flesh.

Two of three are down—but Roman hasn't taken a shot yet.

She is standing motionless, the wind at her back and her HITR steady, braced by her arm strut as she targets the last mercenary. He has his arm around the throat of the civilian; he's holding a pistol pressed to her head.

Dr. Parris is bundled up in a parka with a fur-lined hood and a thermal mask that hides her face. She's a tall woman, which makes her a good human shield. All I can see of the merc is his arm and the left side of his hooded head.

"You'll want her alive!" he shouts.

My overlay gets a voice ID, tags him as Vincent Glover.

I don't argue with him because he's right. I do want Parris alive. I have questions I want to ask her.

I'd like to take him alive too, but I think the odds are against it.

Quietly, I tell Roman, "Take him."

Bam!

One shot. The bullet buzzes in past the civilian's ear, cracks Glover's goggles, and drills him in the left eye.

Dr. Parris is in bad shape. She's sitting on the ice, shaking, exhausted, incoherent. Whether she's suffering from psychological shock or hypothermia, I don't know, but we need to get her out of the weather—and we're still six kilometers from Tuvalu Station.

I consider my options, and then I pop the cinches on my dead sister. "Escamilla, you've run slaved rigs before, right?"

"Not something I want to remember, Shelley."

"Sorry. I need you to do it again."

Exoskeletons are expensive. When soldiers die wearing them, the army wants them back. It's a sergeant's responsibility to recover both the body and the dead sister—which is why it's possible to slave one dead sister to another, so it can be walked off the battlefield even if the soldier strapped into it is dead.

"You're going to strap the civilian into your rig?" Tran asks.

"Yes." Parris is tall, at least six-one. Close enough to my height. I'd rather put her into Glover's rig, but we don't have the control codes for his equipment.

I crouch beside Parris. She's not using night vision, but the clouds have opened up, admitting an auroral light that shimmers across the ice—enough for her to see me, if only as a silhouette. She squints at me past frost-covered lashes as I explain to her what we're going to do. She seems to understand; at any rate, she cooperates while Escamilla helps me strap her to the rig.

Roman stands watch while we handle Parris. Logan

and Tran search the bodies. They empty pockets and packs, strip off hoods and masks, and then lay each soldier out on the ice and take portrait shots so Kanoa can use facial recognition to identify them. We need to know who the enemy is.

Parris waits quietly, strapped into my exoskeleton, but as she begins to recover a little strength, she gets anxious. "Who are you people?" she asks, her voice hoarse, wind-burned. And when no one answers, her tone ratchets up: "Vince killed everyone! You know that, don't you?"

"We know it." I finish strapping into Glover's rig. It feels small and awkward, but a few experimental steps convince me I can make it work. I walk over to Parris. "What were you working on in your lab, Dr. Parris?"

"Who are you?" she asks again. "Are you Canadian special forces?"

I don't answer. I just watch her through the anonymous black screen of my visor. Without night vision, I must appear to her as a looming shadow with mechanical edges; nothing to separate me from a walking machine. I intend it to rattle her, and it does. The pace of her breathing picks up. "You're going to kill me, aren't you?"

"No."

"Because you think I'm part of it."

"Are you?"

"No! Vince stole my work. He had it with him. The microbial cultures were in a black sample case." She tries to move, to turn, but the exoskeleton holds her in place. "I need to recover it."

"Lieutenant?" I ask.

"Got it, Captain."

Logan comes over, carrying a frost-covered, molded-plastic case. I shine an LED light on it so Parris can see. "This it?"

"Yes."

"How deadly is it?"

She's cold, scared, exhausted, sinking into hypothermia. Her earlier confusion returns. "Deadly? I don't understand. What are you asking?"

I rephrase my question. "How fast does it spread? How many will die?"

I'm watching her eyes past the frost that clings to her lashes; they widen as understanding kicks in. "You think it's a bioweapon. *Oh my God!* Is that why you came? You thought I was running a biowarfare lab?"

"What else would you be doing behind all that security?"

"Bioprospecting."

She says it like it's the most obvious thing in the world.

"You want to explain what that means?"

She's strapped into my dead sister so she can't really gesture, but she moves her fingers to indicate the ice below our feet. "That world down there, it's barely explored. The microorganisms on the seafloor—most can't be cultured in a lab. So we analyze them *in situ*. In place. It's a robotic system. Microlabs. Little automated pods with nutrient chips. We grow the bacteria, test it, sequence the DNA."

"All on the seafloor?"

"Yes, but—"

I spotlight the case. "Then what the fuck's in there?"

I swear I see guilt in her eyes. "Well, you see, once we have the DNA sequences, we can synthesize genes. We do that in the lab. And those synthetic genes get implanted into lab-stable microbe strains. But the legal requirements for . . . working with synthetic organisms . . ."

Yeah, now I understand. The only thing they brought up from the seafloor was data. She could have been doing the lab work in Toronto or Vancouver or anywhere else. But there was an advantage to doing it aboard *Sigil*. "You've been sidestepping the rules. You wanted to do the work out here where the jurisdiction is open to question."

"You have to understand. We're in competition with the Chinese, the Russians. If we waited to get permits—"

"You found something worth protecting."

She nods; her bloodless lips crack as she presses them together. "We've been running simulations. We may have an effective treatment for several degenerative brain diseases."

"And that's worth a lot of money?"

"Potential billions. Enough to tempt pirates. The company sent in extra security while we go through the permit process." Her voice goes soft. "Vince knew what we had. We didn't tell him, but he knew. He wanted to sell the synthetic strain. He said he had a buyer."

ETM 7-1 does not exist to referee shares in dragon treasure. "I need you to be straight with me, Dr. Parris. Do the contents of that case have biowarfare applications?"

"*No.* It has nothing to do with biowarfare. I would never work in a field like that. War is immoral. Killing people is immoral. I can't believe what Vince did."

"Goddamn it, Kanoa, is she telling the truth?"

My emotional analysis program, FaceValue, refuses to pass judgment because her face is masked, but Kanoa has more resources. "Voice and pupil analysis indicate yes."

And that means this mission has been a waste of time and lives. All those slaughtered at *Sigil* are dead because we moved in—our presence triggered this disaster—and the only thing that was ever at stake was money.

I hate fucking look-and-see missions.

"Why are you still alive?" I ask her.

"Because it was my project! Vince thought I might be useful. That's the only reason."

"It parses as truth," Kanoa says.

I have another question. "Did he try to call his contact? Ask for support?"

She nods. "After they had to land the helicopter, he made a call."

"And what happened?"

"They were angry. From the things he said, I think they were Chinese. And then they wouldn't talk to him. And we started walking."

I take the case from Logan and step away. "Kanoa, you picking up anything on the military networks?"

"Negative. Nothing so far."

"So what do you think?" I ask him.

"I think Glover's employer didn't want to get caught with a bloody hand in the cookie jar, so they cut him loose."

"Expecting him to die?"

"Yes."

Whatever it is we've been looking for these past months, this wasn't it.

I stash the case in my pack. Palehorse Keep has been a disaster, and it's not over yet. I need to get Parris to shelter, and I need to get my squad safely home.

"What's the status of Oscar-1?" I ask.

"Unknown. We've lost track of him. The base commander was questioning his credentials. It's possible he's been arrested."

If that's true, we are in a really bad position.

Every mission is subject to chance, but if the Red is behind us, mission support usually goes like clockwork. The Red makes sure of it, issuing orders, manipulating schedules, providing access, whatever it takes to let us move and move quietly to where we need to be—but not this time. "It's like the Red pulled out of this mission. The action didn't play out as expected, and we got dumped."

"Something else may be going on," he concedes.

Just a few hours ago, I was chewing out Tran for assuming we could rely on the Red—but that is exactly what we've been doing on this mission. We were relying on the Red to get Oscar-1 past the military checkpoint on Ellesmere, without preparing any alternate means of refueling his aircraft.

Kanoa tries to reassure me. "There's no evidence of an immediate threat."

"Matter of time."

"Roger that. Get to Tuvalu Station and we'll have more options."

I brief the squad, and then we move out. I'm exhausted; we all are. We ran a marathon today, but it's not just the distance that weighs on us. The cold, the wind, the adrenaline—the doubt—each takes a toll. We push on anyway.

At least the ice is flat. The sky remains clear. Even the wind eases a little. Six kilometers isn't far. That's what I tell myself. But it's far enough that I have time to envision new and dire worries.

"Kanoa."

"Here."

"Are we looking at flat ice like this all the way to Tuvalu Station?"

"Affirmative."

"I don't like it. We've got no cover. If we get surprised by a nest of mercenaries—"

"Negative. This is not *Sigil*. It's not a petroleum company. There is no evidence of private security."

"Why is it set up so close to *Sigil*? That's suspicious, don't you think?"

"No, it's deliberate. There's a mutual-support agreement on file that says in case of emergency, they help each other out. Tuvalu is staffed only by a few scientists and pioneer types. Nothing to worry about."

"Scientists aren't harmless," I point out. "They invented nukes, guns, bombs, toxins—"

"Your cerebral wiring."

"Exactly. You can't trust them."

"I think we need to adjust your settings."

Kanoa says it to shut me up and it works. But as I lope behind the squad, my footplates crunching against the ice, I wonder about it. "Kanoa."

"Here."

"Does that happen? Do you sit down with medical, assess the baseline, adjust it . . . change who we are?"

"You don't have enough on your mind? Tie your shit down, Shelley. You're on the easy leg of this mission. I called ahead to Tuvalu, let them know you're coming."

"You fucking *called* them? What did you tell them?"

"The truth. *Sigil* was attacked, the helicopter shot down, Dr. Parris is the sole survivor."

"Are we the good guys or the bad guys in this story?"

"There are no good guys, but they don't know that yet. They expect to treat Dr. Parris for hypothermia, and fly all of you out as soon as her condition improves."

"So we leave her there and take the helicopter?"

"Roger that. I want you back at *Sigil*. There won't be room on that helicopter for everyone in the squad, but you can at least fly the wounded out."

We've been calling Tuvalu a research station, but that term implies a permanence and an importance that Tuvalu lacks.

Deep Winter Sigil was a billion-dollar facility built to last decades and designed to be functional whether afloat in the open ocean or locked up in ice. But as we approach

Tuvalu, it becomes clear that nothing about it is permanent. The buildings I thought I saw in the satellite image
are really just tents. Starlight falls in slick reflections against
the metallic sheen of their fabric, making them shine in
night vision. Two are shaped like Quonset huts. The third
is an expansive yurt-like structure with a round footprint.
Short tunnels link them together. None of the tents have
windows or show any sign of artificial light leaking out. I
see no movement.

Several times I pause to listen. My helmet audio filters
the sound of the wind and quiets the crunch of our footsteps. I hear no other sound. But my helmet does detect
EM signatures—a lot of them, just like at any human outpost.

Kanoa annotates the scene with labels projected in my
visor, expanding on the information with a voice report.
"The round tent is the hangar. The other two are shared-
use—living and research space. You can enter through the
airlock on the central tent."

No reason for all of us to go inside; we're not planning
to be here long.

"Escamilla, I want you to take a walk around the outside
of the facility. Look for anything interesting."

"Roger that, sir."

"Tran, take up a post outside the hangar door. Assuming
there really is a helicopter in there, make sure it doesn't go
anywhere."

"Yes, sir."

"You got a feeling, Shelley?" Kanoa asks.

I look for the skullnet icon. If it were aglow, that would
indicate interference, input into my emotional state, but
it's invisible, so I'm not getting warnings from on high.
"Nothing out of the ordinary."

"You're reading a little tense."

Not really a surprise. Everything on this mission has been a fuck-up, and now we're about to steal a helicopter.

As we near the tents, Escamilla and Tran split off to cover their assignments. The rest of us walk with Parris up to a door of insulated aluminum that opens as we approach. Bright artificial light spills out, blinding me for a full second before my visor compensates and drops out of night vision.

When I can see again, I notice that color has returned to the world—and that without even thinking about it, I've turned the muzzle of my HITR to cover a stocky figure in a bright orange parka who is standing in the doorway. He glares at me from a flat, brown, wizened face framed by an orange hood. My encyclopedia runs an automatic facial recognition routine and tags him with a name: John Parker. I let the muzzle of my HITR drop until it's pointing at the ground. I suspect John Parker is already regretting this encounter, not that he really had a choice.

In a low voice with a soft inflection that suggests a native Arctic heritage, he says, "I have to ask you to take off your exoskeletons and helmets."

Kanoa cuts in right away. "Negative. Take control of the facility."

I let the skullnet capture my response: *Roger that.*

One of the most impressive aspects of human psychology is our proficiency with bullshit. Specifically, the way we use it to reduce violence in the world. I don't want to kick my way inside the facility, and I don't want to directly challenge John, but I need him to know who's making the rules. So I play the concerned and cautious commanding officer. "That's fine, Mr. Parker, but we'll need to check things out first. I'll send my lieutenant in to look around. Logan, take Roman with you."

John's lips press together. He isn't happy, but he's too

smart to argue. He retreats into a vestibule. Logan and Roman follow, closing the door behind them.

It's just me and the civilian left waiting on the threshold. I turn to Parris. The sooner she's off my hands, the better. "Let's get you out of that rig."

She's exhausted and only half-conscious. She doesn't resist, but she doesn't help either as I pull the cinches.

Escamilla checks in. "Shelley."

"Here."

"Found a cache of supplies outside the hangar. Can't tell what they are."

"Leave it."

As I free Parris from my exoskeleton she starts to slump. I catch her, walk her into the vestibule, and help her sit down on a bench. The inner door is closed, but the vestibule is still warmer than outside in the wind.

Logan begins to relay his report. "Large room just inside. Six personnel present. No weapons. No overt signs of hostility."

Kanoa watches through Logan's helmet cams to ensure nothing is missed. "Confirmed," he says. "All six personnel cross-check with known records."

Logan directs Roman to stay in the central area while he moves through the tunnel to the second tent. "Looks like a dormitory."

"Clear the rooms," I tell him.

"Roger that."

I leave Parris to the goodwill of Tuvalu's staff, and go outside again. The dialog between Logan and Kanoa continues as I strip out of the dead merc's rig and get back into my own.

"Room one, clear," Logan reports.

"Confirmed."

"Room two, clear."

I walk toward the hangar, where I meet Escamilla and Tran. "Have we got a way out of here, sir?" Tran asks me.

"Still waiting on that."

A door in the side of the hangar opens. I turn fast, but this time I manage to keep my HITR across my chest instead of targeting the civilian framed in the doorway. Artificial light from inside illuminates a blue parka and hood, half-raised hands, gloved palms turned out, no obvious weapons. My gaze shifts from the hands to the face. She's standing a step back from the door so the light falls at an angle across the bare skin of her face. Black skin, dark-brown eyes, elegant eyebrows drawn down in a fierce scowl, her lip curled in contempt. "You got anything human left under that helmet, Shelley?" she asks me.

Escamilla and Tran both turn their weapons in her direction. Kanoa checks in with a monosyllabic observation: *"Shit."*

And me? Shock hits me so hard it blows every thought out of my brain but one—one that's so strong, so focused, my fucking skullnet picks it up, translates it to audio, and in a calm tone that in no way represents how I feel, I hear my artificial voice say over gen-com, *"Jaynie."*

It's an impossible coincidence to run into Jayne Vasquez here, at the ice-end of nowhere—but then, I don't believe in coincidence. I know better than that.

"Shelley, take it easy," Kanoa warns—as if I would ever hurt her.

Jaynie can't see my face, but she recognized me anyway. We've been on enough missions together. She knows what I look like when I'm rigged. She knows how I move.

I shoulder my HITR and then I reach with two hands for my helmet.

Kanoa protests, "What are you doing?"

I ignore him and take the helmet off. I peel back my thermal hood. The cold hits like fire, but I don't care, because I need to show Jaynie that I am not more or less than what I used to be.

She takes a long look at me. Then she steps aside to let me into the shelter of the hangar.

Inside the hangar, the air is heated to five degrees American—bearable compared to the outside. The round walls surround a small Bell helicopter painted rescue yellow; the span of its blades is only a couple of meters less than the hangar's diameter.

Escamilla follows me in. Roman comes in through the tunnel that leads to the living area. I ignore them both. So does Jaynie.

She pushes back the hood of her parka, letting me see that she is not wearing a skullcap. Her scalp is covered in tightly curled black hair trimmed short in a military cut. I want to ask if she got wired, if she had a skullnet put in, but I know better. "You gave it up, didn't you? No skullcap. No skullnet. You're not an emo-junkie anymore."

That's not what she wants to talk about. "You are supposed to be dead." She watches me with a stonewall expression. "The fucking United States Navy shot you out of the sky. Or was that faked?"

"It wasn't faked." The navy fired the missile that brought down our little spaceplane, *Lotus*. It wasn't a direct hit, but the shockwave and the debris were enough to break us apart. "Kurnakova is dead."

"And you're still here. Still God's favorite."

God's favorite toy, maybe.

Since I'm not wearing my helmet anymore, Kanoa has switched gen-com to my overlay. "This is not what you're here for, Shelley. The only thing you need to worry about is getting your squad safely extracted."

"I don't agree, sir." Dread and anticipation wage war in my head as I look past Jaynie to the tunnel entrance, imagining Delphi appearing there. I kept track of her for a while. I was glad when she partnered with Jaynie. When they set up a company together, I was sure she'd be okay. So I left it at that. I stopped looking back. But now? "There *is* a reason for this," I insist.

"There may be a reason, but it's not one you need to understand. Get that helicopter fired up and get the hell out of there. That is an order."

Kanoa is at least partly right. We need to be gone, and soon, before a call gets through to the Canadian military. So I gesture at Escamilla. "Check for the key, and then get things started."

"You stealing my helicopter?" Jaynie asks, glaring at Escamilla as he opens the pilot-side door and leans inside.

"This your operation?" I don't want to believe it. "Come on, Jaynie. You're not going to Mars."

"Key's here!" Escamilla calls out. He looks in the back. "Seats have been pulled. Cargo configuration, but we can work with that."

"Do it."

Jaynie drops her chin like a fighter. "Mars is the goal we're working on."

"That's fucking crazy."

Escamilla peels off his pack and his helmet. He starts popping cinches on his dead sister because his rig has to come off before he can fit in the pilot's seat.

Jaynie looks at him, looks at me. "I'm not the one walking around with wires in my head, Shelley."

No, she's just the one thinking about going to Mars. And it scares me because it's possible. A one-way, privately funded expedition is under development. A lot of dragons are behind it. It wasn't long ago that I heard chatter in the barracks about the pending launch of an advance robotic mission intended to deliver supplies ahead of a crewed expedition.

"Did you buy in, Jaynie?"

She nods. "I did."

Dragon-scale money was in play on our last mission together. I did my part to see that Jaynie and Delphi wound up with it, because I wanted Jaynie to have the freedom to build a sanctuary somewhere beyond the influence of the Red. Mars fits that description, but Mars is a mistake.

"There is nothing on Mars for you, Jaynie. Not even air to breathe."

"Were you sent here to tell me that?"

I hesitate. Jaynie has a paranoid fear of the Red and its influence over her life, but there is a resonance of truth in her words. "Maybe."

I look again at the tunnel entrance. I want to be sure. "Delphi's not here, is she?"

Jaynie follows my gaze. "She's been looking for you. Did you know that? She never believed you were dead. I kept telling her there was no way—" She doesn't get any further. Her control cracks; her voice climbs an octave. "God*damn* you, Shelley, why didn't you come home?"

Roman is still standing watch, anonymous behind her visor, but I can see Escamilla's face. He's sitting in the pilot's seat, hesitating over the checklist as he waits to hear what I will say. He made the same choice I did. Everyone in the squad made the choice to walk away from the lives they'd lived before. We all share that guilt—and I know better than to apologize for it.

"We are engaged in a war against Armageddon, Jaynie. No one goes home from that."

Escamilla nods in grim approval as he returns to his task, but Jaynie's eyes are glistening. She leans in close. Her gloved hand touches my arm; her eyes plead with me. "*Stay.* We'll make room for you to go with us. We'll get the wiring out of your head. You'll be okay."

I *don't* believe in coincidence. I am not here by chance.

"I'm not going to Mars, Jaynie, and neither are you. It's suicide. A mistake you can't come back from." She pulls away, but I catch her arm. "I need you to listen to me. I need you to understand the way things are, because there is a new standard in the world. It says that everyone has to be visible, everyone accountable. So don't keep your secrets too close or some jackboot like me will kick in your door to find out what you're hiding."

She jerks her arm free of my grip and backs away. "Go to hell."

Logan comes through the tunnel. "Load your gear," I tell him. I shrug off my pack, but Kanoa intercedes. "You've still got Dr. Parris's sample case."

"You want me to give it back to her?"

Jaynie has retreated toward the tunnel, but she's watching me warily.

"We've got no reason to keep it. It's not biowarfare material, so hand it over."

"Jaynie, wait." I get the black case out of my pack. "This belongs to Dr. Parris." I hold it out to her. "It's biological material, microbial cultures. She says it's not dangerous, but you should talk to her about it, use your judgment."

Jaynie crosses her arms, raises her chin, puts on a skeptical expression. "You want me to return that to her?"

I don't want to argue about it. "Do what you want."

"I intend to." Despite her defiant tone, she comes to take the case from me. Her hand is shaking. I think maybe mine is too.

Escamilla calls out, "We need to get the hangar doors open!"

Logan responds, "I'm on it!"

We are pirates, taking what we need. "Jaynie, listen. I'm sorry. About the helicopter. It's just that we need to move fast, so we don't really have a choice."

She draws back. "You're sorry about *that*? Don't worry. It's insured. Now get the fuck out of here." She retreats to the tunnel. But as Logan opens the hangar doors, letting in the rush of the wind, Jaynie turns back. She projects her voice to make sure I hear her. "Hey, Shelley, maybe we'll meet again—on Mars, after the war!" Then she's gone.

Logan steps up to my side. His thermal mask is rolled up to expose his face. "I didn't think that could ever happen."

I tell him what I told Tran before this fucked-up mission started. "*Never* trust the Red."

Never think you understand it.

The wind is in our favor, ferrying the helicopter south to *Sigil*, but it's still strong enough to generate white-knuckle turbulence. Escamilla says nothing, all his attention focused on the controls as he works to keep us on course and steady.

Logan, Roman, and Tran are in back on the floor, crammed in with our packs, our weapons, and the folded bones of our dead sisters. I'm riding in the co-pilot's seat. All of us have our helmets on. Mine shows me the terrain in the green glow of night vision. I'm supposed to be helping Escamilla navigate, but mostly I'm thinking about Jaynie and Delphi and how hard it must be to get to Mars, and how utterly and forever beyond my reach they would be when, inevitably, things begin to go wrong. It's a line of thought that links to a weird, familiar panic and for just a few seconds I'm back on the First Light mission, aboard the C-17, and Colonel Rawlings is telling me the harsh truth: *You can't do anything for her.*

This time, though, I'm forewarned.

My short trip into low earth orbit required a twenty-million-dollar rocket. Mars is literally another world, vastly farther away. I know the transit will involve complex orbital dynamics and gravity boosts, but it will also require a rocket a hell of a lot bigger and costlier than the one that ferried me into orbit.

A rocket like that should be easy to track down.

My thoughts snap back to the present when my skullnet icon flicks on: fiery red veins against a black background. A flood of manufactured anxiety hits me, overwhelming my homegrown fears and bringing with it a premonition that death is on its way. I'm not the only one who receives the warning. Chatter erupts over gen-com as everyone speaks at once.

"What the fuck?'"

"Something's up?"

"What is it? Anybody know?"

"Kanoa, you got anything for me?" I look out the windshield, but all I see is the rugged ice below us, its low peaks and pinnacles smoothed by the recent fall of snow.

Kanoa checks in, grim-voiced, speaking to the entire squad. "Warning, warning. Radar indicates a fighter coming in low and dark. Tracks back to a Chinese carrier off Greenland. Trajectory indicates an intercept. Shelley—"

"Full throttle!" I yell at Escamilla. "Get us into Canadian territory."

I tell myself there is no way a Chinese fighter will shoot us down over territory claimed by Canada, but Kanoa puts an end to my fantasy when he says in a deadly calm voice, "Ninety seconds to missile range."

Dr. Parris suspected Vince Glover had a Chinese

connection. It's starting to look like she was right—and when the Chinese decide to clean up a dirty situation, they don't fuck around.

"Down!" I yell at Escamilla. "Put us on the ice."

"Roger that."

Our airspeed slows; the deck drops away beneath me. I twist around to look in back.

Night vision details Logan, Tran, and Roman huddled on the cargo floor, their opaque visors turned in my direction. "Rig up!" I tell them. "*Move, move!* Claim your compass points, and when we hit the ice, scatter!"

Scattering is the trained response of an LCS under air attack. The more distance we put between each soldier, the harder a pilot has to work to gun us down.

Roman is first up. "North!" she says as she snaps open the folded frame of her dead sister.

Tran is right behind her. "West."

There's not enough room to extend the rigs all the way, not enough room to stand up straight. They strap in anyway. It's a chaos of titanium bones and Arctic camo as they bend and crouch and help each other secure their cinches.

Logan eases his pack on, careful not to knock anyone down. Over gen-com, he says, "Escamilla! You—"

I cut him off. "I'll take care of Escamilla."

"Right, sir. I'm south, then—and you'd better get rigged."

"Clear some room."

They press against the walls. I get out of my harness and climb over the seats. Tran has my rig unfolded, the leg struts bent in a crouch. I cinch up. The deck sways, but Tran and Roman both grab me, keep me from falling. Logan helps me get my pack on. I grab my HITR from the floor and loop it over my shoulder. "Escamilla, you are east. Got that?"

"Yes, sir!"

"As soon as you get this ship down, roll out the door and fucking run for your life. I will get your gear to you."

"Roger that, Shelley."

Logan is crouched by the eastern window. Night vision shows me a slice of sky behind him, marred by a dark mote moving fast between the stars.

"Escamilla, why aren't we on the ground?"

"We need a place to land, sir. There's smooth ice ahead. Maybe twenty seconds."

Too much time.

"Get us as low as you can. Logan, Tran, open the doors."

A sliding door on each side gets slammed back, admitting a blast of arctic air along with the roar of the oncoming jet, audible even over the helicopter's own engine noise.

"Ten seconds," Escamilla says.

I wait with Logan. Roman and Tran are on the other side. The ice, shot through with broken pinnacles, speeds past, five meters below us.

"You are within missile range," Kanoa warns.

"*Rocket!*" Logan yells.

"*Jump!* And not into the fucking rotors!"

A half second of blurred motion, and they are gone. It's only me and Escamilla. I reach over the seat and pop his harness. "Get the fuck out." Then I turn, grab his gear, pitch it out the left doorway—the doorway facing east, the one that shows me the fiery trail of a rocket slaloming toward me—and I follow the gear, rolling out the door, praying I don't collide with Escamilla.

I slam shoulder-first into the ice. My momentum flips me into the air. I come down on my arm struts in an explosion of snow just as the rocket finds the helicopter. Flame enfolds the world and the pressure wave hits, knocking me back in time, all the way back to Dassari: my legs blown off, unable to move, and the fighter screaming overhead, the muddy ground trembling beneath me.

The Chinese fighter blows past and the vibration wanes. The present locks back in. It's not mud I'm clinging to; it's ice. I shove the terror away and make myself scan the squad icons.

Not all green, but none flashing critical red either.

"Escamilla! Status?"

"Moving, sir!" He sounds like he's speaking through gritted teeth. "I think I broke a fucking rib."

I slap the ice with my arm hooks, launching myself to my feet. In the west, night vision shows me the fighter coming around for another pass. "Enemy incoming! If you've got cover, take it!"

I race north, looking for Escamilla's gear. I find it only twenty meters away. The squad map puts him southeast of my position. I scoop up his pack and the folded bones of his dead sister and take off in that direction, the leg struts of my exoskeleton powering me over the rough terrain.

The fighter is roaring in low, hunting us, hunting me. I'm the one in motion. I don't want to lead him to Escamilla, so I look for a ridge or a pinnacle of ice high enough to hide me, but I don't see anything like that. What I see is oily smoke curling over a pool of open water. No sign of the helicopter.

I hear a burst from the fighter's autocannon. The pilot has found a target. My squad map assures me no one else is in motion, so I'm pretty sure his target is me. I drop Escamilla's gear. I think maybe Kanoa is yelling at me, but I'm not listening. How can I listen? Despite the protection of my helmet, the jet's roar is all I hear. It's Dassari all over again—and maybe because I came so close to dying like this before, I opt for a different way out.

No less terrifying.

I drop my HITR and shrug off my pack, throwing it behind me, hoping it will provide a target to distract the pilot. Then I dive, sliding across the ice toward the open water. I'll drown this time rather than being blown apart again.

Given a choice, though? I'd rather live.

Just before I drop over the edge of the ice, I pivot on my belly and hammer my arm hooks into the edge of the floe. My legs hit the water first. The weight of my dead sister pulls me down, plunging me under the surface. I am fully extended, hanging by my arm hooks, knowing that if those hooks slip or if the ice breaks, I'm heading for the ocean floor.

The full impact of the cold is tempered by my thermal layer, which keeps the water away from my torso and my limbs, but as my helmet floods, the water touches my lips, my nose, my eyes. I squeeze my eyes shut, imagining my shocked brain shrinking to a tiny, hot point.

It's not imagination when I feel the ice snap away under my right hook. The hook slips, but it catches again. And then there's a muffled *boom*! The ice shudders. The hook slips a second time.

I want to breathe.

Worse than that, the water is finding its way inside my thermal suit, seeping past the neckline and the wrist cuffs, climbing my thighs—it feels like razor blades slicing away my skin—and I change my mind about the kind of death I prefer.

I haul against the arm hooks, expecting them to slip. If they slip, my only chance is to un-cinch before I go too deep. Down on the bottom it'll be so cold, my body might never rot. Buried in silt, I could become a fossil for some freaking ape to dig up in twenty million years. Or I'll be food for crabs and starfish.

The arm hooks hold.

My helmeted head breaks the surface, the water drains away, and I breathe. Releasing my right hook, I reach across the surface of the floe, jam the point in, and haul myself high enough to get an elbow over the edge. The hooks hold me, so I don't slide back. I reset them one at a time, dragging myself up onto the floe.

I lie there, watching the water drain out of my sleeve, amazed at the way it transforms into thin sheets of white ice before it quite escapes. I notice my body shaking uncontrollably. It's a clinical observation. I tell myself I'll be all right. My thermals are designed to hold in heat whether they're wet or dry.

I make myself focus on the present. First thing: Scan my squad icons. They are green and yellow, but I'm shivering too hard to read the details. I push myself up to a sitting position. The wind is blowing, but I feel it only as a pressure. Maybe I'm too cold to feel colder. Maybe my gear is doing its job.

The night has gone quiet. So quiet, a stray thought questions if I've gone deaf—or maybe the audio gear in my helmet has shorted out? I decide to test it, though my chattering teeth make it hard to talk. "R-roll c-call," I say over gen-com.

It's a relief to hear them respond:

"Logan."

"Roman."

"Escamilla."

"Tran."

"W-where's the f-fighter?" I ask no one in particular.

Then I see it myself. It's in the northeast, a ghostly arrowhead in night vision, halfway through a wide turn that will bring it around for another pass.

It never finishes that turn.

The sky is clear, but distant thunder rumbles in the south—and the Chinese fighter reacts, pulling straight up, rocketing toward the stars like it's intending to leave the planet. In seconds, it's too small to see, and then the southern thunder resolves into the roar of at least two more fighters streaking in pursuit.

I presume it's a show of force, the Canadian Air Force scrambled to defend their offshore claims. I get up, as the two jets pass far to the east.

"Logan, y-you got an injury r-report?"

"Yes, sir. Escamilla thinks he's got a broken rib. Me and Tran are just banged up and bruised."

"Do we have mobility?"

Escamilla growls, "I can walk."

"Kanoa, y-you there?"

"Here."

"We need a n-new extraction plan."

"In process. Stand by."

I make myself stand up. I need to move. Generate some heat. Give my thermal layer something to work with. So I go looking for my pack.

I dropped it as a decoy and I guess the strategy worked, because I find a second crater where the pack should be. A film of newly frozen ice is already forming on the surface of the open water.

I look around, but my squad is hunkered down and I can't see them. I don't see Escamilla's gear either. I've got a feeling the crater swallowed it too, and it's on its way to the bottom.

"Escamilla, I think I lost your gear."

"Goddamn it, Shelley. I can't fucking trust you for anything."

"Something to keep in mind."

I look back the way we came, touched by a new worry.

After its second pass, the Chinese fighter swung much farther north than it needed to. Why? Did we turn Tuvalu
Station into a target just by being there?

I ask Kanoa. He assures me Tuvalu Station is intact, but
maybe that's only because the cavalry arrived. Thinking
about Jaynie as additional collateral damage on this
fucked-up mission sends the chill even deeper into my
bones. I want to get out of here before we make things
even worse.

We're still eight kilometers out from *Sigil*. We start walking. Progress is slow because Escamilla doesn't have his rig,
and we're all exhausted—but a few minutes later, Kanoa
checks in.

"Good news. That Chinese fighter forced the Red to
revisit this mission, and we finally got an order through.
Oscar 1 is on his way."

It's a relief to hear it. Then again, it'll be almost two
hours before Oscar-1 reaches us. We keep walking, and
even with Escamilla slowing us down, we get to *Sigil* first.

The tiltrotor is too big to land on *Sigil*'s helipad so, fighting the wind, Jason Okamoto holds it in a hover while we
load our wounded and our gear. He's in a hurry to leave,
and not just because of the weather. "There's a Canadian
gunship an hour behind me," he tells us over gen-com as
we load Julian's stretcher and secure it to the floor. "And a
no-fly order in effect. So far, I've got official clearance, but
this is not a good time to be flying on counterfeit orders—
especially after that refueling fiasco."

"Get the door closed," I tell Tran.

As soon as it latches, we're on our way, riding the buffeting wind south. Our two prisoners get left behind. Let the
Canadians figure out what to do with them.

It takes a few minutes to tie down our folded exoskeletons, secure our packs, and stow our helmets. We're still linked into gen-com through our overlays. Fadul grabs the empty copilot's seat. The rest of us buckle in to the fold-up canvas seats mounted on the cabin's side rails.

"All secure back there?" Okamoto asks.

"Roger that."

He turns off the cabin lights, and then the deck tilts as he puts Oscar-1 into a steep climb to try to get us above the worst of the wind. It's going to be a hell of a long flight home.

I lean back, close my eyes, cross my arms over my chest, and dial the sensory feedback from my legs down to nothing. It's warm in the cabin. That plus the darkness and the roar of the engines quickly lulls me into a half sleep—until Tran speaks over gen-com. "You know what I don't get?"

I snap awake, my heart racing. He's a shadowy figure, sitting across the narrow cabin between Roman and Logan.

"What do you not get?" Escamilla asks in a surly voice as he stretches his long legs across the cabin's narrow floor.

"I don't get why we're based in Texas. It's fucking unfair, if you ask me."

Fadul is upfront in the copilot's seat, but she's hooked into gen-com, so she's part of the conversation. "No one asked you," she reminds him.

"No, think about it. We are an illicit ass-kicking ghost militia run by an elusive, enigmatic, un-erasable AI. Right? Seems like some cool, luxury-packed, underground hideout should go along with a setup like that."

"Shut the fuck up, Tran," Logan advises as he wads his parka into a pillow.

"You got to read something besides comic books," Roman adds, wriggling around, trying to get comfortable without releasing her harness.

"I think Tran has a point," I say in his defense.

Fadul answers, "That's because you just fucking hate Texas."

True enough.

Strike Squad 7-1 hides in the open, occupying an officially mothballed US Army training facility—the very same facility from which the assault on Black Cross was launched late on Coma Day. We are based at C-FHEIT, the Center For Human Engineering, Integration, & Training—pronounced "see-fight" in army-speak. It's where I trained when my prosthetics were new. I was the test case in an army program aimed at recycling experienced combat personnel who'd had their legs blown off. I proved the program worked, but when the economy cratered after Coma Day, funding was canceled and C-FHEIT was closed.

It's still officially closed, but by some bureaucratic alchemy, Kanoa was able to take it over.

I nod off, dreaming of ice and wind and battles I don't remember fighting.

We stop briefly at the remote listening station on the north end of Ellesmere Island. This time, the counterfeit order that allows Oscar-1 to refuel is accepted, and we're soon on our way. We'll be flying through the night.

I sleep for another couple of hours. When I wake again, I unbuckle, check on Julian, and then move up front, just to be moving. I find Fadul asleep, her head turned to the side. Okamoto is alert as always. He's not wired, but when he flies, he runs a program in his farsights that checks his wakefulness by monitoring his gaze. He's also got a pack of pills taped to the control panel—little doses of speed if he starts to get sleepy. Old-fashioned but effective. And in a few more hours, Escamilla will come up front to relieve him.

I lean over to look out the windshield, but it's night over northern Canada. There's not much to see. Okamoto looks up at me. He's only fifty, but his buzz-cut hair is silver, and so is his goatee. The soft lights from the instrument panel illuminate a grim expression so uncharacteristic of him that I know right away we've got trouble.

It's too loud to talk easily, so I use gen-com to open a solo link. "Something wrong with the plane?"

"No. It's not that." He returns his gaze to the instrument panel. "I'm not asking about the mission. It's not my business what you did up there. But you might want to know— we've got an air war going on in the Arctic."

Right away, I get a sick feeling in my gut.

"It's big and it's getting bigger," Okamoto says. "Rumor on the civilian stations is that China initially scrambled a fighter. They called it a response to terrorism. Canada, Denmark, and Russia all reacted, sending out their own fighters to protect their sovereign interests."

"Is it just posturing? Or are they taking each other down?"

He shakes his head. "Not much solid information."

"Okay. Thanks."

I retreat to my seat and strap in, then send a message to Kanoa, asking him to check on the situation at Tuvalu Station. His response comes back within a minute: All personnel were successfully evacuated by the US Navy.

I hope it's true.

CHAIN OF COMMAND

IT'S MIDMORNING WHEN WE MAKE IT BACK TO C-FHEIT. The news that's reached us overnight is not good. Missiles have been launched and fighters shot down, and there's every reason to believe the air war in the Arctic will get worse before it gets better.

Okamoto shifts our craft's propellers from vertical to horizontal and then, descending in helicopter mode, he delivers us to C-FHEIT's central quadrangle.

Our two-story barracks is on one side of the open area. The gym is directly across from it, and at the far end is the gray, one-story, windowless Cybernetics Center. A flagpole stands in front of it, flying an American flag that waves with easy grace in a chill winter wind.

We left Julian at a private hospital in Michigan; he's scheduled to be flown down to San Antonio later today by air ambulance. Dunahee, Fadul, and Escamilla can all be treated on base. I send them to report to medical. The rest of us work in guilty silence to get the gear unloaded, and as soon as we're clear, Okamoto takes off again, heading for a well-deserved rest.

Our working theory is that a Chinese company was

paying Vincent Glover to pirate Dr. Parris's multibillion-dollar microbes. When Glover realized that deal was about to fall through, he decided to salvage what he could. But he took action only because we showed up. And we shouldn't have been there.

I have glimpsed Armageddon. All of us have. That's why we're part of this outfit. In the nine prior missions I've served with Strike Squad 7-1, I've seen four of our soldiers killed and now two critically wounded—but I always felt the action we took was worthwhile, that we'd made the world at least a little bit safer.

Not this time.

I dump my arctic gear in the corner of my room and set to work cleaning my weapon. We never know when we'll be called out, so we always need to be ready.

As I work, I think—about my own limits and how far I'm willing to go in this holy war.

Eighteen months ago, I left behind everything that mattered to me because I was determined that Armageddon would not happen on my watch.

So how the hell did I manage to start my own fucking war?

ETM Strike Squad 7-1 is housed on the second floor of the barracks. This used to be officer territory, outfitted with suites, but the floor was remodeled and re-divided into ten individual rooms. Support personnel—all but one regular army—are housed downstairs. The one exception is a civilian intelligence analyst.

7-1 hides in plain sight. Like the crew of the submarine, our support staff has worked out who we are. They just assume we've gone dark, while remaining legitimate soldiers loyal to the United States Army.

The truth is more complex. Though we use army resources—housing, communications, transportation, weapons, intelligence—we are fighting a nonlinear war, and that means our interests only occasionally align with those of our host. It's not a fact I'm proud of, but the way I look at it? The US Army has always operated with contradictory goals and interests determined by politicians and generals pursuing their own pet agendas. We're just contributing one more set of objectives.

On the second floor of the barracks is a media room restricted to 7-1. That night—the night after we kicked off worldwide media's newest entertainment offering, *War in the Arctic*—I'm sitting between Fadul and Tran in one of the media room's upholstered armchairs, watching a news-propaganda station.

We're all dressed alike, in uniform T-shirt and trousers. Visible below the sleeve of Fadul's shirt is a long gash on her bicep, held together by wound glue and segments of clear tape. She's slouched in her seat, bare feet propped up on a coffee table, glaring at the huge screen like she wants to take a swing at it. Tran doesn't look any happier. He's slurping his third energy drink of the evening, his legs vibrating with the overload.

The voices of two mediots are discussing lives already lost as a video plays. It's an angel's-eye view of a drilling rig—not *Deep Winter Sigil*—on fire in the Arctic night. A column of flame envelops the derrick. One of the mediots assures us that drilling has not been completed; the well has not reached oil; there is no danger of environmental disaster.

"These clowns don't know what they're talking about," Tran says. "I mean, if there's no petroleum, what's feeding the fire?"

Fadul answers without turning her head. "It's stored fuel, idiot."

"That's what they want us to believe."

No way to know yet what the truth is. What we've heard so far—and maybe it's bullshit—is that a Chinese fighter was shot down after taking aggressive action inside Canadian territory. In retaliation, the Chinese launched a sortie that sank a Canadian Coast Guard vessel. The Russians, who resent the Chinese presence in the Arctic, jumped in to defend the Canadians, while the Danish navy deployed two frigates in defense of its client state of Greenland along with the development deals Greenland has with the Chinese. So far—if the mediots can be believed—the US has managed to stay out of the conflict, held back by a non-interventionist wing of Congress that recently passed legislation restricting the power of the president to engage in military activity outside the borders of the country. That legislation is an overt challenge to long-established war powers, and a Supreme Court review is imminent—if "imminent" is a word that can be used to describe the glacial pace of Supreme Court proceedings.

I flinch as the door opens. A glance over my shoulder shows me Kanoa coming in. Because of his spinal injury, he doesn't work out like he used to, but he's a big man who still packs a lot of muscle—enough to fill up the doorway. His Polynesian heritage shows in his dark skin and his wide, strong face. Tonight he's dressed in a black pullover and gray camo pants. As he sits behind me in the second row, I turn around and ask him, "What the fuck have we done?"

Fadul answers first, with a derisive hiss. "You're always saying we're not on the side of the angels, but you don't really believe it. You still want to be the good guy."

"So do I," Tran says. "That's why I'm here."

"So do we all," Kanoa affirms.

In that case, we've all failed, because good guys don't start accidental wars. I gesture at the monitor, where family

photos of the missing oil rig workers are being shown: the
smiling faces of men and women whose lives never mattered all that much—except to those who loved them. "Is
this a mistake?" I ask Kanoa.

"It's a fucking conspiracy," Tran says, his gaze still fixed
on the screen. "Forces arrayed against us, to undo our good
work."

Kanoa side-eyes him, but Tran is too engrossed with
the reporting to notice. So he returns his attention to me.
"Think about it, Shelley. Would you want it to be a mistake?
Do you think that's any better?"

"I don't like either option. If we kicked off an accidental war, that's a serious fuck-up. But if it's not accidental—
what does that say about what else we might be asked to
do?"

"You starting to think we're on the wrong side of history?"

"No. We're outside of history." When the history of this
age gets written, we won't be part of the story—but I don't
give a shit about that. I just want to know that history goes
on. "Every mission we've done until now has been worth
doing. Not this one."

"My *first* ETM mission," Tran says. "And it was a fucking
mistake."

"Yeah." He's furious about that, and I don't blame him.
"There was nothing threatening going on inside that lab."

"Look-and-see," Kanoa says. His palm slices the air in a
dismissive gesture. "We all know it won't always work out."

I consider again my suspicion that the Red is not a single
coherent entity. If it's a divided mind, with contradictory
goals, that could explain some of the mission's failures.

I jump as Tran's fist hits his armrest. "Holy *shit*," he says,
staring at the monitor.

The mediots have taken a break from their coverage of
the Arctic War to mention other publicity-worthy events

of the day. The secretary of defense is pictured briefly, and
then the story shifts to a security incident on the Canadian
border.

"What?" Fadul asks.

Tran looks surprised that we're all staring at him. "It's
the secretary of defense. Died suddenly."

"Died of what?" Fadul wants to know, like she's trying to
work out a reason she should give a damn.

Kanoa reads more into it. "*Jesus.* That's the second—"

"No, it's the third," Tran interrupts. "The third member
of President Monteiro's administration to die under mysterious—"

"Hold on," I interrupt him. "They're talking to Dr. Parris."

The scene shifts to a recording studio set up to look like
a nineteenth-century library, shelves with wooden shelves
holding neat sets of leather-bound books—a cultural motif
of intellect. Dr. Parris is the sole inhabitant of the stylized
setting; I see her face for the first time as she gazes uneasily
at the camera from her post in an upholstered chair. Her
hair is short and gray, her eyes sunken over sharp cheekbones. There are frostbite injuries on her lips, cheeks, and
the tip of her sharp nose that give her a bruised and beaten
look. The mediot interviewing her gets right to the point.
"Dr. Parris, there has been widespread speculation that your
lab was devoted to biowarfare research—"

That's as far as he gets before she stops him. "*Absolutely*
not." But she's no longer looking at the camera. She's looking away; she's looking remorseful. "Some of the questions
directed at me by my rescuers lead me to believe the attack
on my lab and the murder of my staff might have been motivated by that rumor—which makes it all the more tragic,
because in fact we were working to develop new pharmaceutical applications to improve life around the globe . . ."

It's easy to see she's shocked and grieved at what

happened to her colleagues, but her work remains important to her. She answers the mediot's questions on the objective of her work, though she carefully skirts the issue of
synthetic bacterial strains.

"At least we did one good thing," Tran says. "We saved
Dr. Parris."

But I have to take even that away from him. "Parris
would still be at work in her lab if we hadn't shown up."

Fadul shrugs. "I think it *was* a mistake. All those dead
scientists, the war. But that's how the game is played. Sure,
the Red tries to make shit happen. It's got some secret plan.
But it can't dictate the future. All it can do is shift the odds.
Every move we make is still a toss of the dice."

"Not every move," I insist. "There were elements the Red
could have controlled. Why didn't we know about Glover's
helicopter? What happened to the order to refuel Oscar-1?
Why didn't we get scrubbed from that satellite image? Why
only a few seconds' warning when that Chinese fighter
came in?"

"Why did we run into your old sergeant?" Tran asks.
"That was the weirdest part of the whole mission. It's got to
mean something."

"Not in the way you're thinking," Kanoa says.

The social code among our little coven of resurrected
war heroes is that the past should be left alone. Don't try to
keep track of those we abandoned. Don't talk about them.
Don't hold onto what was. That's why I haven't brought up
the subject of Jaynie, but I think Tran is right. "Why *was*
Jayne Vasquez put into play?"

Fadul answers this question with a stony glare and cold
silence. She crosses her arms and turns back to the screen,
where the video has shifted to show, for about the hun-
dredth time, bootleg video of the dead bodies aboard *Sigil*.

Kanoa likes to say we are ghosts operating in the world

on a temporary dispensation from God. I think he believes that. And if our devotion to the cause ever wavers? He gives us a pep talk, reminding us that we'll get out soon enough, that any mission could be our last, that we are here for only a little while, to do what we can, while we can.

Yeah, this is a fucking cult.

It's disturbing that most of the time, I fit right in.

Not at this precise moment.

I tell Fadul, "I think you're half right. I think the mission was a mistake, but it was *meant* to be." I phrase it that way because I know it'll irritate her—enough to get her to talk to me again. I fucking hate it when she locks me out. "If we'd succeeded in taking *Sigil*, if we'd cleared the lab and gone on our way, I would never have known Jaynie was out there, planning to defect to Mars."

Planning to take Delphi with her.

"It's not going to happen," I add.

"You don't get to decide that," Kanoa warns me.

But I've already decided: I won't let Delphi throw her life away.

That night of the First Light mission, when I was on the C-17 and Lissa was hostage on an enemy aircraft, an uncrossable gulf lay between us. It was like Lissa existed in another dimension, another world. No way to reach her. Nothing I could do. I never want to be that far away again, or that helpless when things start to come apart.

I tell Kanoa, "The Red put this in front of me. That wasn't by chance. There was a reason for it."

Fadul reenters the conversation with the expected lecture. "It doesn't work that way, asshole, and you know it. No mission has a one-hundred-percent chance of success, so there are always contingencies. Backup plans. Alternate missions if the core task goes south—but we can't always tell what those alternate missions are, even after the fact."

She's mostly right. A lot of what we do is play the odds.
Sometimes the order comes down to prep for a general
mission, no details, we just get in position and wait—and
a lot of the time, shit never happens. Kanoa was working a
mission like that, sitting aboard a US Navy destroyer in the
central Pacific with no clue why he was there until orders
came for the ship to proceed with all speed to a specific set
of coordinates. A few hours later, he pulled me out of the
water.

Contingencies, see?

If I'd landed safely back in San Antonio, Kanoa might
have continued his vigil on that ship until a different mission came his way, or he might have been sent back home.

"Maybe Tuvalu was just a contingency," Kanoa says. "Or
maybe it was the primary phase of the mission. Either way,
Shelley, it doesn't mean it has anything to do with you, or a
mission to Mars. The reason might be as simple as putting
Vasquez and Parris in the same room."

Fadul adds, "It's natural to want to see what happened
as your personal drama. Doesn't make it true."

It's my turn to retreat into silence, because I can't argue
either point. They could both be right—though I don't
think they are.

A familiar voice—one with an unpleasant association—
draws my attention back to the TV.

A chill crosses my skin; my heart rate kicks up. Onscreen
is a woman identified in a caption as Yana Semakova, CEO
and principal owner of Torzhok NAO, delivering an
unflinching condemnation of the Arctic hostilities in excellent English: ". . . Torzhok has invested heavily to create
supply lines designed to serve development of Russia's
Arctic resources. Thousands of jobs have been created, all
of them now at risk . . ."

When I heard her speak before, it was not in English

but in Russian. It was not as the CEO of a major corporation, but as a daughter, annoyed and impatient, struggling to hold onto some semblance of respect for a paranoid old man. It was not with the high-definition audio of a major media broadcast, but with the low fidelity of an old-fashioned two-way radio—one owned by Russian billionaire Eduard Semak.

This is his daughter.

Eduard Semak used his wealth to assemble a collection of nuclear weapons the way other wealthy men might assemble a collection of classic cars. On the mission called Vertigo Gate, I visited Semak in orbit.

And now here is Yana Semakova, drawn into the conflict begun with our assault on *Deep Winter Sigil*. I cannot believe her involvement is just coincidence.

". . . all could be lost in the next airstrike. Jobs, investments, lives, all lost. This conflict must stop before that happens. It must stop now, or the consequences will be unthinkable."

"What consequences do you foresee, ma'am?"

Semakova looks straight at the camera. She is middle-aged, on the heavy side, dignified and attractive without the appearance of having ever used the services of a cosmetic surgeon, though she could easily afford to. As she speaks, she's as fierce as her father, but far more convincing than that decrepit old man. "If this goes on, it will bring tragedy," she says. "Environmental tragedy. Economic tragedy. Tragedy of historic proportions. Tragedy that will not be undone by this generation or the next. All peoples must rise up against any power that does not immediately participate in a cease-fire. Do not be caught on the wrong side of history."

The feed shifts back to a studio where a mediot recounts the known losses so far: three fighter jets, two drilling platforms, a coast guard vessel, and a nuclear-powered ice-breaker that was damaged but is still afloat and limping back to port. One hundred twelve lives.

Why? What is it for?

My skullnet picks up the thought and decides to voice it over gen-com: "Why? What is it for?"

"Shit," I whisper.

It used to take a lot of concentration and practice to trigger the skullnet to translate a thought to words—but the skullnet is an adaptive system. The embedded AI that does the work has gotten way too good at reading me . . . or misreading me. This isn't the first time it's mistakenly posted my thoughts to gen-com.

Fadul is not about to overlook it. She slides her feet off the coffee table, turns to give me a withering look. "Got enough noise of my own in my head, Shelley. Don't need to hear yours."

"Yeah. Don't need you to hear it."

"But they're good questions," Tran says. He's still staring at the monitor, his caffeine-jacked legs still vibrating. "They're the kind of questions people should ask more often."

Kanoa raises a skeptical eyebrow. "Put in more time training the AI," he tells me.

"Yes, sir."

I stand up. I need to move. So I pace behind the chairs, waiting for Fadul to track down the reason behind my mental slip. I don't think she's aware of this connection between me and Yana Semakova, but I know her well enough to know she'll look. After a minute I hear a soft, whispered *"Fuck,"* just audible over the mediot's ongoing monologue. I turn to find her staring at me, her dark eyes shadowed with dark circles. "The cache of nuclear weapons you uncovered," she says. "Semakova is linked to that."

I nod. The purpose of Vertigo Gate was to find the location of Eduard Semak's stolen nuclear devices. We succeeded in that. The devices were recovered, but no one living was held responsible. Blame was laid on a deceased lieutenant who had "taken advantage of a frail old man." That was the explanation offered by the family and accepted by investigators. When I heard it, I knew a considerable sum of money must have changed hands to purchase a revised history.

I wanted to blow it open, but there was no way I could do it without revealing my existence and my own involvement. "Let it go," Kanoa advised me.

It was both easier and safer not to argue. What mattered was that the nukes were in responsible hands and scheduled for decommissioning. More than once since, I've wondered if Semakova wasn't grateful for what we did— getting rid of her crazy old man and relieving her of the burden of his nuclear armaments which she surely had no intention to ever use.

I flinch as the door opens; it's Escamilla coming in. "Hey Shelley, going emo again?"

I casually give him the finger while Fadul fills him in. "Shelley's freaking out because the lines of fate are closing in a net around him."

"Two coincidences that aren't coincidences," I say.

"Need to pay attention to that," Tran agrees.

But Fadul rolls her eyes. "What *does* it mean?"

Someone pops the volume on the TV down to zero. Probably Kanoa, because he's got gossip to share. Cracking a rare smile, white teeth shining in the light from the TV, he says, "Vasquez lifted two point five billion dollars in electronic currency from Semak's personal holdings during Vertigo Gate." He looks at me. "There's no need to sweat it, Shelley. Semakova and Vasquez worked out a peace agreement. They've met in person at least three times and share some business interests."

FaceValue tags this as the truth, but I don't want to believe it. Like all of us, Jaynie undertook both First Light and Vertigo Gate because of ideals. It makes no sense that she would turn around and compromise herself by allying with the criminal empire of Eduard Semak.

"That's got to be mistaken intelligence. Jaynie doesn't have anything in common with Semakova."

"Sorry, Shelley. But I've seen their names together in enough DIRs to believe it."

DIRs—Daily Intelligence Reports—are long, detailed compilations of notable events around the world. I rarely look at them, because they don't have any real bearing on what we do. We are assigned a mission and we execute it— or fuck it up, in the most recent case.

Palehorse Keep was different, not just because it got fucked up, but because for the first time, the moral imperative of the mission did not compensate for the fallout. I want to believe there is some hidden benefit to what we did, some circumstance spun off from the chain of events we initiated that will make even a war in the Arctic worthwhile.

But I'm not seeing it.

The next morning, I wake up hurting. It's December 25 and we have the day off. No PT, no studies, no training. But I'm up at 0500 anyway, reminded by every organic muscle and joint I still possess that I ran a marathon and topped it off by jumping out of a moving helicopter. It's not usually a single debilitating injury that ends the service of an infantry soldier. Most of the time, it's the accumulated wear and tear.

I walk in zombie steps to the bathroom, take some pills, and stand under a stream of hot water until the pain eases. While I'm in there, I check my email for an update on Julian's status: still in serious condition, but improving.

I sleep for a few more hours. So it's midmorning before I show my face downstairs.

The support personnel are celebrating Christmas with a tiny artificial tree on the watch desk and a plate of cookies that is nearly empty. The private on duty eyes me warily; they always look at me that way. I don't know why. "There's going to be a party in the Cyber Center, sir, starting at noon."

"Maybe I'll be there."

Like last year, I toy with the fantasy of calling my dad. I try to imagine what I would say, what I could say.

Hey, it's me.

After Vertigo Gate, the Department of Defense issued an official notice that I was dead. No details. Just a statement that the Lion of Black Cross had died in the service of his country. I let my dad believe it, just like I let Delphi believe it.

I'd like to call him, but I know the conversation we'd have wouldn't do either of us any good. So like last year, I drop the idea. Why tear open old wounds?

Outside, the day is gloomy with gray clouds but no rain. I walk quickly to the Cyber Center. Party preparations are underway in the cafeteria, so after I heat a couple of egg-and-bacon meals in the microwave and get supplied with a plate of fancy cookies, I retreat with my spoils to the office of our on-site intelligence analyst, Cory Helms.

Cory is one of the two civilian personnel who make up our intelligence team, and the only one quartered at C-FHEIT. Kanoa brought him in six months ago under a private contract paid by the Department of Defense. He's a small guy, a bit pudgy, quiet and thoughtful and a little awkward, whose thinning gray hair is always neatly parted and combed.

Within a week of his arrival, Logan and I, being arrogant assholes, codenamed him Bilbo.

Every four weeks Cory squeezes aboard the van that shuttles regular base personnel to San Antonio on Fridays, returning the following Monday with a fresh haircut. Otherwise, he's here. Even on Christmas.

His office door is open. Inside, he's got two cheap steel desks arranged in an L-shaped configuration. On top of one are a pen and a large pad of paper marked up with cartoon doodles; on the other are two magnetic levitation toys, one with a small silver ball floating an inch above the base, and the other, a slowly cycling rocket ship an inch long, traveling in an endless circle. Monitors line the walls, all of them active, emitting multiple voices in a cacophony that makes no sense to me, but Cory seems able to parse it. Something is holding his attention, anyway. He's leaning back in a rolling chair, staring at one of the screens, with no idea I'm there until I rap hard on the open door.

He spins around with an expectant look until he realizes it's me, and then his expression shifts to an anxious, appeasing smile. For some reason I've never been able to pin down, I make him nervous too. He knows who I am, of course. He knows what we do. But I've watched him in meetings, and he doesn't have the same reaction to Kanoa, or Logan, or anyone else. Not even Fadul, who is a hell of a lot more intimidating than I am.

I put my food down on the nearest desk and invite myself to sit in the empty chair. Cory's smile fades. "Am I in trouble?" he asks with real concern.

I pick up one of the egg-and-bacon meals. "Should you be?"

"After Palehorse Keep? We all should be."

Can't argue with that.

I attack the food, scanning the monitors as I eat. Running on one is a video of the damaged nuclear-powered icebreaker, with a massive cavity blasted in its superstructure and its charred decks torn open. Another screen shows stock footage of Canadian fighters taxiing on a runway with a vast, snow-covered plain beyond them. A third shows stills of the lab on *Sigil* with a bar caption asking, *Was it biowarfare?* Dr. Parris has already countered that rumor, but I guess biowarfare is a sexier headline than pharmaceuticals.

"What can I do for you, Shelley?" Cory wants to know. He'd like to hurry this session along so he can get rid of me that much sooner.

I take another bite and then nod at the monitors. "We started this war. Do you think the Red planned for us to do that?"

He doesn't hesitate at all. "No."

"Then you think this war got started by mistake?"

He presses a knuckle against his mouth. "I don't think it was predicted. We did the look-and-see because we didn't know what was going on inside—and what was going on was an espionage operation being carried out by a third party without moral qualms."

"Glover's security company."

"The Chinese scrambled a fighter to eliminate evidence of a connection we didn't know they had. And because we didn't know it, their response was not predictable. That tells me the war wasn't planned. But that doesn't mean it was a mistake. Not in the way the Red processes events."

"Then what is it?" I ask as I finish off the first meal, swapping the empty tray for the full one.

"A market adjustment?"

The going theory is that the Red evolved out of a program designed to manipulate both markets and consumer behavior to optimize long-term profits. Long-term profits don't happen at all if the world is annihilated. And that, we believe, forms the basis of the Red's drive to eliminate existential threats. So I'm having a hard time with Cory's casual assessment. "No way does a flash war involving nuclear-armed opponents reduce the chances of Armageddon."

"That's not what I mean. Look at it this way: Because we didn't know what we'd find aboard *Sigil*, the outcome was unpredictable. The only predictable result was that the market would shift—and that's what happened. The Red recalculates and moves on."

"Why hasn't it moved to shut this war down?"

"It hasn't been under way for very long."

I scowl. "You don't think so? What's the death toll so far?"

He frowns down at his hands.

"What is it?" I press.

In a grudging voice, "Two hundred thirty known dead. So far . . . not counting the *Sigil* massacre."

The Red doesn't give a shit. I know that. Two hundred thirty is a trivial number and no doubt an acceptable loss on the way to some newly devised goal.

"It's not about individuals," Cory says.

"I know that."

"New circumstances mean new opportunities to identify and evaluate threats. Maybe the Red is letting this war play out to see what turns up."

"No. That is not what this is about. Something else is going on."

We stare at each other for several seconds. Then Cory asks, in a meek voice, "Is that a guess, or . . ."

I start eating again, glaring at one of the monitors: a replay of last night's burning oil derrick.

"Shelley?" Cory asks. "Is there something you know?"

"It just feels wrong."

I look at him again. To my surprise, he's nodding. "Your feelings count. They've been validated before."

"No, that's not what I mean. This is not the Red talking through me."

"Okay. Then what is it?"

I finish off the second meal, using the time to organize my suspicions into words. When I'm done, I stack the second tray on the first. Then I lean back, crossing my arms over my chest. "Too much went wrong on this mission, and it started in the planning phase. Dr. Parris was doing pharmaceutical research, but we didn't know that. We assumed the increase in security meant they were developing something illicit, something dangerous. Why didn't we consider that they were just cutting corners on a legitimate investment?"

His cheeks darken. FaceValue notes the growing intensity of his emotion and tags him with a little bar graph colored to show 30 percent anger, 70 percent embarrassment. "We *did* consider it," he insists. "But even if we'd understood the goal of the research, with security that tight we would have needed to look to be sure."

"You were following the mission, right?"

He nods.

"When you saw the video stream of that lab, did you think it was a biowarfare operation?"

"It seemed plausible."

"I was sure that's what it was. We've been looking for something these past months. Something bigger than the operations we've turned over. I thought we'd found it. But we got it all wrong."

"Sometimes we get things wrong," Cory says. "It's that simple."

"Nothing about this mission was simple. And there are a lot of open questions. Like why didn't Intelligence know that helicopter was there? That information should have been easy to obtain. How could you have missed it?"

The percentages on the graph don't shift, but the colors darken. Cory is only half of our intelligence team, but to his credit, he doesn't make excuses. "I don't have an answer for that, Captain Shelley. I'm sorry."

I lean forward. "It seems suspicious to me that the helicopter got dropped from our surveillance, but *we* didn't get scrubbed from the satellite image. You know it's supposed to work the opposite way. The enemy is visible. Not us."

"It *is* a concern. We *are* concerned, Captain. And we are looking into it."

"There's more to look into, Cory. Oscar-1 had improper orders. Julian could have died because of that delay. And why didn't the mission briefing include a psych evaluation of Vincent Glover? I don't remember reading any suggestion that he was a cold-blooded killer."

Cory nods, not really looking at me anymore. "These are all questions that we need to answer."

I lean back again, flexing my mechanical feet, curling them and then stretching them out again. It's a bad habit I've gotten into ever since the feet started making noise. As the small joints slide past one another, a series of soft clicks is generated—a worrisome rattle that tells me the joints are no longer properly aligned.

I catch Cory staring in fascination at the intricate mechanical movement.

"Cory, there's something else I want you to look into."

"Sure. Of course." Like he's ready to agree to anything to get rid of me. "What do you need to know?"

"Jayne Vasquez—"

"Oh boy."

"—and Karin Larsen, aka Delphi."

"Major Kanoa isn't going to like this."

I shrug. "If he gives you trouble, let me know and I'll handle it. But I want you to find out for me where Jaynie and Delphi are, what they're doing, who they're working with—every fucking thing you can turn up. I want to know if Yana Semakova is stalking them. I want to know about this Mars thing, if it's real."

That puts Cory on his feet—"Oh, the Mars endeavor, that's real!"

He doesn't mean any harm; it's just enthusiasm. But the motion is so sudden it shocks me. I launch to my feet too, reaching for a pistol in a chest holster that I'm not wearing.

Cory sees me, sees my expression, and his enthusiasm transforms to fear. He backs up against the desk, staring at me like I'm the monster who emerged from under the bed.

"Damn it," I whisper. "Don't *do* that."

"I'm sorry."

I walk to the door. I know he's hoping I'll leave, but I close it and turn back.

"I'm *really* sorry," Cory says. Like he thinks I'm going to tear his head off.

He's operating on antique assumptions. A closed door used to indicate a desire for privacy, but privacy is a dead concept at C-FHEIT and the only thing a closed door means anymore is *don't interrupt.* Kanoa will get a report on this conversation and so will our senior intelligence analyst, Bryson Kominski. They could decide to slap me down or order Cory to disregard the assignment I've given him, but I think they'll leave it alone. 7-1 operates on transparency and trust, both up and down the chain of command. Our senior staff knows what we're up to, but they take care not to meddle in every little aspect of our lives. If we had to live under the rigid discipline of a police state, 7-1 would spiral apart.

I sit down again, hoping that will make Cory feel less threatened.

"You're into this Mars stuff?" I ask him.

"Sh-sure. In general, anyway."

"Tell me."

"It's real. People *will* go to Mars. There's a coalition of billionaires financing an expedition. I didn't realize Jayne Vasquez was involved. It's so cool that she's using Semak's money for a purpose like that."

"You want to go to Mars?"

"I'd love to. It's a new world. Who wouldn't want to go?"

I wouldn't. Unlike Cory, I've been in space—low earth orbit—and it was awe-inspiring, a life-changing experience. But my destination, the Semak Hermitage, was just an ugly little prison cell. I've been locked up in prison. I know what that's like. The Mars module would be a prison without parole. There would be no way out.

But for Cory, Mars is a dream. I hear the ache in his voice when he says, "It's never going to happen for me. It takes money—or skill or connections—and anyway, I'm forty-nine years old." A sad little smile. "Not exactly a hot candidate."

He doesn't understand what he'd have to give up. "Would you be willing to pull your overlay? Jaynie would make you get rid of that before she'd ever consider you. Otherwise, she'd assume you were a spy for the Red."

"I'd be willing to pull the overlay just for the chance to try out."

No hesitation.

His earnestness bothers me. It makes me question his loyalty. He's here at C-FHEIT, working with us. He knows what we do. He *is* a spy for the Red. That's his job. But how immersed is he, really, in our purpose?

I tap my head. "You don't have a skullnet, right?"

"Oh, no. Only select soldiers are equipped with those. They were banned for civilians last year. Too much potential for abuse."

"Abuse? Abuse by who?"

He doesn't like the question. His upper body starts rocking in a stiff, repetitive motion. "By whoever controls the programming." He tries, but he can't quite meet my gaze. "I saw the report you wrote on your kidnapping. You know what can be done to a captive subject. You experienced it."

"That was blatant abuse." Hell, it was torture. "It'd be smarter to be subtle. Keep the interference minimal. Your subject might never be aware of the manipulation."

"No, you would know," Cory says. "The skullnet icon would tell you something was going on."

That's the theory, anyway.

"Who controls the programming, Cory?"

The pace of his rocking picks up. "Your programming?"

"Sure. Let's talk about my programming."

"In the regular army, it would be Guidance. Now it's the Red."

"No one else?"

"No."

FaceValue confirms he's nervous as hell but he's not lying.

"Not that I know of, anyway," he adds. "And I *have* looked."

I get a feeling Cory looks into most things. He's like a human version of the Red.

"Who has access to my programming?" I ask him.

His shoulders hunch. It's not a question he's comfortable answering, but it's also not one he can evade. "Technically,

I do. It's part of my security clearance, but I would never try to adjust your skullnet."

"Unless Kanoa ordered you to?"

"Not even then. I'm not trained for it. It would be a foolish risk."

FaceValue confirms he's sincere. Good to know, though I resolve to talk to Kanoa about who has the authority and the ability to mess with my head.

I decide I've scared him enough. "Find out what you can about Jayne Vasquez, Karin Larsen, and Yana Semakova. Send me a report."

"I will," he says. "I'll do it. It's in the queue."

I head out, leaving the plate of cookies behind for Cory but taking the empty trays with me. The trays go into the recycler. As I walk back to the barracks, I worry over what Jaynie will tell Delphi. I worry that Delphi will talk to my dad; he doesn't need that kind of hurt. I worry over the mission too, considering again all the things that went so inexplicably wrong. By the time I get to the barracks, I'm watching for the skullnet icon, waiting for a flicker that will indicate an adjustment in my brain to bring my mood back from a looming melancholy. But there's nothing.

My mood stabilizes anyway.

Like Cory said, the icon is supposed to glow with any activity in the skullnet beyond baseline, but I rarely see it anymore. I've let myself believe that's because I don't need it as much as I used to . . . but abuse doesn't have to be blatant. Would I know it if the icon failed to report subtle interference?

Tran is coming downstairs as I go up. "Hey Shelley, aren't you going to the Christmas party?"

I tell him the truth. "I'm getting too old. I'm so beat up, I'm just going back to bed until tomorrow."

Tran is actually six months older than me, but I've got

more mileage. He flashes a smile. "Yeah, I got pounded too, but I'm calculating good odds that I'll be able to collect a little Christmas cheer."

I think I know the private Tran is after. Kanoa won't approve of a hookup, but he won't say anything either. He'll just transfer the target of interest before things have a chance to gel. "Good luck with it."

I head upstairs, take another shower, and go back to bed, but I don't really want to sleep. I'm still thinking about what's going on in my head. There's a simple AI embedded in the skullnet, tasked with monitoring and regulating my brain function. It's had two years to learn how I think, and it's gotten really good at interpreting my thought patterns and translating my commands.

Cory said it's the Red that controls the programming behind my skullnet's AI and no one else. But I think he's wrong. Because *I* interact with that AI every time I issue a silent command, every time I use it to sleep, every time I look to it to take the edge off of my anger or my grief. Every time I've ever resented the appearance of the skullnet icon. Just how well does the embedded AI know me?

I decide to test it. I visualize the skullnet icon, willing it to appear.

My skullnet detects the pattern of my thought, the AI interprets it and sends a command to my overlay, where the icon appears: a circle with a black background overlaid with a glowing red web.

I'm looking at it. I see it. But I feel nothing.

The icon should only appear when the skullnet is actively using chemical stitches and staples to hold my head together, but that's not what's going on or I'd feel it.

Monitoring my thoughts, translating them, posting commands to my overlay—none of that should induce the icon to appear, because none of those things requires any interference in my brain. So what is the appearance of the icon telling me?

I will the icon to fade to invisibility and within a second, it's gone.

It's telling me that, absent outside input, the icon is no longer linked to skullnet activity. All this time when I thought I was operating on my own . . . the truth is I'd just chosen not to see it.

Vertigo sweeps over me. I feel lost in my own history. I know I operate on programs. That's not a secret. But I've always known *when* I was operating. Or I thought I knew.

Now? I have to wonder if I've been operating on a rogue program that I accidentally helped to write. And if so, how much has it changed who I am?

I think of another experiment, one that could answer that question. The skullnet has no off switch, but what if I try telling it to stop regulating my mood, to turn off all active interference? Not just to turn off the icon which only reports activity, but to turn off the activity itself?

Could I do that?

Do I want to?

I stare at the ceiling, thinking about it. I've been de-wired before. I know what happens without the cerebral support of constant stimulation. But I want to know who I am.

Identity is not a fixed thing. I know that. Who we are shifts from moment to moment, day to day, fucked-up disaster to fucked-up disaster. And brain-stimulation therapies that are used to treat mental illness do not create a new person . . . they just strip away the scar tissue to reveal what's underneath.

I want to know what's underneath my skullnet. I want to look down there again. I want to know for sure that the choices I've made are mine and that the loyalty I feel to ETM is real.

So I envision the skullnet. I envision its position beneath my scalp, on the surface of my skull. I imagine the electrical processes continuously shooting through it as it senses and modifies the activity in my brain. I envision that activity gradually slowing, descending into stillness.

I sense a shift. It's a change in the state of the Universe. I swear my lungs stop, my heart stops, time stops. The vision I've manufactured of the skullnet ceases all glittering processes and freezes into bright stillness.

Vaguely, I'm aware of a squad icon in my field of view burning in emergency red, but I feel no concern. I feel nothing—until a loud *bang!* kick-starts time. There's a scramble of motion: boots on the floor, voices. A shadow falls across my field of view, a face that I can't focus on. It extinguishes my vision of the skullnet.

"Jesus Christ," Logan says.

My heart slips out of suspended animation and starts pounding again.

"Pulse!" Dunahee shouts in triumph. "He's coming back."

All on their own, my lungs decide to breathe. My body reforms around me, heavy and distant. I let my eyes close like a kid who wants to be somewhere else.

"Shelley, look at me."

Logan makes it sound like a desperate plea, so I do it. I open my eyes again, conscious of my own deep breathing. Logan is leaning over me, staring into my eyes. Dunahee is right beside him. *"What the fuck?"* I whisper.

"You were *gone*," Logan says. "Your icon went red. No heartbeat. No respiration. Residual brain function."

I shut myself down?

I sit up. Logan tries to stop me, but I push him away. "It's okay. I'm *okay*." In truth though, I'm not. A cold sweat slicks my skin and soaks my T-shirt. I peel the shirt off and lean against the wall. "That was a mistake."

"No kidding, brother! What the hell did you do?"

I hesitate, considering whether or not I should say what was going on in my head. "You thought I was dead?"

"You *were* dead."

Through the open door comes the sound of running footsteps. We all look up as the base medic bursts in, wide-eyed, hauling a field kit. Confusion slows her down as she surveys the room. "Who's the emergency?"

"It's me," I tell her. "But I'm okay. It was a mistake."

Kanoa and Fadul come in behind her, and then some of the support personnel from downstairs. As the medic hesitates, unsure what to do, I look at Logan and think, *Secure this floor. No one but us.*

He puts his hand out to stop the medic from getting closer.

"Lieutenant," she says in a timid voice, "you need to let me check on him."

Logan speaks over her without speaking at all, his artificial voice audible in my ears. *Are we under attack?*

No. My fault. Secure the floor.

He locks down his expression, turns to the medic. "I have to ask you to leave, Specialist."

"Sir—"

Kanoa takes over. "Everyone who is not 7-1, clear this floor and keep in mind that everything occurring on this base is classified and may not be discussed between yourselves or with anyone who is not a superior officer assigned to this facility."

Within seconds, every outsider is gone. Kanoa gestures at Fadul. "Confirm the floor is clear."

Logan watches me warily as I get up. "What the hell, Shelley? What was that about?"

"Like I said, it was a mistake." I grab a bottle of water from the little fridge and drink half of it. "I wanted to see what I could do with the skullnet. It didn't work out like I thought."

Kanoa pulls out the desk chair and sits. "You were trying to shut it down, but you shut yourself down instead."

Logan looks at me like I'm insane.

I shrug and sit on the bed.

Fadul reappears in the doorway looking shaken. "We're secure and what the fuck, Shelley? Were you trying to check out?"

"*No.*" It shocks me she would ask that.

"You were dead," she insists. Her hands are shaking. I've never seen her so rattled before.

"It was an accident." I turn to Kanoa—at least he looks composed—and I tap my head. "The icon's supposed to tell me when the skullnet's active, but it doesn't. Not all the time. Not anymore. I want to know about the programming, Kanoa. I want to know who's in control, who sets the baseline, who *resets* it—"

He stops me right there. "No one resets it, and I think that's part of the problem. You're not the same person you were two years ago, but you're running on the same baseline."

"Well, why doesn't it get reset?" Logan asks.

Kanoa looks up at him. "Reset to what? How can we tell where the new baseline is, or where it would be if you weren't using a skullnet?"

Fadul moves closer. Dunahee gets out of her way. "I want to know how Shelley took himself out," she says. "I want to know why."

She's starting to piss me off, but before I can say anything, Kanoa intercedes. "He told you why. It was an accident. As for how, think about the sleep command. That's a physiological cue. It's the first one you learn. But the AI in your skullnet can learn others. It's a back-and-forth that you're probably not even conscious of most of the time." He turns to me. "You were trying to visualize the skullnet?"

I nod warily. "I was visualizing the processes slowing down."

"Never think of an AI in human terms. Your embedded AI can oversee complex functions—nothing is more complex than the operations of the brain—but the AI itself is not especially complex. It does what it does and nothing else. It's not self-aware and it does not contain a model of a skullnet as *hardware*. When you asked it to freeze the processes, you were asking it to effect an action in a dimension it can't even conceive of. So it did the next best thing. It shut down the processes it can control."

"You know a lot about it," Fadul says.

I pick up on her suspicion. "You've done it yourself?" I ask him.

His eyes narrow. "We all make mistakes, but we can't operate without the skullnet."

"That's for damn sure," Fadul says, glaring at me.

"It was just curiosity."

"And did you learn what you needed to learn?" Kanoa asks.

"Yes, sir. It won't happen again."

"If it does," Fadul says, looking at Logan, at Dunahee, "no one bother waking him up, okay?"

Logan says, "Give it a rest, Fadul."

She shrugs and walks out. Dunahee waits for the door to close behind her before he says, "I think she means it."

I know she does.

After a few more minutes they decide it's safe to leave me alone. I take another shower, and then I sleep for the duration of Christmas.

The next morning, I'm feeling better. I check in with Julian and talk to him for a few minutes. He's healing, but he tells me the physician has advised him he'll never be one hundred percent again, and he's distraught at the real possibility that he won't be with us on any future mission.

"Hey," I tell him. "You never know. Look at me."

That makes him laugh, which hurts. I tell him to rest, and we say goodbye.

The news from the Arctic is mixed too. The shooting is on hold, but fighter pilots are still challenging each other, while troops, no doubt poorly equipped, are being moved to encampments. I wonder who'll get the blame when they start freezing to death.

After breakfast—after walking to and from the Cyber Center, listening to my feet clicking like a slowly shuffled deck of cards—I decide to see what I can do about it. I get out cleaning wipes, cotton swabs, and a can of pressurized air. Then I sit on my bed, detach my right leg, and start hunting in the joints of the foot for dust and debris. But I don't find much. I think the joints are just misaligned. Joby Nakagawa, the engineer who designed and built my legs, swore I wouldn't be able to break them, but he never promised I couldn't wear them out—and the legs have seen a lot of action.

I've switched to working on my left leg when an alert pops up in my overlay. An email from Cory, with the report I requested. I fit the leg back into the knee joint and lock it in place. Then I open the report.

It's daunting—forty thousand words with no summary. Cory must have hired out the research, because there is no way he could put this much material together so quickly on top of his other tasks.

I push the cleaning supplies out of the way, lie back on the bed, and start skimming.

Over the next half hour, I learn that Jaynie and Delphi invested most of their stolen assets in a holding company they created. Kanoa is right about their association with Yana Semakova. Through the holding company, they have a significant investment in Torzhok NAO, an engineering and supply firm founded by Semakova and operating in the Arctic. My initial suspicion is that Semakova blackmailed them to secure the investment. But the facts dispute that. Torzhok has existed for seven years as a highly profitable company involved in cutting-edge projects in the Russian Arctic. It's privately owned, much admired, and nowhere can I find any hint that it deals in weapons and armaments. So at least Semakova has not followed in her father's footsteps.

Jaynie has another significant investment. She's extended her military experience into the private sector, creating her own legally registered security company. A band of mercenaries, to protect her holdings and maybe her person. I hope they're loyal.

Larger than either of these investments is a ten-percent share in a company called ShotFusion, Inc.—a privately held corporation created to launch a one-way Martian colonization expedition. They are well on their way to assembling the technology. A massive prototype rocket housed at the spaceport in San Antonio is undergoing extensive testing. The first crew could leave within two years.

My gaze sweeps over a list of twenty-four names: all those who presently hold a seat among the first three crews. Right away, I find the names that matter to me: *Larsen, Karin* and *Vasquez, Jayne*. So there's no doubt. Jaynie and Delphi both are planning to leave.

But at least now I know—and in time to do something about it.

I go over the list in more detail, looking for familiar names, the names of dragons, but I don't see any. I don't see Yana Semakova's name. But then I spot a name I never expected: *Flynn, Mandy*. My temper spikes. Private Mandy Flynn is no dragon. She's still a kid, just twenty. Too young to throw her life away on a one-way venture to a dead planet.

I search for Aaron Nolan's name—he's the only other surviving member of the Apocalypse Squad—but to my relief, he's not on the list.

At least one of us has some sense.

I go again to visit Cory in his office. This time he's expecting me. He probably set up an alert to warn if I'm around. "Was there a problem with the report?" he asks when I walk in.

"No problem, but I'd like to expand on one aspect of it. I need a detailed assessment of security at ShotFusion's facility in San Antonio."

"Physical security?"

"Yes. Security at the physical location where the proto-type rocket is housed. What would it take to run a mission there? One with a viable exit strategy?"

He looks perplexed. "We haven't received orders for a mission like that."

"Not yet," I concede.

"Then why—"

"Look, you know the Red isn't straightforward. It's like some fucking oracle, hinting at this, warning at that. That's why I've learned to trust my feelings—and I've got a bad feeling about this Mars colonization project."

He's looking worried. "What kind of a bad feeling? Are they under threat?"

"No. But the more I learn about the Mars project, the more I think they *are* a threat. It's a matter of time before the order comes through. So I want you to work up a plan in-house—don't contract it out—on the easiest, safest way to end development."

"No. I . . . I can't do that." He starts to stand up, changes his mind, and sits back down again. "The Mars projects are not an existential threat."

"I think they are."

"Why?"

I don't tell him my reasons. Instead, I explain it to him in a way I know he'll understand. "Everyone visible, everyone accountable. Right?"

He gives me a reluctant nod.

"The only reason Jayne Vasquez is invested in this is because she wants to be invisible—out from under the influence of the Red—and that's not acceptable."

This time, he stands up. He takes three steps across the room. "Mars is the future," he says, turning back.

"Maybe. But we need to secure this planet first."

"If you think we're going to get official orders—"

"I think we are. Orders will come through and then you'll be ready. I'm just asking you to do the research. I'm not asking for support. Look at ShotFusion's security. Find me a way in. You don't need to do more than that. Not until it's official."

He's worried and unhappy. "I'll talk to Kanoa about it."

I nod. "No secrets here."

It's a simple mission. No reason Kanoa wouldn't approve.

Twenty minutes later, I'm in Kanoa's office.

"Sit," he says, glaring from behind his desk: government-issue gray steel with a paper map of North America on the top, pressed under a plastic panel.

I sit.

"You've let the incident at Tuvalu Station get under your skin."

"What happened up there happened for a reason."

"We had this discussion the night you got back. And you do *not* get to decide what Vasquez does with her money or her time. You do not get to develop your own missions. And you do not get to utilize 7-1's analysts for your personal research. Is that understood?"

"So just do as I'm told and nothing more?"

"Come on, Shelley."

"I need this. Karin Larsen's name is on the crew list—"

"Your ex?"

"Yes. And there is no way I am letting her go."

He leans back in his chair, crosses his arms, and in a clinical voice he asks, "Are you fucking crazy?"

"Yes, sir. Yes, I *am* fucking crazy. I wouldn't be here if I wasn't fucking crazy. I'd be with her."

"Tuvalu really shook you up, didn't it? You need to remember that *you* left her. You made that choice."

"Was it a choice?"

"Don't play that game now, Shelley. Not after all this time. No one forced you into this organization. You knew what was required of you from day one, and you made the choice. I don't remember that it took a lot of persuasion."

I want to argue with him: that I was not in my right mind that night; that I'd been too close to death too many times to think I had any right to a real life; that the Red had engineered the decision for me. But I remember how I felt then, both the slow, shaking recovery from hypothermia and the passionate conviction that I had been called to this duty, that it was necessary and honorable, that I would give what I had, do what I could.

I still don't know if that was *my* decision. I do know I haven't changed my mind.

Kanoa speaks in a conciliatory tone. "It could be years before they leave."

He means I could be dead long before it happens.

He adds, "Sometimes we want incompatible things."

My gaze has wandered. I make myself look at him again. "I still think we'll get this mission. And if we do, you're not going to be able to trust Cory Helms to do his part."

"I need you to get your head together, Shelley."

I know he's right. I do want incompatible things.

"And Shelley? Stay away from Cory Helms."

At 1202, bandwidth vandals jam access to GPS along a stretch of Interstate 35 on the outskirts of San Antonio. Safety overrides programmed into an autonomous tanker truck fail to properly execute, leading to a fiery collision with a semi, also autonomous, that is hauling custom components for ShotFusion's Mars project. No one is killed, but both vehicles are destroyed, and ShotFusion's development program is predicted to be delayed for months. Cory is convinced it's my fault.

I am summoned back to Kanoa's office.

This time, Cory is there, standing to one side of Kanoa's desk, an angry blush to his cheeks as he glares at me. Kanoa is leaning back in his chair, looking aggravated. He spends a lot of time tracking potential ETM recruits. That's what he'd be doing now if we weren't wasting his time on absurd personnel issues.

I sit down in the same chair I used before. "I did it. I hacked those trucks."

Kanoa rolls his eyes. "For the record, Shelley. Did you have any advance knowledge of the I-35 incident, or anything at all to do with sabotaging ShotFusion's Mars project?"

"No, sir. I did not. It was a coincidence."

I watch his focus shift as he checks my physiological status, confirming I'm telling the truth. He looks at Cory. "You satisfied?"

Cory doesn't believe in coincidence any more than I do. "You wanted it to happen," he says. "And when you put the idea out there, you *made* it happen."

He might be right. I think maybe he is. And if so? I'm not sorry. "Everyone visible, everyone accountable," I remind him.

"If you think this will stop them, it won't."

"It's enough for now," I counter. "The project's delayed. There's time for a new element to come into play."

"Or for an old one to be taken off the board," Kanoa growls. "Shelley, get the hell out of here."

I go, sure that Kanoa will be able to talk Cory down and convince him that this is just a setback, not the existential disaster he thinks it is. But later that afternoon, a notice goes out to direct all information requests to Bryson Kominski, our senior intelligence analyst, who lives and works off site. Cory has decided to take a few days of leave.

I don't like it, but Kanoa thinks he needs time.

The personnel van departs in the late afternoon, with Cory the sole passenger aboard.

0531. I awake.

The abrupt transition—deep sleep to full awareness in the time it takes to open my eyes—tells me the event is not natural. I've been awakened by an alert sent through my skullnet, and that means we've got an active situation.

My heart initiates a fast march, fired by a guilty suspicion that the Arctic War has taken a turn for the worse.

I throw off the thin blanket, get to my feet, grab my pants. I'm pulling them on when an order comes through my overlay, spoken in Kanoa's voice: *Squad meeting, 0540, conference hall.*

No order to rig up in armor and bones. So the threat is not imminent. I resist the urge to shoot questions at Kanoa. Instead, I link to an audio newsfeed, listening to a summary of world events while I get my uniform on. The lead story is the winter bases being set up across the Arctic ice by the Russians, the Canadians, and the Chinese, while the chairman of the Joint Chiefs of Staff is due in front of Congress to argue for our own "permanent" presence—a request that the non-interventionist wing is expected to vigorously reject as part of their ongoing assault on the president's wartime powers. The next bit is backgrounded with an enraged Arabic speaker. My skullnet starts to translate, but then the mediot is speaking in English, something about the biowarfare lab in the Arctic—a story that just won't die.

I drop the newsfeed and step into the hallway. Tran is just exiting his quarters. His dark eyes turn to me in anticipation. "We going out again?"

"I don't know what's going on."

More doors open. Roman and Dunahee fall in with us, but Tran waves off their questions. "He doesn't know." We descend the stairs and head outside.

Dawn hasn't reached us. The night sky is a hazy dark-gray vault set with muted stars. Right away, I am aware of the metallic taste of dust in the cool air—a factor I rarely notice in the heat of the day. No wind blows, and I hear no sound except our own footfalls and the annoying clicking of my feet. Impatient to learn the reason for the call-out, I move into a fast trot. Tran, Roman, and Dunahee keep up, falling naturally into formation, two by two as we follow the illuminated sidewalk to the Cyber Center.

On the way I think *map*, and the squad map pops up in the corner of my vision. A glance shows Logan, Fadul, and Escamilla coming behind us. We push past the Cyber Center's light-shielding double doors. The conference hall is just inside.

Kanoa is already standing at the podium, his uniform neat, his expression unreadable. I check his icon as I take a seat in the front row. Kanoa is an iceman. The worse the crisis, the calmer he reads. Right now, his blood pressure and heart rate would reflect well on a Buddhist monk.

He waits until everyone is seated. Then he begins without preamble.

"Forty-two minutes ago, a modified YGH-77 missile was launched from a BXL21 road-mobile missile launcher in Kazakhstan. The missile struck and destroyed a target in low Earth orbit using a non-nuclear kinetic warhead.

"The attack is considered an act of terrorism. The Kazakh government has captured the missile launcher and is currently attempting to recover the terrorists who operated it.

"Immediately prior to the attack, a message appeared across social media attributing the imminent strike to the Shahin Council, a name I'm sure you've all heard many times before."

Too many times. The Shahin Council is a transnational terrorist network—or an underground drug and weapons cartel. It gets hard to tell the difference. "The immediate damage caused by this strike is somewhat minor. The implications are not.

"An object in low Earth orbit is not an easy target to hit. The satellite in question was about four hundred kilometers above the Earth's surface and moving at seven and a half kilometers per second when it was struck—demonstrating that accuracy in guidance and targeting is no longer limited to elite militaries."

His gaze locks on me. "The Semak Hermitage was the target. It's been obliterated."

Eighteen months ago I visited Eduard Semak at the Hermitage. Two days ago, Eduard's daughter and heir, Yana Semakova, spoke on global television, arguing against the Arctic War.

I don't believe in coincidence.

"They chose that target because she spoke out."

"According to the posted message," Kanoa says, "the target was chosen because it was unoccupied. 'A merciful demonstration of sophisticated capabilities.'"

"It's more than that."

"It doesn't matter," he says. "What matters is that every satellite at a similar altitude must now be considered vulnerable—a huge section of our communications infrastructure. But there's more to it. The Hermitage was a large satellite. Some of the debris will fall into the atmosphere, burning up on reentry, but a large part will remain in orbit—a debris field that will gradually expand upward and outward, posing a collision hazard for other satellites. There is a deeper message: that the situation in LEO could get much worse, real fast.

"Right now, most satellites can be moved out of the path of known fragments of debris. But that will get harder if the amount of debris increases—say, after another habitat gets hit. At orbital speeds, every fragment, down to a single screw, has the potential to collide with a working satellite, striking with the energy of a bomb. And every collision creates even more debris. Given time and malice enough, LEO could be filled with a cloud of fast-moving particles so dense that no rocket could be successfully launched through it. It's called the Kessler Syndrome, and it has the potential to lock us out of all access to space for centuries to come."

"That's *fucked*," Tran says, sounding personally offended. "Who the hell would want that?"

Fadul knows the answer. "Psychopaths. Every time."

"The claim," Kanoa says, "is that it was done as retaliation, to hit back at those who sponsored the biowarfare project recently discovered in the Arctic."

"Ah shit," Logan says. "That rumor again? That's been disproven."

"The mediots keep pushing it," I tell him.

Kanoa nods. "And the Shahin Council has reason to exploit it. Last week, one of their members collapsed on stage while delivering a speech. A young and healthy man, he was dead within half an hour. Maybe he was murdered. Maybe God struck him down. Frankly, I don't care. The significant fact for us is that we had no warning of the orbital strike until the Shahin Council's announcement. Our intelligence network picked up no hint, no rumor that it was going to happen—"

"Wait," Tran says, sounding rattled. "You're saying the Red didn't know anything about this?"

Kanoa nods. "That's what I'm saying, Alex. Our most optimistic interpretation is that this operation was set up in some sort of shadow world that the Red couldn't perceive. Not visually, not electronically, not through spies or statistics or behavior studies."

"I got a feeling it's figured things out now," Fadul says. "Even if these clowns have another launcher, they're going to get slapped down hard."

"Agreed," Kanoa says. "And every legitimate government in the world is going to be on this."

"You said that's the optimistic interpretation," I remind him. "What's the pessimistic read?"

Kanoa's answer is grim. "That the Red facilitated this attack as part of a long-term strategy to limit access to space."

"Do you think that's likely?" Logan asks. He gives me an uneasy glance. "I mean, after what happened to the Mars rocket . . ."

"No," Kanoa answers. "I don't think it's likely. I don't think it's remotely compatible with the Red's strategy. Satellite communication and surveillance technology are part of the Red's sensory system. Sacrificing them to prevent future expeditions to Mars doesn't make sense."

Logan nods willing agreement. "And the Red's already shown it knows how to slam the Mars projects without slamming the world."

"So we're back to the optimistic interpretation," I say. "If you really want to call it that. The Red got blindsided by the Shahin Council, and we have no idea how. And we were blindsided in the Arctic. That whole mission, it felt like the Red didn't really know what was going on, or it was distracted, or it was of two minds . . ." I hesitate. Not for the first time, I wonder if we're wrong to think of the Red as a single entity. Why would it have to be? "You think these two incidents could be related, Kanoa?"

He ponders this for several seconds. "It's too early to say—and we have more immediate concerns. Records show that at least nineteen missile launchers have been sold into questionable hands."

"That's a lot," Escamilla says. "You think we'll get orders?"

"It's possible."

ETM 7-1 operates under the paradigm *Everything visible, everything accountable.* But if the Red can be distracted or manipulated to the point that a look-and-see mission escalates into a regional conflict, or if it can be altogether blinded to a large-scale operation, then we're going to lose the war.

It's discouraging. It takes so little to constitute an

existential threat to the world, while relentless, merciless action is required to push back against that threat. If nineteen missile launchers wound up in "questionable hands," then how many lesser, but still lethal, weapons do the terrorists, the crusaders, the dragons of the world control? All wanting to impose a restricted existence or outright death on those around them.

There is no end to this war.

Maybe it's true that most people want to live in peace—I have my doubts—but most people never get to make a choice. "Most people"—whoever they are—have always lived at the whim of those willing to use violence to get their way. Most people, throughout history, have gone along with it, willing to be entertained by the spectacle of a beheading, the horror of a living person set on fire, the thunder of shock and awe. Nothing has changed in the modern world except that each of us has the potential to generate more destruction than ever before. And nothing *will* change. Evil intent will always be with us, and there will always be another battle to fight.

Nine hours later, I'm in the cafeteria, brooding over an empty plate. Fadul is at the opposite end of the table, brooding on tragedies all her own, while Tran has invited himself to sit down across from me with a freshly microwaved meal steaming on his tray. He looks up in feral anticipation as we all get linked into gen-com—Tran can't wait for the next mission—but Kanoa kills his enthusiasm with a grim announcement: "Strike two."

Another dragon lair has been hit. This time, there are five people aboard, and there's video.

"Push it through," I tell Kanoa.

The video was recorded by an STS spaceplane on approach to the habitat. "Was this a scheduled run?" I ask.

"No. The spaceplane was sent to evacuate the inhabitants after a specific threat was made against them."

The video runs silently in my overlay. Digits in the lower right corner count down distance to the habitat. The spaceplane is 104 kilometers away when the missile hits. It comes so fast I can't even see it. The habitat just explodes, ripping apart in a burst of high-definition destruction that kicks debris in every direction.

A large fragment—possibly an airlock door—hurtles out of the void. For a split second it looks like it's coming straight at me. I jerk to the side. Across the table, Tran ducks and swears, *"Holy shit!"*

The shrapnel strikes the STS plane's fuselage and wheels out of sight.

"That wasn't a catastrophic hit," Kanoa assures us. "The plane is intact—it's still up there and communicating."

"It must have been damaged," I say.

"No report on that yet."

I remember when I dropped back into the atmosphere aboard another STS plane. The thermal shielding on the hull held off the quiet heat death that enveloped us. "If the heat shield has been damaged, it won't be able to land. Does STS even have another plane?"

It's not Kanoa who answers my question. To my surprise, it's our senior analyst, Bryson Kominski, who only rarely participates in gen-com. "They've got one additional plane, presently on the ground in San Antonio."

I've never met Bryson. I don't know where he's based. My guess is San Antonio, but he could be in DC for all I know. His low, gravelly voice and midwestern accent lead me to picture him as a stocky Caucasian in his senior years.

"I'll bet there's a bidding war on," Fadul says, "with every dragon in orbit screaming for a ride home."

"They've got emergency escape capsules," I point out.

"Each one equipped with only two reentry couches," Bryson reminds me. "And most of the habitats have at least three residents. Not that the unfavorable math is slowing the exodus. Two capsules have already popped off."

The high frontier is in retreat.

Escamilla breaks in—I check the squad map and locate him in the gym along with Roman—"When does this get to be our mission?"

"You want this mission?" Fadul asks him.

"There is no mission without a target," Kanoa says. "We are looking for one. So is every intelligence outfit around the globe—and I'm guessing a lot of black-market arms dealers are looking into the situation too."

"This can't last," Bryson says. "These missile launchers get one shot. After that, we know where they are. And the Shahin Council cannot have more than a handful hidden around the world."

"How many shots does it take to end the space age?" Roman wants to know.

"No data on that," Bryson admits. "Maybe there's already enough debris up there to initiate a slow cascade of collisions."

"Fuck it," Fadul says. She gets up from the table, grabs her tray. "It was always a game for dragons anyway."

"It's not just about dragons," I tell her. "You want to operate in a world without satellite communications?"

"We have EXALT."

EXALT is a distributed network of aerial communications towers, each self-powered by solar and wind. It's a more rugged system than what we had before Coma Day, and it came up fast, when the Red got behind its development. But EXALT has limits.

"What about GPS?" I ask her. "You want to live without that?"

She scowls at me, while across the table, Tran looks horrified. "That'd be fucking medieval—like all those dystopian novels I used to read."

"Block the chatter," Kanoa says. "I want everyone to prep their gear. Then hibernate so you'll be rested and ready if a mission does come through."

He closes gen-com, dumping us all back into our own local spaces. The squad map winks out.

"*Shit!*" Tran says, his fist thumping the table. "This is real, isn't it? We're looking at eternally fucked-over communications. Who would want to live in a world like that? Shelley, we need to take these crazy beaters *down*."

"Eat," I advise him as I get up to dump my tray. "And make sure your gear is ready."

He can't let it go. "What's it all about anyway? Money? Virgins?"

"A pastoral utopia," Fadul sneers. "Where the women work the fields and the men smoke their weed."

I head for the door, but behind me I can still hear Tran. "You'd *have* to be stoned to stay sane in a shit-primitive mud hole with no satellite uplinks and no GPS."

And Fadul, baiting him. "Then you'd better consider laying in a supply for the apocalypse, Farmer Joe, and hooking up with some passive woman who won't cut your throat when you slap her around."

"Jesus, Fadul. You must have had one hell of a home life."

"Don't you know it."

It's dusk and I'm out on a run, still two miles from the barracks and in violation of regulations because I am both unarmed and alone.

That is, I'm alone except for the angel that's watching

over me. I can't see it, but I know it's there. The fact is, I am never really alone.

There is a slight catch, a hesitation in the flexion of my right foot every time it meets the asphalt road. It still works though, and I run fast. Hell, if I run far enough, maybe the joints will wear smooth again.

When I came to ETM, I imagined the legs would outlast me. It's not working out that way, but I think they're still good for another mission or two. If I make it that far, I'm going to have to break cover and give Joby Nakagawa a call.

The light is fading fast, but the road is a straight line, easy to follow as it bisects a plain of dry grass—a rustling ocean washing around groves of small trees. Only a few vehicles ever come through here—mostly supply trucks and the personnel van. Lack of traffic has left the road looking abandoned, with dust, dry grass, and dead leaves collecting on the asphalt. To the north, coyotes yip and call. They've come in close a few times to look me over with their cold brown eyes. I should probably carry a pistol just in case.

A link request pops up in my overlay. The overlay's reader, set to speak in a crisp, educated, masculine voice with an American accent, identifies the caller for me: "Karin Larsen."

Delphi.

I pull up so fast, I almost trip over my clicking feet.

For most of a minute I stand there, alone in the middle of Texas-fucking-nowhere, sweat leaping off my face into the dry air and the grass rustling around me. I'm having a hard time getting enough oxygen as I stare at the icon tagged with her name.

There is no way Delphi should be able to call me. My overlay was wiped and reformatted the same night Kanoa pulled me out of the Pacific Ocean. Only a very short list of known contacts are allowed to connect with me, and Delphi is not on that list.

The coyotes sing out in the hue and cry of a hunting pack, the link disappears—and anger sets in.

Is the Red playing me?

Using my gaze to manipulate menus, I access my call log. Delphi's address is there at the top of the list. I commit the string of digits to memory. Then I clear my overlay and start walking.

I want to know if it was really her. I want to know how she got on my contact list. I want to call her—but I don't. I consider instead what has changed, what might have slipped, what could explain how she found her way in.

Two possibilities occur to me. The first—that I was with Jaynie those few minutes at Tuvalu Station, but no way could Jaynie have hacked my address. And second—I asked Cory to do some personal research for me, to look into Delphi and Jaynie's situation. I expected him to be subtle—it's his job to slide anonymously through the Cloud—but what if he made contact? The easiest hack is the social hack. Cory left C-FHEIT yesterday on the personnel van, saying he needed to take a few days of leave. He could have arranged to meet Delphi; she could have bribed him.

I need to report the call. It's a security breach. It's my duty to report it—but it's not my priority.

I walk, thinking things over, waiting for darkness to collect around me as if that could hide who I am, what I'm going to do. I wait for the coyotes to go quiet. Stars appear in ever-greater numbers. Satellites move among them. It's hard to imagine that a few broken satellites in all that vastness could have the impact predicted by the Kessler Syndrome.

In the gathering darkness, the land looks the same in all directions. No lights mark C-FHEIT's buildings, because we've got a permanent black-out protocol. Windows in the gym and the barracks use one-way opaque glass, while the

Cyber Center doesn't bother with windows at all. I rely on GPS to tell me where I am.

One mile out, I stop again. And I send a link request.

She picks up right away, adds a visual.

Her eyes are shadowed with dark circles and worry lines that weren't there before, but she's beautiful anyway with her bright blue gaze and shiny blond hair pulled back from her face—and I have never felt so damned and lost in all my life.

I'm not sitting in front of a camera and I've got no icon, so she doesn't see me.

"Say something," she urges me.

"I'm sorry." Sorry for a hell of a lot.

Little wrinkles appear between her eyebrows as her gaze shifts away from the camera. She's frowning past me when she says, "Keep talking. I need more to confirm a voice identification."

She's operating in handler mode: cool and efficient. I try to do the same. "How much did you pay Cory Helms to access my address?"

"It *is* you." She looks at the camera again. "Were you behind what happened on the freeway yesterday?"

Of course she would want to know. "Is that what Cory told you?"

"His email said you wanted something like that to happen—and it did."

"He emailed you?"

"Yes, and he wasn't looking for money. He's angry and he's scared. He sent the email hours ago, but it went to my public account. That's noncritical stuff. I don't look at it until I have a chance to sit down, and with the incident yesterday—" She catches herself. "Shelley, he knew things about you."

Cory knows things about everyone here. "Do you know where he is now?"

"No. There's just the email."

And it's been hours since he sent it. "I have to go."

"Shelley!" Her sharp tone freezes me. "I need to know. Are you a prisoner?"

I wish I had that excuse, but I shake my head there in the dark where only the angel can see me. "I want you to know—I didn't know that was going to happen yesterday. Mars is a mistake, but—"

My overlay shuts down. The link to Delphi winks out. Everything goes: the icons, the tags, the connections. My display is wiped clean, leaving me no way to call out. For nine seconds I stand there with nothing in my field of view except the starlit sky. I am silently praying for my system to come back when a tiny orange-yellow light ignites in the lower left corner of my vision. I've seen it before. It's a counter, monitoring a reformat of my overlay. Progress so far: *10%*.

That can't be right.

I've had my overlay reformatted twice and it takes hours—but I have to commend Kanoa for decisive action. A brain-wipe is the nuclear option for stopping an electronic tryst. "Fuck you anyway, Kanoa," I mutter. I memorized Delphi's address for a reason.

Not sure yet if I'll call her again.

And fuck me for not seeing Cory as a threat. He set me up, and now I can't even report him as a security risk. Not until I get back to base.

The counter ticks over to 20 percent. That is too damned fast. What the hell is going on?

It's gotten so dark, I can't see the road. I take a best guess at where it is and start back, walking as fast as I dare. The counter hits 30 percent. My anxiety rises with it. I still can't see where I'm going, but I start jogging anyway. I want to get back. I want to find Kanoa. I want to slam him up against a wall. Let him bust me for it. What the hell do I care?

40%.

Just stay the fuck out of my head.

I run off the road. I can't really feel textures with my titanium feet, but I can sense the difference when my right foot impacts the hardpan on the road's shoulder. I steer back onto the asphalt.

50%.

I hear the clatter of footplates striking asphalt some-where ahead of me. It's the sound of soldiers running—more than one—running fast, toward me.

I can't help myself. I pull up sharply as instinct insists that I am prey. Blind in the night, unarmed and unarmored, dressed only in PT shorts and T-shirt, I am at the mercy of even a single rigged soldier—and I hear at least three.

Why? What's happening? Is this a disciplinary action?

60%.

It's true I'm in violation of unit regulations and I expected some sort of punishment in addition to my brain-wipe. But not this. Not an overwhelming assault out of the dark.

"Logan!" I shout, because I don't like being afraid. "Is that you? What the fuck is going on?"

"Shelley!" His voice reaches me, sounding closer than I expect. "Sitrep! Why the hell did you drop out of sight?"

70%.

They clatter up out of the dark, surrounding me with the soft hissing and creaking of their dead sisters' joints, along with the smell of fresh sweat, gun oil, and lubricant. "Are you okay?"

"What is going on?" I ask him again.

"Suspected security breach. I don't know the details, but

Bryson called it. He ran passcode resets for everyone. Yours
didn't go through." Logan is the half-seen silhouette looming in front of me. "You dropped off the map. We thought
someone came after you."

"No one came after me. Who's with you?"

From the figure on my left: "Me. Tran."

And from behind me: "Roman."

Logan speaks again. "Kanoa says to get you undercover
ASAP."

80%.

"I can't see a damn thing out here. You have a light?"

"Yeah." There's a rustling noise, then a red LED switches
on at waist height. He hands it to me. "What happened?
Why did you shut your overlay down?"

With the red light pointed at the asphalt in front of me,
I slip past him and start walking. "Kanoa's reformatting it."

"*What?*" He catches up with me in a stride. His dead
sister hisses softly beside me, footplates striking in short
steps so he doesn't leave me behind. "Why would he order
that?"

"And Cory is the security breach."

"Is that a guess or do you know it?"

"I know it."

90%.

"Bryson," Logan says. "You heard that? Shelley says it's
Bilbo . . . No, he's fine . . . He's offline, yeah. Kanoa's reformatting his overlay . . . *shit*. Well, shut it down, Bryson!"

The raw panic in that request sends a chill up the back of
my neck. I pull up, staring at the counter. *93%. 94%.* "Shut
what down?"

95%.

Logan surges past me before he realizes I've stopped.
"Your reformat! Kanoa didn't launch it. The code came
from outside."

I've been down this road. I've had my head hacked before. My hands shake, but I manage to keep the fear out of my voice. "I'm at ninety-eight percent."

"Bryson, come on! Reinitiate! Factory reset. *ASAP*."

99%.

The tiny counter disappears. I stop breathing, waiting for the payload to launch its poisonous code.

But then the counter reappears.

1%.

The number hangs in my vision second after second like it's supposed to, while I gasp at the cold night air like I've just finished a sprint.

"Shelley?" Logan's voice is shaking. "Bryson wants to know—"

"Yes, it reset. It's going slow this time. Like normal."

"Good."

I shine the light on the asphalt and start walking again. The AI in my skullnet operates on a baseline algorithm. That's not nearly enough interference to keep my temper in check. Without warning, I turn around. Roman has to jump sideways to keep from running me over—and that just makes me angrier for no reason at all.

"What the *fuck*?" I shout at their shadowy figures—Logan, Roman, Tran—like it's their fault. It's not; I know that. But I am feeling so shaken and betrayed, I don't give a shit. "Cory Helms was supposed to parse as loyal!"

"Guess Bilbo got his mind changed," Logan says in a tone that promises retribution.

Bilbo got his mind changed by me.

"Everyone else is reset?" I ask.

"All of us," Logan says. "He can't get in again."

"We going to try to recover him?" Tran wants to know. "I mean, he knows everything."

I turn the light of the little LED back to the asphalt,

wondering what payload would have been delivered if the reformat had finished. I always thought Cory was a decent guy. Guess I was wrong.

"Captain Shelley, sir?"

I pause halfway across the barracks lobby to look at the kid on duty at the watch desk. He shrinks from my gaze, just like Cory. It doesn't improve my mood to know I've turned into an asshole who terrifies people just by making eye contact.

Logan, Escamilla, and Roman, rigged and armed, don't merit a glance from the kid as they clatter past, heading for the stair. His wary eyes are fixed on me as he holds out a scrap of paper in his faintly trembling hand. "From Major Kanoa, sir. He said to give this to you."

Fucking hell. I hate being cut out of gen-com.

I take the note and follow my escort upstairs, but it's a weird dissociative moment in which I glimpse myself as the kid must see me: a half human monster parading around on robot legs, scaring the shit out of innocent people.

Fuck me.

At the door of my apartment, I open the note: *My office. 1900.*

"Logan!" I bark because his apartment door hasn't closed yet. "What time is it?"

"1850."

Shit.

I take a two-minute shower, throw on a fresh combat uniform, and jog over to the Cyber Center.

"You're late," Kanoa says when I walk into his office.

"Add it to the list of infractions. Do we know where Cory is?"

He studies me from behind his gray steel desk. "Why are you so sure Cory's involved?"

His question catches me by surprise. Doesn't he know I talked to Delphi? I answer cautiously, not ready to volunteer the information. "Cory left the base last night." I sit down in the same chair I always use. "Have you been able to contact him?"

"He hasn't responded yet, but we know where he's been. We know where he is. No one's grabbed him."

"Do you know who he's been talking to?"

"No. But it doesn't add up. He doesn't have the personality profile to turn traitor overnight and launch a cyber attack that vicious against you. He's never been comfortable around you, Shelley, but he respects you, he respects what you've done."

"It's the Mars thing. That's his first loyalty."

"Maybe. But he went to see Julian this morning, visited him in the hospital, stayed for an hour. If he was planning to turn around and fry your brain, why would he bother?"

But he did betray me. He emailed Delphi and gave her the means to reach me.

Granted, that was a few steps below burning my overlay.

"Logan told me Bryson picked up a security breach."

"He got an event notice—a first-time call to your overlay. You didn't pick up on it though." He waits to see if I will say anything. I don't. "Bryson checked the records. Cory had added the caller's address to the approved list. So he called Cory to ask about it. Didn't get through. He figured better safe than sorry and initiated a reset of everyone's security. But your update didn't go through."

"Did he force the update?"

A forced update would have dumped my open link and initiated an immediate reset. Kanoa's gaze shifts subtly before returning to me. "Bryson says no."

"The security reset was queued, then." Queued while I talked to Delphi. And that allowed a window of time for the attack on my overlay.

For too many seconds, Kanoa just watches me.

I know what he's doing. He's letting his emotional analysis program work. He's aware now that something else happened. "Now would be a good time," he says.

"All right. Cory was fucking with me. That first-time call? It was from Delphi . . . Karin Larsen."

"Your ex."

"Yes. He gave her my address. Put her on my contact list."

"You didn't take her call."

"I called her back."

His fist hits the desk. "God*damn* it, Shelley—"

"It's the Mars thing," I say again, cutting him off. "He wanted to warn her. I think he hoped she could change my mind." I tell him about the email. "He sent it to an address she doesn't usually check, so it's been hours. Maybe he didn't launch that cyber attack, but sometime during those hours, he must have been involved with the party that did."

"We'll know soon. We've got an FBI agent on the way to pick him up. Suspicion of disseminating classified information."

"You want the FBI talking to him?"

"Better that than leaving him loose. Once he's in custody, we can contain the damage." He leans back in his chair. "Let's talk about Larsen."

"Let's not."

"You let her believe you were dead. That's not going to feel good. Then you appear out of nowhere and threaten her—"

"I did not threaten her."

"That cyber attack could have been her attempt to protect both herself and the Mars project."

"That's bullshit. Delphi would not do that."

"How sure are you? How sure are you that Vasquez isn't part of this?"

I understand what he's doing. I understand the psychology of it. He's introducing doubt. He wants to use that doubt to destroy the trust and loyalty I still feel. And it doesn't matter if I understand it. It's still a goddamn effective play.

"I'm sure enough," I say, but we both know that's a lie.

"You got anything else to tell me?"

I think of Delphi's address, locked up in my organic memory—but I'm not going to share that. "Let it go, Kanoa."

He doesn't push it. He's too skilled at this game to overstep. "Holiday's over," he says. "Make sure 7-1 is ready to deploy. I've got a feeling you're going to be busy again—and soon."

Logan is waiting for me in the hall. He's wearing his combat uniform, but he's taken off his armor and bones. "I'm still not seeing you on the squad map."

I check the counter in my overlay. "I'm at forty-five percent."

He frowns at his display. "It's like you're dead. Or gone."

"Not yet." We head outside. "Kanoa thinks we're going to get a call-out soon."

"I've been thinking about that, and it's not going to work. Julian is out. Dunahee and Escamilla need at least a few weeks to heal. Fadul won't admit she's hurt, but she's got a hole in her arm. We don't have enough personnel."

"We've got you, me, Roman, and Tran. And Fadul's going to want to play regardless. Let's make sure we're ready."

We inventory our equipment, weapons, and ammunition. We keep a lot of gear on hand to allow us to work in different environments, and we do a lot of training, in and out of simulators. *Be ready for anything.* That's what Kanoa likes to say. We use the inventory to work up a resupply order that might get filled in a couple of days or a couple of months. You never know.

At 2110 in the evening, we're back at the barracks, and my reformat has reached 96 percent. Logan heads upstairs. I stop at the desk. A different private is on watch. She eyes me warily but gets out of my way when I slip behind the desk, sitting down at the Tactical Operations Center.

From the TOC, I can access data from the angel that watches over C-FHEIT, as well as from the perimeter sensors and cameras. But I can also pull up a personnel map. Normally, I'd do that through my overlay, but that's not an option right now.

The map comes up onscreen, marking the locations of everyone on base. Most of the support staff is in their barracks apartments. A few are in the recreation room. Tran and Escamilla are in the media room upstairs. Fadul is alone on the technical range. I want to see Fadul.

I head out again, cross the parade ground, enter the gym, and take the stairs down to the range, where I pause at the heavy glass door. Beyond are six shooting lanes. They're used mostly for calibrating weapons, but Fadul is on the range practicing her manual skills. Instead of using her helmet and onboard AI, she's shooting with just safety glasses and bright-orange earmuffs. Through the door I hear a faint *pak-pak* of gunshots as she cradles her HITR, its stock braced between shoulder and cheek.

I grab my own earmuffs from a rack, slip them on, and open the door while she continues to shoot in a steady cadence, nailing the same hole in the target every time. The door closes. She can't hear me. Maybe she senses a shifting air current, I don't know, but she pivots, bringing her weapon to bear on me, lip curled as she glares down the length of the barrel.

If there is anyone in this unit more fucked up than me, it's Fadul, but she shows exquisite self-control, snapping her weapon up so the barrel points at the ceiling. With one hand, she wrenches off her ear muffs. I take mine off too.

"What the hell?" she demands in a high, breathy voice. There is a layer of sweat glimmering on her cheeks, and a faint tremor in her throat.

"Sorry."

"*Sorry?* I don't got you on my map, Shelley. I didn't know you were there. You fucking scared the shit out of me. Do not test God like that. It's considered a sin."

"Kanoa thinks we're going to be busy. How's your arm? You going to be up for it?"

She makes a dismissive noise. Turning back to the range, she places her HITR carefully on the shelf before looking at me again. "You don't got to ask me that." She crosses her arms just below her breasts and asks, "Something else going on behind those pretty eyes?"

Her posture, her question: both are a warning not to come any closer. We are brothers and sisters in arms, and sex isn't supposed to happen inside the squad, But Fadul and me, we don't trust strangers. So a few times we've turned to each other. It's not something we ever talk about, and it's not why I'm here.

"You ever think about going back, Fadul?"

"Ah, *Jesus.*" She turns away, shaking her head.

"Do you?" I press, because I know what she left behind.

Her dark eyes return to me, narrow, angry. "The dead don't get to go back."

"Sure, that's what we tell ourselves. But if one of your kids saw you on the street, ran up to you and said, 'Mama, please come home'—"

Her eyes flash as she cuts me off. "You leaving us, Shelley?"

I don't have an answer for that, but she has an answer for me. "I'd tell that baby I wasn't real. That I was a dream. My kids don't need some fucked-up, wired zombie feeding them breakfast every morning. They do need a guardian angel, and that's who I am, even if they never know it. That's who you are."

The counter hovers at 99 percent. I watch it until it disappears, replaced by an array of icons that wink into sight and then slowly fade.

"You back with us, Captain?" she asks me.

"Yeah. I'm back."

For the second night in a row, I'm launched again out of a dreamless sleep. I check my time display: *0334*. Bryson speaks on gen-com, "Alert. Alert. Strike Squad 7-1, new orders. All personnel are to report immediately— unarmed—to a unit inspection at the west end of the parade ground. Do not rig up. Repeat: *do not* rig up. All weapons shall remain secured in lockers."

The link to gen-com drops and a red X pops up in my overlay, indicating lockdown, no connections allowed.

I roll out of bed, sure that Bryson is compromised. I step into my trousers while I try to link back into the base network. I can't even get a menu. I try to link into gen-com, hoping for a point-to-point connection, but gen-com is not responding either.

No doubt now.

I pull on a T-shirt, grab my HITR from its charging rack, cross the room in two strides, and hurl the door open. "Rig up!" I shout into the corridor. "Armor and bones!"

I stomp the length of the hall, shoving doors open,

confirming everyone is up and awake and strapping into their dead sisters. "Anyone got access to gen-com?"

"Negative, sir!"

"No, sir!"

Only Kanoa is missing.

I race down the stairs, scaring the private manning the TOC—another private, wide-eyed and not quite twenty years old. "What alerts have we got?"

"None, sir. Everything's quiet."

I cut behind the desk, drop into a chair in front of the TOC, call up the current status of perimeter sensors.

All the sensors are off.

Fuck. This is exactly how we got through the Apocalypse Forest to hit Thelma Sheridan. "Status listening," I say to alert the TOC to voice input. "Display angel sight."

The monitor goes black except for a caption: *C-FHEIT SECURITY DRONE LIVE FEED. CHANNEL: NIGHT VISION. CHANNEL CLOSED.*

"We are on our own!" I shout up the stairs. The upper floor rumbles with activity: shuffling feet, the thumping of plastic locker doors, grunts, and soft curses. I spin out of the chair, circle the desk, and sprint to the door. I open it cautiously. Just outside, the night is quiet, but farther off I hear the rumble of a small armada of heavy-duty helicopters, probably Black Hawks.

I close the door and turn around. "Private, I want you to roust everyone on the first floor. You will get them down into the basement within two minutes. Understood?"

Her eyes are wide, her mouth a small round O, but she snaps off a determined "Yes sir!" and runs for the dorm rooms, shouting and banging on the doors.

I look up the stairs to see one of my soldiers—I'm pretty sure it's Tran—fully rigged, HITR in hand. "We've got at least three Black Hawks incoming," I tell him. "Get everyone down here. We need to issue heavy weapons—"

The front door opens. I jump out of the way and bring my weapon up, training it on Kanoa as he comes in.

He's half-dressed like me in trousers and T-shirt. He's got boots on, but they're still untied. "What part of 'unarmed' do you not understand, Captain?" he barks. "Put that weapon away."

He stomps across the lobby. I follow on his heels. "Major, we are under attack—"

He catches sight of Tran at the top of the stairs. "What the *fuck* are you doing rigged?"

"Gen-com is down," I insist. "Bryson's been compromised."

"Gen-com is locked down pending the result of an imminent inspection."

He trots up the stairs. I follow him. We find 7-1 in the hall, rigged and ready.

"Get out of your gear!" Kanoa roars,

"Major, you cannot be accepting Bryson's communication as a legitimate order."

He turns to face me, inches away, as the sound of the Black Hawks becomes audible through the insulated walls. Kanoa isn't any taller than me, but he's a bigger man all the same, and he's furious. "We don't have a choice, Captain. Mr. Helms has relayed a full report on our existence and activities. I just got off the phone with the colonel in charge of the oncoming forces. They are US Army. *Legitimate* army. If we engage, we will be fighting our own. We will be fighting against overwhelming forces in a battle we cannot win."

He turns again to the soldiers of 7-1 as the Black Hawks' muted thunder trembles in the walls. "Stand down, all of you. Leave your rig and your weapons in your quarters. Form up downstairs in uniform only, no armor. Move!"

The hallway empties as my soldiers duck back into their apartments. Kanoa cuts past me, shoves open the door of his own room, and disappears inside. It's only me and one rigged soldier left in the hall.

"Let's move, Fadul. You heard the major."

She lifts off her helmet and looks at me. Not exactly with panic. Call it a desperate suspicion. "What the fuck?" she asks. "Did the Red just cut us loose?"

"I don't know. Maybe." For damn sure, we've been betrayed—by Cory, Bryson, Delphi, or the Red—who knows? "Get out of your rig. Get ready."

I return to my room and rack my HITR. I get on a jacket and a cap. I don't think about wearing boots until Kanoa sticks his head in the door. "Footgear!" he shouts.

A minute later we are all downstairs. The TOC is unmanned. Kanoa has gathered the regular army personnel along with 7-1. No one is to stay behind in the building.

"We will report as a unit," Kanoa informs us. "In good marching order." He eyes me. "We will obey all orders issued by our superior officers." He opens the door and leads the way as we exit into the roar of the approaching Black Hawks.

Their lights are on, three blinding white beams focused on the parade ground. I half expect to be gunned down there on the sidewalk, but it doesn't happen. We march to the flagpole in front of the Cyber Center, where we form up, facing the quad and the oncoming gunships, with 7-1 in the first row and the support personnel behind us.

We brace against the buffeting of the gale-force winds generated by the Black Hawks as they settle to the concrete. Troops pour out. None of them are rigged in dead sisters, but they're wearing helmets and visors, and they're armed with HITRS. They spread out in an arc, facing us. I count twenty-four, everyone with their weapon trained on our formation.

It's impossible to hear orders over the roar of the engines, so gen-com gets switched on again—a one-way link that allows a gruff male voice to speak directly in my ears. "You were to present yourselves unarmed."

Of course they're using standard threat detection to scan for hidden weapons.

Kanoa is on my left. He turns to look at me, but I'm not the one who's armed. Fadul is standing on my right, staring at the massed troops in front of us. The Black Hawks' blinding white searchlights are reflected in her eyes and in the sheen of sweat on her cheeks. Her lips are trembling.

I raise my hands slowly, palms out, the gesture of surrender, of no resistance. Then I lean over, put my lips close to her ear so she can hear me. "Give it up."

She turns to look at me, her eyes wide, the only soldier in 7-1 more fucked up than me. "Why is this happening?" she shouts over the noise. "Why are we going along with it?"

"Give it up or we're dead."

"Maybe that's better." She starts to reach inside her jacket.

"No!" It's like I can feel the pressure of twenty-four fingers tightening on triggers. "Remember where you are. This is not the Sahel." I know what she went through. I've felt her hidden scars, thick under my fingers. There are scars in her mind too that no skullnet will ever heal. But tonight we are not facing a mob of untrained teenage irregulars jacked up on speed and hate. "You don't have a reason to kill any of these soldiers."

"It's over for us, Shelley."

"Only if you're stupid."

That earns me an angry glare.

But then she turns her gaze back to the array of weapons directed against us, and she raises her hands into the air.

I feel like I can breathe again.

"Facedown on the concrete," the voice on gen-com says.

We do it, and then gen-com gets shut down again.

Lying prone, my cheek pressed against the concrete, I don't have a good perspective on the activities around me. I can see a soldier—rank of specialist—a few feet away, with a HITR trained on Fadul. I assume there's another watching over me with similar focus.

I see other soldiers cautiously entering the barracks, using the muzzle cams on their HITRs to survey the interior before they advance inside. It pisses me off, knowing my room will be searched, my clothes pulled out, my gear, my weapons, and my rig inspected. But there's bitter satisfaction too, because that's all they'll find. There's nothing personal to me in the barracks. The stuff that defines me is all in the Cloud—videos, photos, music, books, messages—all stored in encrypted files where they can't get to it.

After a few minutes, the Black Hawks shut down. My guess? The ongoing inspection has turned up no immediate threats, so the ability to make a quick getaway is no longer a priority.

In the relative quiet that follows, we are issued orders by direct voice. "You will not move until your name is called. When your name is called, you will stand up slowly. You will remove your jacket and let it fall to the ground. You will place your hands on your head and await further instruction."

They call my name first. *James Shelley.*

I do as instructed. I stand up. I look to my left for Kanoa, but he's not there anymore. I get my jacket off, but when I start to put my hands on my head, two MPs step in with new instructions—"Hands behind your back." Quickly, efficiently, they use padded cuffs to lock my elbows and wrists together. Leg shackles go on next. "About-face."

I turn, to find that the support personnel have already been taken away. Kanoa is there instead, with his hands behind his back. Maybe he's cuffed, I can't tell, but he's not wearing shackles. He's standing beside a colonel. Automatic facial recognition identifies him as Colonel Jason L. Abajian, United States Army.

Like his troops, Colonel Abajian wears a desert-brown combat uniform bulked up with chest armor. But his helmet is old-style—no visor, no electronics. He's wearing farsights, though, with clear lenses. His gaze is fixed on me, his expression an odd mix of annoyance and greed.

If he's running standard facial recognition, he won't find my name or the names of anyone else in ETM 7-1. We've all been scrubbed from the usual databases. But a custom query that compares my face to a known image of James Shelley will confirm who I am. It takes him a few seconds, but he gets there. "My God, it's true." He turns a fierce look on Kanoa. "What did I just step in?"

"You didn't step in it," Kanoa says. "You waded in. You're up to your hips in it."

The colonel raises a bushy eyebrow above the glittering lens of his farsights. "No, it's worse than that. Whatever the fuck this operation is that you're running here, it is *swimming* in bullshit. This is beyond black ops. This is alternate-dimension, voodoo ops. This base is supposed to be *closed*. Will, you are supposed to be dead. I went to your funeral.

"And now here you are, claiming to be in command of ETM Strike Squad 7-1, which does *not* exist. You do *not* belong to anybody. *No one* has stepped up to claim this operation. There is no chain of command. And I am told by those who profess to understand these things that there *is no explanation for your budget.*" He lifts his chin. "Or maybe you funnel that in from another dimension too?"

"I'm not in finance," Kanoa says. "I just operate on the budget I'm given." His hands are still behind his back, so he probably is cuffed, but that hasn't intimidated him. The way he addresses the colonel, it's obvious they've known each other for years. "Damn it, Jason, my people did not have to cooperate with this boondoggle. We did so only out of professional courtesy and regard for the lives of your soldiers. I respectfully request the same courtesy be shown to us in turn. Take the shackles off, and we can talk."

"We can talk," Abajian says. He signals the officer in charge of the MPs. "Captain, move the prisoners inside."

We are taken into the Cyber Center, where we're sorted into separate rooms. Most of the office space has never been occupied or even furnished, so there is no lack of little bare windowless cells. A chair is brought in for me and I'm told to sit, but the cuffs and shackles remain on. Two MPs stay in the room with me, flanking the closed door. They are silent and anonymous behind their black visors, but they're not rigged—I haven't seen any soldiers in Colonel Abajian's operation wearing dead sisters. And perhaps as a gesture of fraternity or professional courtesy or some bullshit like that, they left their HITRs outside and are armed only with service pistols.

I check gen-com, but it's still shut down, and my overlay still shows a red X with no menu options.

I occupy myself by looking up Colonel Abajian's

biography in my onboard encyclopedia and confirm that he and Major Kanoa share a similar background in military intelligence.

After only a few minutes, one of the MPs speaks. "Captain Shelley, we've received authorization to remove your restraints. If you would stand up, sir."

I do it. No point in being an asshole—especially when I know Kanoa is trying to negotiate a deal. After the cuffs and shackles come off, I'm asked to sit down again. I do that too. Twenty-one minutes go by.

"If you'll come with us, sir."

They escort me to the conference room we use for debriefings. It's furnished with a rectangular table and ten chairs. Abajian is at the head of the table. He's removed his helmet, but he's still wearing his farsights. Kanoa is at his right hand; Cory Helms is at his left.

I read fear in the angle of Cory's hunched shoulders, guilt in the tentative glance he throws in my direction. Cory was supposed to be on our team, but he went outside the circle. He gave us up. That's not something I can easily forgive.

Logan is brought in behind me. He freezes when he sees Cory. *"Shit,"* he whispers.

Kanoa says, "Sit down."

I take the chair at the foot of the table. Logan sits at my left hand. Cory stares down at his laced fingers, hands clenched so tightly they're white-knuckled.

The MPs close the door, remaining outside in the hall. It's just the five of us—but Abajian doesn't appear at all concerned that he's outnumbered. He leans back in his chair, crossing his arms over his chest. "Gentlemen, Mr. Helms ignited some concern yesterday afternoon with his report—a full report, I should add—on the existence of a rogue militia openly occupying C-FHEIT, which records show to be a mothballed base." His gaze fixes on me. "Is this a treasonous organization, Shelley?"

"Not so far, sir."

Kanoa gives me a dark look, but Abajian nods. "Points for honesty. I've reviewed the missions you've conducted and I'll agree they have not been directly treasonous. The fact remains that you are unaffiliated with the United States Army and are operating independently of the chain of command."

"The official chain of command," Kanoa says.

"That's the only one I know about."

I trade a look with Kanoa. I want to confer with him over gen-com, ask him what he's already discussed with Abajian, but despite the lack of restraints, we are still prisoners and a private conference is not an option. Kanoa senses my question anyway and answers it aloud, "Colonel Abajian has already been fully informed of our operations." I can't help it. I look at Cory. But Kanoa ignores him. "Consider this a debriefing. Speak freely."

That's when I decide that I am here to help recruit Abajian, to bring him into our network, because only with Abajian's cooperation can we reestablish the appearance of legitimacy that has let us operate this long.

Returning my attention to the colonel, I speak as directly as I can. "We do not operate under the chain of command, sir. Our orders are issued by the Red."

Cory snatches his hands off the table. Kanoa leans back in his chair, looking resigned. Logan exhales in a soft hiss, while I continue. "You've heard of the Red, sir. Maybe you're one of those who prefer to pretend it doesn't exist, but you *are* aware of it." I look at Cory. "And I'm sure Helms has informed you that we believe we are not the only ETM unit in operation. It's likely there are other squads in other sectors around the world."

"But you have no direct knowledge of these units?"

"No, sir."

"And assuming these additional units do in fact exist, do you have any concerns about the threat they may represent?"

I consider his question. My instinct is to answer with a cynical *Yes, sir!* But the truth is otherwise. "The Red, by its nature, limits the threat any ETM unit represents. You've already seen our armaments. There's nothing unusual here, and there are only a few of us." I pause, wondering if Julian has been arrested too, but I don't want to give him up, so I don't ask. "You have a hell of a lot more to worry about in this world than us, Colonel."

"ETM," Abajian muses. "Existential Threat Management." He pronounces each word with sarcastic precision.

Kanoa says, "If the missions we undertake could be handled officially, 7-1 wouldn't exist. But sometimes the chain of command is too slow or too cautious. That's where we come in. We get our orders, and we go."

"No questions asked?" Abajian wonders.

I answer him: "We ask questions. That doesn't mean we get answers."

"You execute anyway. Perfect, obedient soldiers."

"Maybe not perfect."

"That's right. You managed to start a war in the Arctic. Was that the goal of your mission?"

"It was not," Kanoa says.

"Just a side benefit, then?"

Logan speaks up for the first time. "We operate in the real world. There's always a risk."

Abajian looks at me. "You have a different assessment?"

He catches me by surprise. I didn't think my doubt showed, but I don't deny it. I answer him honestly. "We are not on the side of the angels, and in the right circumstances,

I don't think the Red would hesitate to start a small-scale war. But this was something else. These past months we've been looking for something critical. It's felt that way. But this time when we were sent to look, it was like the Red switched sides. We went in with bad intelligence and we almost didn't get pulled out."

"Every mission has problems," Kanoa says.

"Not like this."

"The Red did not switch sides," Kanoa insists. "It backed you. Shelley, you were operating. It was the Red that got you on scene. It was the Red that helped you disable that helicopter. It was the Red that finally cleared Oscar-1 to move north."

"Oscar-1 was detained and there shouldn't have been a helicopter at *Sigil*. I think we make a mistake when we think of the Red as a single mind, a single entity. Why should it be? Why can't it have competing versions? Because I swear it was helping us *and* getting the fuck in the way, from the start of Palehorse Keep straight through to the end."

Turns out the ravings of a madman can induce a long, awkward silence. I lean back in my chair and wait for the reprisals.

It's Cory who steps up first. "I think the Red would reintegrate," he says thoughtfully. "Eventually, anyway."

Is he agreeing with me? Or telling me I'm wrong? Either option irritates me. It doesn't improve my mood when I notice that Abajian is watching me with a level of attention more appropriately directed at a zealot holding the trigger on a suicide vest. "Where do you draw the line, Shelley, between intentionality and random fucked-up luck?"

"I don't, sir. That level of analysis is above my pay grade. I just work with what I'm given."

"What is your pay grade? Do you earn a paycheck?"

It's an insulting question; it trivializes what we're doing.

I get paid just like I would in the regular army, but that's not why I'm here. "I'm dead, Colonel. What the fuck do I need with money?"

"It's that easy?"

"It's not easy. It never has been."

"But you keep at it. Don't you ever want to say no to a mission?"

I study him, puzzled, wondering if he gets it, if he gets what we do here. "What happens if I do say no?"

"You tell me."

"We get a little closer to midnight."

He trades a look with Kanoa, and I know I've said something wrong—but I haven't said anything that isn't true.

Kanoa turns to me. "Cory contacted Colonel Abajian because he was concerned that 7-1 was on the verge of going rogue, of operating on the basis of personal vendetta rather than on carefully considered orders, of overstepping our mandate, such as it is."

This is too much for Logan. He leans in. "We've done more good here in the nine months I've been part of ETM than I saw done in my four prior years in the regular army. Cory wants to lay the blame for a freeway accident on Shelley. But Cory compromised our security and out of his own personal vendetta, he orchestrated a cyber attack."

"That was my operation," Abajian says. "I hoped to quietly neutralize ETM so we wouldn't have to come in with the heavies." He turns his hands palm-up. "But you got your security restored before we could pull that off."

So it wasn't Cory who attacked me. All he did was hand over the keys to the enemy.

He's sitting with hunched shoulders, but when he notices my gaze, he reacts. "You've changed, Captain Shelley. I don't deny your heroism and that you've saved tens of thousands of lives, but that does not give you the right to dictate to others—"

"Mr. Helms," Abajian interrupts in a tired voice. "No one is innocent in this operation, and we have another mission to discuss."

My skullnet icon winks on, its appearance reflecting the ignition of a program in my head, one that tells me, *Listen.* Because this matters. This is the reason for tonight's raid. It's the reason Abajian was allowed to come here.

I hear a catch in Logan's breath. We look at each other. I see my own ready state reflected in his eyes. "You operating?" he asks, mouthing the words.

I nod a subtle *yes.*

This mission Abajian has come to discuss—it's our mission. Or the Red wants us to believe that anyway.

Kanoa doesn't feel it. He's looking puzzled. Abajian has no idea at all as he proceeds to explain why he's come to me.

"My analysts have examined your records, your conduct, Shelley. They have identified in you something of a messiah complex, but they assure me that despite this, you are quite sane, and that you continue to be both a bold and intelligent officer. All of these characteristics recommend you as the ideal candidate for the mission in question."

A messiah complex? I look to Kanoa for an explanation, but he won't meet my gaze.

"This mission would involve you," Abajian continues, "and at most two others. You would not be operating as a squad. You would not be operating as a military unit. You would not be anonymous."

"What does that leave? Is this a PR deal?"

This induces a snort of amusement. "No, it's not a PR deal. I need you on a field team tasked with locating a missile launcher that may be next in line to target LEO."

So. Kanoa warned we'd be heading out soon. Maybe he was operating too.

"What I'm about to tell you is classified information, not for dissemination," Abajian says. His eyes narrow in an imitation of an ironic smile because it's a joke. *Everything I've been involved with over the last year and a half is designated classified, legitimately or not.*

That's as far as the joke goes.

"There are at least three missile launchers still at large in the hands of rogue operators associated with the Shahin Council. We know where two are housed. Allied powers are preparing operations against them. We know less about the third launch platform. Though we feel certain about the general region where it's located, we need an operative who can go in, confirm its presence, and communicate its precise location. It has been suggested that *you* are the person best suited to do that, Captain Shelley."

"Suggested by who?"

"A consultant."

FaceValue doesn't flag a lie, but none of this seems likely to me. My existence isn't entirely unknown, but that doesn't mean my name shows up on anyone's roster of available personnel. I trade a look with Logan. The suspicion in his eyes reflects my own.

"Slide it back, Shelley," Kanoa warns. "There is a reason your name was put forward."

"What reason?" Logan wants to know. "If this is an official mission, it can be carried out by official troops, legitimate special forces operations, or CIA operatives."

"No, we're the best ones for it," I say, "because they expect this mission to fail. And when we don't come home, who's going to notice we were even gone?"

"You are oversimplifying, Captain." Abajian glares across the length of the table. "Time is of the essence, and if we expected you to fail, I would not waste time recruiting you. This mission has highest priority. *Highest*. You will receive all the support we can provide.

"That said, there are political considerations. The election that followed Coma Day shook up Congress and brought in a large contingent of non-interventionists who want to abandon all American military action abroad. They've left us operating under a severely weakened Authorization for Use of Military Force. We will do what we need to do to prevent another orbital strike, legal restrictions be damned. But it's essential that we obtain solid intelligence on the location of the missile launcher before we act. We cannot afford a mistake. If we don't get this right the first time out, an impeachment hearing will be called against the president. Monteiro is vulnerable—an unelected president with no political base, and with many potential enemies." He raises an eyebrow. "I trust you don't count yourself among those enemies, Captain Shelley?"

"No sir, I do not."

Before Susan Monteiro was appointed to replace the sitting vice-president, she was Colonel Monteiro, who presided as the judge over the court-martial of the Apocalypse Squad. When the president resigned, she became his handpicked successor. She has tried hard to impose the rule of law instead of the rule of money over the country, and I admire her for that.

Abajian gives a short nod and continues:

"We believe the missile launcher has been transported in pieces to its current location—probably a UGF, an underground facility—where it's been reassembled, ready to be rolled out when the stars align." Another joke. He cracks a half smile. "Once you pinpoint for us the location of this facility and confirm the presence of the launch platform, we will deliver a cruise missile strike to permanently close the facility's doors."

"That's all?" Logan asks. "You just want confirmation of the location?"

"And of the presence of the missile launcher."

"It's hard to believe the Red doesn't already have that information," Logan says.

"Do you know something I don't, Lieutenant? Is the Red behind this mission?"

"Why else would you be here, sir?"

Cory speaks up in a soft, uncertain voice. "Lieutenant Logan, you can't assume this is the Red's mission."

I answer for my lieutenant: "It's not an assumption." Then I turn to Abajian. "Colonel, I want to know how this target can remain unknown. An underground facility big enough to hide a missile launcher must have attracted notice when it was under construction. There's got to be a history somewhere."

Abajian responds with admirable patience. "Shelley, Intelligence is searching for that history, for any kind of data, but we are talking about a region where secret projects have been undertaken for the better part of a century. A large, rugged, remote region. Given time, we might be able to find it, but we don't have that time. This mission needs to go tonight."

"That's a tight schedule."

"But we could do it," Logan says.

My messiah complex must be in remission, because doubt is pushing out my initial programmed enthusiasm. "Let's hear the rest of it."

Abajian complies. "A terrorist cell codenamed Northern Sword is known to be affiliated with the Shahin Council. Northern Sword operates within the target region and we believe they are in control of a BXL21 road-mobile missile launcher.

"Mission 'Arid Crossroad' has been adapted from a plan already under development. It calls for you to work with a civilian asset who will put you in contact with key elements of Northern Sword. Our analysts have modeled the personalities of those elements and they believe that you have a good chance to gain access to their facility—but there is an issue of timing. We cannot hold off the strike indefinitely. The political situation in the host country is unstable and we will be operating there without permission. We prefer to act only after we receive your confirmation that the launch platform is present, but we will act in any case at the slightest sign of hostile intent."

Logan follows the subtext as easily as I do. "So, the plan is to track us to the facility, and if we're still there when you start shooting, oh well?"

"It gets better," I say. "If things go south, no one will be able to prove we are legitimate US soldiers operating under orders, because we're not."

Abajian doesn't deny it. "You are correct, Captain Shelley. You will be presenting yourselves as private sector, minimizing risk to the president."

I appreciate that he's not lying to me, but I don't like the setup.

I feel like *we're* being set up.

Arid Crossroad is a rogue mission, ultra-dark, and there's no guarantee Abajian is on our side. He might decide the best course is to track us to the facility and take his shot as soon as we enter. Waiting longer, waiting for us to get out with confirmation of the presence of the missile launcher, is a risk he might decide not to take. Maybe he already has decided.

Kanoa watches me. I feel like he's reading my mind.

"This is not how we operate," I tell him.

He nods. "The element of trust is missing." Leaning back in his chair, he says to Abajian, "Let's get it all out front. Bring her in."

A spike of fear slams through me. I turn toward the door, certain it will be Delphi walking in. *Not here,* I think. *Not like this.*

The door opens—and I breathe again. It isn't Delphi. It's an older woman, fiftysomething; I should know her, but my shocked brain doesn't come up with a name right away. My overlay is more efficient. It consults the onboard encyclopedia and tags her after just a couple of seconds: *Yana Semakova.* She is dressed in a finely tailored blazer and brown pants. There is only a little makeup on her face. Her brown hair is short, styled in a simple perm.

She looks straight at me and without waiting for a formal introduction, she says, "We *can* be allies, Captain Shelley. We have a shared interest. I suggested you for this mission, and if you are willing to do this, I will prepare the way. They already know your name. They know you killed my father and stole his money. They respect that—and they will let you in."

Abajian holds up his hand. He doesn't want her to say more—not yet. "Will you consider the mission?" he asks me.

I look at Semakova, shake my head, and say, "No."

It's gratifying, seeing the surprise, the consternation on their faces. They thought they had me modeled with that messiah complex—but my fanaticism is strictly limited.

To my surprise, Cory is the first to argue. "You said the Red's behind it!"

"I don't care if the Red's behind it. I don't care if Ms. Semakova has a way in. This parses as a suicide mission, and that's not going to work for us. I need to believe we have a real chance to get out."

Abajian's answer is both straightforward and grim. FaceValue confirms the sincerity of his words. "We are all allies here, Captain Shelley. Not enemies. This is *not* a suicide mission, but I won't bullshit you. Given the nature of the enemy, this operation is extremely high-risk. But we will do everything we can to support your extraction. You are a creative officer. You have a knack for survival. This is *your* mission—if you are willing."

I look at Logan. I might have a knack for survival, but I've led good soldiers to their deaths. "What are you thinking?"

He shrugs. "Never trust the Red. That's what we always say. But if it gets behind us—"

"No," Semakova interrupts. "Where you are going, there is no outside influence, no Red. You will be on your own."

"We haven't agreed to do it," I remind her.

She turns her eyes briefly skyward. "I am not here on some little chance that you will agree. I have made a study of you since you visited my father. I have spoken with those who worked with you on that mission and before. And I say to you that this is only a dance of words. You will do it. The only one who pretends to doubt is you."

I don't know if Logan has a messiah complex, but after more discussion, we agree together to do the mission. Abajian wants to limit it to the two of us. I want to take Escamilla.

"Broken ribs," Logan reminds me.

"Fadul, then."

"No women," Abajian says. "Not where you're going."

"The army doesn't restrict where women can fight."

"You won't be army," he reminds me. "You'll be private sector—and they're a hell of a lot more conservative than we are."

Semakova has taken a seat at the table. "This mission is not a political statement," she says. "It is a slam."

No women. So Roman is not an option. Kanoa's back is too fragile for field duty, Dunahee has a broken shoulder, and Julian is still hospitalized, which leaves—

"Alex Tran?" Logan asks doubtfully.

Palehorse Keep was Tran's first mission with us, but he proved himself.

"Bring him in. See if he's willing."

Tran arrives, his dark face drawn and worried. He takes a second to scan the room. I know what he's doing. He's counting up friends and enemies. He likes the odds. When his gaze lands on me, he mouths the words *We on?*

I give a slight sideways shake of my head.

Kanoa doesn't miss this little drama. In an irritated voice, he says, "Sit down, Alex."

Tran waits for my nod of approval, and then takes the seat at my right hand.

"We're being offered a mission," I tell him. "Just the three of us."

"High risk," Logan adds. "You in?"

To my surprise, Tran looks uncertain. His gaze shifts between me and Logan. He's got FaceValue, but he still has to ask, "This is real? You're not joking?"

"Of course we're not joking," Logan says.

That's all Tran needs. He lights up with a smile. "Then hell, yes. I'm in." He hooks a thumb in Cory's direction. "Just tell me why Bilbo is sitting here, after he gave us up."

"Mr. Cory Helms is consulting," Kanoa says. "Now shut up and pay attention."

Colonel Abajian explains the mission profile.

"Northern Sword is a small but financially sophisticated organization of anti-western activists eager to see American freedom and power erased from the world. They are ostensibly interested in installing a new government in central Asia, one with the usual draconian religious restrictions to be applied to everyone but themselves. A Russian citizen known as Maksim Abaza is their leader. It's believed he's a key figure in the planning and development of 'Broken Sky'—what we in the West call the Kessler Syndrome. It's his assertion that without satellite surveillance and communication, drone warfare becomes far more difficult to carry out successfully, requiring costlier face-to-face engagements—"

"He is right about that, at least," Semakova interrupts.

Abajian scowls. "It's not as simple as that, but it makes a solid sound bite." He turns back to me. "Here's the story. Maksim Abaza is imaginative and ruthless. That's what's allowed him to thrive. But he's also arrogant and ambitious, eager to advance his own name by whatever means, and that's where you come in. He'll want to benefit from your celebrity. You, James Shelley, the Lion of Black Cross—a warrior as clever and ruthless as Abaza himself. You proved that when you took down Eduard Semak. You went dark after that conquest, but now you're back and ready to strike out on your own in the business of war. The money you stole from Semak will let you develop an inventory of arms at a time when Northern Sword has armaments to sell and is in need of cash. The broker bringing the two of you together is Leonid Sergun—Ms. Semakova's uncle. He is the individual who suggested this mission and he's well known to Maksim Abaza."

"Well known for what?" I ask, certain I won't like the answer.

"Leonid is an arms broker," Semakova says. "And for many years, he was my father's 'fixer.' He did what needed doing. 'Not on the side of the angels,' as you are known to say, Mr. Shelley, but he is changed. He is not a young man anymore. Now he lights candles and kisses the icons and makes promises. He wants the angels and the saints on his side—and he will do what he must to buy their favor."

"He's afraid of death?"

"He's afraid of Hell."

Is it possible to make up for a lifetime of murder and terror with acts of contrition in your last years? Fuck if I know, but if Sergun wants to bribe the angels by showing us the way into Northern Sword's den, I won't be the one lecturing him on too little, too late.

"Leonid Sergun has worked with us before," Abajian adds. "He's reliable. Now we need to get this operation launched. You've got twenty minutes to collect your gear. Weapons are acceptable, but leave your rigs behind. Do you have civilian clothing suitable for outdoor use in cold weather?"

The three of us share a suspicious look before I answer. "No, sir."

"Noted. Suitable clothing will be provided en route, along with the Arid Crossroad mission plan."

He starts to stand up, but I have one more question. "Colonel Abajian, in the hypothetical case that we see an opportunity to destroy the missile launcher ourselves, are we authorized to take such action?"

Abajian settles back into his chair, his hand resting on the table. He speaks carefully. "All we are asking you to do is to play your role. Locate the facility, confirm the presence of a BXL21 missile launcher, and leave. That said, you are the commander in the field and it is up to you to determine how best to serve the overall goal of this mission."

I nod. "Yes, sir." I can work with that.

He stands up. We all stand up, even Semakova, with a cacophony of chair legs scraping. Abajian holds his hand out to Kanoa. "If anyone questions your operation again, send them to me." They shake hands, and then we salute. "Twenty minutes, gentlemen," he reminds us. "I want Northern Sword's missile launcher taken out of the equation before they have a chance to use it."

We scramble to collect what we need from the armory and the supply closets: ammunition, first aid, food, water, communications gear. Abajian ordered us to leave our rigs behind. Without helmets, we won't have tactical AIs, so I pick up an optical scope for my HITR. I make sure Logan and Tran do the same.

"With no helmets, we aren't going to have hearing protection either," I add. "So grab earplugs. Maybe we'll get a chance to use them."

"We've got these HD pistols," Tran reminds me.

I turn to look. The Stonewall Home Defense 9-millimeter is designed to be consumer friendly, with sound suppression built into the extended barrel, ensuring the concussion can't cause permanent hearing loss. The barrel makes it an awkward size, but we've got shoulder holsters to fit.

"Bring 'em."

Not that I'm expecting trouble.

We grab weapons cases and then return to the barracks to collect our HITRs.

I'm stepping out of my room again when my network icon goes green. I'm automatically logged into gen-com, but I get icons only for Logan, Tran, and me.

Tran is waiting in the hallway. *You linked?* I ask him.

He doesn't speak out loud, but his response arrives over gen-com. *Roger that.*

"I'm linked too," Logan says as the door to his room opens.

We head downstairs to find Kanoa waiting for us. He looks grim, worried. No one else is in the building, so he

goes ahead with an impromptu meeting, standing in front
of the watch desk. "I don't like the way this came together,
but I believe it's a legitimate mission. Abajian's ambitious
and he knows how to play hard ball, but he's a good commanding officer, and he'll back you as far as he can."

"Meaning he *will* cut us loose if he has to?" I ask.

There's still a little artificial Christmas tree on the watch
desk. It casts a red light on Kanoa as he crosses his arms
over his chest. "That's how I read it. He's protecting the
president first, as he should. But you need to make this
work, Shelley, regardless."

"We will. Are you going to be linked to gen-com?"

"No. You're not going to have a handler. A continuous
link would be suspicious—and you probably won't have
connectivity anyway."

It's easy to see he's worried about it. I surprise myself
by trying to reassure him. "I've worked without a handler
before. We'll be okay." I eye Logan and Tran. "We'll back
each other up."

"The job will get done," Logan agrees. "And if we get
lucky, it won't even be a fighting mission."

Tran cracks a half smile. "You mean if *they* get lucky,
LT. You ask me, it's going to be hard to walk away without
finishing the mission."

Logan gives him a dark look. "We do what the situation
calls for."

"You do what you need to do," Kanoa says. "Just make
sure you're focused on *this* mission. Do not worry about
your status or what the future of ETM 7-1 will look like
going forward. We'll figure that out when you get back.
Until then, good luck."

He offers his hand. I put my pistol case down on the
watch desk long enough to shake it. "I'd like to see the rest
of the squad, sir, before we go."

"Negative. That won't go over well, especially with Fadul. I'll fill them in on what they need to know after you're gone."

He shakes hands with Logan and Tran, and then he gestures with his chin toward the barracks door. "Move out."

It's 0522 when we board one of the Black Hawks. We are the lone passengers. I stow my pack and the gun cases, then strap into a canvas seat between Logan and Tran. I look for the green network icon, which brightens under my gaze. I'm toying with the thought of calling Delphi, but when I play it out in my head, I know it's just a stupid fantasy. *Yeah, hi. I've got another mission. I might not be back.*

I left her for a reason. I'm not going to put her through that again.

The Black Hawk's crew chief hands out flight helmets and then closes the side door. After a few minutes, we lift off, flying northeast toward Dallas.

Another mission. Another opportunity to do what I was put on this Earth to do. That's how I look at it. *Shit.* Maybe I do have a messiah complex. People used to call me King David. But it's not God I serve. Not directly, anyway.

I never used to spare a thought for God, but I've read most of the Bible now. That shit doesn't make any sense to me, but I think a lot about God anyway—a mystery figure, moving in mysterious ways. Guiding me, maybe.

I guess I trust God more than I trust the Red, which isn't saying much.

I want to do the right thing, but there are so many wrongs in the world. There are so many people we need to get rid of, so many means of bringing Armageddon down on the billions who only ever wanted to live their own quiet lives, make something of themselves, see a fucking movie now and then, and get drunk with their friends.

I want to give them that chance.

NONLINEAR WAR

"HOLY SHIT," TRAN WHISPERS. "THEY'RE SERIOUS, aren't they?"

It looks that way.

Abajian's Black Hawk delivered us to Dallas/Fort Worth International Airport, where we were met on the tarmac by an army major with no interest in conversation. A short ride in the backseat of an SUV has brought us to an immense open-front hangar.

I lean forward to get a better look out the front windshield.

Sunrise is still half an hour away, but the hangar is bright with artificial lights that illuminate the dual fuselage of a gigantic carrier plane. Each of the carrier's two aircraft bodies look like the long, narrow fuselage of a normal jet, but they're fused together by a shared wing. Suspended from the center of that wing, two meters above the hangar floor, is a sleek little suborbital plane. Ground crew wearing Sidereal Transit Systems shirts are working in calm haste to clear tubes and cables from beneath it. A steep staircase leads to the suborbital's open door.

A suborbital is a dragon's transportation: fearsome speed

at fearsome cost. A lifetime of earnings for many, burned up in a single transit to the other side of the planet.

The major turns to issue terse instructions: "This is a chartered military flight. The other passengers aboard are on business of their own. They will not question you. You will not question them. Understood?"

I study the plane and wonder: *Who are they? Why are they in a hurry to get to the other side of the world? Are they involved with our mission? Who the hell is paying for this anyway?*

But all I say is "Yes, sir."

"After exiting this vehicle, you will proceed without delay up the staircase. Once inside, take the three open seats and strap in. Your gear will be loaded separately and returned to you in Riyadh, where you will transfer to a private jet. Your requested civilian clothing has been placed in the overhead bins. You will change in-flight, leaving your current uniforms behind."

The pre-mission support is damned impressive, I have to admit. I just hope Abajian has got a plan to handle us post-mission too.

"Go," the major says. "And good luck."

There are eight luxury seats aboard the suborbital, four on each side. It's the first three on the left that are open. The other passengers all have the outward appearance of civilians, but they are hard-bodied and hard-eyed. We glance at each other and look away.

My face is well known and I suspect they recognize me, but they won't get any confirmation from facial recognition, and my own automatic routine doesn't come up with any names for them. None of us are in the usual databases. It's an absence that conveys critical facts about our occupations and our connections.

I take the front seat—and realize there is no cockpit. I can see straight ahead, out through the narrow windshield.

Logan is sitting behind me. His synthetic voice comes over gen-com. *Is this a robotic plane?*

I answer in the same silent way. *Looks like it.*

I flinch as a voice, female and friendly, issues from the cabin speakers: "Welcome aboard, ladies and gentlemen."

The cabin door closes on its own and the carrier plane begins to roll, ferrying us with it.

We don't know if any of the other passengers are using amplified audio, so Logan plays it cautious, shifting from gen-com to text. He sends a group message to me and Tran. *The army can't be paying for this. There's no way this could be hidden in a black budget.*

I put together a text of my own without speaking. *We're flying on dragon money. It's got to be. They're scared of Broken Sky and they want it stopped.*

Tran whispers his response over gen-com. "I've been thinking. This is really just another look-and-see mission."

Logan doesn't like that idea at all. "Bullshit. We're going to find bad guys behind the door for sure this time, and we know what we're looking for."

"But do we know what we'll find?" Tran asks. He shifts to text to make his point. *Anything could be in that UGF. The BXL21 might not be our only target.*

I turn to look out the little round window beside my seat. Outside, I can see the left fuselage of the carrier plane and the runway beyond it. The sky is glowing, but the sun is not quite over the horizon. We've been looking for something these past months—something a lot smaller than a missile launcher. It *is* possible we're still looking. "Tran could be right. We'll know when we get there."

Another text comes in from Tran. *IF we get there. It'd be*

ironic if this vehicle turns out to be the next target for Broken Sky.

This pisses off Logan. "Shut the fuck up," he says, loud enough to be heard on and off gen-com—but I laugh. I can't help it. Because it *would* be ironic. I'm not too worried though. We're suborbital—a one-shot deal with a trajectory and timing that won't be known to the enemy until it's too late to aim.

Granted, I've been wrong before.

The initial flight feels the same as any passenger jet taking off. Suspended between the dual fuselage of the carrier plane, we are far from the engines doing the heavy lifting, but the cabin is still noisy with a dull, distant roar.

Once we're away from the airport, I get up and check the overhead compartments, where I find duffels labeled with our names. A couple of our fellow passengers eye me as I head to the back of the plane, but no one speaks out loud. I change my clothes, putting on heavy khaki slacks and a long-sleeve athletic shirt—quality garments, appropriate for a fledgling dragon heading into the field—and then I put my army boots back on to cover my robot feet. There's a coat, but it's too warm to wear now. My uniform gets stuffed into the duffel, and then I return the bag to the compartment.

Logan and Tran change clothes after me.

By the time Tran comes back, we've received the mission briefing for Arid Crossroad.

I read it on my overlay while we climb higher into the atmosphere. At first I just skim, then I go back to read for detail. The mission begins with a flight from Riyadh to Islamabad, where we will be met by Leonid Sergun, our agent in this fictitious arms negotiation. In this scripted drama, I am a newly minted and ruthless dragon, out to expand the fortune I stole from Eduard Semak, while Logan and Tran are hard-ass mercenaries in my employ.

Sergun has brokered a deal that will allow us to purchase a mixed lot of missiles, explosives, and programmable automatic weapons being offered at a bargain price to a buyer willing to close right away—because Maksim Abaza and his Northern Sword soldiers are on a tight schedule.

You really think anyone's going to believe this shit? Tran texts.

Logan is not convinced either. *Backstory seems a little thin.*

I compose my own text. *Look at it from Abajian's point of view. Story only needs to hold up until we get there. By then we'll have shown him the way.*

Logan: *IF we get there. If they don't kill us on the road.*

I try to put a positive spin on it. *Sergun thinks it will work.*

Tran: *I don't get why we trust HIM.*

I don't know either. But if we're going to do this mission, we've got to trust somebody.

The intelligence team feels that the rush to conclude this arms deal is strong evidence that Northern Sword actually does possess the missile launcher, and that they intend to use it very soon. Afterward, they will need to abandon their present location. Better for them to turn unused armaments into cash—which is why we are being allowed to visit at this critical time.

Leonid Sergun claims to be well known to Abaza and trusted by him. Abaza has agreed to transport us from Islamabad to . . . wherever it is we are going. Intelligence believes it's a UGF in a sparsely populated region to the north.

The cabin's disembodied voice speaks again. "Please

confirm that all of your personal items are secure. Launch will initiate in two minutes, thirty seconds."

Camera eyes watch us, confirming that we aren't doing anything stupid or leaving any gear lying around. The warning repeats every thirty seconds, until the last thirty seconds, when we're treated to a countdown. The synthesized voice bubbles with excitement as we reach the final seconds. ". . . three, two, one, zero!"

The rockets fire. Their force slams me back into the seat—maybe not as ferociously as my flight aboard *Lotus*, but it's a thrilling demonstration of power all the same. The cabin shakes, the clouds race past and then disappear, and soon the sky goes dark. As we reach our maximum altitude just above the top of the atmosphere, the exhausted rocket engines fall into silence—and with nothing holding us up, we begin to fall.

Free fall.

The sensation of weight disappears as I float against my harness.

"*Holy shit,*" Tran murmurs in a high-pitched voice. He's not the only one. Our stoic fellow passengers are whispering excitedly too.

But not Logan. "Ah, *fuck*," he says.

"If you're going to puke," I warn him, "puke into a bag."

"You are free to leave your seats," the cabin's joyful voice announces, "and enjoy the wonder of zero gravity!"

So we do, while the suborbital glides through a long, smooth arc back to the constraints of Earth.

Our stop in Riyadh is brief. I check in with Kanoa, and then we move with our gear to a chartered jet. The pilots are non-uniformed, but facial recognition identifies them as American Air Force officers. We settle into the seats. This time, we're the only passengers. That makes it easier to relax. I take my boots off. Flight time is six hours, so we sleep.

It's 0400 local time when we finally approach Islamabad. As the plane descends toward the runway, I gaze out the window at a vast, well-lit city. We won't be staying long.

After we land, the plane taxis to a hangar apart from the main terminal. The hangar is open on one side, the interior lit by dim red lights. We roll under the roof and stop. I turn on the record function in my overlay and then peer through the window. No one around. "Tran, you're communications for as long as it lasts. I want you to turn on your satellite link."

"Yes, sir."

We crowd the aisle as we get our gear out of the bins. Tran wakes up his satellite relay. As soon as I get a signal, I check in using gen-com. "Kanoa, you there?"

He responds in just a few seconds. "Roger that. Status?"

"Stage two. No welcoming committee."

"Instructions are to go through the passenger lobby. The civilian asset is on the way and will meet you on the other side."

I get my coat on, shoulder my pack, grab my gun cases, and wonder: Are we being set up? The money and effort that have been expended to get us here argue against it. If the point of this operation is to kill us or create an international incident . . . well, there are cheaper ways to get it done—and that's a twisted substitute for a comforting thought.

Logan is behind me in the aisle, loaded with his own gear. "You going barefoot?" he asks.

I flex my robot toes. "They wanted the fucking Lion of Black Cross. I want them to know for sure that's what they've got." And anyway, I don't like wearing shoes. They inhibit the usefulness of the feet.

The pilot and copilot emerge from the cockpit. We

shake hands and they wish us a gruff "good luck." Then they get the door open and we disembark under the shelter of the hangar's roof.

Outside, the temperature is a few degrees above freezing, but the wind is light, so it's not too bad. According to the mission plan, we are "prescreened" for customs. I guess it's a dragon's privilege to pay off officials and enter a country, no questions asked.

There's a glass door with Arabic script. My overlay translates it as a welcome message, so that's where I lead my squad. The door is unlocked. On the other side is a richly furnished lounge lit by dim cocktail lamps. Again, no one is around. I'm hoping that's on purpose, that Abajian paid for privacy.

We stop long enough to enjoy the gilt restrooms and to get our weapons out and loaded. Then we move to the main doors. I go first. I hear a lock disengage as I push one of the glass doors, opening it just a few inches. Outside is a patio lit with daylight bulbs and furnished with marble benches. Twin formal gardens are on either side, each with a small fountain. A portico shelters the patio and the gardens, extending over an elegant driveway that branches from a wider road running past the main terminal.

Sunrise is hours away, but Islamabad is awake. As the scream of a departing jet fades, I hear a dull, river roar of distant road traffic and, closer, the squeal of brakes from the main terminal, and the shout of eager voices.

Logan steps up beside me in time to see a large vehicle turning from the main road into the driveway. It stops at a closed steel gate beneath the blue halogen glow of a streetlight, so that I get a good look at it: a battered brown American-made LTV—a light tactical vehicle—basically an agile armored truck.

"You with us, Kanoa?"

There is no insignia on the LTV and I find myself imagining that it was bought, stolen, or captured from the Afghan National Army.

"Roger that. Confirming your welcome."

I am on edge, standing in the partly open doorway. From the mission briefing I know that this vehicle and the men inside it—other than Leonid Sergun—are part of Northern Sword and loyal to Maksim Abaza. My grip on my HITR tightens as the gate rolls back. The LTV surges into motion. It rumbles around the curve of the driveway. I imagine a gunner leaning out the window, hidden behind the glare of headlights.

"Take it easy, Shelley," Kanoa warns.

I make sure the muzzle of my HITR is pointing at the ground. "It's all about trust, right?" The LTV comes to a stop in front of the patio.

"Don't trust anyone outside the squad," Kanoa warns. "And stick to the mission plan. I'm dropping out of gen-com now per procedure, but we are observing. Good luck."

"Tran, shut down the link."

"On it, Shelley."

I hear the rustle of his equipment. The connection to Kanoa closes, but my network icon remains green. As I eye it a tag slides out, informing me I am linked to an EXALT network. Maybe the Red is watching too.

I push the door all the way open and step outside into the artificial light.

We are on our own.

The image of Leonid Sergun included in the mission plan showed a dour, scowling, heavily muscled man, sixty-three years old, with white hair buzz-cut in a flattop above a thick-jowled and weathered face. In that image, he must have been putting on a fierce pose to impress his terrorist clients, because it's a different sort of man who crosses the patio to greet us. His smile is warm, his blue eyes twinkling. He's sending off waves of good nature so intense they must surely register on some local EM sensor.

"James Shelley!" he exclaims in a marked Russian accent. As he sticks out his hand, he casts the expected glance at my robot feet. "No introduction needed, of course. It is an honor. An *honor*." FaceValue flags him orange: questionable, a difficult read. After a hearty handshake, he turns to my "bodyguards," who have emerged behind me from the lounge. He offers them a quieter greeting. "Ray Logan, Alex Tran, welcome. All is in order."

I am eager to cross the patio and get inside the LTV where we will be out of sight of any watchers, but Leonid doesn't share my philosophy. Instead of hurrying to get us under cover, he extends the introductions, turning to the two men who have come with him.

These are Abaza's men. The first is maybe thirty years old. He has a long face, light brown skin, closely trimmed ginger hair, and a neat beard of the same color. He's dressed in military camouflage patterned in green, brown, and gray—forest colors. He's armed with a pistol in a chest holster and a high-end automatic rifle held snug in the crook of his arm. It's a Lasher Biometric 762. Like a HITR, it's coded to its owner and will lock up if anyone else handles it.

"This is Luftar," Leonid says. "He is here to ensure we arrive safely at our destination, though all the world burn down around us."

I'm not sure Luftar understands this, but he smiles. "*Konechno*, Papa," he says, seeming happy to take on the role Leonid has assigned him. I have a suspicion he's got heavier gear stashed in the LTV.

Luftar's companion is much younger. He looks barely

twenty, slender, with dark-brown skin and a bright grin. "Damir is our driver," Leonid says. "You may direct all your curses at him for every bump we hit in the road—as I have already done many times."

Damir puts on a look of anguish at this insult. Turning his hands palm-up, he protests, "Papa, the road is what it is, and we must not be late." His English is excellent.

Leonid puts his large hand on the kid's shoulder and sadly shakes his head. "Make your excuses as you will, you will have no forgiveness from me." And then he grins and gives Damir a good shake, rattling loose a laugh from the kid.

But when he turns back to us, he is serious. In a low mutter, with one heavy eyebrow raised in question, he asks me, "You are recording what you see?"

I am here because Maksim Abaza wants to gain from my celebrity. So I shrug and say, "It's well known."

"It's why you are here," he agrees. He gestures at the road, the terminal, the distant buildings. "Look up. Look around. Let the watchers see your face. Let them know you are here, and that you're not afraid to undertake this business venture."

This request goes against every instinct. I don't want to be seen or noticed. I want to be anonymous, out of sight. But it's too early in the game to second-guess Leonid Sergun, so I do as he asks. I look around, surveying again the road to the main terminal and the buildings beyond, but this time while standing in the light.

"Enough," Leonid says as the roar of an arriving jet fades. "Get inside before someone puts a bullet in your head."

FaceValue's orange flag of uncertainty hasn't changed.

Though it's called a light tactical vehicle, the term "light" is relative. With its armor and its powerful engine, an LTV

masses over fourteen thousand pounds. This one is even
heavier, given the armored fuel barrels strapped to its back
bumper.

I look inside at an interior that's been highly modified.

The two front seats are standard, divided by a console. Empty steel-frame gun racks are mounted overhead.
Behind the front seats, the setup gets suspect. There's a
blackout screen that prevents anyone in back from seeing
out the front windows, and the small windows in back
have all been painted out, ensuring that no prospective
buyer—or prisoner—confined in the back will be able to
see a damn thing that's going on outside.

I'm pretty sure this LTV has been used more often for
prisoners than buyers.

The back seats are gone and the floor has been leveled. A
thin mattress has been put down as a concession to comfort—I decide to ignore a large but faded bloodstain, and
climb in. At least there's heat.

Logan and Tran come in behind me. Despite the outward size of the LTV, there's not a lot of room.

"Kind of a step down from our recent transportation,"
Tran observes.

Leonid is standing in the open door, with Luftar beside
him. "I'm sure this is true," he says. "But at least it cannot
be shot out of the sky."

I'm stunned he said it, that he would drop any hint
of our real interests. But he goes on in the most natural
tone. "I understand you were eager to make this deal and
there was little time, but when I heard what you would
undertake to arrive so quickly"—he shakes his head—"I
am not ashamed to say I worried. But here you are safe,
as it was meant to be, and as soon as Luftar has inspected
your gear—and we have stored your long guns—then we
can be on our way."

My grip tightens on my HITR as I side-eye Luftar. "You want us to turn in our guns?"

"Only the assault rifles. Luftar will secure them in the open racks in the cab." He shoves out his lower lip. "It is not polite to enter another man's house armed for war."

I'm a fucking arms dealer. Why shouldn't I be armed for war?

Leonid reads my resistance. FaceValue flickers briefly through an undecipherable sequence of moods as his expression becomes grave and solemn. "You do not know me. But I ask, Shelley, that you trust me as your guide, your agent. We *are* on the same side."

Are we?

My own words come back to me: *We are engaged in a nonlinear war, with no sides, no real allies, no fixed enemies, no certain battlefield.*

Leonid is playing his own game. Semakova said he is here in the service of God or of the Angels, or maybe just the Russian Orthodox Church, while Maksim Abaza and his crew also claim to serve God but under a different flag. And me? I work for the Red.

I force a thin smile, check the locks on my HITR, and hand the weapon to Luftar, who murmurs a quiet thank you.

I gesture at Logan to hand over his HITR, too. He gives me a doubtful look, but he does it. Tran looks rebellious, but what choice does he have?

Luftar disappears with the weapons.

"You may keep your pistols," Leonid says in a conciliatory tone. "We are all friends here."

Of course we are. For now, we all have things to gain by pretending our trinity of faiths can get along.

"Now your gear," Leonid says. "Luftar will inspect your packs and your gun cases, and remove any satellite devices, which he will hold until our transaction is complete."

This request is easier to accept. I turn over my pack to
Luftar, knowing there's nothing in it to excite interest—not
in the company of mercenaries anyway. Luftar pulls everything out—clothing, ammunition, rations, water, first aid
kit, and my satellite uplink, which he keeps. He works efficiently and respectfully, and then repeats the process with
the other two packs. Last of all, he gives the empty gun
cases a quick look before stowing them between the blackout barrier and the front seats.

Another commercial jet screams in. After the roar of its
engines drops to a bearable volume, Luftar asks, "*Nu poy-
edem*, Papa?" My overlay translates. *Well, ready to drive, Papa?*

Leonid climbs in with us, then gives our armed guard
a thumbs-up. Luftar closes the passenger door, latching it
from the outside—and my green network icon goes red.
At the same time, the passenger compartment goes dark.
The only illumination left comes from a few narrow shafts
of artificial light seeping through pinholes in the black
window paint and leaking around the edge of the blackout
screen—just enough light to reveal a problem.

"*Shit,*" Tran says. "I can't get a signal in here."

"Neither can I," Logan growls.

I have a different complaint. "Where the fuck is the
door handle, *Papa?*"

Leonid has brought a cushioned backrest with him. I
watch him in the murky light as he arranges it against the
closed door. He leans back, seeming unconcerned as he
stretches his legs across the width of the cab. The LTV
lurches forward. "You must understand, Shelley. Those
who do not take reasonable precautions do not remain in
this business long."

"We still have our pistols," Tran says.

"Be careful shooting in here," Logan advises. "The ricochet could kill you."

"And me," Leonid says, looking at peace with his eyes closed. "I prefer to survive this transaction. Let us strive for patience and to keep our tempers in check." I see a glint as one eye opens. "Try to get comfortable. This will be a long drive—and we have pressing business to undertake as soon as we arrive."

I arrange my pack so I can lean against it. My Stonewall pistol is in a chest holster, a cold weight against my heart. Closing my eyes, I use my overlay to check GPS—but of course I get nothing beyond a message, *searching for signal.* I open my eyes again. "Can either of you get location data?"

Logan sounds disgusted. "No."

Tran hooks a thumb at the roof. "It's the armor. We'll get nothing while we're in here."

"Precautions," Leonid repeats. "We all have many enemies."

He doesn't need to say what is obvious: that there will be camera eyes in this prisoner wagon, watching us, monitoring every word we say—but not the words we leave unsaid.

I focus on a phrase, *We still linked?*

The signal goes out over gen-com on an encrypted line-of-sight link. Logan says nothing. He doesn't even look at me. Nothing to give us away—but his flat, synthetic voice tells me what I need to know. *Still here.*

And Tran: *Roger that.*

I've got a detailed map stored in my overlay. I study that, I note the road conditions, I listen, and I try to guess where we're going.

At first the road is paved and smooth, but we move slowly, with horn-honking traffic all around us, and rumbling diesel engines. The glare of artificial light lances through the pinholes, transiting swiftly across our compartment. It

scatters against Logan's tense face, but where it passes over
Tran's dark skin it disappears, leaving only glints. Leonid is
revealed in sporadic flashes. He is looking at me, his gaze
stern and resolute, no longer the jovial host who greeted us
just minutes ago—but FaceValue still calls it bullshit orange.

"Do you have an overlay, Papa?" I ask him.

This earns a derisive *tsk*. "I am an old man." Light flashes
over a face that's now amused. "And now you are thinking
to yourself, *So was Eduard Semak*."

That's exactly what I'm thinking. "Semak wore an overlay and he was a lot older than you."

"So I am younger. I should be more adaptable, yes? But I
am adaptable. I learn from those around me and I learned
many things from my brother-in-law. I learned the business. And I learned a thing he did not mean to teach me:
Know your limits. Eduard overstepped his. Not a path I
want to follow."

"Why don't you use farsights?" Tran wants to know.

"I do use farsights—when I need to navigate an unfamiliar city or find a face in a crowd. But we are going to see
friends. I don't need a device to tell me their names."

"Or to measure their sincerity?" I ask.

"No one is sincere in this business, Shelley."

"Maybe that's why FaceValue can't figure you out. It
wants to flag everything you say as bullshit, but it won't
flag anything as a lie."

This makes him laugh. "My nephews rely on FaceValue
and they have complained of the same thing. But it's not
me. It's this machine mind you use, programmed to neatly
divide the world into truth and lies. The AI is correct when
it reports I don't lie. Why should I lie? I live my life among
friends and I am fond of them all. And if I think half of
them are idiots, should I tell them? But a fond insincerity
must be difficult to parse."

"Yeah, I guess it would be."

I looked up Leonid Sergun in my encyclopedia, but the entry was just a stub. There was no history of him in the mission plan. But I remember what his niece, Yana Semakova, said of him: *He did what needed doing.* No doubt among his many friends were some who discovered late in their lives that Leonid Sergun did not count them as friends anymore.

But he is changed, Semakova said.

I sure as fuck hope so.

The traffic jam outside the blacked-out windows eases, and Damir makes the engine growl as we pick up speed. We leave the city behind. I can tell because no more light is leaking in. Hard to see anything in our compartment, and the road gets rough. Not that we slow down.

I mutter my own curses at Damir as I grope for grab bars and tie-downs. Everyone is forced to brace to keep from being bounced around. I allow the map to fade from my overlay since I can't read it anymore. Instead, I think about Colonel Abajian.

He's got eyes on us. Satellites won't give him the continuous, real-time surveillance he needs. So he'll be using a drone.

Drones can be tiny—as small as my thumb. They can be the size of a hawk. The drone we use when we operate as an LCS is a three-foot crescent wing, but of course drones can be a hell of a lot bigger than that, faster, higher-flying. A solar-powered electric drone equipped with excellent optics and soaring quietly at thirty thousand feet stands a good chance of tracking a moving subject even in steep, forested terrain—and providing highly accurate targeting data for a cruise missile strike.

Abajian won't need us to report the location of the facility. He'll know where it is the moment we disappear inside. From that point on, he'll have the data he needs to target it, but we are trusting him to wait.

After a long time, the sun finally climbs into the sky and daylight seeps into the back of the LTV. It's a gloomy illumination, but at least we can see. There's no comparable improvement in the road. We bounce and jar and rattle. And then we bump so hard there's a hammerblow clash of metal on metal. Tran and I are tossed into the ceiling. Logan manages to hold on and so does Leonid, but even his patience is exhausted. With his huge fist, he pounds furiously on the blackout screen, cursing Damir—and the LTV slows to a less-insane speed.

Tran rubs at a lump sprouting on the back of his head. "Fucking driver needs to learn to drive!"

Damir knows how to drive. He just has his own fearless style. The engine revs madly. We heave over terrain so rough I wonder if we're still on a road at all. We brake hard and then shift back up through the gears, over and over again, climbing and descending and crawling around what feels like hairpin turns.

At one point the LTV slides sideways. Luftar shouts useless advice as Damir works the gears, gunning the engine. God knows how far we'll fall if the road collapses from under us and still it's not fear I feel. It's a weird, low-grade anger. I *do not* want to die on the way to the UGF. I want to get there. I want to find it. I want this mission to prove worthwhile. I feel the desire like an obsession that leaves me chemically armed with attitude. I look over at Logan. The intensity of his glare makes me think he's charged up the same way.

The tires get traction. We shoot forward. Tran kicks the blackout screen with the sole of his boot like he's trying to kick it out. "Don't get us killed before we get there, dumbass!"

I can't help myself. I start laughing. We are fucking robots, programmed, and eager to execute.

Four hours and nine minutes after we leave the airport, the LTV finally rolls to a stop.

I hear wind outside. Nothing more.

I need to piss.

Logan's artificial voice arrives over gen-com. *We here?*

I ask the same question out loud, addressing the man who should know. "Papa, are we here?"

"No, it's too soon." He sits up, pulling his cushion away from the door.

I draw my pistol.

"Take it easy," he adds irritably. "We are guests. They want to impress us, not kill us."

The door swings open, admitting a blast of freezing air along with the glare of daylight, blinding after the gloom of the LTV. I squint at the face of our driver, the smiling young madman, Damir, as he peers inside. Damir's smile widens into a grin when he sees my pistol. *"Bang,"* he says, targeting me with a finger gun. He laughs and then waves at us to join him outside. "Come, sir. Come, Papa. We can rest here."

Leonid goes first, clearing the way. I holster the Stonewall, grab my coat, and follow. Logan and Tran pile out behind me, both with pistols strapped to their thighs.

A thin layer of snow frosts the ground. Behind the LTV I can see our muddy tire tracks, but on the unpaved road ahead of us, the snow is clean and undisturbed.

We have stopped near the bottom of a deep, narrow ravine, just at the edge of a scattered cover of young evergreens. A stream runs below the road. Wooded slopes rise above it, framing a sky layered with high, gray clouds. A light wind rocks the treetops. It's goddamn cold.

I glance into the cab, confirming our HITRs are secured in the ceiling racks like they're supposed to be. Then I get my coat on.

GPS coordinates come in, telling me what I already know: We are in a rugged region with no towns or villages close by. The road we are on is a ragged scratch in the mountains, without a name or a number.

I dismiss the map so I can watch Luftar. At the airport he wasn't wearing farsights, but he's wearing them now. He has his Lasher Biometric slung over his shoulder, and an SA-40 angel in his hands—a pricey surveillance drone with self-adjusting wings, designed for mountainous environments with erratic winds. He carries it out from under the trees, and when there's open sky above him, he flicks on the SA-40's electric engine and lets it go. Its quiet propellers carry it swiftly up and away, in the direction we're driving.

Luftar doesn't watch the angel. He moves back under the trees, where he stands with his head cocked, studying the display on his farsights. "Floater," he growls in English, returning to the LTV.

Damir steps up beside me, an excited glint in his eyes. "Do you see it?" he asks, gazing skyward.

"See what?"

He takes my arm, urging me out into the open. I go with him, crunching through the snow on my titanium feet, with Logan following behind.

"There." Damir points. And then I do see it. A large bird, maybe a hawk or an eagle—or a drone designed to mimic a raptor.

I turn at the sound of a door slamming behind me. Luftar has traded his Lasher for a Light Fifty. Tran moves in, watching with an incredulous expression as Luftar sets up the sniper rifle, resting the bipod on the high hood of the LTV. Over gen-com, Logan says, *No way.* Even if Luftar has an AI to help him aim—and I don't think he does—it's a crazy shot.

But Luftar looks confident. He crouches behind the Light Fifty, aims high, and squeezes the trigger. The shot echoes off the valley walls as I turn my head in time to see the bird—the drone?—pitch and then tumble, shedding glittering bits of feathers or plastic as it falls, dropping out of sight in a swift arc.

Beside me, Damir erupts in a celebratory whoop, his ecstatic voice echoing in the ravine.

Luftar looks up with a proud grin. "Smart bullet," he says. "Never miss." I should have guessed. He was using a self-guided projectile, not ordinary ammunition. He looks so damned pleased, it's impossible not to smile in return.

"Do you know who fielded the floater?" I ask him.

It's Damir who answers. "It doesn't matter, sir. If it's not ours, it's the enemy's."

"And we have many enemies," Leonid proclaims. He walks up to Luftar and gives him a hearty slap on the back. "But we are well guarded."

I look up again at the sky. Luftar's SA-40 is still up there somewhere. Colonel Abajian will have eyes in the sky too, but the drone he's using will be high-altitude—something subtle, sophisticated, untouchable.

"Careful, Shelley," Leonid says in a gently mocking tone. "The floater is gone, but look up too long and a satellite might log your face."

"Long odds on that."

To identify an individual in a deep ravine like this, a high-resolution spy satellite would need to pass almost directly overhead during these few moments when my face is exposed—and I don't always photograph well.

"Ah, my friend, unlikely odds kill men all the time."

I turn to look at him. He's still under the trees, standing alongside the LTV. Despite his easy tone, his face is serious. I realize he's trying to warn me, to counsel me that I'm making a mistake. I glance up once more at the sky. I'm out in the open with Damir. I'm not too worried about it because I want Abajian to know where I am; I want his invisible high-altitude drone to mark my presence. But James Shelley the arms dealer would not feel that way. He would be more cautious.

I nod and, signaling Logan to follow, return to the cover of the trees.

From where we've stopped, I can see the road ahead as it climbs a steep slope. Seventy meters on, it jogs around a sharp turn and disappears.

I'm suspicious of this road.

Abajian's report said the missile launcher was transported in pieces and assembled on site. It would have to be, because this roadbed couldn't support either the weight or the width of the BXL21. I'm not sure it could support the trucks that would be needed to ferry its components.

I look again at Leonid—*Papa*—but if he is suspicious, he reveals no hint of it. He's smiling, joking in Russian with Luftar, feigning a large rifle held against his shoulder. He mimes pulling the trigger and then throws his hands up in pretended shock, stumbling sideways as if the recoil has almost knocked him over. He laughs. Luftar and Damir laugh with him. Hell, I laugh. Leonid is an arms broker. I know he is a bad-ass, stone-cold killer, but it doesn't show— and he's fucking funny when he wants to be. Maybe it's his self-deprecating humor that has let him stay alive so long.

Luftar puts the sniper rifle away and then hands out cans of sweetened tea, bread, and cold roast lamb. We eat standing up under the trees, and then Damir smokes a cigarette.

After a few more minutes, Luftar speaks to Leonid in a soft, apologetic tone. Leonid listens closely, nods a grudging agreement, then turns to me. "The SA-40 has sighted a patrol in one of the valleys ahead of us. Luftar would not be concerned with meeting them, except that you are with us, Shelley. Questions would be asked."

"Okay. What do we do?"

"We stay here. This is a good place. Later in the day, when the patrol has passed, we move on."

So we sleep in the LTV, with the door partly open. When I don't want to sleep anymore, I walk under the trees. The SA-40 returns twice. Luftar swaps out the battery pack and sends it out again. The third time it returns, he decides it's okay for us to move on.

"Do you know how far we're going?" I ask Leonid when the door is closed.

"Only halfway to Hell," he assures me.

I watch the time tick past in my overlay as I sit braced against the bumps and turns of our crawling progress. The pinpoints of light leaking into the back of the LTV gradually fade as night arrives. On the other side of the blackout screen, I hear Luftar speak. My overlay doesn't catch what he says, but the tone is positive. A few seconds later, Damir whoops and pounds on the steering wheel. We come to an abrupt stop. Again, I reach for my pistol, though I'm thinking longingly of my HITR in the gun rack on the other side of the blackout screen.

There is the sound of one of the front doors opening, slamming closed. Seconds tick past. Almost a minute. The LTV lurches forward again. Moving slowly, we bump over a low obstacle, rolling onto a smooth, level surface. We continue for a few seconds and then stop again.

Even over the LTV's climate control I can hear men outside, speaking. There is a thud. Maybe a heavy gate, or door,
being firmly closed. Needles of bright, artificial light shoot
again through the pinholes in the blackout paint. But it's
still too dark inside to see faces, so I do a sound check.
"Logan, you ready?"

"Roger that."

"Tran?"

"Yes, sir."

"We are among friends," Leonid warns, his low voice
weighted with caution.

"We look forward to meeting our new friends, Papa," I
answer.

"Yes, Shelley. Exactly so."

I think, *Be ready for anything.*

The door swings open.

At first I imagine we are in a garage. It's the daylight
bulbs that mislead me. They're mounted to the ceiling, but
it's a ceiling of chiseled rock, not concrete. The lights are
bright, but the area they are required to illuminate is large
and there is too much distance between the bulbs. The
result is a grid of shadows. The air is moist and cold, but
not as cold as it was out in the wind. Somewhere, a generator is purring.

Damir is standing at the door, looking in, still smiling.
Behind him I count twelve men, including Luftar. There
are no women.

Like Luftar, most of the men are dressed in forest camouflage—military garb but not American. A few wear
black sweaters over olive-drab pants. They are a weathered,
sun-hardened crew, but still young. Half have thick, shaggy
hair and beards—black, brown, ginger, blond. The rest
have buzz cuts and beard stubble. None show any gray hair.

My overlay tags one of the brown-haired buzz-cuts

as Maksim Abaza, leader of this terrorist coven. Abaza is Caucasian, sharp-featured and lean, his face still showing a remnant of brown tint from a fading tan. A pleased half smile conveys a sense of victory as he eyes me.

My overlay fails to tag any of the other men, but my system will remember their faces.

Luftar cradles his Lasher 762. Three others carry the same weapon. I should take that as a threat, but as they crane to see into the LTV's dark interior, all I see in their expressions is curiosity. Leonid signals me to exit first, so I do, climbing out with my pack in hand. I am met by a murmur, with random words chosen for translation by my overlay, mostly the equivalent of *See his feet? It's him.*

Just like Abajian promised, I'm a celebrity, even here.

Wherever the hell here is.

Abaza steps forward, proffering his hand in an American greeting. "Shelley!" He nods at my feet. "No question it is you, alive as promised, though rumor insisted you were dead. I am honored, sir. Honored."

I reach out to shake the hand of my terrorist host and am pulled into a bear hug, while behind me Leonid protests, "Maksim! I swore I would bring Shelley to you! Did you doubt me? I am wounded! *Wounded.*" He grips at his heart to prove it while we all laugh. We are a merry bunch, bent on returning the world to the primitive communications of the 1950s.

I shake hands with the muscle, while my own toughs clamber out of the LTV, packs on their backs and pistols on their thighs. Logan and Tran glare, narrow-eyed. They are behind the curve on our program of international friendship. I ignore them, and so does everyone else.

Everywhere is raw, gray stone without any concrete. The floor is flat but gritty, and there's a lot of open space— enough to easily turn the LTV around. Ours isn't the only vehicle. Three pickups, all with PKM machine guns mounted in the cargo beds, are backed up against a wall directly in front of the LTV. An empty flatbed truck is backed against the far wall. So my initial impression of a garage wasn't completely wrong. But the missile launcher I'm looking for isn't here.

That doesn't mean our intelligence is wrong. A tunnel leads away from the lighted area. It's wide enough to drive a tank through—or a road-mobile missile launcher—so it's possible our target is stored in another part of this complex.

I don't know much about mining, but my guess is that this UGF was never used as a mine. I'm imagining some paranoid government or well-heeled revolutionary army deliberately carving it from the guts of a mountain to serve as a hideout, a fortress, a bomb shelter.

Just a few meters behind the LTV is a massive gate, closed now, but that must be the way we came in. The gate is made of heavy, riveted plates of black steel, and like the tunnel, it's big enough to drive a tank through. I'm going to assume Colonel Abajian's surveillance drone successfully tracked us to that gate. Our job now is to confirm the presence of the missile launcher, but whether we succeed or not, this sanctuary has become a marked target.

Abaza notices my interest in the gate. He grins, showing off yellow teeth. "Come have a look."

I follow him. The gate towers over our heads, its surface cold under my palm. Abaza spins a mechanical lock. I listen to its smooth, well-oiled mechanism. He's taunting me, making sure I understand that we're trapped in here. "Steel bolts bigger than an elephant's dick hold the doors. No one in. No one out, until our business here is done."

Leonid joins us, laying his big arms around our shoulders. "And we should get to business, my friends. There is much to do and, I think, not much time?"

Abaza scowls, not appreciating the reminder. "There is time enough, Papa. Come. We will have coffee and a last meal." He shrugs out from under Leonid's arm and stalks off toward the tunnel. I watch him go, wondering if there are more men here, or if the thirteen we've seen so far are all of Northern Sword.

Leonid's grip on my shoulder tightens. "Patience, my friend. There is much to assess, much to do. These things always take time."

We follow Abaza into the tunnel, his men trailing behind us. Spillover from the garage lights illuminates the first several meters. More light comes from a side opening twenty meters along. Past that, I can see the black outline of another side chamber or tunnel, though it's unlit. Without night vision, I can't see any farther, though I can hear the low rumble of a generator. Louder than the generator are the echoes of our footsteps. Both the echoes and a slight breeze hint that the tunnel runs a long way into the rock.

Abaza disappears into the lighted opening. We follow, and find a deep chamber cut back at an angle to the tunnel. Barrels along one wall probably hold water, or maybe fuel. There's a workbench with a propane stove and two microwaves. Cushions surround a long, low table, and there are clusters of thin mattresses with crumpled sleeping bags. I count nine, less than the number of men here. Maybe they have a watch rotation, sleep in shifts. But this is definitely a barracks room.

Abaza invites us to sit at the table while his men brew coffee and heat prepackaged food. Across the table, he speaks in Russian with Leonid. My overlay tries to translate, but after I decide they're discussing business terms, I ignore it and look around instead, trying to estimate the size of the chamber.

Logan is ahead of me in working things out. *Tank tunnel,* he says.

I glance at him, sitting beside me. Then I consider our surroundings again. A tank tunnel is used to hide tanks and other battlefield assets, and to secretly deploy them close to or across a contested border. This chamber is easily large enough to house a tank. It's probably possible to park two in here, end to end. The angle of the chamber would make it easy to roll a tank out into the tunnel. We don't know for sure that there are more chambers, but my guess is there are. I imagine a series of them, hollowed out in a herringbone pattern. A chamber of this size would be big enough to house the missile launcher.

Where the hell are we, that the politics and geography make a tank tunnel worthwhile?

I pop my regional map back into my overlay and scan the terrain, but there's no obvious candidate for our location, so I close the map again, not wanting to call attention to myself with a vacant-eyed stare.

Steaming plastic trays are set out on the table. Coffee is poured. We eat, until after a few minutes Abaza speaks, this time in English. "Shelley," he tells me, nodding toward one of his soldiers. "My friend is curious. He wants to ask you about the women soldiers in the American army."

I feel my stonewall expression slide into place. Around the table, everyone is watching, waiting to hear what use we make of women on the front lines.

The man with questions speaks. My overlay starts to translate, but I stop it, holding out for Abaza's version— Abaza, who leans back, putting on a cold smile. "When my friend fought in Africa, the older men told him that some of the American soldiers were women. He thought they were making a fool of him and he refused to believe it."

The man speaks again. Abaza and the others laugh. I feel Logan stiffen beside me, while Leonid purses his thick lips and turns to Abaza. "You insult your guest?"

"It is not an insult," Abaza says. "It is a fact." He looks at me, wanting me to know what his man has said. "He refused to believe the women soldiers were more than propaganda, until they took one prisoner. Women do not belong on the battlefield."

He doesn't say more. He doesn't need to.

I look at him, I look around at his men, and I wonder: How many American soldiers have they killed? How many women have they beaten and raped? How many innocent civilians have died at their hands?

They are the enemy. It's a fact I don't want to forget.

Abaza frowns down at the table. He has to be desperate for this deal, desperate for cash. There's no other reason he would risk my presence here. I hope it worries him that I'm angry. But he offers no apology, choosing instead to pretend that nothing is wrong, Turning to Leonid, he says, "Damir will show you the stock. Take what you will. Take all of it! It won't matter. Just be ready to go by dawn."

Dawn is at least ten hours away. I hope Abajian is willing to wait that long.

Damir is tired from the road. He comes to us yawning, a young, mad stoic who accepts his fate with grace and veiled pride. "Maksim gives me these tasks because of my English skills. That is the burden of knowledge."

"Your English is excellent, my young friend," Leonid assures him. "It is only your driving that needs practice."

Tran laughs, but for once, Damir does not find Leonid's

joking funny. "You may leave your things here. We will not be going far."

I pick up my pack by the shoulder strap. "We may need our things."

Damir shrugs. "Come, then."

Luftar tags along too, cuddling his Lasher as Damir leads us deeper into the dark tunnel. A dim green light gleams beside the dark chamber mouth we saw before, marking the location of a light switch. Damir turns the lights on inside a chamber identical in size, shape, and angle to the barracks room.

"Not much here," he observes, and he's right—the room is mostly empty. There's a half-pallet of what turns out to be Iraq-War-era AK ammo, and a full pallet of fairly new Russian RPGs. Nothing more.

Logan and Tran stand watch on either side of the entrance, while Luftar idles in the hall, smoking a cigarette and watching every move we make. I open the crates. Leonid gets out a tablet, which he uses to log and photograph the contents. He asks my opinion and feigns interest in the little I have to say. When the crates are closed again, he straps sealing tape over the seams and affixes RF tags to each piece.

He explains, "When these goods reach my warehouse they will be scanned again. When all the tags are accounted for, then the money you have placed in escrow will automatically transfer."

Advanced banking for terrorists.

I haven't placed any money in escrow, of course, but I think someone has. It's possible to fake all kinds of data including a death—I should know—but from what people like Bryson and Cory have told me, even the Red insists that money should be real. I don't know whose money we're playing with and it doesn't matter, because these terrorist toys that Leonid is so carefully inventorying will never make it to any warehouse—I will blow them up on the road if I have to—and no money will ever change hands.

I wish Leonid would hurry the fuck up. I want to get a look at things farther down the tunnel, determine if the missile launcher really is here.

"Damir," Leonid says. "Bring a forklift. These are ready to be loaded on the truck."

Damir slips out past Logan and Tran. I follow with Leonid. As we leave the chamber, Logan shines a little LED light down the tunnel. "Looks like at least two more chambers."

"More chambers with more goods!" Leonid declares. "I would not subject you to such a day of misery for a single pallet of RPGs."

I've stopped paying attention to FaceValue because Leonid has defeated it. Emotional analysis is useless to gauge the intent of a man whose every word reads as a half-truth steeped in subterfuge—but it's hard not to like the old bullshitter. I only hope we really are playing the same game.

Leaving on the lights in the first storage chamber, we move deeper into the tunnel. As we move, I watch the floor in the beam of Logan's light, searching for any hint that tank treads ever rolled through here, but the floor is smooth.

The chambers are staggered on opposite sides of the tunnel. Tran clicks the light switch for the next one—and I stifle a groan. This one is full of pallets—but still no missile launcher.

"Ah-ha," Leonid croons. "Look at this. Look at all this. We have found the armory."

I turn to Luftar. He nods, as if to say *I'll wait*, and lights another cigarette. I watch the smoke drift back toward the garage. Is the launcher here? If I asked Luftar about it, would he tell me?

"Shelley!" Leonid calls. "There is more here than I antic-
ipated. More than will fit on the truck!"

This is Leonid's way of reminding me that I am here
as an arms dealer and I need to play that role. I signal
Logan and Tran to again take up posts on either side of the
entrance. Leaving my pack with them, I join Leonid.

We work quickly, inventorying crates of AKs, grenade
launchers, boxes of C-4, and pallets of ammo. Other
crates hold body armor, some used, some new, and
antique night vision gear, incendiary and fragmentation
grenades, antipersonnel mines, and shoulder-launched
surface-to-air missiles. And then Leonid hesitates at an
open crate. It holds gas canisters labeled in Arabic characters. My overlay translates the writing, but it's just a
manufacturer's code. "Probably Syrian," Leonid decides.
"From before."

My skin prickles. "Wait . . . you think it's sarin?"

"*Da.*"

This is a yard sale at the Devil's house.

I look over my shoulder. Luftar is still watching from
the hall. He gives me a smile and a slight nod. If there
were other men here, apart from those I've already seen,
there would be some indication of them, lights or noise,
but there's nothing. I conclude there are only the thirteen.
If we could arm ourselves adequately and hit them without
warning, we might win a firefight. Luftar is on watch to
make sure that doesn't happen.

"Where is that boy?" Leonid growls. "Damir!" He
stomps out and yells up the tunnel. "Damir! Where—"

He breaks off when he realizes someone up there is yelling too, dark and dirty Russian. It's Abaza. Leonid goes still,
listening to a furious tirade. "*Shit,*" he whispers.

And I think, *Abaza must know.* He must know who
we're working for and why we're really here.

I move to the chamber's entrance, to stand with Logan and Tran. Luftar is looking away, toward the disturbance out front. I edge closer to him, my hand drifting toward the pistol in my chest holster.

I don't want to kill Luftar. He seems like a decent guy. But then, so do I, most of the time. The overriding fact is that he is the enemy, assigned to stand over us with a Lasher.

I can't give him a chance to use it.

Take him? Logan asks.

We have only the three Stonewall pistols between us. When Luftar goes down, his Lasher won't do us any good, because it's registered to his biometrics, but we have a room full of weapons behind us—enough to start a war.

I review in my mind where the RPGs are stashed; I calculate the number of seconds it will take me to reopen the crate and distribute the weapons.

Violence of action has won battles for me before.

So I say, *Yes.*

Logan and Tran both reach for their pistols. I take a step back toward the RPGs. From deeper in the tunnel, someone speaks a question.

I don't understand the words. I don't know who it is. I turn, my pistol out, aiming the Stonewall's long, fat barrel into the darkness. Someone yells. Everyone yells—Logan, Luftar, Tran, Leonid, the unknown voice, and me—all of us agreed on one thing: *"Don't shoot!"*

For half a second, all is silent, and then Abaza's voice booms down the tunnel. "What the *fuck*? What the *fuck*?"

I don't turn to look at him, knowing Logan has my back. I keep my attention on the unknown. In the dim light spilling into the tunnel I see a young man, mid-twenties. My first thought is that he is no soldier. And my second: *Can I use him as a hostage?*

His eyes are hidden behind farsights that gleam faint green. The narrow lens rests above sharp cheekbones and a prominent nose—Middle Eastern features framed in a short mane of thick black hair. He's dressed like a civilian with money who's decided to spend a week in the mountains: khaki pants, lug boots, a dirty sage-green thermal coat for warmth, and several days of beard stubble. No weapons that I can see—but there is a look of shocked recognition on his face—an *oh holy shit* expression that I don't like at all.

He turns to run. I go after him. I catch him in two steps. Get him by the shoulder. Shove him back against the tunnel wall, the Stonewall under his chin, the ruby glow of its laser sight so bright it looks like it's burning a hole in his skin. "Who the fuck are you?" I growl, trusting Logan and Tran to cover me against Luftar, Abaza, and his men.

"No one," he whispers. English, this time, with an American accent. "I'm not armed."

Leonid moves in to talk me down. "Shelley, my friend—"

But Abaza has caught up with us, and he takes over. "Shelley!" I hear panic in his voice. He's almost breathless with it. "*Shelley*, please. I have wanted to kill Issam many times—but I ask you not to. He is harmless, and I need him."

"Let him go, Shelley," Leonid says. "It was a misunderstanding. Nothing more."

The tunnel is crowded now with Abaza's men and the advantage of surprise we might have had a moment ago is gone—but so is the sense of threat that nearly brought us to a firefight.

I holster my pistol. But I don't let Issam go, not yet. Instead, I push his farsights up, away from his eyes, giving my overlay a clear look at him—and it finally identifies him. It tags him as Issam Salib, an American citizen, born in San Jose, Stanford educated, with a doctorate in computer science.

"You've got to be fucking kidding me." I mouth the words more than speak them, but Issam catches on. He gives a slight shake of his head. It's not so much denial as a gesture of helplessness or hopelessness—and it makes me wonder how deeply he believes in the radical cause.

I let him go and step back a pace. "What the fuck is he doing here, Maksim? Coming up on me like that in the dark?"

Abaza strolls closer. I watch him warily. He's holding his Lasher 762 casually, in one hand, and he's looking at Issam, not me. Still, I move back, putting more distance between us.

"No," Abaza says, turning to me with a hurt expression. "Come." He beckons me to follow him deeper into the tunnel. "Come, I will show you why he is here, why we have only a few more hours."

"You have had news from outside?" Leonid asks him. "Bad news?"

Abaza answers in Russian, but my overlay whispers a helpful translation: *Nothing that will concern our work here.*

Only a minute ago, Abaza's furious rant was echoing down the tunnel. He's quiet now. His anger is under control, but it's still there beneath the surface. I feel it. I see it in the tension of his muscles—and FaceValue confirms it. The worst move I could make now is to look like I'm afraid of him. Better to look like a jackboot instead. So I grab Issam again, by the arm this time, and drag him with me as I follow Abaza—who looks back, evaluates the situation, and barks a short laugh. I am a man after his own heart.

I pull Issam closer. "What were you thinking when you saw me?"

"I . . . I thought you were here to kill me." His voice is breathy, pleading. I've done a good job of terrorizing him—and Abaza's okay with it; he's enjoying it. Issam is not in a good position here—and maybe that's something I can use.

"Why would I want to kill you?"

Abaza laughs again. "Because you are a hero of the West, and Issam will strike the next blow against your empire of satellites."

So our intelligence was mostly right. The missile platform is here, but it's not Abaza who is the intellectual power behind it. It's Issam. Does that change the equation?

Logan sticks close behind me as we walk into the dark. It's his light that lets me see where I'm going. I assume Tran is with him, and Leonid. There are others, but I don't look. It's Abaza who worries me.

We reach the next chamber. Abaza pauses beside the green glow of the light switch. "I do not trust you, Shelley," he says. "I trust no one. Not even our friend, Leonid. But I don't need to trust you, because you cannot betray me. Soon we move out. You return with Leonid, and tell the world what you saw here, what I did here, how I succeeded when they failed in Sudan and failed in Bolivia."

Abaza. He likes to play the silent tough guy, but it's an act. Behind that act, he's a little kid who wants the world to fear and admire him.

Works for me.

I release Issam, expecting him to flee, but he just stands there, rubbing his arm.

I ask Abaza, "What happened in Sudan? In Bolivia?"

"Betrayal. Failure. But it won't happen here."

Colonel Abajian had said allied operations were preparing to hit the known locations of two other missile launchers. My guess is that Northern Sword is the last holdout.

Abaza turns the lights on, revealing what I expect: the BXL21 road-mobile missile launcher—and it's *huge*. I knew its dimensions, but to be there in front of it, to see it filling the chamber with not even a meter of free space on either side—the sight transfixes me with its gravity, its implied power.

The vehicle is backed in, so I am looking up at the glass windows of the cab, with the cargo bed and its four cradled missiles behind. It takes a fleet of wheels to support the combined weight of the launcher, its stabilizing legs, and the YGH-77s. I count eight fat tires on this side alone. The four missiles rest in separate hydraulic lifts that will raise them to a vertical position for launch. They are over twenty feet long but lithe and narrow. Fins flare above the first-stage booster.

Our only assignment was to locate this facility and confirm the presence of the missile launcher. We have done that. We could depart with that knowledge and call this mission a success, but it's not truly done until this device is destroyed. Colonel Abajian has promised to do that, but in war, nothing is certain. The least chance could be the difference between success and failure.

I flinch as Abaza puts his hand on my shoulder. "The balance of power is shifting. The BXL21 is not part of our deal, but the stock you are buying will be worth even more because of it. There will be a time of chaos as the world rights itself. You will grow rich."

I don't give a fuck about Abaza's scrapyard collection of military artifacts.

And I don't want to walk out of here leaving the missile launcher intact. Abaza might need less than an hour to roll the platform outside and set up. Issam might have a hundred targets lined up for him to choose from. There's a good chance that Colonel Abajian's cruise missile strike will come too late.

I don't think the BXL21 would be all that hard to destroy right here, where it sits.

An idea is brewing in my head. What if the rockets can be ignited here, inside the UGF? The warheads they carry are nonexplosive—kinetic weapons designed to destroy their target with mass and momentum alone—but why should that matter? They carry their own oxygen in the propellant mix. If I could ignite all four rockets, surely they would dump enough heat energy to blow this place apart?

Colonel Abajian gave me a free hand to determine how best to serve the goals of this mission. Destroying the BXL21 while ensuring that this UGF could never be occupied again would more than satisfy the mission goals.

Leonid's manufactured enthusiasm erupts into what has become a suspicious silence. "Maksim!" He pushes past me. "You *are* part of it." Like he's so amazed, so impressed. "I wondered. I wondered at the reason you had agreed to sell. I knew it was something big." He steps around an obstacle on the floor: a mattress with a sleeping bag. Issam must sleep here. An outsider among Abaza's people.

Leonid begins to circle the vehicle, inspecting it, his eyes round with wonder as he lays down the shit so thickly, I can't believe Abaza doesn't shoot him in disgust. "You amaze me, my friend. Your determination, your cleverness, to bring this huge, intricate device here, and no rumor of it anywhere." He pauses as he reaches the rear of the vehicle. "But Maksim . . . Maksim, my friend, you must know that after this, they will never let you rest. They will hunt you without mercy."

"It won't matter," Abaza snaps. "Not if we cripple them."

Leonid nods somberly. He passes out of sight behind the vehicle. We all wait in silence, listening to his footsteps as he returns, unseen, on the other side. When he steps into sight again, he looks at me. "You are making an excellent investment, Shelley, but only if we move quickly."

"They will not find us," Abaza says. "Not in time. In a few hours, we will go. Three will stay with Issam to serve God."

I turn to look at Issam, wondering how a Stanford-educated genius stumbled into shit this deep and sticky. He returns my gaze. FaceValue confirms his quiet panic. He wants out. He wants me to get him out. He knows no one else will. "I've kept us hidden from the Red," he says, turning his farsights over and over in his hands.

"You've studied the Red?"

"I needed to get outside its reach. I went too far."

"You went where God intended," Abaza tells him. "You will do as God intends."

"Yes, of course. That's why we are here." Issam turns his vulnerable, dark eyes to me. "Do you want me to show you how it works? It's really cool, I promise. And God-level scary."

I am being flirted with, enticed on a date. Leonid sees it too and tries to interfere. "We need to finish the inventory."

"No." I shift my gaze to Abaza. He has to know I'm recording everything I see—and that means he can't afford to show me fear or doubt or weakness. So I dare him. "I want to see it. Not often I get to see a gun this big."

He draws himself up, puts on a stern expression. "This is more than a gun, Shelley. This is God's will."

Issam touches my arm. "Come sit in the cab. You won't believe it. It's like you own the world up there. You own the skies, anyway."

"You own nothing," Abaza says. "The driver is just a driver and it does not matter who sits in the cab, because the missiles are not controlled from there." He reaches out, catches Issam behind the neck; pulls him close as a lover, even as Issam shrinks back. "Shelley is a handsome man."

Issam stares at a spot above Abaza's shoulder. He makes no answer.

"I know what you are doing. You want to beg him to take you with him—back to America! So go. See what answer he gives you."

He shoves Issam backward, directly into me. I could step out of the way, but I don't. Instead, I catch him by his shoulders and hold him close. I'm not sure if Abaza is jealous of Issam or of me, but it doesn't really matter. Either way gives me what I want: a few minutes in the quiet of the cab, to hear what this desperate American expat has to say.

"Show me, Issam." I pitch my voice low, like a lover, just so I can see the flush of anger in Abaza's face. "I won't have a chance like this again."

I climb up behind him into the cab. He slides into the driver's seat, his shoulders hunched, chin dropped, a submissive posture. "Close the door."

I slam it behind me and lean forward to look at the console—a posture that hides my face from the watchers below. I turn to Issam. He is eyeing me with an appeasing smile. It's an attitude not reflected in his voice as he speaks swiftly, his lips barely moving. "There are no listening devices here." FaceValue tags it as truth. "You are safe to speak. Did the Red send you here?"

"What do you know of the Red?"

"Enough that I kept this facility secret for seven weeks. Twice as long as the last time I ran a cover. The method works."

"What method?"

"It's a system using locally integrated AIs. Complex. It would take more time to explain than we have, but it works. It *can* work, to affect local goals. Did Maksim invite you here?"

I nod. "I thought Maksim would be the one controlling the missile launcher."

"Maksim? Maksim couldn't point his finger up his ass without help. He's an idiot. A vain, psychotic idiot." Issam gives me a helpless shrug and then mimes pointing out the gauges on the dash. "I thought it was over when I saw you, our security cracked, this site no longer hidden—but I guess he just gave it away."

"You're sorry?"

"*No*. It's just . . . intellectual pride. The only pride I have left. Maksim didn't lie to you. I'm begging you. Get me the fuck out of here. I will give you all my work. Everything I know."

"Ten minutes ago, you thought I was here to kill you."

"What else could I think? I know how the Red operates. If it can't observe or influence a local system, it sends in a physical manifestation to reformat it."

"A jackboot to kick in doors."

"Hey, I'm not criticizing. Look who's holding my leash. But everyone knows you're a soldier of the Red. Abaza knows it. He has to, but he's vain. He wants to share your fame."

I sit up again and look below. Leonid is talking to Abaza, distracting him. I see Logan out the side window, walking with Luftar around the platform.

"Maksim wants to show the world that he defies the Red. That he doesn't fear it. But he should fear it. You know it. I know it."

Down below, Leonid gestures at Damir, who trots

toward the base of the ladder on my side of the cab. Tran intercepts him. Takes over as messenger, while I imitate Issam, speaking quickly, with only a slight movement of my lips. "Why are you here?"

"Because I am a fool! And a coward. They beheaded my friend with a fucking sword! And he was one of them! They decided he'd betrayed the cause. He was a troubled man, but not a bad man. I'm only here because I listened to him, followed him, and now I'm trapped in this circus of murderers. I don't want to be here, Shelley. I want out. I want you to get me out."

I hear the thump of Tran's boot on the first rung of the ladder and speak quickly. "The entry gate is locked. We need Abaza to open it."

"There is a back way out."

"You know that? For sure?"

He nods. FaceValue shows no deception.

"You're able to reprogram the launch, aren't you?" I ask. "Set it to go off at any time?"

Issam studies me. His focus shifts to the screen of his farsights. Probably scanning the notations of his emotional analysis app. It's telling him that I want this very much. "Yes. I have full access. No one else understands how to program a launch."

I slide closer to the door, getting ready to go. "You might have only a minute."

"Time enough."

I nod, envisioning incandescent fire. It's a miracle that I remember to ask him, "Is there anything else here? Any WMD?"

Tran pops into sight outside the window. I give him a thumbs-up. *Coming.*

"No. No nukes. No bio. This is just a conventional cache. Can you get me out of here?"

"Maybe, but it's going to take a new plan. Be ready for anything."

"You think it'll be soon?"

Tran drops back down the ladder. I open the door and step out. "I've got a feeling."

Leonid again insists we finish the inventory. This time, Abaza backs him. He wants me away from Issam. And he wants his money; he'll need it when he's on the road. The forklift operator comes to move some of the tagged pallets out of the armory room, giving me a few minutes to think.

A long time ago, at the start of the First Light mission, Jayne Vasquez said something that's stuck with me ever since:

I think most of the people who know anything about this stuff don't want to get rid of the Red. They want to control it, because whoever figures out first how to do that gets to run things.

Issam's "locally integrated AIs" might be a step in that direction. Charts of real-time activity in the Cloud—supposedly the activity of the Red—diagram disparate elements, and it's been my impression that the Red is not a single, unified presence. It's more complicated than that.

And Issam's machinations have worked. He kept this place secret, almost to the zero hour. He's kept himself secret. I want to know how he did that. I want to know more about what he knows: The hazard of it, the possibilities. There is only one way that will happen. My skullnet translates the thought. *We take Issam with us.*

Tran is on watch at the armory's entrance, opposite Logan. Two of Abaza's men are just outside, smoking, not paying much attention. Luftar isn't with them; maybe he's gone to sleep.

Tran turns his head to look at me; white teeth flash as he cracks a half smile. I remember that same smile back at C-FHEIT, right before we left, when he told Logan, *It's going to be hard to walk away without finishing the mission.*

We get to finish the mission now, because the only way to take Issam with us is to take the UGF first.

Logan is too disciplined to risk suspicion by making eye contact. He taps the butt of the pistol holstered at his thigh and asks, *How?*

Not *why?* He didn't get to talk to Issam; he doesn't know what's at stake. But he trusts that I have good reasons to extend the goals of this mission.

Doing so will let us ensure this hidden fortress is destroyed along with the missile platform and Abaza's cache of war toys. Under the new paradigm, everyone should be visible, everyone accountable, and that means all places like this, hidden away and isolated from the Cloud, need to be eliminated from the world. That's the core of what we need to do. It's a bonus that we'll be able to take Issam with us. He has knowledge we need.

Leonid is not hooked into gen-com, but he's a wily old monster who has no need of FaceValue because he long ago learned to read minds. He leans in close to me and says, "Stop brooding. You've done your part."

"It's not enough."

He looks alarmed, but I ignore him. We need to do this. I know it as clearly as I did at Black Cross when I defied all orders and walked outside. And we need to move quickly.

If we take Abaza alive, we might force him to open the main gate. If that fails, we could probably uncrate enough explosives to blow the gate open, although in this confined space the backblast could kill us or consume all the oxygen—or trigger Colonel Abajian to launch his cruise missile. Yeah, that's not an option I like. If Abaza is dead, it's better for us to retreat down the tunnel. Issam said there is another way out.

"Be very sure," Leonid says, his voice a sullen growl as he seals another crate.

I *am* sure. I'm too sure. So sure, I know I'm operating on a program that's running in my head, even if I don't see the skullnet icon—but that certainty doesn't change the way I feel.

While Leonid works, I engage in silent discussion with Logan and Tran to clarify a plan. It takes a few minutes. In that time, a forklift comes to take away another pallet. I wait for it to leave. Then I call out, "Tran, go for coffee."

"Yes, sir."

One of the two men in the hall goes with him as he follows the forklift out of the tunnel. Logan maintains his post at the armory's entrance, giving no sign that anything is up.

Tran will go as far as the barracks room. From there, he should be able to get a signal to his HITR, still in the cab of the LTV. He will order the weapon to fire remotely: a three-round sequence that will cause everyone in Abaza's crew to look in the wrong direction.

Out in the tunnel, the remaining guard stretches, muttering in a language my overlay identifies as Turkish, interpreting his words as *Long night.* Leonid turns an accusing stare on me. I shrug, waiting to see what he will do. If he's going to betray us, now's the time.

His lip curls. He doesn't like it, not at all. But he's adaptable.

He nods, letting me know he's in. Still, I don't turn my back to him when I stoop to yank the sealing tape off a crate of single-shot RPGs. Leonid follows my lead and unseals a second crate, one containing M4 carbines—weapons with no biometric locks to slow us down. Ammo comes from a different crate, already open for inspection.

I expect the guard to question us, but he doesn't notice; he doesn't even look.

It *has* been a fucking long night.

I toss Leonid a pack of earplugs, tear open a pack for my own use, and pop them into my ears. In a few seconds they react with the air, making a tight seal, good enough to blunt the worst of what's coming.

I pull my pistol from the holster. The tired guard paces past the entrance, singing under his breath to stay awake. I activate the laser sight, take aim at his ear, and fire. The Stonewall's built-in noise suppressor reduces the volume, but the report is still loud, even past the earplugs, as it echoes against the tunnel walls.

My target jerks sideways. His knees fold. Logan moves at last, darting into the tunnel to catch him and drag the corpse into the chamber.

As I holster my pistol, I hear Tran's HITR fire—three shots triggered by remote command. The sound is like cannon fire, reverberating against the rocks. It's followed by the much softer report of Tran's pistol.

"Get your earplugs in," I tell Logan.

"Roger that."

His voice is muffled, but I can hear him.

I grab a pair of single-shot RPGs, while Leonid loads two M4s with brutal efficiency. He hands one to Logan. "Fast and hard, or we are dead," he warns.

"That's how we do it," Logan assures him as shouts and outraged questions echo down the tunnel.

Logan and I bolt for the door. Leonid is on our heels, demanding to know, "Do we have a plan?"

"Hell, yes!"

Logan turns, sprinting deeper into the tunnel. He is to secure both Issam and the BXL21, while Tran and I, and Leonid if he's into it, get to eliminate the opposition.

I look up the tunnel, to see a spray of red blood on the chiseled wall just outside the barracks room. On the ground beneath it is the corpse of the guard who thought it was a good idea to escort Tran.

"Tran's in the garage, recovering the HITRs," I tell Leonid as I crouch to pick up my pack from the floor. "Don't shoot him. Everyone else is fair game."

"That is not a plan!"

"Improvise." I shrug into my pack and then start after Tran, but I slow down long enough to add, "Try not to kill Maksim. We might need him to open the front gate. Take him down, but don't kill him."

Leonid brings his rifle to his shoulder. For a second I think he's aiming at me. "We are never going to get out of here," he growls. I duck against the wall as the weapon goes off with a *crack!*, sending furious echoes bounding back and forth through the enclosed space of the tunnel—but he's shooting past me. Up front, one of Abaza's soldiers, stumbling confused from the barracks room, goes down.

"Logan!" I shout over gen-com. "Status?"

No answer. He probably doesn't hear me. Radio communication is going to be unreliable in these deep chambers with their thick stone walls—but I need to know that Issam is not in the barracks room.

Leonid is shooting steadily, once every two seconds, discouraging anyone from leaving the barracks room. I sprint forward under his covering fire, pass the intervening chamber. The chambers are angled. That lets me see partly into the barracks room before I reach it—but Leonid's shooting has driven everyone out of sight. The booming echoes of his gunfire mix with echoing shouts—orders, questions, furious

threats—to create a cacophony of noise with no direction, all
of it muffled by my earplugs. I can't tell how many soldiers
are inside the barracks, or if Abaza and Issam are among them.

And I can't shoot until I know.

As I crouch, my shoulder pressed against the wall, Logan
answers one of my questions. *Issam is here.*

"Roger that."

A clarity of purpose comes over me. What I want to
do, what I *need* to do, is eliminate the opposition—quickly,
efficiently, brutally. They outnumber us, and that means
we will lose this action if I let them get the upper hand.
Sometimes, you have to give up a goal, and the goal I give
up is Maksim Abaza. If I worry about his safety, I put us all
in jeopardy, so to hell with him.

I step out from the wall far enough to get an angle on
the chamber and launch an RPG. It explodes with a concussion that shudders through the floor and dazzles my
eyes. I duck back as high-pitched screams echo up from
Hell. Rifles hammer, bullets buzz through the stinking air,
stone cracks, and fragments of copper, tungsten, and rock
patter against the floor.

Staying low, I move up a few steps and fire the second
RPG. It goes off—and a secondary explosion follows.
Maybe a propane tank. I don't know. An incandescent curtain cuts off any view into the barracks room. I fall back
as the heat sears my face. With fire roaring behind me, I
sprint back to Leonid. I'm seeing black around the edges of
my vision as the oxygen is sucked out of the air. Leonid is
still shooting—at what, I don't know. "Don't shoot Tran!" I
remind him as I duck into the armory.

"You think Alex is still alive?"

"Fuck, yes!"

The air in the armory is better than what's out in the hall.
I breathe deeply, taking advantage of it while I can.

A grenade goes off somewhere. No way to know for sure, but I take it as a signal that Tran has recovered his HITR from the LTV.

I grab a rifle, load up on ammo, and go out again, in time to pick up the tail end of a transmission on gen-com.

"—get to him."

"Tran, is that you? Say again!" The inferno in the barracks room has almost burned out.

"Abaza's out front, but I can't get to him."

So Abaza is still alive, still dangerous.

"What's your status?"

"Pinned down inside the LTV. Abaza's behind the flatbed. At least three with him. I can put a grenade into the cargo and blow the truck, but then we all cook."

Or suffocate.

"You've got your HITR?"

"Roger that."

It's a fucking complication, not having Leonid part of gen-com. I yell at him as I head back up the tunnel. "At least four still alive and we can't afford to blow them up. Not yet."

"I'm happy you understand that," Leonid roars as he lumbers after me.

He'd do better to save his breath. There isn't oxygen to spare, and the air tastes poisonous with a residue of burned petroleum, plastics, and flesh. I need to end this soon, or we are all going to suffocate.

"Tran, we're giving up on Abaza. I want you back in this tunnel."

"It's a fucking long way from the LTV, Shelley."

"You can't drive the LTV?"

"Negative. It needs keys."

Damir had the keys.

I look ahead to the barracks room. Scattered fires burn

feebly inside. Charred debris, some of it bodies, clutters the floor. Damir is probably not in there. He was dealing with loading the flatbed. He's almost certainly up front with Abaza.

I pass the wide entrance to the barracks room. Just as I get to the other side, shots are fired from the garage. Bullets ricochet off the wall in front of me. I drop to the floor. Leonid spins into the barracks room, standing just behind the shelter of the wall. "Negotiate," he tells me.

Good idea.

I'm twenty meters from the tunnel mouth. I can see about half the garage. The flatbed truck is backed against the left wall. Its cab and half its cargo bed are visible to me. The pickup trucks, with their machine guns, are hidden behind the wall to my right. The LTV is parked between them and the gate. Tran is inside it, ready to shoot down anyone who tries to get to the machine guns.

"Maksim!" My voice echoes against the stone. "Leave your weapons. Come out in the open. I want you face-down on the floor or I blow up the truck."

"Idiot," Leonid growls at me. "Don't make threats you're not willing to carry out."

"Who said I'm not willing?"

Two or three seconds pass as he considers this, and then he asks me, "Is it like that?" But he doesn't wait for an answer. "Maksim!" he shouts. "You know who my client is. You know he is haunted. It is not always his own will that drives him. That madness is awake in him now."

"Then kill him!"

I turn a startled gaze on Leonid, but to my relief, he's ignoring this advice.

"No, Maksim. I have made my choice. Now you choose. Do we all die or do we live?"

For many seconds, there is only the sound of lingering fire hissing in the barracks room, and the distant generator. Then Abaza says in a bitter voice, not even bothering to yell, "I will open the gate for you. That's what you want! I will do it if I can leave first with my men."

What I want is to set this cavern on fire, to ignite every piece of killing hardware Maksim Abaza has stashed in here and turn his hidden fortress into an oven hot enough to melt the copper in the bullet casings.

But not yet, I remind myself. Not while we're still here.

With my sleeve, I swipe at the sweat on my forehead. Then I look up at Leonid. "Can we deal?"

He shakes his head, narrowed eyes searching for any sign of movement in the cavern. "If you let him leave first, he will blow up the truck before we can get out."

Logan checks in on gen-com. "Shelley."

"Status?"

"Issam is cooperating. He'll put the missiles on a delayed ignition. Give us enough time to get to the other end of the tunnel before they go off."

"Perfect." That should be enough to bring the mountain down on this UGF.

It's almost an afterthought when I ask, "How far is it to the other end of the tunnel?"

"Unknown. Issam hasn't been to the other end, but he's seen others come through."

"Okay. We assume it's locked like this end. We'll need to bring explosives."

"Roger that."

"Let me know when you're set up."

"We're ready now. Countdown starts on your order."

"Stand by, then."

No reason to hold back anymore. No reason to play games with Abaza. I need to take him out before we go,

or he could get into the missile chamber, abort the countdown, and win this contest after all.

"Papa."

"Da?"

"I want you to go back to the armory. Remember those
smoke grenades we saw? Bring me a case. Then collect
enough explosives to blow the next gate, and join Logan."

"What are you going to do?"

"Convince Maksim to let me have Tran. Now go. Hurry."

For a huge old man, Leonid makes good speed down
the tunnel.

"Maksim!" I shout, my voice echoing. "I want you to
send your men out into the open, one at a time, no weapons."

No response, not for half a minute or more.

"Movement," Tran warns me.

A few seconds later, a trembling figure comes into sight
around the hood of the truck. It's Damir, looking like a
scared kid. "Face-down on the floor," I tell him as Leonid
returns.

Leonid crouches behind me, putting an open case of
white-phosphorus grenades on the floor at my feet. "If you
don't have Maksim in your sights, you've got nothing," he
warns me.

"I understand. Now go."

Damir is down on the floor. I feel bad for the kid, but
Tran matters more to me. The mission matters more.
"Logan, let me know when Leonid is with you."

"Roger that."

"Shelley," Tran says, sounding worried at last. "What are
we doing?"

I use my gaze to modify the link, taking it to a private
channel. "We're going to blow up the truck."

"Ah, *fuck*."

"If we don't do it, Abaza will."

"But—"

"Just listen. You're going to have about four seconds to get over here, no second chances. And then you fucking *fly* down this tunnel—"

"Goddamn it, Shelley, I don't have my rig!"

"—*don't wait*, because if the firestorm doesn't kill us outright, it's going to suck all the oxygen—"

"I know that! I know."

"Are you ready?"

"Yes. All right. Fucking do it."

"Stand by." I switch back to gen-com. "Logan?"

"Waiting on Leonid . . ." Another thirty seconds go by. "Okay, he's here."

"Confirm he has the explosives."

"Roger that. He has them."

"Okay. Trigger your countdown. And run. Tran?"

"Here!"

"When you see the smoke, run."

In quick succession, I pull the pins on three of the grenades and toss them across the floor so they bounce toward the truck. With luck, at least one will lodge against a tire. All three ignite into spinning columns of burning white phosphorus spewing a dense white smoke.

Damir looks up in shock, while Tran breaks from behind the LTV, sprinting all out for the tunnel, his pack banging against his back. He's got one HITR in his hand and two more strapped to the sides of his pack. The smoke is a screen hiding him from Abaza and his crew, but the smoke is already rising toward the low ceiling, and the grenades will burn for only fifteen seconds.

Shouts erupt from behind the truck. I see sparks as bullets ping against the floor. They're aiming at the grenades, not at Tran. They're trying to keep the incendiaries away from the truck, which I admit is a smart move. Through the smoke I glimpse Damir retreating toward the locked gate. He's got a pistol in his hand. It's aimed at me.

I dive across the tunnel. Rounds crack where I was just standing, skimming the walls and the floor, kicking up shrapnel. From my position on the floor, I look for Damir—but he's hidden by the smoke. I fire three rounds anyway, just to discourage him.

The smoke is at its densest around and beneath the truck. I can't see if any of the grenades have lodged against the tires, but that just means there's no way Abaza can see Tran. That's what I tell myself. But where is Damir?

And then Tran stumbles. He goes down, skidding on his belly, just as one of the grenades bursts into a roaring white incandescent fountain. A bullet must have hit it and kicked it out from under the truck. Burning white phosphorous sprays across the garage and someone starts screaming.

Not Tran.

He's on his feet again, racing for the tunnel.

"Don't stop," I tell him. "Don't slow down."

Blood gleams on his right pant leg, from hip to ankle, a blazingly bright hue of red in the white phosphorous light. He reaches the tunnel, charges into it, but as he races past me, he starts to slow. "Shelley!"

"Go!"

One by one, I pull the pins on the next set of grenades, but this time I stand up and heave them directly onto the flatbed. As soon as the last one leaves my hand, I turn and run—but my right foot sticks as I push off on it. It must have been hit with shrapnel. I didn't even notice. But now the joints are locked at a crazy angle. I run anyway, balancing on the heel, hoping the foot doesn't fall apart. I imagine I can feel the joints in the left foot grinding.

I'm still better off than Tran. He's loping, favoring his wounded leg. I catch up to him and scream, "Fucking *run!*"

He tries. He does. Burdened by the weight of his pack and three HITRs. Far ahead, I see Logan's light in the darkness of the tunnel. And then the truck blows up.

It's a series of explosions. The first one is small. The second is massive. I lose count after that.

A blast wave picks us up and hurls us another five meters along the tunnel. I crawl into the shelter of a chamber. Tran scrambles in behind me. We stay down, pressing our faces against the rock until the roar subsides.

Air swirls around us, rushing out of the room, out of my lungs. I gasp for a breath. It's like breathing air out of an oven. And it stinks. Tran coughs. I cough. I don't think we've got much time. My lungs are twitching, burning in the noxious air.

So I get up, grab a strap on Tran's backpack, and haul him up. He's still got two HITRs secured to his pack, but his own weapon, the one he had in his hands, is gone. My rifle has disappeared too. And the tunnel is cluttered with debris. Chunks of hot metal and plastic and—for all I know—body parts. I don't look too closely. I just try not to trip over my bent foot as we stumble together deeper down the tunnel.

Back in the garage there's another explosion, but it's not a big one. I hope like hell the munitions still in the armory don't get hot enough to go off on their own.

The fiery light from the garage fades quickly as lack of oxygen extinguishes the flames. We're limping into deeper darkness anyway. The fucking plugs are hurting my ears, so I pry them out. We reach the missile chamber. I glance inside to see a few amber lights high above me and a glow against the back wall. I don't stay to see more.

The air gets a little better after that. Our pace picks up. And then I see Logan's light ahead of us.

"Watch out!" he shouts, waving the light up and down like he's trying to blind me. The beam catches against swirling smoke. "Slow down, slow down! The tunnel stops here."

Coughing and wheezing, we stumble to a halt in front of a wall of solid rock. I reach out to touch it, harboring a delusional hope that it isn't real—but of course it is. Despite the fiery air, it has a cold solidity that sends a chill of horror through my nervous system. Tran's not doing any better. *"Holy God,"* he breathes.

But then I look at Logan and realize he's alone. "Where's Papa?" I have to force the hoarse words past my raw throat. "Where's Issam?"

"I sent them ahead."

"Ahead where?"

"There's a test bore." He's speaking quickly as he turns his light, sweeping the beam at the wall behind him until it plunges into a dark rectangle in the stone, only four feet high. "Whoever built this UGF, they didn't finish."

"You sure that goes somewhere?" Tran wheezes.

"It's not like we've got a choice! We need to *move*. This air is killing us."

I glance at Tran's icon, yellow in my overlay. *Fuck.* My icon is yellow too. "Logan, you've got the light. You're first."

"One of those HITRs is mine." He unstraps one of the weapons secured to Tran's pack. I grab the other one, but it turns out to be Logan's gun, so we trade. As soon as I have my HITR in hand, its icon activates in my overlay.

That's when Tran realizes, "I dropped my HITR!" He looks back like he's thinking of going after it. Fucking oxygen deprivation. I grab his shoulder to make sure he doesn't move.

"Go, Logan."

He's still got the M4 from the armory. With that in one hand and his HITR in the other, he slips into the borehole, stooping low to clear his backpack. I shove Tran after him. "You've still got your pistol. Now get your ass in there. We'll take care of your leg when we're the hell away from here."

That much talking sets off another coughing fit, but I move in behind Tran anyway. The tunnel is narrow. My shoulders scrape the sides, my pack drags the ceiling, and the butt of the HITR knocks against the floor.

A wind is blowing past me. I want to take hope from that, because a breeze means there's an outlet somewhere, right? But it's a hot wind, blowing out of the burning cavern. It brings no relief, just poisoned air. I'm short of breath, coughing every few steps past a raw, dry throat. I trigger gen-com. In a hoarse whisper I ask, "Logan, how much time? Before the roof caves in?"

"Twelve minutes." Logan sounds short on breath too "Ten seconds."

"You think"—I pause to breathe—"we can get out . . . by then?"

"Issam thinks so . . . but I've got . . . no fucking clue."

We push on with all the speed we can muster. My back aches, my knees ache, my lungs feel like a rotting swamp, set on fire and smoldering. I have to stop after a minute to hack up a wad of phlegm. Tran isn't doing any better. With blood loss on top of toxic air, he starts to stumble, and it begins to dawn on me that we are in a really bad situation.

"Tran, you have to move faster." Four rockets are going to ignite behind us, each with enough energy to punch a satellite out of orbit. "We have to get out of this fucking tunnel."

Tran does his best. Bent over, with hands braced against the walls to keep from falling, he staggers after Logan, wheezing with every breath. As I trail behind him, coughing in a cramped Hell of heat and darkness, my mind starts wandering hopeless paths. Issam thought he saw strangers coming out of this rathole, but if he was mistaken we are utterly fucked. We will die here and no one will ever know what happened to us. Delphi will never know . . . and I think it will always haunt her, wondering if I am dead or if I just abandoned her a second time.

Five minutes more until the rockets ignite. We keep going. Four minutes. Three. There are noises ahead. A low, angry voice.

"*Shit,*" I whisper. "That's Papa."

I don't want to say what I'm thinking, but Tran says it for me. "Something's stopped them." There's a desperation in his hoarse voice that I've never heard before. "The fucking tunnel must be blocked."

"It's not blocked." I don't know if that's true, but right now we need to believe it. "We are going to get out of here."

Two minutes to go and I hear Leonid more clearly, "Move! Faster. You want to breathe clean air again? Don't stop."

"Behind you!" Logan calls out.

"Come on, then!"

"Can you see the end?" Tran wants to know, his voice a raspy whisper echoing against the walls.

"There's no fucking end. No fucking fresh air."

Issam says nothing, but I hear him, a desperate whooping gasp at each indrawn breath.

One minute left.

No way to know what's going to happen when the

rockets ignite. That will mark the successful completion of the mission—but will it also mark our deaths? What the hell was I thinking in there, so confident we could get out?

That confidence is gone. In my morbid imagination, I envision a torch funneling out through this borehole or a rush of superheated air and fucking nothing we can do but scramble on, putting one more meter and then another behind us because I was so sure we could handle an expanded mission that I never weighed what we could accomplish against the lives of my soldiers—

A deep, rumbling wave of sound rolls in from behind us. The tunnel walls shiver under my hands. "Don't stop!" Leonid yells. "Go, go, go!"

The walls continue to vibrate, and then I hear the low, throaty roar of approaching wind, louder and louder until it catches up with me. I cringe as it sweeps past my shoulders. I am expecting heat. Extreme heat. Killing heat. And it *is* hot. Hot as the inside of a closed-up car on a summer day. Hotter maybe—but not hot enough to kill us outright.

Then the wind heats up and I get scared all over again. Ahead of me, Tran stumbles, crashes to his knees. *"Fuck!"* he screams. *"Fuck!"*

"Get up!"

He does.

And then there's a thunderous *crack!* behind us. The sound hurts. It hits like a hammer inside my skull and I drop.

For three or four seconds—hell, maybe it's three or four minutes; I don't know—I just lie there, stunned, held down by the weight of my pack, with my HITR underneath me, jammed against my chest, and my cheek pressed against the dusty stone. Tran is down too. I see the vague outline of his body, defined by Logan's little light, and I hear the painful wheeze as he breathes. At least he's breathing.

The air is brown with dust. No wind blows. I think the cavern might have collapsed. Or the borehole caved in behind us. Something has blocked the tunnel back there, because I feel no more heat from the inferno.

I make sure I'm linked into gen-com, and then I rasp, "Roll call."

"Holy fuck," Logan whispers. "I'm still alive."

"Me too," Tran concedes, stirring a little, lifting his head.

I should probably get up too. "Papa!" I croak.

He answers: *"Da.* Goddamn you, Shelley. This was *not* a plan."

"Yeah, I don't know what the fuck I was thinking. Issam alive?"

"So far. I still might kill him."

"We need to move."

"Da. Get up, little boy. You don't get to die yet."

I hear Issam wheezing like an asthmatic. If I could do something to help him, I would, but all we can do is move on.

In the mission Colonel Abajian assigned to me, I was to play my role as an arms dealer to the end, leaving as I came in the company of my bodyguards, with Damir driving the flatbed truck. There was no contingency for a post-inferno evacuation, or for rescuing an asthmatic Stanford scientist who'd gotten himself in with the wrong crowd.

Issam makes it only a few more steps before he collapses. "Papa," I call, "just get past him, go on ahead."

I send Tran forward too. As he squeezes past Logan, he notices the extra M4. "LT, let me carry that."

Logan hands it over with a warning. "Don't lose it."

Tran really doesn't need the extra weight, but I guess he needs the comfort. Carrying the M4 in one hand, he clambers over Issam and then follows the light that Leonid carries.

I move forward with Logan. As we crouch beside Issam, my broken foot slips, pitching me to my mechanical knees. *"Shit."*

"Steady," Logan says.

I don't think he's noticed the condition of my foot yet.

We help Issam sit up. His farsights are askew on his face and every breath is a labored gasp. I take his farsights off and fold them up to put in my pocket—but then an idea occurs to me.

Logan?

Here.

Back me up.

What?

Gangster shit.

"Issam," I say out loud. Then I have to turn my head to cough. "Look at me, Issam."

He opens his half-closed eyes, focusing on me, his chest still heaving.

My throat hurts. My lungs ache. I have to talk in a low, hoarse voice. "I want you to unlock your farsights."

At this request, Issam's eyes widen even farther, so I know he understands me. Logan settles back on his heels, the harsh shadows cast by his little LED exaggerating his brief, cold smile. Issam's farsights almost certainly contain extensive data gathered over two years among his "circus of murderers." That is an invaluable intelligence asset. I don't want it locked up and out of reach.

I speak gently, use a reasonable tone, and make sure he understands his vulnerable position. It's a technique of persuasion I learned from a mercenary. "Unlock your farsights for me, Issam. No secrets anymore, okay?" I take a slow, shallow breath, struggling not to cough. "You need to give it all up if you want us to get you out of here, get you home."

He takes the farsights, holding them in two hands as if he doesn't know what to do with them. "I have personal things . . ."

"No." I shake my head. "Nothing stays personal or private in this world. You know that better than most."

Still, he hesitates.

I cock my head to listen. "Logan, can you still hear Papa?"

"No. They're too far ahead. We can't wait any longer. We need to catch up."

I start to get up.

"Don't leave me," Issam says.

"Unlock the farsights," Logan growls, "so we can get the fuck out of here."

Issam looks from Logan to me and back again. I think he suspects it's an act. But why risk it? Why risk pissing us off? I watch the decision get made. He nods and slips the farsights on. His gaze shifts subtly. He mutters. ". . . select. Select. Yes. Yes, I'm sure!" He slides them off. Hands them to me. "No secrets," he says. "All yours."

I put them on and check the security settings. Wide open. All biometric identifiers deleted. No passcode required. I shut off the network access and then I stash them in an inside zip pocket of my coat. "You're going to be okay, Issam." Logan helps me get him on his feet; I get his arm over my shoulder. "You're going home."

In the narrow tunnel, we have to crab sideways. My pack keeps hitting the wall; the muzzle of my HITR scrapes the roof. Issam tries to help, but after a minute he's dead weight, so I put him down again. Logan takes his shoulders, I take his knees, and we carry him.

We stop every minute or so to breathe and to make sure

Issam is still breathing. In the tight, low-oxygen environment of the tunnel, carrying him is an exhausting, dizzying chore, and I know I'm not thinking clearly. I'm not thinking of anything but the next step, so it's a few minutes before I realize that we're breathing cleaner, cooler air.

Leonid and Tran have moved far ahead, but the borehole is straight, so Tran's voice reaches us easily on gen-com. "Shelley, Logan," he warns. "Stop where you are and hunker down. We're going to blow the gate."

We lay Issam down, and then we lie down beside him. Soon after, I hear our forward contingent stampeding madly back toward us. Leonid barks, *"Drop!"*

I duck my head, throwing a protective arm over Issam's unconscious face.

The explosives go off.

"Roll call," I growl when the dust settles.

"Logan."

"Tran."

"Papa, you still with us?"

"Da." He doesn't sound happy about it. "This was *not* our mission. This was beyond our mission. Far, far beyond it."

"I know."

"I think the angels must be watching over us, that we are even alive."

"So far anyway," Logan growls.

I spend several seconds coughing. When the fit passes, I hold my hand above Issam's nose and mouth, and am rewarded by a warm flush of exhaled breath—which makes me aware of how cold it's gotten. I have to guess that the door out of Hell has been successfully blown open. I look up to confirm it. Through a fog of dust, I see a faint purple glow. "Let's just get the fuck out of here."

Under the influence of the cool air, Issam starts to waken. I leave him to recover, advancing with the others the last few meters. The twisted shards of a steel gate hang from broken hinges with a lavender twilight beyond and glinting stars. I'm still limping to the gate when a network icon flares in my overlay. A tag slides out, identifying the network.

"EXALT!" I murmur in astonishment.

"I've got it too," Logan confirms, a step behind me. "An EXALT network *here*."

I thought we'd be isolated, with no way to get word out, since we had to turn over our satellite relays to Luftar. They're burnt to ash by now.

It's a thought that brings a flush of primal fear to my skin despite the cold.

I liked Luftar. He seemed like a decent guy. But it's not smart to think of the enemy that way.

Gen-com responds automatically to the presence of the network, opening a link to the Cloud, seeking links to the rest of our squad and to our handler. While I wait for Kanoa to check in, I push past Tran and join Leonid at the entrance.

It's 0546 and the sky has just begun to lighten. A thin frosting of snow lies on the ground.

"Is that a path, Papa?" With the half-light and the snow it's hard to be sure, but I think there's a path leading into a forest of evergreen trees that might be cedar.

"Looks like it," he says. "Not well used."

Steep, heavily forested slopes rise on two sides, ending in snow-frosted gray peaks that frame a narrow valley. I see a shimmer and then a tiny white flash just above the eastern ridge. I think it's the EXALT node. Easier to see is a plume of dust and white smoke from the explosives Leonid used to blow open the gate. The plume is drifting south, a marker indicating to anyone watching this region that something of interest is going on here.

Drones have surely been watching. Did they see evidence at the main gate of the conflagration we ignited?

Colonel Abajian warned he would respond to the slightest sign of hostile intent.

I check my overlay. Gen-com still shows only me, Logan, and Tran linked in. Where the hell is the rest of my squad? Where is Kanoa?

"Echo tango mike 7-1. Someone out there?"

No one responds.

Abajian might still have my squad on lockdown—but that doesn't explain Kanoa's absence.

"Wait here, Papa." I slip outside.

Despite the steep valley walls, my overlay immediately latches on to signals from a constellation of GPS satellites. In seconds, my position is pinpointed. I'm in a valley with a name I've never heard of and can't pronounce. Eleven kilometers south is a narrow road that might offer us a way out of here. There's a much bigger, modern highway well to the north, past the ridge that separates us from the front gate of the UGF. I don't know why the underground facility is here. I can't imagine what it was intended for. Maybe it was a make-work contract designed by some Cold War defense contractor who bribed an official to gain the approval.

"Echo tango mike 7-1," I repeat. "ETM 7-1. Kanoa. Abajian. Whoever's there. Mission accomplished, but we need a ride out of here."

Still no answer.

Before we left, Kanoa said I was not to worry about the future of 7-1, but I'm worried now. Abajian said he was our ally. But what if he changed his mind? Now that the mission is done, he might see 7-1 as a political liability, too dangerous to keep around.

I duck back into the tunnel where Leonid and Logan are waiting, Logan with his HITR, Leonid with the M4 he took from the armory.

"Where's Kanoa?" Logan wants to know.

I tell him my theory. He does not take it well. Leonid growls like an irritated dog, and then he mutters, "I will see what I can arrange." Pulling his tablet from a pocket, he moves to the door.

After another coughing fit, I turn to Tran, who's sitting down, leaning against his backpack, his arms around his M4, eyes closed, his dark skin frosted in dust. More dust has mixed with the blood soaking his pant leg, and his chest is rising and falling with fast, shallow breaths. He needs to be evacuated, transported to a hospital and treated. But for now, all we can do is clean him up and close his wounds.

Logan helps me. The blood on Tran's pants is cold, sticky, coagulated. We ease his pants off and manage not to restart any major bleeding. I use water from my pack to clean his leg. That lets us get a look at his wounds: seven lacerations, six of them on his thigh, one on his hip. "You look like a yeti got hold of you."

"Shrapnel," he growls through gritted teeth.

Logan and I work as fast as we can, pulling out bits of rock and metal before gluing each wound shut. The glue has an anesthetic that gets Tran feeling good enough that he puts his shredded, blood-soaked pants back on himself. I help him with his boot.

"We have to move out," I tell them. "Drones will have marked the activity here. Depending who they belong to, we could be a target."

"I'm good," Tran says. "I can do it."

I think he's trying to convince himself.

Leonid comes back inside the tunnel.

"Got us a ride?" I ask him.

This earns me a dark scowl and an untranslatable Russian curse. "The details are being worked on. Also, fighter jets are coming this way."

Even as he says it, I hear their low roar. I squeeze past him to the entrance. The remains of the shattered gate are vibrating in sympathy. Logan and Leonid crowd behind me. Together we search the sky.

"There," Logan says, pointing to where three jets are racing in from the southwest. At first they're just distant gray points beneath a deck of high clouds, but they draw closer with startling speed. My overlay tags them as Pakistani.

Leonid makes the same assessment. "They are out of Islamabad." He adds, in an ominous voice, "It has been only thirty minutes since you blew up the truck. Less since the missiles ignited. It is possible these jets were already in the air, but is it likely? Or are they here to intercept an outside threat?"

"*Ah, fuck,*" Logan says "You think Abajian already launched his cruise missile?"

Colonel Abajian might have launched it an hour or more ago when the news came that the other missile sites had been captured—a preemptive strike to stop Abaza taking any desperate action.

The fighters scream past our position, barely a half-klick to the west. The Pakistanis don't have a lot of tolerance for American cruise missiles in their sovereign territory. I watch them pass over the shoulder of the mountain. I wait a few seconds for their roar to fade and then I say, "Let's get the fuck out of here, get into the trees. I don't want to be underground when that missile hits."

I go back for Tran, but he's already made it to his feet. He's bracing himself against the wall, a grimace on his face. "Help him, Logan."

"I don't need help," he protests. "I'm good."

"Then go outside."

I squeeze past, and hobble after Issam. He's dragged himself to a sitting position, but he doesn't look like he's good for much more than that. I kneel beside him. He gives me a desperate, frightened look. He's sticky with sweat and dust, and stinks of fumes just like the rest of us, and he's breathing with a faint wheeze—but at least he's breathing. "How badly do you want to go home?"

"You said you'd get me out," he whispers.

"I will. But you're going to have to help."

I get him on his feet. I'm trying to get his arm around my shoulder when the ground shudders, a vibration that rises up through my titanium legs. I drag him stumbling to the tunnel mouth. Everyone else is already out. We emerge as a rumble of thunder rolls in from the north, a deeper register than the jets' engines.

Logan, Tran, and Leonid are all looking back at the mountain. The rising light picks out the dirt and dried sweat on their upturned faces, the mud and smoke stains on their clothes, and it hits me again how close we came to dying—and we're not safe yet. Boiling up behind the mountain is a column of gray smoke.

"*Abajian*," Logan growls, using the name like a profanity. "That was his cruise missile, wasn't it?"

And Tran—his voice ravaged, but his attitude still practical: "Good thing we didn't stick around and try to get out the front door."

Amen to that.

Tran is holding tight to his M4, but he's given up his pack to Leonid. "Tran, you okay to walk?"

"I told you, Shelley, I'm good."

He sounds like a petulant kid with a sore throat. I hope he's not bullshitting me.

I know I sound pretty bad too, but I'm still functioning. "Logan, take point. We'll try for the highway and maybe Papa will have a cab waiting for us."

"A helicopter," the old man growls, waving Tran ahead before following Logan on the path beneath the trees. He's carrying his M4 across his body, ready to use on short notice. "And if not a helicopter, we hijack a—"

One of the fighters screams overhead, west to east, barely above the treetops.

"Move, move!" My hoarse shout sets off another coughing fit, but I keep going anyway, balancing on my broken foot while holding on to Issam to make sure he doesn't fall behind. We stagger and stumble and trip down the trail. We put maybe a hundred twenty meters behind us as the jet swings around. On its next pass, it comes in from the south. "Get under cover!"

I drag Issam off the path; shove him into a tangle of dead branches at the base of a tree. "No movement," I warn him.

The pilot uses his autocannon. Bullets nail the forest, but all he hits are trees. Maybe he knows we're here, but I don't think he's really aiming at us. How could he be? He's got a fucking mountain in front of him demanding his attention, and judging by his flight path, he's lining up to put a missile right through the tunnel's mouth—

Another jet screams into the valley. This one comes in from the east. Huddled on the ground without my rig, my helmet, my handler, without angel sight, I feel weak, blind, and helpless. I struggle to see through the tree-tops, to understand what's going on. My overlay records enough to tag the second jet as American. It dives right at the Pakistani fighter. I swear the two almost collide. The American fighter pulls out south. The Pakistani banks away to the northwest with no missiles fired.

What did I just see?

I swear the American fighter just kept the Pakistani from blowing our escape route to dust. Is Abajian on our side after all?

In the relative quiet, I order our little party back onto the trail. We limp and stumble for fifty meters. Then the fighters return. This time they're above the cloud deck. We can't see them, but we feel the bone-shaking thunder of their engines. I think there are three, maybe more, undertaking crazy maneuvers. They start shooting, but not at the tunnel we just left behind and not at us. Judging by the sound, they are hunting each other. It's a fucking dogfight going on above our heads. So close, I'm afraid we're going to be collateral damage. But then they swoop away. There are explosions, another deafening pass, and then a high-pitched dopplered scream of engines, drawn out and lingering for ten seconds or more.

Through the trees I see a dying fighter plunging toward the ridge on our west, the red, white, and blue air force star logo visible in the gathering light. The fighter hits the ridge and explodes on impact, shaking the earth, shaking my soul.

Have we started another war?

"Oh my God," Issam says. "Oh my God. Oh my God."

I want to tell him to shut the fuck up, that a terrorist tool like him should not be shocked by violence, but I'm distracted by the sight of the pilot dropping out of the sky beneath a partly open parachute.

I leave Issam and hobble through the trees, tripping and stumbling over deadwood as I strive to keep the pilot in sight, to record the descent with my overlay and mark the point where the parachute passes out of sight. The exertion leaves me gasping, my breath steaming in the cold air.

Another fighter roars in, sweeping the area where the

pilot vanished, firing its autocannon. It makes a single pass.
Then it screams away. I think there's another dogfight in
the distance, but no more explosions. Just engine noise,
receding into silence.

Logan speaks over gen-com. "You get a location on that
pilot, Shelley?"

"Maybe. For damn sure—" I catch my breath. "You and
me . . . are going to look."

The trail we're on is not marked or visible on the GPS-
generated map that pinpoints my position, but studying
that map along with the image of the descending pilot lets
me guess at the drop site—a point I estimate to be at least
three kilometers away. If I had an angel, I could confirm it
in a couple of minutes.

I could confirm if the pilot is alive or dead.

Probably dead. That's what I tell myself to forestall dis-
appointment. The chute failed to open fully; a strafing run
followed.

We are going to look anyway.

We move out again. I've got no way to know the specifics of the political situation playing out around this incident, but I can guess at the general situation. Either the
Pakistanis are furious because our mission was carried out
without their knowledge or approval, or they are furious
that a component of Broken Sky was exposed under their
watch, and they want to eliminate all evidence that it ever
happened.

We are part of that evidence. The way I see it, it's just
a matter of time until attack helicopters come hunting us,
or an infantry squad rigged in dead sisters. Abajian isn't
going to risk another fighter in our defense. So we need to
evacuate from this region as soon as we can, but first I need

to confirm the status of the pilot. I won't leave an injured warfighter behind.

As we continue on the trail, I watch landmarks, and when I think we're close to the drop site, I take Logan with me, and we go to look.

"Shouldn't be too hard to find the parachute," Logan says.

That's all we need to find. If the pilot is in good shape, he'll be long gone by the time we find the drop site. If he's dead, we'll record the scene and move on. And if he's wounded but unconscious, we'll assess and figure something out. The most dangerous scenario for us is if he's wounded and functional. Fighter pilots fly with a pistol secured in a shoulder holster.

"Let's keep up some chatter," I decide. "If we talk American, maybe the pilot won't shoot us."

We set up search transects using GPS. This lets us blunder through the forest and negotiate the uneven terrain while maintaining a consistent thirty meters between us. We go for a kilometer in a straight line. I pretend I'm okay, but my foot is locked at an awkward angle, my fingers are freezing, my lungs are hot, and I feel like I'm breathing through a coarse, wet rag stuffed in my throat.

After a kilometer, we turn around, shift our lines south, and go again. We try to keep up the chatter over gen-com, but mostly it's Logan talking, because my voice is getting worse.

We're reminiscing about our favorite fast food from before the Coma when a voice speaks to me from out of a bush I've just hobbled past—not a burning bush, fortunately, although it is rattling with old dry leaves. "Identify yourself."

American accent. Female.

I freeze, envisioning her with a finger on the trigger. I

don't want to give her any reason to squeeze. "James Shelley, captain in an irregular militia known as ETM 7-1."

"Is that Special Forces Operations?"

"Darker."

Logan speaks over gen-com, "I've got her in my sights."

Do not shoot.

"She's safe," he says, "as long as her pistol isn't aimed at you."

I make sure the muzzle of my HITR is pointed at the ground when I turn to look at her.

She's standing behind the bush, dressed in a flight suit and jacket, and carrying a small emergency pack on her back. There's a compact pistol in her upraised hand, but its stubby barrel is aimed at a corner of the sky. She is Caucasian and tall, close to six feet, with short brown hair. I put her age in the mid-thirties. She's studying me through colorless farsights resting on a prominent freckled nose. Civilian farsights would have a green light to indicate they were recording. Hers are military field issue.

"It *is* you," she says, suspicion in her voice, like she still isn't sure this is a straight deal. "I was told to find you. We're supposed to be on the same side."

"Yes, ma'am." I cough. It's a wet cough. "You pulled that fighter off us. I think we can be allies for a while."

"I'm Captain Helen Thurman. United States Air Force." She comes out from behind the bush and bravely offers to shake my hand.

I have to turn away, coughing—a brief fit that ends when I spit a wad of rotten lung tissue into a patch of snow.

She lowers her hand, eyeing me in concern. "Something I need to know about?"

"Noxious fumes."

"Sounds like onset of pneumonia."

"I fucking hope not. But enough about me. Are you injured?"

"I got hung up in a tree. Strained my back. Minor concussion." She slides her pistol into a shoulder holster. "I'll live."

Logan says, "I'm coming in."

I relay this information to Captain Thurman. "My lieutenant's joining us. Don't shoot him."

"Agreed."

We both turn at a crackle of dead wood to see Logan approaching through the trees.

She taps her farsights as her gaze returns to me. "Orders are to remain at large until they can pull us out. That might be two to three days. There are a lot of hurt feelings out there in International-land. Under no circumstances are we to turn ourselves in to the Pakistani military."

"If it happens, it won't be voluntary. I promise that."

She nods to Logan as he joins us, taking in his dirt-smeared face, his smoke-stained coat. "There are supposed to be four of you."

"One of my soldiers is injured. He's with our local asset. And we've acquired a civilian."

She looks at me. "Identity?"

"I'm going to hold back on that information."

She's not in a position to argue, so she shifts the topic. "I'm supposed to hook you into my satellite relay. Command picked up your attempted communication, but they won't respond on a wild network. They'll only use a network they can control."

I look at Logan, who rolls his eyes. That is not how we operate. We use the facilities available to us, and in any case, the EXALT network is a trusted resource. Kanoa must be on a tight leash if he's following some other protocol.

Thurman dictates the address of her relay, and then a passcode. Gen-com listens for it, transcribes the data, and relays it between me, Logan, and Tran. Twenty-one seconds later, Kanoa links in. "Mission status?"

I'm so relieved to hear him, I almost let him know, but I catch myself in time to preserve my reputation. "Mission accomplished, and then some."

"Shelley? Is that you? What's wrong with your voice?"

"Smoke inhalation."

"Damn. All right. You got a summary for me?"

"Captain Thurman is present," I say, eyeing her. "I don't think she's cleared for this discussion." Thurman crosses her arms over her chest and glares. She does not step away. "Tran can fill you in, but I've got some data for you. You want me to upload?"

"Do it."

I get the farsights out. Thurman has a cable, so I use that to link to the relay, and let Kanoa handle the download.

"Your vitals look like shit," he informs me after the data begins to flow. "Tran too."

I don't like the reminder, especially with my eyes watering as I resist another coughing fit. "You need to get us out of here."

"We're working on that. The political situation—"

The cough I've been fighting escapes. Harsh, but it doesn't last for more than a few wracking spasms. Logan takes over as I gasp and wipe my face on my sleeve. "We have to get out, Kanoa," he says. "Tran needs to be in a hospital. Shelley too. He's not going to be on his feet much longer."

I back up Logan's argument by saying, "You know this place is going to be crawling with enemy in a matter of hours."

"We are working on a deal," Kanoa insists. "But until that deal is concluded, you need to stay out of sight. The president's reputation is on the line. So, elude the enemy, resist if you have to. Do not give yourselves up."

"Major," Logan asks, "do you think you could at least send us an angel?"

"Not in time to do you any good. I'm going to talk to Tran while the download finishes."

He links out.

"This is bullshit," Logan says. "We need to get you and Tran to a hospital."

"Fuck it. Fuck all of them. We'll get out of here on our own. I mean, we've got Papa. A fucking wizard of the dark arts." I stop my tirade to breathe, hearing a wet gurgle in my throat. "He *will* conjure a helicopter, and when he does, I'm getting on it. I don't give a fuck where it's going."

My rant ends in another coughing fit, which does not improve my temper. By the time it's over, Captain Thurman has unplugged the farsights. She hands them back to me. "Your data transfer has finished."

I stuff them back into my coat pocket. "Much more of this shit and I'm . . . I'm going to . . ." I finish in a whisper. ". . . hunt down a Pakistani patrol and *let* them put me out of my misery." Thurman looks like she's entertaining second thoughts about the virtue of our company. "Welcome to Existential Threat Management," I rasp.

"Mission first," Logan adds. He flips a finger at the sky, on the excellent chance a drone is watching us.

But Thurman takes away the sweetness of defiance. "The Pakistanis took out our drones. We took out theirs. Which means we've got a window of opportunity. Until they get new equipment up here, we can move where we like, with no one watching."

That probably gives us at least an hour, maybe more. Plenty of time for Leonid to work magic. I check my squad map, get my bearings. "Let's hook up with the others."

On the way, Thurman relays what she knows. "This is a SARS-K region. Permanent habitations abandoned. So there's not an immediate danger. On my overflight, the only human presence I picked up was a small party at the head of the valley. I assume that was you."

"Yeah, that would be us."

"What were your orders?" Logan asks.

She doesn't answer. We walk on in silence for twenty or thirty meters before she speaks again. "Stop me if you've heard this. Right before we got the order to scramble, news came in. The White House announced two illicit BXL21 road-mobile missile launchers were found and destroyed. That's the weapon used to attack objects in orbit."

"Yeah, we're familiar," Logan says.

"I thought so. These were found in Bolivia, and in Sudan. That's what you're working on, isn't it? You went after another one here?"

"I think that's going to remain dark," I say.

This is confirmation enough. She nods. "We were scrambled early. Then we burned fuel for forty minutes, waiting, until orders came through to move in and protect friendlies. The Pakistanis didn't like it. Three of them, two of us . . . things got complicated fast."

"They would have gunned us down if you hadn't shown up. So thanks for that."

"No problem. It only cost my career and a sixty-million-dollar plane—but at least my wingman got away."

Thurman and Leonid study each other warily. I know she's used her farsights to work out his identity when she turns to me and asks, "You're sure about this?"

"Absolutely. Papa's our local asset. Been essential to the success of our mission."

"You call this success?" he asks, his heavy brows drawn low.

"We're not dead yet," I remind him.

He grunts, unimpressed. "Not dead. Just abandoned by your command."

"We will be extracted as soon as practical," Thurman insists.

"No one will come! How can they, when all civilian aircraft are grounded by military order?"

Okay, so we aren't going to be able to fly out.

A feeling of exhaustion settles over me. I can't pretend anymore that I am going to be okay. I hoped my lungs would clear up in clean air, but it hasn't happened. And Tran is no better off. "It's going to be a farmer's truck, then," I conclude, contemplating dismal hours spent bumping on a frozen road to God knows where.

Captain Thurman dissents, for different reasons. "The closer we are to the highway, the more likely we are to be picked up."

"The closer we are to the highway," Leonid lectures her, "the more difficult it will be to distinguish us from civilians. And no, Shelley, I am *not* riding on a truck. Not after no sleep, a gun battle I did not anticipate, shock waves, toxic fumes, more running about than I have done since I was forty, and a local garrison that is criminally underpaid."

"Papa hired a military helicopter," Tran explains in a raspy, whispery voice. His eyes are watering, the whites turning yellow. I wonder if I look as bad, but I don't really want to know. "He negotiated the deal with the district commander."

At this news, Thurman's eyes get big. She shakes her head. "*No*. This is not going to happen. We will follow orders, remain in the field until—"

"Stay if you like," Leonid interrupts. "Perhaps you will live." He turns to me. "Your link to your bosses. Are you able to shut it off?"

"Why?"

"Need-to-know. And they do not need to know the specifics of our movements. I have contacts to protect."

I am still angry with Abajian and Kanoa. Leonid is the only one trying to get us out of here, so it isn't hard to agree to his request. "Roger that. Let's go closed-network, point to point only."

"Kanoa's going to be pissed," Logan warns.

"Not for the first time."

"We do what we need to do," Tran rasps. "And what we need to do is get the fuck out of here."

So we lock down, allowing connections only to one another.

But Thurman is still not displaying a positive attitude. "You *can't* be serious, Captain Shelley. This man is a criminal, engaged in deals with other criminals, none of whom can be trusted."

"I trust him." And I realize it's true. "If Papa has bought the local garrison, I'm willing to ride out on that ticket."

"You have a duty, Captain Shelley."

"Yes, ma'am. I need you to turn over your uplink."

"What?"

"Turn it over and I will turn it off."

She puts her hand on her holstered pistol. "That is not going to happen."

"Or you can stay here."

Leonid mutters another untranslatable curse. "There is no time for this! We must be at the rendezvous point when the helicopter arrives. And that means we go *now*." He sets the example, starting again down the trail, long, swift strides, rifle in hand, and Tran's pack on his back. He doesn't check to see if we're following.

I hook a thumb at Tran. "Get going." Then I extend a

hand to Issam, who has found a seat among a tumble of snow-frosted stones at the side of the trail.

He waves me off. "I'm doing better now. I can walk." He gets up on his own, and then he gives me a worried frown. "Do you want me to carry your pack?"

I guess I look like I'm dying. "Just go."

He follows Tran, leaving me and Logan to deal with the stubborn air force captain. "Last chance," I tell her. "If you want a ride out, you will turn it over."

Logan takes a different approach. "You don't want to be captured out here, Captain. And you aren't going to be able to defend yourself against what's coming with just a handgun and limited ammunition."

It takes a few minutes, but he persuades her to turn over the device. I guess even an air force pilot can show *some* adaptability.

I fall behind.

It's fucking embarrassing.

The altitude, the thin air, are wearing me down. It doesn't help that my right foot is broken. And I'm so tired of listening to the metal-on-metal scraping. I've still got my boots in my pack. I think about putting them on to muffle the noise, but I don't think my broken foot would fit. And anyway, there's no time.

I'd be okay if I was rigged.

Logan and Thurman wait for me by a bend in the trail. I stomp up to them on my creaking, dysfunctional legs, a heavy-breathing zombie with rotting lungs.

"Give me your pack," Thurman says. "You can carry mine. It's lighter."

Pride makes me lie. "I'm not that far gone." I try to shoulder past them.

Logan puts out a hand to stop me. "You're slowing us down. Just do it."

We all look around as the distant drone of the helicopter is suddenly audible over the whispering of the trees.

"Now, Shelley."

"*Okay.*" I hand over my pack, taking Thurman's in trade.

"And your HITR," Logan says.

"Don't push it." The weight I'm carrying has already been cut by sixty percent. We move out, and I'm able to move a lot faster. It's like I picked up an energy boost. But it doesn't last. My chest aches with every rasping, rattling breath and black spots swarm in my vision. The noise of the approaching helo gets steadily louder—and I worry we might have another kilometer, maybe more, to go.

Then, as the trail descends alongside a stream, we see it: a battered, dark-green, single-rotor helicopter. I think it's a European model. It settles into a winter-brown pasture just below the forest's edge, maybe two hundred meters away in a straight line. Its arrival frightens a herd of white goats that had been chewing on the dead grass, sending them scattering downstream.

Leonid is below, already at the meadow's edge.

"Tran," I say, "hold up."

His answer comes back over gen-com. "Roger that."

We lope down the trail. Well, Logan and Thurman lope. I stumble. But we catch up with Tran and Issam.

I struggle not to cough, to maintain silence, as we gaze through the trees at Leonid, who has crossed the pasture and is almost at the pilot's door. I raise my HITR and stare down the optical sight as that door opens.

A woman in coveralls jumps out. Leonid meets her under the turning blades. They shake hands, the fabric of their clothing rippling in the gale. She gestures like she's shouting a question. He turns to look back, to where we are hidden in the trees. His brow knits in a scowl; he raises his index finger and mouths words that I can read clearly: *One fucking minute.*

What the hell. We can't stay here.

I lower my weapon. "It looks okay, and we've got one minute to get down there. Let's go."

I expect a short flight, but I'm wrong. The helicopter is in the air sixty-seven minutes. I have a headset on that lets me listen to voices speaking over the radio. As my overlay translates, it becomes clear there are other craft in the air, hunting for us—or pretending to. From what I can understand, they are hunting for us on the ground.

I use GPS, following our location as it shifts across the map. When the helicopter finally sets down at an airfield, there's a small, battered twin-engine turboprop waiting to meet us. Captain Thurman walks around the little plane, inspecting its condition. She doesn't look impressed, but she boards anyway. The copilot's seat is empty, so she gets a thumbs-up from the pilot to sit there.

The plane's interior is rugged, with a bare aluminum floor and well-worn, thinly padded seats. I collapse into one of the two-passenger bench seats. Across the narrow aisle are single seats.

Once we're in the air again, we dig out rations from the bottom of our packs, but after the first bite, I don't want to eat anymore. It hurts going down and sits like poison in my stomach. I make myself drink water. I tell Tran to do the same.

I lean against the wall, looking out the large window at an astonishing array of towering clouds while I listen to my breathing. It's fast and shallow and easily audible over the turboprop's engine noise. Every few minutes, I am wracked with coughs. Tran isn't coughing as much as me, but I worry that's because he's in worse shape and his body is already shutting down.

Turbulence buffets the plane. Nothing too dramatic, but it makes me flashback to my last minutes aboard *Lotus*, when the US Navy shot our little spaceplane out of the sky.

We've been in the air an hour when Leonid invites himself to sit beside me. He's a big man, a looming presence, and I'm feeling squeezed. "I have been talking to Issam," he says. "You risked a lot to get him out. Given that, I think you should talk to him too, about this thing that haunts you. And not just you. Your men as well. He has thoughts on it."

"You mean the Red."

A lot of people are uneasy talking about the Red; they don't like to name it, as if by naming it, they invite the spirit in.

"*The Red.*" Leonid mouths the words as if he's trying them out for the first time. "Are you aware of it when it uses you?"

If this was Issam questioning me, or Thurman, I would invite them to fuck off. But it's Papa, and I'm pretty sure I'm going to owe him my life. "Sometimes. Not all the time."

"Why didn't we just leave the facility as we had planned?"

"I don't think that was ever the plan." From the beginning, it was in my mind to do more. Why else did I secure approval from Colonel Abajian to do all that I thought was necessary, even before we left C-FHEIT?

Though we haven't been speaking at any great volume, Logan picks up the thread of our conversation from his seat in front of me. He gets up, turns around, leans on the seatback, and offers his opinion. "We couldn't just leave the facility, Papa. We had to finish the mission."

Leonid leans back, his weight making the plastic frame of our bench seat creak. "The mission was to locate the missile launcher."

"No," I say. "That was just the mission Abajian gave us. There was more."

"I saw the mission plan. There was nothing more."

"There *was* more," I insist.

Our conversation draws Issam's interest too. He is across the aisle from Logan, but he leaves his seat, to look on with an interested gaze. He should be interested. We risked our lives to get him out of Maksim Abaza's hands. That was never part of any plan.

Looking at him, I notice he's wiped the dirt off his face, and he's not having any trouble breathing anymore. Calm and unafraid, he appears a different man. A lucky man. Lucky that we showed up. I hope he knows it.

I return my gaze to Leonid. "There *was* more to the mission. It wasn't written, but when the time came, we knew. We all knew." My eyes water as I struggle to suppress a cough. I talk quickly, breathing in sharp, shallow inhalations. "We needed to destroy the missiles *and* the UGF. Places like that, isolated from the Cloud, are dangerous. Too dangerous to exist."

And then I have to turn away to clear my dissolving lungs. I wish all of them would go away, leave me alone, but I don't get my wish.

"Too dangerous for who?" Leonid asks. "For what?"

Logan answers for me. "For our future."

I nod full agreement. "The only way this works is if everyone in the world is visible, everyone accountable. *No one* gets to take the system down."

Leonid looks up at Issam, who raises his eyebrows in

a smug expression. "Like I said, if you want a man to do unforgivable things, give him a righteous cause and a powerful belief."

This pisses me off. It's like Issam is comparing me to Maksim Abaza and his crew. "Did you know they had nerve gas in there?" I ask him.

"No, I didn't know that, but I'm not surprised."

"'A circus of murderers.' That's what you called them. But you were working for them. You—"

"I'm a coward, Shelley! I admit it. I was out of my depth. I was scared. I kept telling myself that at the last moment, I would do the right thing, but I don't know if that's true." He looks aside. "It's probably not true."

"Yeah." It's never an easy thing to trade your life away. "Look, I don't deny we did unforgivable things in there, but we did have a righteous cause."

"And a powerful belief?" Leonid asks me. "Shelley, my friend, think about what really happened. At what point did you make the decision to go beyond the mission plan and destroy the missile launcher?"

I shrug. "It was always an option. Colonel Abajian left it to my judgment."

"*When*, Shelley?"

"I don't know! I don't remember. I just knew we had to act. There was no time."

"There was time."

"Abaza was getting suspicious."

"He was not."

Despite my fatigue, I draw myself up. I don't need this shit. Not even from Papa. I'm tired, and I don't want to answer any more questions. My glare is intended to convey that, but Leonid is not an easy man to intimidate.

"Does that work with your soldiers?" he asks me. "Because for myself, I am too old to be frightened by dark

looks. Do not forget, I was there. I saw it all. Maksim
wanted you there with him. He wanted you to tell his
story. He wanted the celebrity. You were in no danger
from him."

I look up at Logan, still leaning on the seatback. He
returns my gaze with a troubled expression. "It was the
only way we could get Issam out," he reminds me. "We
needed to establish control of the facility."

"You failed in that," Leonid says. "You never had control. You didn't have a real plan. It's only luck we didn't all
die trapped under that mountain." He leans over, taps my
chest. "Though you may yet die from the damage you've
done to your lungs."

It's a slight touch, but it sets me coughing again. Leonid
waits for the fit to pass. Then he pushes his point home.
"You were haunted, Shelley. You were not thinking ratio-
nally. You were not thinking as a man who values his life
and the lives of his soldiers. It's true we would have left our
new friend behind"—he looks up at Issam with an apologetic expression—"and for that I would have been sorry.
But it was the rational option. You chose instead a suicide
mission."

"It was *not* a suicide mission."

"You made it one when you attacked Maksim without
a plan."

"We had a plan. We had options. Issam was cooperating.
He promised there was another way out."

"A vague promise. A means to justify what you'd already
decided to do."

I turn to Logan again for backup, but he's looking confused.

Is that what happened? he asks over gen-com.

Is it?

"If you are a berserker," Leonid says, "a suicide jihadi, so be it, but don't lie to yourself about it. Know who you are, what you are. Know the truth behind what you do."

"That is *not* who I am, Papa. That's not who we are."

He lifts one heavy gray eyebrow. "Then it is possible you are subscribed to the wrong god."

I try to go to sleep; I'm exhausted. But when I nod off it's only for a minute, two at most. There is a thick, putrid mass in my lungs that is suffocating me. When my chin slumps, it gets even harder to breathe. I jerk awake, gasping for air.

I told Abajian I wouldn't go on a suicide mission—and then I made it one.

What the fuck was I thinking?

I didn't see the skullnet icon, but I knew a program was running in my head—and it didn't matter to me. I had clarity of purpose. What mattered was getting the job done, taking out the UGF, *mission first!*

Leonid warned me, *Be very sure.*

I'm not sure anymore.

I go over the video I recorded, fast-forwarding through the night, looking again through my own eyes at what I did, what I said—and it doesn't make sense to me. I burned everyone in the barracks room, knowing Maksim Abaza might be among them, knowing that if he was, I had just eliminated one of only two tenuous options for getting us out alive—and I was too arrogant even to worry about it. Moments later, after confirming Abaza was still alive, I warned him I would blow up the truck. Leonid cautioned me against making threats I was unwilling to carry out. And my answer? *Who said I'm not willing?*

Papa knew then who was in control. Maybe I knew it too, but I didn't care.

Never trust the Red.
I think I've heard that one before.

Never trust the Red.
How many times have I said it?
I trusted it anyway, with my mind and my soul.
And it sent me on a suicide mission.
I stare like a zombie at the back of the seat in front of me, chasing that thought around and around in my exhausted brain, until the spell is interrupted by a question from outside my feverish mind. "You're wired, aren't you?"
I turn my head, puzzled, and discover that Issam has replaced Papa in the seat beside me. I scowl and press my hand against my coat, confirming the farsights I took from him are still there. He gives me a half smile. "Papa says he'll throw me out of the plane if I give you any trouble."
I draw in a deep breath. The rattle of my lungs reminds me to check Tran's icon and then my own. Yep, we're both still breathing.
"Papa's exaggerating," I tell him in a soft, hoarse voice. "You're a valuable intelligence asset."
"Just like my farsights."
I nod.
Issam returns to his original question. "You *are* wired, right? You have an embedded neuromodulating net?" He presses his fingers against his scalp to illustrate. "Here? Implanted against your skull?"
"Yes."
"And an overlay, too. That's a dangerous combination."
"It's how I work. Anyway, you were Maksim's pet technician. Did you get hazard pay for that?"
The question is meant as a jab, but he takes it seriously. "I haven't been paid since Coma Day."

"Yeah. Coma Day changed everything." It changed all of us. We all have our stories. "Where were you?" I ask him. "Still at Stanford?"

"No. I wish I'd been there. But I was on a flight over the Atlantic, bound for Switzerland. The defense department was trying to recruit me for a 'Manhattan Project' focused on AI. It didn't feel voluntary. They were going to protect us. Isolate us. I didn't want to play. So, I got in touch with an old friend."

"The one you told me about?"

"Yes. He arranged for me to get to Canada and then to Europe. It didn't go the way I expected."

"Can't trust anyone."

"I couldn't get back home. I wanted to, but I kept getting pulled deeper and deeper into . . . well, into things I didn't want to be part of."

Not the most compelling story I've heard. "You're clear of it now—and if you're telling me all this because you're worried I'll testify against you, forget it. I can't testify because I don't exist. None of us do."

"What I really want to tell you is that I used to be wired, too."

·"Say that again?"

"I used to be wired. Like you. It was a cutting-edge thing. Popular in the AI community." FaceValue does not flag a lie. "Interface with the Cloud, tailor your own emotions. You had to go to Japan to get it done, but . . ." He shrugs.

I tell him what Cory told me. "It's illegal now. For civilians."

"Is it?" Issam shrugs. "Congress was slow and senile and so focused on the next election that there weren't any laws against it when I had it done. But when the DOD came knocking on my door, I panicked. I thought they'd lock me up when they found out. In hindsight, my fear doesn't make any sense. There was no legal basis. They probably didn't know what a skullnet was, but I was scared, and I just knew I had to run."

"You think that was the Red? It got inside your head, made you panic?" Only then do I realize what he's really telling me. "Wait . . . you said you *used* to be wired?"

"Yes. I had the skullnet taken out. I told my new 'friends' I regretted it, that it was an abomination. It's a simple surgery to remove it. I had the overlay taken out later." His brow wrinkles, reflecting complex thoughts. FaceValue says that he's sincere. "I've run a lot of scenarios and done a few studies. All of it shows how impossible it is to escape the influence of the Red. It doesn't really matter how far you withdraw or where you hide. We are all part of the world and sooner or later the Red reminds us of that. Still, influence can be resisted, challenged, turned. We're not puppets. Not until we let it inside our heads. Once you do that, you never know who's in control. That's why I took my wire out. The next time I do something terminally stupid, I want to know it's all me."

I think this plane won't ever land.

Logan comes back to sit with me, though we don't talk. Not at first.

I study his icon. His vitals are running hot. Elevated heart rate and blood pressure. Elevated muscle tension. He's on edge.

"You're worried," I say. My voice is not much more than a whisper and I move only my lips, knowing that any other motion risks setting me coughing again.

I feel his eyes on me. "This plane is so damn slow."

"And Tran's not doing any better."

"Neither are you."

Not something I really want to think about.

"You think Papa was right?" he asks. "We weren't meant to get out of there?"

"We were meant to destroy the place. Compelled to. You remember feeling that way?"

"Yes."

"And whatever happened after that . . . just didn't fucking matter."

He's silent again for most of a minute. "We were set up. And then thrown away."

"We were."

"It pisses me the fuck off."

Everyone in ETM shares a basic personality type. I could call it a propensity for service, but fuck it. We're circle-jerking, self-righteous cumwads with a tacked-on messiah complex and an addiction to risk. Intellectually, we've always known that in the calculations of the Red, no individual matters all that much. But emotionally, it's hard to overlook being shoved into the fire. And it's not the first time for me. It happened at Black Cross, when the Red walked me outside. It happened at *Sigil*, when I stood up on that block of ice and made myself a target.

I'm stubborn, but I can learn.

"This is a nonlinear war." I turn my head, enough that I can see him. "Alliances shift depending on circumstance. That's how the Red operates. We need to operate that way too. Be on our own side. Think for ourselves."

"We *do* think for ourselves." He's speaking quietly, urgently; there is fear behind his words. "Most of the time. And I don't want to quit what we're doing. We've done good things. Worthy things—"

Unforgivable things.

"—but the Red is changing. It wasn't like this before. Last time out, we started a fucking war. This time, we were meant to be sacrificed for a minor tactical gain. Where does that leave us? We can't just go along with it. Next time could be worse. But quitting is a lousy choice too. Shelley, I know you're thinking that if Issam could get rid of his skullnet, we can too. Close up that vulnerability. But—"

"We don't have a choice."

Not what he wants to hear. "There's always a choice."

"No. Like you said, next time could be worse."

"So, take out the skullnet? That's what you're going to do?"

"What else can we do?"

His hand coils into a fist. He looks like he's going to start punching the seat in front of him. "It's not going to work for us. You know it. We can't make the transition. If we take out the skullnet, we'll crash so hard, there's not going to be anything left."

Yeah. That's how it works. The skullnet is addictive. The brain gets used to its input and when that input stops, the system crashes, and we go down hard. I've been there. I know.

Something else is lodged in my mind, something else Logan said. *The Red is changing. It wasn't like this before.*

Guess I should have known it would go this way.

Guess Jaynie was right.

We land in Budapest. There's no reason we should be allowed into the country, but Leonid makes it work. We're met on the tarmac by a black van with heavily tinted windows. There is a bodyguard in a business suit who takes up a post outside the plane.

The van's driver boards the plane to help with our gear.

He offers to take my HITR, but I am tired, hurting, angry, and worried—and that means I want the security of being well armed. So I insist on carrying it myself. The driver shrugs. The bodyguard doesn't flinch either as I slide into the van's backseat, hugging my weapon.

Tran is too far gone to move under his own power, so Logan works with Captain Thurman to get him into the van's front bench seat. Leonid makes sure all our gear is off the plane.

I press my head against the cold glass of the window, listening to Thurman talking to the driver just outside the van's open door. "US embassy first, understand?"

And Leonid: "Yes, fine. But stop in the street to let her out. Do not park or try to enter the grounds."

She climbs into the back of the van to sit beside me. "You and your soldiers don't have to stay with Sergun," she says. "You'd be better off coming with me to the embassy."

"No." It's a whisper, my eyes watering as I struggle not to cough.

"I know you're unsure of your status, but Command is aware of you. I was told to link up with you, remember? We're on the same side."

"It's complicated."

Leonid and Issam climb into the middle seat. The van door slides closed.

Thurman speaks in a softer voice as the van starts to roll. "I'm not going to keep any secrets when I debrief. I don't know what that's going to mean for you."

Leonid turns around, his elbow on the back of the seat as he looks at me. "You have intelligence to offer, Shelley. You are not without value. If you turn yourself in, do it in your own time, on your own terms."

I nod and then whisper, "What Papa said—assuming I'm not dead by morning."

We drive beyond the *No Stopping* signs in front of the American embassy and then pause at the curb just long enough for Thurman to jump out. I turn around to look as we pull away. She's still wearing her flight suit, which draws immediate interest from the guards on duty in front of the gate. The last I see of her, she's holding her ID up for their inspection.

I continue to watch the traffic behind us, anxious to know whether we're being followed, but I can't pick out a vehicle. Probably, a drone has been assigned to watch us.

A few minutes later we descend into the basement parking area of a private hospital, coming to a stop in front of the glass doors of a brightly lit lobby. Hospital attendants in white coats wait with a gurney. Tran is moved onto it. They start to wheel him away. When I realize we're being separated, I panic. "Logan, go with him!"

Speaking sets off another coughing fit. When I look around again, Logan is leaning into the backseat in defiance of my last order. "Damn it, Lieutenant, I told you—"

"Shut up, Shelley." He slides my pistol out of my chest holster. "Give me your HITR too." I don't exactly hand it over. It's more like he takes it. "Can you get out on your own?"

"Fuck, yes."

This turns out to be an exaggeration, but more attendants are waiting outside the van and they manage to catch me before I fall onto the concrete. "Logan," I whisper, "don't let Issam get snatched."

It's a fucking relief to get strapped into an oxygen mask. It's even better when an injection takes the pain in my chest away. There are scans and assessments and a doctor talking to me in worried tones about scar tissue in my lungs. She makes me breathe a vapor of regenerative hormones and then I get to sleep, for what feels like the first time in days.

When I wake up, I look past the foot of the hospital bed to see Logan sitting in a cushioned recliner, feet up and eyes closed, lightly snoring. He's cleaned up and dressed in new civilian casuals. I'm surprised to note that he's holding his HITR across his lap. I push myself up until I'm sitting. There's a nightstand between me and a second bed. Tran's there, under the windowless far wall. He's hooked up to an IV and out of it, but he's breathing. I test my own skills, cautiously filling my lungs. Still hurts a little, but I'm not going to complain.

A cup of water is waiting on the nightstand. I drink some. It's fortified water. My throat is still raw, but bearable. I don't put the cup down, until it's empty.

On the facing wall, next to Logan, are two closets with white cabinet doors. One of the doors is open. There's gear inside. The pack I can understand. But along with it are two M4s, my HITR, and the three Stonewalls in their holsters, hanging from a hook. Trust Leonid to find us a hospital with such a relaxed weapons policy.

A monitoring sleeve wraps my right arm. It must have reported my waking to an alert staff, because I hear the door open as I swing my robot legs over the side of the bed. Logan startles awake, kicking out of the recliner and targeting an attendant as she comes into the room.

"Easy," I warn him, my voice still raspy.

She freezes—a small woman, brown-skinned, with black hair confined against her head in heavy braids. But she recovers faster than Logan. Scorn washes out the shock on her face as she confronts him, launching into a verbal reprimand in a language my overlay doesn't know. I start to wonder if she went to drill-sergeant school. Logan lowers the muzzle of his weapon, but he holds onto his dignity, fixing her with suspicious attention even as she waves him out of the way.

I get the impression this hospital has dealt with mercenaries from time to time.

She switches to English as she addresses me, but her tone isn't any kinder, leading me to suspect that I've been sorted into her mental category of 'idiot soldier.' "You were *not* thinking of standing up on your own, I hope, *sir*? I will walk you to the toilet. We do not want you to fall."

Her size doesn't inspire confidence in her ability to hold me up, but I've been down this road before and size doesn't tell everything. Anyway, I know better than to argue.

She holds on to me, but before I shift my weight to my artificial legs, I try flexing the feet. The left one moves more or less as I want it to, though the joints grind and click. The right foot is obviously misaligned, and I can hardly get it to move at all. I look at Logan. "I need maintenance."

"No shit." He looks tired.

"You been on watch since we got here?"

He shrugs.

"Come on, sir," the attendant says. "Let's get you moving."

With her assistance, I manage the trek to the toilet. The feet are stiff and awkward, but I can still get around on them. I'm returned to my bed, where I'm given an inhaler with instructions to use it every hour while I'm awake. There is a promise that food will arrive soon, and then we are left to our own company.

"I haven't linked into the Cloud," Logan tells me.

I check my overlay. "I'm still locked down too." It surprises me. "I thought the Red would have turned us back on by now."

"It probably doesn't need us yet." There's an edge to his voice. "But it's a matter of time. Before it happens, we need to decide what we're going to do."

Time for a sitrep. "No contact from Kanoa?"

"No. Of course the only way he has to get in touch is

to physically send someone—but there haven't been any visitor requests. He's got to know where we are, though. It's been eighteen hours since we dropped Captain Thurman off at the embassy. Plenty of time to debrief. So, Kanoa knows we arrived. Abajian knows."

We stare at each other for several seconds while I consider the jeopardy of our situation. "They have to see us as a security risk."

Logan nods. "If we're lucky, they'll want to debrief us."

I reach for my coat pocket, where I stashed Issam's farsights, but of course I'm not wearing the coat. I'm wearing pajama pants and a hospital shirt with shoulder snaps.

"I've got the farsights," Logan says. "But that data's already been shared, and it isn't going to buy us any favors. Right now, I'm wishing we hadn't sent it to Kanoa."

"We needed to send it in case we didn't get out. Just tell me you've still got Issam."

"Papa put a bodyguard on him. He's staying in a hotel across the street—it's part of the medical center, connected by an underground tunnel. But he stops in here every couple of hours to sit by your bed. I think he's in love with you, Shelley. Must like your brutal approach."

"Reminds him of Maksim."

"Yeah? Well, he's not grieving."

"Why hasn't Abajian sent anyone after us? We're either assets or targets, and either way, we should have had visitors by now."

Logan cradles his HITR. "Maybe he just can't get to us. Papa swore this medical center was secure, including the hotel." But then he shrugs. It's a casual dismissal of Leonid's assurances. Logan has been keeping watch for a reason. "Maybe they don't want to draw attention."

"Where is Papa? Did he take off?"

Logan looks startled. "I fucking hope not, because *I*

can't pay your medical bills. And if Kanoa has cut us off, we're in a really deep hole."

Money *is* a problem. I've got a personal account under a fictitious identity. There's a fat chunk of cash in it but probably not enough to cover what our treatment must be costing, and if Kanoa is really pissed at us, he'll deny our access to ETM's corporate account, leaving us essentially broke and homeless. The fate of many American patriots before us.

After all we've been through, the thought that we might be undone by a lack of funds strikes me as painfully funny and I laugh. Laughing starts me coughing, but it's a shallow cough and over quickly.

Logan gets up to check the door, then returns to his chair. Something in his expression puts me on guard. "One more thing you should know. About Issam. He has this theory about locally integrated AIs."

"I've heard some of that."

"A local AI kept Abaza's UGF dark."

"Issam designed that AI."

"He wants to redesign the Red."

Tap-ti-tap. Tap-tap-tap.

It's a complex knock on the door, like a code. I'm sitting cross-legged on the bed, my HITR laid out in front of me, disassembled for cleaning.

Logan is sleeping again in the chair, but he starts awake at the noise. I drop the cleaning rag I'm holding and reach for my pistol.

"It's okay," Logan says. "That's Issam's knock."

I hear the door sigh on its hinges, then Issam comes in. He's acquired new farsights. "Oh, you're awake," he says when he sees me. Logan leans back and closes his eyes again. Tran is still asleep.

"Where's your bodyguard?" I ask him.

"Outside in the hall."

He grabs a white plastic folding chair from a corner, sets it up by the bed, sits, and then gets right to the point. "I'm in a lot of trouble. I've got a revoked passport. My name's on the terrorist watch list. And I've got money problems, as in no money. My assets were seized. My parents can't send me anything, or they'll be arrested. You know. For financing terrorism."

I smile to myself as I pick up the cleaning rag again and get back to work. The legal net that's caught Issam is constitutionally questionable, but sometimes it does work.

"Shelley, I was hoping with your connections, you might be able to . . . adjust the record?"

"My connections?"

"You're a soldier for the Red."

I trade the cleaning rag for a soft brush. "You think I can just requisition a change to the terrorist watch list?"

"I don't know. How does it work for you? How do you get things done?"

"I just do what I'm told . . . more or less." But I scowl as I recall what happened to the Mars rocket in San Antonio. Maybe sometimes I *do* get what I want—but I'm not going to tell Issam about that. "Like I said before, you're an intelligence asset. And that means you're not going home. Not until things play out."

He glances uneasily at the door—thinking of the bodyguard on the other side? "You said you'd help me get home."

"I did?"

"*Yes*. Were you lying?"

"I guess so." I would have said anything while we were in that tunnel, just to keep him moving.

"*Shit*," he whispers. I glance up to see his hands clenched by his mouth, his eyes staring ahead into a future of years spent in prison.

"Come on, Issam. You've got value. We just need to make sure you get picked up by the right party."

"You'll help me with that?"

I shrug. "I don't know what's coming. But if I can, I will."

He's quiet for a time, but he's restless, like there's something he wants to say but he needs to work up the courage. I don't want to hear a confession about a bad case of Stockholm syndrome, so I shift the subject. "Logan said you're working on some way to get rid of the Red."

"Huh? What? *No*. I don't want to get rid of it."

I stop what I'm doing to look at him.

He nods, speaking quickly, like he's desperate to hold on to my attention now that he has it. "The Red is the most amazing phenomenon to arise out of human science. It's unarguably an entity. Not inherently evil, but not remotely human either. Intelligent, with a will of its own, with goals, loose in the world, affecting everyone—and of course we're terrified of it. It challenges our conceit of free will, and the first thing most people want to know is, how can we get rid of it?"

He shakes his head. "I don't think we can, not without carrying out a scheme like Broken Sky aimed at crashing civilization. But more than that, I don't think we *should*. We need the Red. We need our cyber-guardian. What else is going to pull us back from the abyss?"

I go back to cleaning, disappointed, dissatisfied to hear Issam express my own pessimistic views. "We're too damned stupid to stay out of the fire."

"Collectively? Yes. After what I've seen, I don't think we have a chance without outside intervention."

"So this is our foreseeable future. Some asshole, somewhere, trying to slag the world, and if we're lucky, the Red figures it out in time to intervene." I put aside the rag and the brushes and start reassembling the HITR. "That's why I joined up—and if that's all it was, I could live with it. But the Red doesn't really give a fuck about peace. If things get too quiet, it just sends us out to fire up another conflict."

"Another conflict? What conflict?"

"You've heard about the Arctic War?"

"Yes."

"It started from nothing."

"Wasn't a biowarfare lab uncovered?"

That rumor again. It won't die.

"It wasn't biowarfare. It was pharmaceutical research. But either way, the war shouldn't have happened. Worst case, a ceasefire should have been called within twelve hours. But last time I checked, the conflict was escalating."

"And you had a role in it?"

Not a question I want to answer. I ignore it, checking the electrical connections on my HITR instead. I switch it on, inventory the ready lights. Raise it to my shoulder and sight down the optical scope.

"What really pisses me off about the Arctic War," I say, "is that it doesn't make any sense. All that territory, all those resources. It's too much to fight over. There's too much at risk and it doesn't make any fucking sense." I load the grenade magazine, and then the 7.62-millimeter rounds. "It feels like war for the sake of war. Another manufactured war."

"It probably is," Issam says.

I lay the HITR down. "Because there needs to be a war going on somewhere, right? The fucking Red is supposed to choke back the dragons, the defense contractors, the contracted politicians. That's how it started. That's why we did First Light. Now we're back where we began, only this time the conflict is more dangerous than the Sahel, more dangerous than Bolivia. When this idiot war succeeds in fucking up the Arctic, the whole planet is going down."

My rant wakes Logan. "We on?" he asks as he sits up and drops his footrest.

"No. Sorry. Go back to sleep."

He squints suspiciously at Issam. Then he leans back, closes his eyes, and turns himself off again.

Issam watches him. "That is so creepy."

I shrug.

He looks at me again. "Don't take this the wrong way, but there *are* strategic reasons to continue the Arctic War. Not for those fighting it, but for outside groups. The Shahin Council might like to see America involved in that war, because after the damage done on Coma Day, a war could destabilize—even bankrupt—the country. And a war would stop Arctic crude from ever reaching the market, keeping the price higher for everyone else."

"Are you saying the Shahin Council is involved?"

"No, I'm not saying that. They could be. I just don't know."

FaceValue doesn't flag a lie. "It still doesn't make sense to me that the Red is allowing this to escalate. It's too dangerous. It *is* an existential threat."

"Remember I told you I've been working with locally integrated AIs? I know I'm not the only one."

I start packing up the cleaning kit. "Okay, maybe you could explain that."

He nods. "I'm going to use metaphors, not mathematics, okay?"

"Works for me."

He gets up, paces a few steps, raises his hands as if he's trying to grasp the proper words. "The human brain—your brain—is a physical system that generates 'you'—your personality, your thoughts, your feelings, your memories." He looks at me to make sure I'm following along. "It's a crude analogy, but think of the Red as an entity, like you, existing across the computational resources of the Cloud, the way 'you' exist across the physical organ of your brain."

I think about it, and shake my head. "No. The Red isn't everywhere at once. It comes and goes."

Issam shrugs. "Maybe *you* aren't everywhere at once in your own mind. You can't recall all your memories at once. You can't consider multiple problems at the same time. And what you think about can be dictated. You're an LCS soldier." He taps his head. "That means you've got neuro-modulating microbeads in your brain tissue."

I nod wary agreement, wondering if I'm giving something critical away.

"You'll agree that the activity of the microbeads influences who 'you' are. They can be used to affect your persona to some extent, your emotional empathy, and your ready state, that is, whether you're asleep, alert, calm, or hostile."

"Sure, but the microbeads are only active if they're stimulated from the outside. By a skullnet or a skullcap."

"And you have a skullnet that's always on, providing a constant, baseline level of stimulation. Am I right?"

Grudgingly: "Yes."

"An interesting aspect of bio-inspired AIs like the Red is that over time, they interlink. As they compete for computing resources, they set up cooperative pathways between one another that can influence both the pace and the nature of activity in their linked network. A local AI, given a repeating sequence of specific tasks, can expropriate local resources, restricting the influence of other entities within a given area. Because it's a learning system, those entities may eventually just transfer tasks to the locally dominant AI. Think of it as your brain giving up on regulating some neurochemical because that function has been taken over by the microbeads."

"So control of who I am is handed off to an outside system . . . which works through the embedded microbeads."

"Exactly. And in an analogous way, neighborhoods in the Cloud can be influenced by the activity of aggressive local AIs."

I see where this is going. "You kept the UGF hidden by using one of these L-AIs to modify the behavior of the Red to . . ." To do what? "To suppress evidence of the facility? But you weren't even hooked into the Cloud."

"Not directly, but being off the grid is not going to make you invisible. It doesn't take a direct connection to deduce that someone, something, or someplace exists. Most objects in the world, animate or not, have a kind of metaphorical gravity that influences elements around them, so the existence of a hidden location or organization or whatever it is can be detected from its effect on other things. The UGF was decades old to begin with, forgotten in most records, and remembered by only a handful of people who learned a long time ago to keep their mouths shut. So before Maksim got there, it had very little gravity. But our presence in there, all the activity, it was sure to be noticed. Trucks on the roads. Heat signatures. EM transmissions. Lights. So, I tasked an AI with obscuring or corrupting evidence of activity, and diverting queries and investigations."

"But you'd need to crack into all kinds of systems to be able to do that."

He shakes his head. "Not necessarily. You've seen maps of the Cloud, with nodes of activity charting the density of information packets. Some of that is the Red or linked to the Red—because the Red is not a single, simple system. It's being rewritten constantly and constantly forges new links to other parts of the system."

"Including your AIs."

"They can share access, just like they share tasks."

"So your L-AIs are hacking the Red to accomplish their tasks—and the Red has already hacked most of the world."

He flashes an awkward smile. "Not exactly a secure system, is it?"

I pick up my HITR again, holding it in the crook of my arm, because maybe there is no security and who the fuck knows what's going to happen next?

Issam sits again in his chair. He looks up at me with his vulnerable dark eyes, and he says, "The L-AIs are just like the microbeads in your brain tissue. They change the personality and affect the goals of the Red. I think someone is using an L-AI to continue the Arctic conflict. Why, I don't know. Sell more armaments, maybe. Restrict petroleum development. Or maybe it's more subtle than that."

"Could that L-AI have been used to launch the conflict?" I ask him.

He gives me a curious look. "Do you have a reason to think that's what happened?"

I don't say it aloud, but yes, every anomaly on that mission gives me a reason to think an L-AI was involved. "This Arctic AI—it's not one of yours?"

"No. But this is a big world, with billions of people, maybe a million smarter, more clever than me. Someone else was bound to work it out. I mean, if you can manipulate the Red, eventually you'll own the world. Right?"

Issam is too important an asset. I decide I want him where I can see him. "You're staying with us," I tell him, "until we figure out friendlies and hostiles and what we're going to do."

He nods, looking relieved. "Sure. That's fine."

When Logan wakes up, I have him request a cot. There's a fee. Logan tells them to add it to the bill.

It's a big room, so we're able to set the cot up between the foot of Tran's bed and the closets.

Despite the presence of the bodyguard outside the door, we're uneasy all afternoon, tensing every time we hear footsteps in the hall. 1800 rolls around and Logan orders dinner—room service from the hotel across the street. God knows what that costs.

He sends the bodyguard home.

Just past 1930, Tran finally wakes up, surprised to find himself still alive. As he sits up, a slow smile spreads across his face. "Hey, this means we get to do another mission."

I contemplate holding a pillow over his idiot face until he stops kicking.

Logan would probably interfere.

"Is it okay if I open network access?" Tran wants to know.

Logan and I answer together, *"No!"*

We set up a watch rotation. Tran volunteers to go first. I let him, though I'm suspicious it's a scheme to get access to Issam's farsights so he can get out in the Cloud without directly violating orders. As I set a wake-up signal, I hear him asking Issam to look up reviews of *The Shattered*, which I'm pretty sure is a comic.

"Don't log into anything," I warn him.

"If I do, I'll make a new account."

I cut that idea off at the roots. "Issam, don't let him use your farsights, and if he threatens you, just wake me up."

Tran rolls his eyes, but Issam frowns, not at all sure if we're joking. I shut myself down—

—and wake up on schedule.

The room is dim but not dark. Despite his leg wound, Tran is up, pacing between the foot of the cot and the door, his M4 held muzzle-down in the crook of his arm. He looks over at me. "You're early."

"Just a couple of minutes."

Logan is asleep in what was Tran's bed, while Issam is snoring on the cot.

"Sitrep?" I ask Tran.

"Nothing to report."

I clomp and creak to the toilet. "How's the leg?" I ask him when I come out again.

He flashes a grin. "Like I keep telling you, I'm good."

I shake my head as I get out my HITR. "Secure your weapon, soldier, and go to sleep."

Tran takes over the bed and checks out. I sit in the recliner with the HITR across my lap, listening to activity in the hall. After forty minutes or so, Issam starts dreaming. It's a bad dream. He's twitching and breathing in little gasps. I watch him for a few seconds. Then he sits up so suddenly he startles me out of my chair. Even in the dim light, I see the whites of his eyes, wide with panic. His right hand grabs at his throat, and then he's on his feet. His gasps change to constricted whoops as he lurches past me toward the door.

I'm so shocked, I step out of the way. But he doesn't make it to the door. Outside the toilet, he goes down. He's on hands and knees, drool running from his mouth as he struggles to breathe. I step past him, lean into the bathroom to hit a call button I remember seeing there, and then I hit the light. Issam lifts his head, looking at me with bulging eyes, his throat swollen. I don't think he's getting any air at all. I step past him, throw the door open, and yell down the hallway, "Emergency! We've got an emergency!"

The nurse on duty comes running. It takes only seconds for her to reach us, but Issam is already on his back, on the floor, his whole body trembling with spasms. The nurse is speaking out loud, using her farsights to summon an emergency team while she tries to establish an airway.

By this time, Tran and Logan are both awake and all the lights in the room are on. There's nothing we can do, so we stay out of the way while the medical team works.

In the end, there's nothing anyone can do, and Issam's lifeless body gets wheeled away on a gurney.

"It's like the secretary of defense," Tran says as a janitor cleans the floor. "Remember I told you about that? He collapsed while giving a speech and nothing the paramedics did could revive him."

"Did you ever hear what he died of?"

"Yeah. I looked it up before we left. Acute asthma attack associated with a severe allergic reaction."

"*Shit*," Logan whispers, because that's exactly what Issam's death looked like—and the attending physician confirms it when he stops by later in the night to talk with us.

I ask him what caused the allergic reaction.

He doesn't know. He can't even guess. He's never seen anything like it before.

At this point we all just want to get out of the hospital, but we are asked to wait until morning when the administrative staff comes in. So we sit in the room and talk about what happened. None of us believe it was an accident. But why was Issam the only victim? Why are the rest of us still alive?

Tran says, "It was like that with the secretary of defense. Just him. No one else, in a crowded auditorium."

"Maybe Issam was poisoned earlier," Logan says. "Maybe it was the bodyguard and it just took time."

Maybe.

In the morning, we're reclassified as outpatients. They provide me and Tran with decent-looking civilian clothes, and we get to move across the street to the associated hotel. Issam spent a night there—that worries me—but he only died when I insisted he stay under my protection.

A private subterranean tunnel connects the two buildings. We emerge in a small underground lobby furnished with chairs, a propane fireplace, and a check-in desk staffed by two smiling men and a dour woman. There is no direct access to the outside, but there is a single elevator, and across the room from it, a closed, windowless door labeled with a sign in many languages advising *MAIN LOBBY THIS WAY*.

Safe to assume this is the secure entrance. Convenient, since we're transporting our HITRs open-carry and our pistols on display in their holsters. The dour woman at the desk greets us in excellent, if unsmiling, English. "Welcome, sirs. Your suite is ready. We do politely ask that your weapons be restricted to your rooms."

"Yes, ma'am."

She doesn't ask for IDs, biometrics, or account information, so I have to assume we're still operating on Leonid's credit. We're handed key cards. They're an old-fashioned means to open a door, but they have the advantage of being anonymous, unlike biometric locks.

"You are on a secure floor," the woman tells us. "Access to your room is only through this lobby. The elevator will not accept any unregistered guests or stop on any other floors."

We step aboard the elevator. There is no keypad. The doors close and we ascend nonstop to our room on the thirty-second floor.

We are in a one-bedroom suite at the end of the hall, furnished in simple, modern luxury. There is only one window. It's floor-to-ceiling, but it's just twenty centimeters wide and made of heavy glass. Hard to shoot through. Probably hard to blast through.

We investigate the suite with weapons drawn.

There is a bathroom off the front room, another off the bedroom. We clear them all and check the closets. When we're done, Tran looks around in satisfaction. "This," he announces, "is a step closer to a superhero hangout. Beats the hell out of the barracks at C-FHEIT." He grabs the remote, flops on one of the two beds, and turns on the TV. "How long are we here for?"

"Tonight, if we're lucky." I head back to the front room.

"Hey, they have sex workers here," he calls after me. "Licensed, bonded. Come to the room. Is that a security violation?"

"Yes." I project my voice to make sure I'm heard. The effort makes my throat itch and threatens to start me coughing all over again, so I step back to the door to escape the need to shout. Tran has limited his search to women. He's scrolling through their profiles. Logan is looking too. It's an impressive selection. "Issam is dead. We don't know how they got to him. We don't want them getting to us."

"Yeah, but we can't squat in this room forever."

"We've been here five minutes. Anyway, I want to wait for Papa to turn up."

Tran pauses the selection. He looks at me with a wary gaze. "You're not trying to cut some deal to work with Papa?"

"No."

"Good. Because we are ETM—if Kanoa doesn't kill us."

"Kanoa already left you for dead," Logan says, surprising me with his bitterness. "Your corpse would be food for crows by now if Papa hadn't gotten us out of there."

Tran returns his gaze to the TV. In a quiet voice he says, "For right now, I'm gonna believe he didn't have options, okay?" He resumes scrolling, but his enthusiasm is gone.

I go back to the living room, where I turn an armchair to face the door and then occupy it with my HITR in my lap and my pistol in a chest holster.

"Logan!"

"Sir!"

"There's a TV out here too. Check if it can access feeds from the hallway security cameras."

I'm not paranoid.

Well, I am.

Why shouldn't I be? We have enemies and I don't even know who most of them are. All I know is they're out there. They got to Issam. They can get to us.

I fix my gaze on my encyclopedia icon and think, *Search skullnet.* A list of articles displays, but I want the manual. I hear Logan moving and then the soft electronic sigh of the monitor coming to life.

He says, "We need to make peace with Kanoa."

"Just now, you didn't sound like you want peace."

"I don't want him hunting us down."

"We'll work it out."

"Confirming cameras in the hallway. *Nice.* They allow alerts. I'm setting it to go off anytime someone appears on the floor."

I hope this isn't a party floor.

I lean back, my creaky robot feet stretched out in front of me, and I start to read about my skullnet.

A skullnet has two discrete tasks: reading brain activity, and adjusting it. Reading is a passive function that lets it track emotions and monitor patterns of thoughts flashing across the brain's neural synapses. It's what lets me "talk" in a telepathic sense, converting simple thoughts into synthesized words. In contrast, adjustment is active: It signals the microbeads to affect mood, or ready state. Adjustment is what lets the Red reach into my head and play me like a puppet.

After an hour reading through the manual, I decide I don't need to get rid of the skullnet after all. I can keep the skullnet's passive functions. I can even keep the active functions, the ones that *I* control with my thoughts. All I need to do is stop the Red from getting inside my head, and I can do that by snipping out the skullnet's receiver.

It's a simple solution. Elegant. Easy. Except that right now I'm existing on a baseline level of brain stimulation overseen by the embedded AI residing in the skullnet's hardware. It's the AI's task to continuously monitor and adjust my mood to keep me humming along no matter what unforgiveable acts I commit. I could just leave that function in place, but I don't really know what the limits of the program are—and once the receiver is out, I won't be able to adjust it. I decide it's safer to shut the baseline function down. The idea scares the shit out of me, but what else can I do?

A well-equipped first aid kit is part of the standard gear any soldier carries. I get mine out of my pack and go through it, making sure I have everything I need. Scalpel, scissors, gloves, sterile wipes, gauze, wound glue. After patching up Tran, I'm low on wound glue, but there's enough left for what I need.

Tran is still in the bedroom, watching something on TV. But Logan is stretched out on the couch. He lifts his head, gives me a suspicious look. "What are you doing?"

"Enhancing security." I gather what I need, head into the bathroom, and close the door.

My lifestyle choices aside, I'm not a fan of pain. As I contemplate what I'm about to do, my heart rate and blood pressure climb.

I take off my shirt. Put a hotel towel around my shoulders. Then I run my finger along my scalp above my right ear until I find two slight bumps just under the skin, a centimeter apart. The one in front is the skullnet's transmitter, positioned for easy communication with my overlay. I don't want to damage the transmitter. The other bump is the receiver. I scrub the area with a disinfecting wipe. Then I break the scalpel out of its sterile wrapping.

The mistake most people make about the Red is to think of it as something human. It's not. It doesn't get frustrated, angry, or vindictive. If a tactic doesn't work, if a pawn refuses to cooperate, if a task fails to execute, the Red learns from it and moves on. If the Red was human, I'd probably get dropped from ETM for what I'm about to do. But my guess is the Red will just recalculate my specs as a useful tool in its inventory.

I lean close to the mirror.

Deep breath.

I get the scalpel into position to cut, but the angle is bad and working in the mirror is disorienting. So I straighten up again and, working as fast as I can, I make two shallow incisions by feel, slicing loose a flap of skin above the receiver. Blood wells out, oozing in bright red streams that drain past my ear, down my neck, and drip onto the towel. *Hurts.* I try not to think about it, but *shit.* So many nerve endings in the skin. Pain is relative, for sure. I've felt pain a lot worse than this, but I'm not going to deny this *sucks.*

I stick a fingertip under the flap and probe for the receiver. It's smaller than a rice grain. I try to get my finger under it, but it's embedded in the meat. I try to get the tip of the scalpel under it, but I can't see what I'm doing.

The bathroom door opens. It's Logan. "Your stress levels are going crazy—*Jesus!*" he says when he sees the blood. "Have you finally cracked?"

I get the impression Logan does not approve of self-mutilation. He makes a quick grab for my right wrist, wanting to get the scalpel away from me, but I fall back. Blood drips on the floor. "I need your help."

He is outraged. "Are you trying to take out your own skullnet?"

"Fuck, *no.* I'd need a surgeon to do that. I just want to take out the receiver." I move back to the counter, trying to see the incision site in the mirror. "I thought it'd be easier than this."

By this time, Tran has picked up on the excitement. He's crowding in behind Logan, eyes wide. "Holy shit."

"You can't take out the receiver," Logan says.

"I can. I am." The pain is backing off. That'll be my skullnet, pumping me up on adrenaline and natural pain-killers as it follows its baseline program. I'm going to miss that.

"How are you going to make adjustments to the skullnet?" Logan asks.

I tell him the truth. "I won't need adjustments. I found a program in the manual that will wind down the baseline until it hits zero. So that'll run, and then I'm on my own."

"You're serious?"

I press a square of gauze against the wound to slow the

bleeding. "It'll take twenty-one days for the program to run. Time for me to adjust. But the skullnet will still be there. It'll still be able to assess my physical status, monitor my thought patterns. I'll still be able to hit gen-com."

"So you're not dropping out of ETM?" Tran asks.

"No. I have the overlay. I can get orders that way. I just don't want the Red inside my head, making me think it's okay to drag us into another suicide mission."

Tran trades a look with Logan. Then he asks, "What if you can't handle things on your own?"

That's the part that scares me. I scowl at my image in the mirror. "If it doesn't work, I'll just get rewired, right?" I turn to Logan again. "Come on. I don't want to make another decision like I made in the UGF. This is the compromise solution."

"Think what you're giving up," Logan says. "You won't get any help staying focused or staying awake. You won't get any narcotic effects. No stress abatement. No automatic sleep."

"I'll get by. Just like I used to when I was a civilian."

"You're not a civilian, Shelley. Civilians don't pump RPGs into rooms full of people."

"Just do it for me. I don't want to cut my ear off."

He still hesitates, while my blood seeps through the gauze and my temper flares. "You know what, Logan? Do it. That's an order."

"*Fuck* you." But he grabs the pack of wipes anyway and cleans his hands. "Give me that." He takes the scalpel. "And put your fucking head down on the counter." I do it, pillowing my skull against the blood-soaked towel. "I should just cut your throat," he says.

"Probably better all around."

"Shut up."

I feel his fingers press against my head. He's not making

any effort to be gentle. He trades the scalpel for the scissors. There's a faint *snip!* and then he drops a tiny black lozenge on the counter in front of my eyes. "Hope we got the right one."

I hope we did too. I think, *You there?*

"Gotcha," Tran says.

And Logan, sounding disappointed: "Yeah, you're still linked."

He uses the wipes to clean up the blood, and then he glues the incision closed. The glue's anesthetic kicks in right away. Other than numbness at the site of the incision, I don't feel any different. Not yet.

By the time I get out of the shower, I'm ready to take the next step. "We need to find out where we stand with Kanoa," I announce. "Let's get our network access back on."

Tran has taken over the armchair facing the door. "Thank you, God!" he proclaims. "This living-in-my-own-head shit is killing me with boredom. And I need to order a new HITR. Express delivery. Why the hell did you let me drop mine, Shelley? I don't know what I'm supposed to do with this stupid M4 if we get in serious trouble."

"Aim?" Logan suggests.

He's stretched out on the couch again, hugging his HITR. I push his feet off and sit down. My overlay is independent of my skullnet, so it's unchanged by my recent modifications. I look for the network icon. It brightens under my gaze and a menu pops out. I return myself to full network access. Gen-com automatically links home.

Logan sits up in a hurry. "Gen-com's updating."

"Same here. Tran?"

"Yes."

The update completes. Gen-com restarts. I get automatically linked in again. So do Logan and Tran. I see their icons in my overlay.

But it's just the three of us, like it's been since we launched on Arid Crossroad.

"*Shit,*" Tran says. "Where's the rest of 7-1?"

Nervous tension makes me check the monitor on the wall, but the hall outside remains empty. "We're here if Kanoa wants to talk."

"If he *can* talk," Logan says. "Maybe Abajian's got him locked down."

"Yeah." I'm worried about that too. "I'm just going to call him."

I try it. The call links, but then it drops. No option to leave a message. It's like I'm not on his approved-contacts list. "I'm going to try Fadul." Same thing.

Logan and Tran give it a shot, but their connections drop too. We try everyone in the squad: Fadul, Escamilla, Dunahee, Roman, Julian. But we've been locked out.

Tran says, "I'm going to order a weapon."

"Do it."

If Kanoa is in trouble, then so are we. We might as well be ready.

I pick up my HITR and head to the bedroom, closing the door behind me. I lie down on the bed. I am used to being part of an organization, one geared to handle security and supplies, to sort through intelligence, to assign tasks. I like it that way. I don't like being on my own. The last time I was out in the world without supervision was my brief and disastrous stay in Manhattan after my court-martial.

That's when I hooked up with Delphi—and I guess that was disastrous too.

I should call her. I memorized her address the evening she contacted me at C-FHEIT. I should call her back. We didn't get to talk for long.

I whisper her address to my overlay and mark it priority,

so if she ever calls me again, she won't get dropped. Then I highlight her address and think, *Link*.

To my relief, the call is accepted. A synthetic, androgynous voice answers, inviting me to leave a message. "Delphi, it's me. If you want to talk, authorize my address. I'll call again."

I grab the remote control Tran left on the bed. I need to distract myself before my elevated stress levels make Logan come after me. So I turn on the TV and pull up feeds from the hotel's security cameras—the hall outside, the elevator, the secure lobby. I see one of the smiling men behind the front desk. No one else.

A link request opens in my overlay. The overlay's masculine voice names the caller: "Karin Larsen."

I swallow against a dry throat and accept the link. A video feed opens.

"Can you see me?" she asks.

"Yes." She's wearing a tank top. No bra. Her blond hair is loose and wispy around her face. The light is dim. "Did I wake you up?" I ask.

"I want to see you, Shelley."

"Okay." I open a video feed that lets her see what my overlay sees. Then I get up and go into the suite's second bathroom, meeting the gaze of my reflection in the mirror. What I see is a brown-skinned man with a stubble of black hair and guilt in his eyes, and regret.

She sees something else. "You look good, Shelley."

"Where are you?" My voice is hoarse. That's from the fire.

"San Antonio. You?"

"Budapest."

"Guess we can't meet at the corner coffee shop."

The only place I want to meet is in a bedroom, with the door closed and locked and Delphi naked and demanding beneath me. I don't like my expression, so I turn away from the mirror, return to the room.

"Okay," she says. "Bad joke. Look, I really don't understand what happened between us. If you wanted to leave, I wish you'd just told me—"

"It wasn't like that."

"—but that was all a long time ago. I'm glad you're alive. I am so happy to know that."

She's moved on. I sense it. But I don't ask. I don't want to know. Because if she hasn't found someone else, then it's my fault for fucking up her life, and if she has . . . *shit*, I don't want to know.

I sprawl in a chair, staring at her image, with the TV playing in the background. "I don't want you to go to Mars. That's a mistake."

She gives me a dark look. "Did you use your influence with the president?"

"What?"

"Monteiro issued a temporary order suspending all orbit-crossing flights pending a new licensing system, and that means we're grounded. God knows for how long. Government-contracted flights are still on schedule, but the rest of us have to line up and wait for a turn to explain why we should have free use of our own assets."

"Huh." I don't want to sound happy, but I am.

"Did you have something to do with that?"

"How could I? I'm not sure the president even knows I'm alive."

"She knows."

I sit up straighter, alarmed at what those words imply. "How do *you* know that?"

But she's distracted. "Shelley, are those security feeds you're watching?"

I close the video feed of Delphi to look at the TV. There

are at least six civilians in the lobby, but they're the sort of civilians with straight spines, stern expressions, and military haircuts, all wearing long black coats good for hiding weapons. They aren't doing anything except milling around, eyeing the under-street tunnel, the door to the public lobby, but mostly the elevator.

The feed from inside the elevator shows Papa, riding up alone.

"Delphi, do you know Leonid Sergun?"

"I know of him. I know you had a mission with him. That's him, isn't it?"

"He's got a small army downstairs. I don't know where this is going."

Leonid steps off the elevator onto the thirty-second floor. I hear the programmed alert go off in the front room. Over gen-com, Logan says, "Papa's here."

"Roger that." I get up. Grab my HITR. "I've got to go, Delphi."

"Call me again. If you can."

RULES OF
ENGAGEMENT

I GO TO THE FRONT DOOR AND OPEN IT, KEEPING my HITR out of sight. "Papa."

He's dressed in a black sweater, black slacks, black boots, and a tailored black coat. He walks with his back straight and shoulders squared, but his heavy, wrinkled face is haggard. FaceValue confirms an emotional strain. I've never seen him so transparent before.

Suspicion kicks in. Something critical has changed. I need to know whose side he's on now. "Papa, who are your friends downstairs?"

This earns me a glare and then a shrug. "At least you are learning caution." He waves me back. "Let me come in. I am not here to kill you."

I step back, opening the door wider and then closing it behind him. He sits on the couch, eyeing the monitor, though this one shows only the empty hallway.

I sling my HITR over my shoulder and pick up the remote, bringing up the other two feeds: one of the elevator, one of the lobby and the men waiting there. "You came in with them, didn't you?"

"Yes. Though they are more your friends, than mine."

He leans back, eyeing Logan who is frowning at the monitor, and then Tran, who is standing near the front door with his M4. "They are American," Leonid says. "They had hoped to meet you before you left the hospital, but it seems you departed earlier than expected."

"You heard what happened to Issam?"

"Yes."

"Are they here to arrest us?"

"They would like to take you into custody. Not as an arrest, but for your protection. The three of you, and myself."

"Abajian sent them?"

He shrugs, an expansive, rolling gesture than encompasses his whole upper body and is tinged, somehow, with a pessimism that feels generations old. "I cannot say. This network of relations—who works for who, where loyalty is owed, or favors—it does not seem so important to me now. It seems my niece, my sister's child, Yana Semakova, has suffered the same fate as our friend Issam."

"*What?*" I don't want to believe what he's telling me. I sit down in the chair facing him, wanting to know more.

"I am told that in both cases it was a sudden, severe allergic reaction."

"That's bullshit," Tran says.

Leonid nods.

"She was my niece. That was dangerous enough, but she was no compliant woman. She had enemies of her own. She spoke against the Arctic War, named names, shamed those who would not or could not stop the conflict. I want to know who proposed to the 'circus of murderers' that the first orbital habitat to be targeted should be hers. Did the wish trickle down from the Russian government? From the Canadians? From the Chinese? Or did the Shahin Council decide on their own?" He

leans over abruptly, as if crushed by an unbearable
weight, held up only by his elbows resting on his knees.
His hands tremble, his jaw works, his muscles go taut.
And I realize he does not know how to grieve. *Shit.*
Neither do I. My skullnet never allowed it. Grief just
gets overwritten.

"I'm sorry, Papa."

Logan and Tran mutter their own condolences.

"No," Leonid says. "No sympathy." He purses his lips,
sits up again, heaves a huge sigh. "I deserve none. I have
caused grief enough in the world. I will say only that I
loved my Yana, and of all my mad family, she at least might
find her way to God."

If Semakova was a target, is there a danger for Delphi
too? And Jaynie? They were all business partners. I get up
and pace on my creaking legs, whispering a text message to
Delphi. *Semakova is dead. Be careful.*

When I turn back, Papa is watching me as if he knows
what I am doing. He says, "Our American friends have
asked me to let you know there is another mission under
consideration. They would like to discuss it with you."

"Here?"

"No. They will escort you to a secure base in Germany."

"When?"

"Now." He waves a hand at the monitor. "They are waiting."

I study Leonid, letting FaceValue work, asking myself:
Could he have saved our lives, brought us here, paid for
our treatment, only to set us up for assassination? Maybe.
Maybe it's a complex deal.

FaceValue flags no lies, just a complex of unreadable
emotions.

Leonid raises a heavy gray eyebrow. "Shelley, what was it
you told that fighter pilot about me?"

I stand up on creaking legs, wondering at my own suspicion. "I told her I trust you."

He stands too. "And do you?"

Nonlinear war: no real allies, no fixed enemies, no certain battlefields. "Are you involved in this mission?" I ask
him.

"A planning and support role. I have operated in the
region before, so I have access to intelligence and local
assets unavailable to our allies."

"Why involve yourself?"

His chin comes up, his eyes narrow. "You ask that only
now?"

"Tell me."

"A simple, foolish reason. Some time ago, I had a
dream that my brother-in-law, Eduard, had bought his
way into Heaven, only to have an archangel, full of vengeance, cast him out. I chose to believe this dream was a
message, a warning, that success in this life buys nothing
in the next . . . but I could still serve God as this archangel does."

I turn away, having nothing to say to this. I step to the
narrow window and peer at the city outside, where a new
day has begun. I have done unforgivable things. How can
there be redemption for that?

Tran has a more basic worldview. "So now you're all
about rooting out evil?"

"Also vengeance," Papa says.

Logan asks, "Is this mission vengeance for Yana's
murder?"

"It may be."

My lieutenant is not satisfied. "We need to know more."

"Then you will need to come to Germany. Come in any
case. Accept this offer of protection. You are not safe here."

I step away from the window. "You know that? You've

heard something?" More than ever, I want to know where Kanoa is.

He gestures at the air-conditioning vent. "The enemy has engaged a new weapon, a targeted, airborne poison."

"That's what killed Issam? And Yana?"

"Yes."

"And you're going to Germany?"

"*Da.* Yes. Didn't I say so? I want to go on living. A proper revenge takes time."

I look at Logan. *Yes?*

He nods agreement.

"Pack your gear," I order. "Tran, did you put in your weapons order?"

"Yes, sir."

"Cancel it. We're moving out."

My decision is confirmed by a text from Delphi that arrives as we vacate the room: *Confirming Semakova's status. Suspected airborne bioactive. Multiple victims in dispersed locations. All key figures. This is the first stage of a war, Shelley. Take shelter now.*

With Leonid accompanying us, we are rushed aboard a US Air Force business jet, which is granted an immediate take-off. I text Delphi to let her know we're okay. She responds, saying not to worry, but for security, she's going dark.

An hour and a half later, the jet touches down on a concrete runway at a US Army garrison in southern Germany. It's a former garrison according to the history I can find. I pull up a satellite image that shows an intact fence around the perimeter. There's clear ground for ten meters inside the fence, and then a belt of evergreen trees looking thick enough to screen the facilities from outside observation.

The facilities include a runway flanked by two hangars, a small housing area, a cluster of larger buildings—probably administrative—and a lot of concrete pads where other buildings used to be. I count only a few vehicles.

Looking out the jet's window, I see the belt of trees from the photo. They are a tall dark-green hedge fronted by a narrow field, white with a light blanket of snow. As the plane makes its turn at the end of the runway, the hangars come into sight. We taxi to the farthest one. On the way, I try Kanoa again. Still nothing. The engines shut down. A two-person ground crew works to get us towed inside, and then the copilot appears from the cockpit. "You may disembark now," she says. "Take all your gear with you."

We shoulder our packs. Then, with our weapons in hand, we file out. At the base of the stairs, an army captain waits for us—Captain Montrose, by his name tag. My overlay's facial recognition routine confirms it.

Montrose isn't armed, but he doesn't need to be. Behind him, standing in a half circle, is a squad of six military police rigged in armor and bones, armed with HITRs, and made anonymous by the black visors of their helmets. Parked behind them are an army SUV and a van, both vehicles with heavily tinted windows.

Captain Montrose takes charge. "Security considerations demand that we move quickly. No personal firearms are allowed on base, so my first requirement is that all weapons and ammunition be turned over to Sergeant Remick."

I step up beside Leonid, not liking the direction of this conversation at all. "No, sir. I don't think so."

"Shelley." Leonid's tone is stern. "I have worked with Captain Montrose before."

"You trust this situation?"

He scoffs. "There is nothing certain in this world. Every day, we make bets. This is my bet."

I turn to Montrose. "I want to know where William Kanoa is. I want to talk to him."

"You will turn over all weapons and ammunition, Captain Shelley. This is not a matter of negotiation."

"You have made your bet too," Leonid reminds me, one eyebrow cocked.

The sergeant in charge of the MPs steps forward to enforce Captain Montrose's request. "No personal firearms are allowed, sir."

"These aren't personal. They're officially issued."

"You are required to turn them over, sir, along with the ammunition."

In my mind, I go over my options: Turn the weapons over, or get into a firefight we don't want and can't win. Not really a choice. I address my next thought to gen-com. *Turn over your weapons.*

Roger that, Logan responds.

Tran's answer is more succinct. *Shit*

But he cooperates. So do I.

I check the locks on my HITR and then hand it over, cursing Kanoa as I do it. He is supposed to be our commanding officer. He is supposed to take care of us.

I hope like hell he's still alive.

"Thank you, Captain Shelley," Montrose says. "Sergeant Remick will escort you to your quarters. Mr. Sergun, if you could accompany me."

"Wait. Where are you taking Leonid?"

"Mr. Sergun has been assigned to separate quarters."

"Papa, what the hell?"

"There are details to be worked out," he says.

I have no idea what that means. I don't know what his status is, or ours. I don't know if he's on our side anymore,

or if he's made new friends. He looks grim as he gets into
the SUV with Captain Montrose.

As they drive off, Sergeant Remick directs me, Tran, and
Logan into the van. The driver is a husky youth wearing
farsights and a neat army service uniform. "My orders are
to check you into guest quarters," he tells us as the doors
close.

The MPs jump onto the running boards. The kid waits
for a signal from Remick and then we roll, with the MPs
riding on the outside of the van.

Guest quarters turns out to be a furnished, three-bedroom,
seventy-year-old home in the last surviving cluster of officer housing at the old garrison. Sergeant Remick informs
us that we are to stay inside with the blinds closed.

"How long are we scheduled to be here?" I ask him.

"I have no information on that, sir."

"Under whose orders are we here?"

"I have no information on that, sir."

"I need to be put in touch with my commanding officer,
Major William Kanoa."

"You are to remain within the premises as I have
instructed, sir, where you will await further orders."

He withdraws but leaves a guard unit of three MPs
outside. Logan watches them past the edge of the blinds.
"Protective custody doesn't feel all that different from
prison."

"It's different," I tell him.

"It's a fucking downgrade from that hotel Papa put us
in," Tran grumbles, slinging his pack onto the sofa. "No
room service, no sex workers, no TV." He stomps into the
kitchen and opens the fridge. "Drinks only." He checks
a cabinet. Over his shoulder I can see it's full of familiar
manufactured meals, crammed onto every shelf. Tran
groans. "Microwave shit. Enough to feed us for weeks." He

looks over his shoulder at me. "I'm not sure coming here was a good idea."

I don't like it either, but at least we're still alive.

I claim a bedroom by upending my pack and dumping out everything I've got left on the bed. There's not a lot. T-shirts, rations, my dwindling first aid kit. Clinging to it all is a toxic, burnt smell that puts me back in the UGF with my heart racing. I give the skullnet a few seconds to smooth things over. The icon glows . . . and I remind myself that the baseline program is winding down and I'm not going to have that kind of assistance much longer.

The T-shirts get tossed toward the door—I'll wash them later and maybe the smell will go away. Clothes are going to be a problem if we have to stay here more than a day. With that in mind, I take off my civilian shirt and hang it up in the closet. Might as well keep it fresh a little longer.

All my other gear gets neatly repacked despite the smell. I want to be ready if anything happens.

Next step: figure out what *is* happening. I settle down on the bed, pop open my encyclopedia, and start reading the newest posts harvested from the Cloud—and it's not good news.

Lines are being redrawn in the Arctic War. Yesterday, the last day of the old year, Russia escalated the conflict by claiming sovereignty over an immense undersea ridge, using the argument that at some point in the planet's geological history, that ridge was part of the Siberian continental shelf. Russian fighters are patrolling the newly declared border, Canadian and American fighters are rising to challenge them, while international shipping companies, backed by Chinese money, are lobbying hard for a peace treaty to be hammered out before the spring thaw.

There have been no more strikes against orbital targets, but the damage is amplifying anyway. A small observational satellite in a known debris path was moved out of the way, only to be struck by an unmapped fragment. Now its shattered parts are adding to the hazard, and more incidents are expected.

Closer to Earth, the Pakistanis are sending fighters to taunt US Navy ships patrolling off their coast—aggressive behavior that has drawn out sorties of Indian Shikras ready to engage them. I imagine defense contractors coaching both sides, encouraging a hot conflict—hot enough to sell some armaments, but not so hot that either side is tempted to use the nukes they've kept stored for decades.

The Americans are saying little, and mainstream news sites make no mention of Captain Thurman or of a lost American fighter. But at fringe sites, armchair investigators are piecing together a scenario from seismic data and local gossip that is surprisingly close to the truth.

Two other raids against Broken Sky took place, one in Sudan and the other in Bolivia, but both have gone almost unremarked by a world long tired of war in both places.

After a couple of hours, Tran sends me a text. *Read this! It's all crowdsourced research, unfiltered by mediots, government, or dragons. The Angel of Death is real.*

There's a link, so I follow it to another fringe site where there's a list of "influencers"—people of power, decision-makers—who have died in recent weeks. I look for the secretary of defense and he's there. I look for Yana Semakova and find her name. But they are only two on a list of more than two hundred. The number shocks me. *Two hundred.* Spread out over four months. I cross-check a few names with other sources, just to make sure, and confirm their deaths are real.

The list includes politicians, corporate types, religious

figures, scientists, and military officers. Twenty-three are
Americans. Others are British, German, Chinese, Japanese,
Saudi . . . most relatively young and healthy. All were single
deaths—a sudden collapse in a crowded office building or
among thousands at a political rally or on a busy sidewalk.

Tran's right. It's like an angel of death has been wandering through the capitals of the world, the financial centers,
the military bases, the think tanks, striking down select targets—and sowing fear in those who go untouched. We're
an example. We were so shaken by Issam's death that we
fled Budapest and agreed to protective custody.

I send a text to Delphi, wanting to know she's still okay,
but I get no answer.

Tran links over gen-com. "Are you looking at it?"

"Yes."

"I think it's a slow-motion decapitation of the world's
leadership."

Delphi called it the first stage of a war—but if so, it's
a quiet war, an undercover war, and it's not clear who's
waging it. "None of the mainstream news sites have linked
these deaths together."

"It's being suppressed. Governments don't want it known
they're vulnerable. They make sure cause of death gets listed
as 'natural' or 'undetermined' or some equivalent shit."

"Logan?" I ask. "You listening?"

"Roger that."

I tell them, "You know how these last months, we've
been doing these look-and-see missions? Even Arid
Crossroad. I'm starting to think we've been looking for the
angel of death all this time, or anyway, for the lab he uses."

Tran says, "That would be a fucking slam if we found it."

Logan is operating from an opposite emotional pole:
"Who's to say the Red's not the angel of death?"

I look at the list again. I don't know most of the names

on it or what they stood for or what the impact of their deaths might be—but if those deaths put us closer to midnight or consolidate power in the hands of a few, then the Red's not behind it.

Evening comes, with no communication from Leonid or Captain Montrose or Colonel Abajian or Major Kanoa or anyone else. No clarification of our status. No further orders.

No idea what's coming next.

Whatever's coming, I'm not ready. Not physically. I've been using the inhaler as prescribed and my lungs are healing, but my body is beat up and it's going to take time to recover. My robot legs, of course, are not going to recover at all. I close the door of my bedroom. Time to deal with that.

The irony of the modern world is that instant global communication is useless if the person you want to talk to limits contacts, like I do. I want to talk to Joby Nakagawa about my legs. I've still got his address. The problem is, my address has changed, so I won't be in his contact list. Instead of calling, I decide to email: my name, the serial number of my legs, and my new address, with a short message, *call me*.

It's still afternoon in San Antonio. Forty minutes later, I get a link request from his address. I accept.

"What the *fuck*?" His tone is icy, somewhere between caution and fury.

"Hey, Joby. Remember me?"

"Jesus! *Fuck!*"

"I'm going to assume that's a yes."

"You're *dead*," he objects. "You're supposed to be dead."

"Yeah, sorry. I keep getting that part wrong."

"You asshole. You've been active all this time, and I've got no data on the performance of the legs. That's why you're calling, isn't it? You're having problems with the legs. That's the only reason you'd call."

"You said no one else was allowed to work on them. Only you."

Suspicious: "What'd you do to them?"

"A lot of wear and tear. Some bullet impacts. Shrapnel. I can still walk, but some of the joints are bent or broken."

"The knee joint?"

"No, that's fine. It's the feet, the lower legs."

"You want new ones?"

"Hell, yes. Can you do that?"

"There's a private manufacturer now. Expensive. I can put in the order for you, if you've got the funding."

"Do it. Forward the invoice and I'll pay it."

"You got a physical address for the delivery?"

"Not yet. I'll let you know."

"Okay. It'll take a few days. After you make the swap, send me the old legs so I can assess the damage."

"Sure. Not a problem."

"Jesus, Shelley, I can't fucking believe you're alive. You know, you might want to consider staying out of the line of fire."

I think that's the nicest thing Joby's ever said to me. "Hey, thanks. But this stays between you and me, okay?"

"No shit, dickhead. I'm not an idiot."

The invoice comes in a few minutes later. *Holy shit.* I check my personal account. I have about two dollars left when I'm done, but I manage to cover it.

We set up a watch rotation. Tran goes first and then Logan. I've got the last watch, so I go to bed early. Lying in the darkness of an unfamiliar bedroom, I think about my skull-net. It's been less than a day since I loaded the shutdown program. I try to decide if I can feel any difference, but I can't. Not yet.

Anyway, better to sleep—and that's still easy. Though my skullnet can't receive outside input anymore, I can still communicate with it using my own thoughts. Maybe, in time, I can train it to generate a variety of mental states on command . . . but for now, I issue the standard instruction: *sleep*.

Hours later, I wake to an earbud alarm. I kill it and sit up, feeling groggy. If I'd used the skullnet to wake me, I'd feel alert, but I can't do that anymore.

A furnace is running, heating the house. A glance past the blinds shows the street illuminated by fog-glazed moonlight. There are no lights in any of the other houses. No cars parked along the street. One of the rigged MPs stands on the sidewalk, the white vapor of an exhaled breath riding forced air currents out beneath the blank, black face of a visor.

I let the blind drop back into place and then hobble out of the bedroom, into the kitchen. Logan is sitting at an empty table, wide awake because his skullnet keeps him that way.

"Status?" I ask him.

"Nothing to report. What's *your* status? You feeling any effects yet?"

"Waking up is harder."

"I remember that."

"Go get some sleep."

I make coffee—something I don't usually do—but I'm worried about nodding off. Everything is quiet until dawn. At 0705 I hear the soft *clomp* of footplates on the concrete outside, followed immediately by a loud, harsh concussion on the door. I know that sound. It's the arm strut of a dead sister hammered against the wood. We used to do that in Bolivia to scare the shit out of people on the other side.

Given that my heart rate just vaulted to racing speed, I'd say it works as intended.

I whisper over gen-com, "Send a wakeup call."

There is nothing in this house that will protect us if our guards come in shooting. Our only chance is to counter-attack as they enter—and if they have cameras on us, or they're scanning through the walls, we won't even get the benefit of surprise. I scramble for the kitchen, grabbing the biggest knives in there—little steak knives with four-inch blades. I hand one to Tran as he bolts from the hall, wearing shorts and a fighting expression. The hammerblow repeats as Logan comes behind him.

"Identify yourself!" I shout at the door. I signal Logan and Tran to move up with me. We position ourselves to make a grab for whoever we see there when the door opens.

My request is answered by a woman's voice, muf-fled through the door. "Lieutenant Andrea Ashman, Intelligence. I am going to open the door, Captain Shelley. I am unarmed."

I hand off my knife to Logan and wave him and Tran to move back.

The knob turns. The door opens slowly, just a few inches. Lieutenant Ashman and I stare at each other through the gap, both of us gauging the threat we pose to one another. She is dressed in an army service uniform. Standing behind her is one of the rigged MPs.

"We *are* on the same side, Captain Shelley."

Are we? That has not been made clear to me. Eyeing the MP, I stand aside. "Come in."

She closes the door behind her. Ashman is tall, almost six feet, thin, with a gaunt face. "I am here to conduct interviews on your recent mission. One of you . . . Alex Tran?" She consults a tablet, looks up at Tran. "What is your rank?"

"Tran left regular service as a staff sergeant." I gesture at him. "Put the knife away and get a shirt on."

"Yes, sir."

I turn back to Ashman. "I want to see my CO."

"I'm sorry, Captain. Colonel Abajian is not currently available."

"Colonel Abajian is not my CO, Lieutenant. Major William Kanoa is my CO and we are not consenting to interviews until I've seen him."

"Captain Shelley, the details of your operation are critical to assessing—"

"I want to see my CO. You get Kanoa here, and I'll tell you anything about the mission you want to know."

She opens her mouth like she's going to argue with me, but she decides against it. "I will communicate your concerns to Colonel Abajian."

"Thank you."

Abajian decides to ignore us. We get no further visitors that day or the next. We sleep a lot.

On day three, my inhaler runs dry. Maybe it had a mood enhancer in it, maybe I'm just starting to feel the decline in support from my skullnet, but frustration kicks in, turning quickly to anger.

Delphi is silent, Kanoa is silent, Leonid is gone, and for all I know, Abajian could have been sacked for carrying out an illegal operation—making it more likely we'll be arrested than offered a mission.

I need to know where this is going. So on day three, I step outside to talk to the MPs.

By this time, we've figured out that except for our guards, we're alone in this cluster of housing. There is no activity at the other residences, no vehicles on the road. It's possible

other areas of the base are still populated, but this corner
is a ghost town.

I open the front door. The snow that frosted the ground
when we first arrived has melted, but the lawn in front of
the residence is brown, the air is cold and crisp with a chill
wind, and gray clouds fill the sky. I hear the distant roar of
a passing airliner but nothing else.

Only one MP is in sight, strolling the sidewalk. That
one turns an anonymous black visor toward me as I step
out onto the covered stoop. A sudden crouch and three
long, bounding strides puts the soldier in front of me. It
takes every bit of idiot stubbornness I possess not to flee
into the house. I've been behind that black mask, rigged
in titanium, bulked out in chest armor, and heavily armed.
It's fucking intimidating, facing that down.

The MP speaks in a man's voice. "You are required to
stay inside, sir, with the door closed and blinds drawn."

"No, Specialist. I demand to talk to my commanding
officer, Major William Kanoa. *Now.*"

It's not smart to defy a direct order issued by an MP
rigged in a dead sister. I know that, but what the hell else
can I do? The specialist uses his arm hooks, forcefully
escorting me back through the door. The only thing my
venture earns me is bruised biceps.

I curse Kanoa, Abajian, Leonid. Myself. We should have
taken off on our own from Budapest and made them hunt
us down.

Right.

Without ETM behind us? They probably would have
picked us up as soon as we hit the street.

Joby forwards an email to me, saying my legs are ready to
ship. The manufacturer just needs a name and address. So

I use GPS to work out the address of the house where I'm imprisoned and I give it to them. Fuck security. The name I put on it is ETM 7-1.

Two days later I'm lying on the sofa, streaming music on my overlay—something loud and angry to match my mood—when the front door opens. A figure looms against a glowing backdrop of wintry light. I am so startled I launch over the back of the sofa. The only thing I can say for myself is that I manage to land feet-first. But then the joints in my broken foot slip, and I end up on my ass. I kill the music and scramble up as Kanoa comes in, closing the door behind him.

"Nice reaction time," he says, setting a midsize suitcase down on the floor.

"Where the *fuck* have you been?"

I am six days in on a gradual withdrawal from my skull-net's baseline maintenance, and I'm definitely feeling it. I give up my hiding place and come out from behind the sofa. "And why the *fuck* are you not signed into gen-com?"

"I am. Different unit."

That shuts me up for a few seconds. It tells me we've been cut loose. And why the hell am I surprised?

Logan and Tran charge into the living room, but they pull up short when they sense my mood. "We did what we had to do, Kanoa. A program launched in our heads and we executed it. And then we did what we had to do to stay alive. If you're going to let us go because of that, I don't give a shit. We're better off."

"It was for your own protection," Kanoa says. "I thought you might have figured that out."

"You know me better than that. I'm no optimist. I thought you were dead, or in prison."

He grunts. "Fair enough, and not all that far from the truth. Abajian has the keys to ETM 7-1. You know that. Cory Helms is in his pocket, and he wants to use us as his personal voodoo operators. I've been encouraging him to back the fuck off. Part of that was putting you at a distance. I had Bryson set it up so that when you finally came back online, your software would update to ETM 7-2 to lock Abajian out."

"I'm going to guess that didn't make the colonel happy."

"He buried me for a few days, but he still doesn't have the keys to 7-2."

"So, where are we now?" Logan asks.

"Same place we've been since Abajian stopped in at C-FHEIT. He has jobs he wants done, but that is not the way we work. We did Arid Crossroad because the Red was behind it."

Tran asks, "If things aren't settled with Abajian, how did you manage to get here?"

"The colonel can recognize a stalemate." Kanoa cracks a cold smile. "I heard that both sides of ETM 7 were proving uncooperative, demanding to see their CO. That made him think I might still be useful."

Tran laughs. "He must have figured out quick it's not a good idea to get Fadul mad."

Since Tran was recruited into 7-1, I don't think there's been a day at C-FHEIT that he hasn't found a way to piss off Fadul. "Tran? Serious question. Why haven't *you* figured that out?"

This gets a cocky smile. "Just a dumb grunt, sir."

I sit at one end of the sofa and ask Kanoa, "Are they okay?"

He sits in an armchair. "Julian is improving, but he probably won't return to active duty. Dunahee and Escamilla are out for another two weeks. Roman and Fadul are fine."

"So we're still understaffed. Papa says—" I catch myself. "Leonid Sergun—he says there's another mission. Do you know anything about it? We were brought here to discuss it, but that was a lie. No one's talking to us."

"I heard you refused to talk."

"I refused to debrief. I wanted to know what the hell was going on. *Is* there a mission?"

"There's talk of one. I only know about it in general outline and I don't know if it's meant to be ours. But if it is? We're not ready for it."

He gets up again, picks up his suitcase. It's a gray hardshell that doesn't appear to be very heavy. I jump as he lofts it onto the sofa next to me. "This caused some commotion when it was delivered to the front gate this morning. It came packed in foam inside a cardboard shipping container. Explosive Ordnance Disposal was called in. They considered blowing it up."

"*Fuck*," I growl, realizing what it has to be. I grab the suitcase by the handle and stand up with it. "Do you know how much this cost me?"

"Yes, actually, I do, since I was reviewing the accounts on the flight over here."

I head for my room, hobbling on my broken feet for the last time.

Tran is right behind me. "What is it?"

I throw the suitcase on the bed, pop the hasps, and open it.

"Holy shit," Tran says. Then he turns to yell back into the living room, "Hey Logan, Shelley's got new feet."

I sit on the bed, and with Tran watching, I slide up my trouser until I expose the knee joint on my right leg. I pop the leg off and drop it on the floor. Then I examine the joint. The connections look clean, so I snap the new leg in place. I grunt against a pulse of pain that shoots up my spine, but it's gone as soon as it comes.

"Let's see you move it," Tran says. "Does it work?"

I stretch my toes. Stand up. Put weight on the new leg. Walk around in a circle. It feels perfect.

Logan is standing in the door, arms crossed, watching me with a severe expression. "You ordered that?"

"No." I drop back onto the bed to swap out my left leg. "The engineer who designed these legs ordered them for me."

"And you made contact with him? You told him you were here?"

"I told the manufacturer—although Joby probably got a copy of the shipping notice."

"That is a fucking security violation, Shelley. Anyone paying attention knows where you are."

I snap the new left leg into the joint. This time, I'm ready for the flash of pain. "Being unfit for duty is a violation too. I wasn't going to let my CO nail me for that."

"Like you care what your CO thinks?" he asks in a low voice.

I let this pass without comment while I take a minute to pack up the old legs. They need to get shipped out to Joby. Shooing Logan out of the doorway, I head back to the living room.

Kanoa is waiting by the front door. "You ready?"

"Are we going back to C-FHEIT?"

"Now? No. We're staying in Germany. This is our base of operations for the next few weeks."

"The rest of the squad is coming in?"

"Depends on events. Depends if we take the mission. For now, you three *are* the squad. ETM 7-2, remember?"

"Three soldiers do not make a squad. We can't operate without more personnel."

"I know. But we're not moving forward at all unless

each of you passes a medical evaluation. Get yourselves cleared for duty, and then we'll see about bringing in 7-1."

I'm worried. What if I don't pass medical? My new legs give me the mobility I need, but what if my lungs don't hold up?

The MPs salute Kanoa as we walk in a group to a white SUV parked at the curb. Logan and Tran get into the back. I take the shotgun seat. Kanoa slides behind the wheel. But instead of starting the engine, he turns to me. "You feeling okay?"

"What? Why?"

His gaze drifts. He's looking at something in his overlay. "You're showing a lot of anxiety. We might need to get Bryson to adjust your baseline after all."

My skullnet's receiver is gone, but the transmitter works fine. It sends regular reports on my physical state, which Kanoa can pick up when I'm logged into gen-com. I cast a warning glance over my shoulder. Logan looks to heaven for comfort, Tran smirks, but neither says anything. I tell Kanoa, "Yeah, we'll probably need to talk about that."

I use my overlay to pull up a colored graph of my neurological status. The only time I ever look at this graph is when I want to teach the skullnet new routines. Then, the shifting colors can measure progress. I think *calm*, I imagine calm, I synthesize *calm* in my brain, and the graph reacts with a calm, light blue hue pushing out the anxious red.

I'm surprised it works that well—but then, the embedded AI has studied me for a long time.

Kanoa drives out of the housing area on a concrete

road tufted with dry weeds that sprout from jagged cracks. It's about four hundred meters through a brown field to the cluster of administrative buildings I saw on the garrison's satellite image. The first building we pass is a three-story monster with boarded-up windows that probably served as a barracks seventy years ago. Across the street from it is a newer structure, a sprawling one-story that looks like it dates from the 1960s. A flagpole stands in front of it, but no flag is flying. "Welcome to the command center," Kanoa says, pulling into a parking space in front of it.

There is no signage to support the building's identity, but there is a rigged MP on duty just inside the glass doors, HITR held across his body. He steps aside to let us pass.

The lobby is empty, the building silent except for our footsteps, but it's clean, the lights are on, and the air is fresh and warm.

We take a stairway down to the basement. Medical is behind an unmarked door. There is no receptionist, no assistant. Just the physician, who runs her tests, and then docks me for lingering damage in my lungs, claiming my lung capacity has been reduced by six percent. Tran doesn't show any pulmonary deficits, which isn't fucking fair because he was worse off than me coming out of the UGF.

"It's all in the genetics," Tran crows. "The primal power of my African side combined with the spiritual potency of my Asian ancestry has blessed me with superhuman recuperative powers. You're just too much of a blend, Shelley. Average all around."

I think I'll put him on point for the next mission, for a more direct test of his superhuman powers.

I'm allowed to pass though, out of deference to my

"superior physical condition," which is bullshit. The real
story, I suspect, is that the doctor is under orders to pass
us so long as she feels we won't collapse on the battlefield.

We return to the house, to find that our LCS gear has been
delivered in our absence.

Our helmets and dead sisters have been brought in from
C-FHEIT. Logan and I get our original weapons reissued,
absent the ammunition, while Tran gets a new HITR to
replace the one buried under the weight of a mountain.

There are new uniforms too. As always, they have no
rank insignia or emblems. The camo pattern isn't one I've
seen before. It's charcoal and brown—darker than day-use
desert camo, but way too light for night patrols. There are
new packs and armored vests in the same pattern.

Tran holds up a jacket, a skeptical eyebrow raised high.
"This is ugly as shit."

I have to agree. "What's this pattern designed for?" I ask
Kanoa. "Some dirty urban center?"

"That, among other things."

"So we're heading into urban combat?"

"The mission has not been designated."

I assume that's a yes. "I did urban combat in Bolivia. I
hated it."

"It's the worst," Logan agrees. "Kids and civilians everywhere."

There were kids at Black Cross too. Not something I
want to remember.

"It's supposed to be a new fabric," Kanoa says. "Light-
sensitive. Hold the jacket under a lamp, Tran."

The blinds are still closed, so all the living room lights
are on. Tran holds the jacket directly under a table lamp.
As soon as the bright light hits it, the pattern's meandering

charcoal lines fade and the fabric takes on light desert
colors. When Tran pulls it away from the direct light, the
dirty hues return. I reach over and turn off the light. Logan
switches off two more. The room dims to twilight, and the
camo darkens to charcoal-black.

"Edge," Tran says. "I like it."

We want to make sure everything is in working order. So
we rig up, strapping into our dead sisters, pulling on our
helmets, checking out the links in our new linked combat
squad. ETM 7-2. I watch the squad icons line up across the
bottom of my visor. Three strong. What bullshit. "Kanoa,
you and Abajian need to work out your differences, or we
are all fucked."

"Roger that. You won't be getting a mission until we do."

That night, after the moon rises, Kanoa sends us out on
a conditioning run. I am required to wear athletic shoes,
sweat pants, and a hoodie to disguise who and what I am.
Logan and Tran opt for the same, given that there's a light
fog, with the temperature below freezing.

Despite the fog, there's enough light from the moon to
see the road, the dark shapes of the neighboring houses,
and the silhouettes of two watching MPs. Neither makes a
move to interfere with us.

As soon as we hit the street, a faintly luminous blue path
appears in my overlay, marking the route Kanoa wants us
to run. We follow the projected path through the housing
area, toward the airfield.

"Check the two houses ahead," Logan says. "Lights."

He's right. It's just a hint of light, seeping out past blackout blinds. I turn to look back at our own residence, and
it's the same: only a trace of light visible, though we left
lights on in the living room.

"Kanoa's probably housed in one," Logan says. "But who's in the other?"

"Want me to knock on the door?" Tran asks.

Tempting. But we're already past. "It's probably where the MPs are staying," I say. "Let's keep going."

Our breath steams in the night. We reach the airfield, run the length of the runway in both directions, then loop around to pass the haunted-looking old barracks and the command center. There are no other lights anywhere, but twice we glimpse MPs rigged in dead sisters patrolling beyond the road.

We repeat the route three times. By the time we're done, my GPS logs a seven-mile run.

Kanoa shows up again the next afternoon. FaceValue confirms my initial impression: He's worried.

"What's going on?" I ask him.

"Stop trying to mind-read me."

"Something's off," I insist.

"Colonel Abajian is here. He wants to see your squad run through an urban combat exercise. Tonight."

"Can't do it. I don't have a squad."

"I know, and that was the subject of a vigorous conversation. But for tonight's exercise, you are to assume the mission has gone south and your squad has been reduced to three."

"At which point we should get extracted."

"Extraction has failed. The mission still needs to be completed. Highest priority."

"Air support?"

"Negative."

"So he wants to see how far we can get before we're gunned down?"

"He wants to know he's offering this mission to the right squad."

"*What* mission?"

"Survive tonight, and maybe we'll find out."

At 2100 we rig up in armor and bones and trot over to the hangar, where Captain Montrose—the same officer who met us when we got off the plane from Budapest—goes over the scenario for the evening. "Insertion is by a stealth Black Hawk, but since we don't have access to one for this exercise, we're using a standard Black Hawk instead."

Tran snickers. "Nothing stealthy about that."

"Shut the fuck up," I advise him.

Montrose continues. "You will be inserted six blocks from the target, a distance designed to protect the gunship from ground-to-air defenses. You will make your way past resistance—"

"Professional?"

"Irregulars."

"Got it."

"The target is a basement-level biowarfare lab."

We're hunting the angel of death, Tran says over gen-com.

Montrose's gaze shifts to Tran, which tells me he's monitoring gen-com, but he doesn't comment, just continues with his briefing. "You will take control of the facility. Collect intelligence and transmit all data to Command. Relaying that data is your highest priority. We must collect evidence of the specific bioweapons under development. You will then hold the facility until Command authorizes you to destroy it."

"Then we get extracted?" I ask.

"Assuming you get that far, the exercise is over."

I trade a skeptical look with Logan. Our last two

missions had deficient extraction plans. But this is just an exercise.

"This is a timed operation," Captain Montrose adds. "The goal is to get in, get the data, and transmit it within sixteen minutes."

It takes longer than that to discuss the details and to issue nonlethal ammo.

It's just an exercise. I remind myself of that as the Black Hawk puts down on the cracked and weed-grown concrete outside the hangar, because my heart is racing, powered by a cocktail of anxiety and anticipation.

"Combat-hyper?" Kanoa asks over gen-com. He's along virtually as our handler.

"I like it that way."

The Black Hawk's side doors are open. We board. Gunners are in place at the forward windows. There are no seats, but then, we don't need any. This is going to be a very short flight. At the crew chief's instruction, we sit in the right-hand doorway, feet dangling into space as we lift away from the concrete. We roar over the base, just above the treetops, with no lights visible below us.

But we're high enough to see beyond the perimeter fence. Just a few kilometers away, the lights of surrounding towns blaze in night vision. Cars are in motion on the streets and highways. It's a different world out there.

The crew chief speaks over our helmet audio. "Fifteen seconds to insertion."

We come in low above an ugly sprawl of concrete block buildings—some burned out, some broken—a mockup of a war-torn urban combat zone. We're greeted by simulated gunfire, blazing in night vision. The Black Hawk's gunners open up in response as we drop with stomach-curdling speed toward a small square. But our descent is a feint. The square isn't big enough for the Black Hawk to land. The rotor wash sends debris spinning away below us as we skew sideways toward a flat rooftop spiked with antennas and netted with empty laundry lines. A low wall encloses it. The pilot settles a skid on the wall. The crew chief barks, "Move out!" And I jump. A horizontal evacuation, keeping my head low, landing in a crouch. Logan and Tran come down beside me.

I sweep my HITR in a half circle, letting the muzzle cams scan the scene so my tactical AI can assess the surroundings. I do a simultaneous visual assessment, noting that the laundry lines are low enough to snag our helmets. Debris is skipping across the roof, remnants of chicken coops and cardboard boxes that pile up against the enclosing wall. Off to my right, there's a break in the wall that the map shows as leading to an exterior stair.

The dim glow of a projected path appears in my visor, pointing to the suspected stairway. The Black Hawk lifts off behind us. One of the gunners resumes firing, the sound either suppressed by my helmet or simulated by it, I don't know.

We are operating without a dedicated angel because the insertion was too precipitous to allow us to deploy one. But we do have data from a high-flying observational drone that allows the battle AI to continuously update a map of the neighborhood. We also have seekers—army-issued microdrones with sound-damping technology, designed for urban surveillance.

I shift my HITR to one hand, open a chest pouch, and pull out the first of the two seekers I carry. "Deploying Seeker-1."

"Roger that," Kanoa says. He'll be handling the device. I hold it clear of my body. He signals the seeker's helicopter blades to deploy on their struts and spin up. As soon as I feel a tug of pressure, I let it go. The seeker streaks away, buzzing softly as it follows the projected path.

"Street and stairway show clear," Kanoa reports. "But it won't last."

"Roger that. Logan, move out."

"Moving."

He scuttles along the path, bent over, his HITR scanning for targets. Tran and I fan out to either side of him so that we can cover him on the stairway. But I pull up when I see motion on the roof across the street.

The rules of engagement limit aggressive action to known combatants. We are not to fire on civilians, even armed civilians, unless the battle AI designates a target. But if we're being shot at, we can shoot back.

"Kanoa, across the street, what am I seeing?"

"Undetermined."

Whatever it was, it's gone.

I move up to the wall, peer over. We are three stories up. The stairway is a steel fire escape that descends in six flights. The street below is clear.

A stealth helicopter isn't quiet. It's just quieter than a standard Black Hawk, so we assume the enemy is aware that we have arrived in the zone. That means speed counts for more than stealth. Logan jumps the first flight of stairs, coming down with *bang!* on the landing. The rusting bolts holding up the stairway twitch. He turns and jumps again.

Tran moves to follow.

"Tran, hold up." We watch the street. No enemy in sight. The drone has already turned the corner to the south. The staircase shakes as Logan hits the third landing. "Okay, *go.*"

With the weight of two soldiers on the stairs, the bolts jump harder. I try not to watch them, keeping my attention on the street.

"Cross street clear," Kanoa says.

"I've got movement to the north."

Night vision shows me the muzzle of an automatic rifle scanning around a corner at street level. A targeting circle pops up on my visor. Whoever is holding that gun is still out of sight. I shoot anyway. A simulated spark jumps off the tip of the muzzle as I'm awarded a hit. The weapon vanishes from sight.

Logan reaches the street. He drops into a crouch, covering the north end. I start down, bounding after Tran, not caring at this point if I bring the stairway down. I want to move out before enemy forces have a chance to trap us.

"Tran, take point. Move south."

"Yes, sir."

The seeker is out ahead of us, sniffing for explosive chemicals, listening for motion, scanning the rooftops and windows. As soon as I reach the street, I turn to follow Tran.

"Clear to cross the intersection," Kanoa says.

"Roger that!"

Tran sprints, making it across in three bounds. He continues down the block, but at a more cautious pace. I keep my interval, ten meters behind him. Logan follows.

That's one block down, five to go, before we reach the entrance of the target lab.

The seeker pulses a motion alarm, highlighting a second-floor window on the left side of the street. Tran hurls himself against the wall, his HITR aimed overhead. Nothing happens. No target posts on my visor.

"Unconfirmed," Kanoa says.

By this time, I've caught up with Tran. "I'm taking point."

I move out, sprinting to the corner. I crouch there while the seeker reconnoiters the cross street.

"Clear to cross the intersection."

We get past the next two blocks with no opposition. Then all hell breaks loose.

Gunfire erupts from a third-story window across the street from me. There's more gunfire from the rooftop above. I want to stay in this war game, so I throw myself sideways, diving through a broken window into the shelter of the closest building—a burned-out shell—landing on my shoulder and rolling to my feet.

Two strides take me back to the broken window. I've got my HITR raised to shoot high. My AI marks the third-floor site where the shots originated, but before I can return fire, a grenade takes out the target window in a white flash, the muffled boom echoing off the buildings.

Over gen-com, Tran pronounces a single word of quiet triumph. "Slam."

I shift my aim to the rooftop, where the second shooter was positioned. I can't see a target, but I can at least discourage any further gunfire. "Grenade," I tell the AI. "Set distance."

For the exercise, we use flash-bang grenades: light and noise but not generally fatal.

A green light flares in my visor, indicating the next grenade in line has been programmed to go off at the requested distance. I pull the second trigger on my HITR, but I don't stay to see the result. I jump through the window. As the grenade goes off overhead, I'm sprinting to the end of the block. When I get there, I glance at my squad map, confirming Tran and Logan close behind, and then I bound across the intersection.

I'm ahead of the seeker now. That's bad, because I see motion a block farther on. I crouch behind the charred hulk of a car. "Kanoa, I need eyes."

"We've lost the seeker."

I reach into my chest pouch to get the next one, but my gaze, and most of my attention, is on the street a block ahead where night vision shows me what I think are two soldiers—no, three—rigged in armor and bones.

I get the seeker out, set it on the dirty sidewalk. "Deploying Seeker-2."

"Roger that."

The little device buzzes to life and lifts away, streaking south.

"Do we have allies here?" I ask Kanoa.

"Negative."

"Who are the rigged soldiers?"

"Unknown." He sounds angry. "Best guess from Intelligence—the competition."

"Another outfit trying to take this lab?"

"Roger that."

"I can't believe Command brought in a squad of LCS soldiers to run against us." It doesn't make sense, because there is always a shortage of LCS squads in the field. "If they can do that, why the fuck don't they bring in the rest of *my* squad?" Something else occurs to me. "Or are these hired guns?"

"Unknown! But you are cleared to engage."

"Roger that." The ROE says we are not to fire unless fired upon, but that rule exists to protect civilian lives. These are not civilians.

I check the squad map. Tran is a few meters back, sheltering behind the corner of the building. Logan is farther away, beyond the intersection.

"Logan, move to the opposite side of the street. Then cross the intersection. As soon as you reach the curb, we're both going to hit that block with grenades. Got it?"

"Roger that."

"Tran, you stick with me."

"Yes, sir."

Logan crosses the main street in two bounds. He draws the interest of the enemy. A grenade goes off in the street. It's not a direct hit, but Logan's icon goes yellow, indicating he's taken shrapnel. The battle AI designates it a minor wound; it doesn't lock up his rig. He transits the cross street next, takes cover behind the corner building, and using his muzzle cams, he lines up a shot. So do I.

I stand up long enough to launch a grenade over the roof of the wrecked car I've been using for shelter. Then I drop down again. I wait for the double explosion—my grenade and his. Then I take off, running hard the length of the block, with Tran a few meters behind me.

"Target overhead," Kanoa says.

I throw myself back against the closest building. Tran crouches at my feet. He starts shooting south down the street while I look up.

A gold glow projected on my visor marks a fast-moving target. I cover it and shoot.

The battle AI registers a hit.

"Enemy seeker down," Kanoa says.

"Good. Tran, you got anything?"

"Negative. No visible targets."

"Logan?"

"Negative."

I flinch as an explosion goes off. I don't see it directly, but I see the flash, hear the *boom*. It's from the cross street at the end of the block. Gunfire starts up from the roof of the target building. I look for the rooftop shooters, but I can't see them. I can't see any muzzle flash.

"Shooters are on the opposite side of the building, aiming south," Kanoa says.

Aiming at our competition. Can't ask for a better opportunity than that.

"Advance!"

We run the block, cross the intersection, and we're there. It's a big building, filling up the entire block, and like the rest of our simulated city, it's a wreck—but we're supposed to interpret that as camouflage for the high-tech lab in the protected basement.

We are to enter through a basement door in the middle of the block.

The gun battle around the corner rages on, but not all of the building's defenders are engaged. Through the seeker, we watch one of the rooftop shooters falling back to cover our side of the building.

"Enemy on the roof," Kanoa says.

Tran covers me while I step away from the building, just far enough to get an angle on the figure three stories above—but the defender disappears before I get a shot off, and I get tagged with a nonfatal in the helmet. That would have given me a nasty headache if this was real.

Logan is already past us, advancing on the target: a steel door at the bottom of a half flight of stairs. "Confirm target," he says over gen-com.

"Target confirmed," Kanoa responds.

Logan tosses a grenade down the stairs, falls back as the flash and *boom* go off.

"Tran," I order, "cover us."

I catch up with Logan at the top of the stairway.

The door looks intact.

"Consider it open," Kanoa says.

I use a hand signal to instruct Logan to take point. He jumps to the bottom of the stairs, tries the door knob, and the damn thing just opens. He pushes it back only a couple of inches, just far enough to pitch another grenade through. After it pops, he sticks the muzzle of his HITR in, scanning the scene with his muzzle cams.

"Image," I tell Kanoa.

He posts the video feed to my visor. Inside is a small, barren lobby with charred walls, empty of everything but a few bits of debris. Across the lobby is another steel door that should lead deeper into the building. Logan moves in. I jump down the stairs. "Tran, come in behind me."

If I had more personnel, I would leave at least two soldiers outside to hold the door, but Tran's not going to be able to do that on his own, and our priority is to get to the lab. So Tran comes with us.

Logan crosses the lobby, tries the next door, and again the damn thing just opens. He scans the other side with his muzzle cams. The feed shows a corridor that runs the width of the building. We are at one end. It's hard to see any detail because it's dark, even for night vision. I can make out two side doors, one on the right and one on the left, about a third of the way down. I can't see anything beyond that. So I get a tiny LED light out of one of the pockets on my vest. As Logan pushes the door open, I switch on the light and pitch it.

It spins end over end, its light flashing in my visor and bouncing off the floor, the ceiling, the walls. For a fraction of a second I can see all the way to the corridor's end. Two-thirds of the way down, there's a second set of side doors. Both are open, with a rigged soldier emplaced in each. All I can see of each soldier is an arm strut, and the HITRs they're holding, aimed up the corridor at us.

Grenades launch from both weapons with a *whump* amplified by my helmet. I try to duck back into the lobby. Too late. The flash-bangs go off in my face. My visor blazes red—and the battle AI takes me out of the game. The joints of my dead sister lock up and I go down hard on the floor. My helmet audio shifts to white noise, my visor goes black, my overlay's display blinks out, and I am dumped from gen-com.

My hands are strapped to my frozen rig, but I still manage to clutch my HITR with a finger curled over the first trigger—not that it matters. The weapon will have been deactivated too.

Panic stirs and tries to make an escape. I feel like I've been transported back to Black Cross after the EMP knocked out all my electronic systems.

And my skullnet is down to 60 percent of baseline support.

I listen to my own harsh breathing. It's up to me to keep a grip on a rational state of mind. No outside assists. I work at it. I push back against the fear. *It's just an exercise. No one is going to hurt me.*

Logan is probably as dead as I am, but the flashes of light seeping around the edge of my visor hint that Tran is still fighting. Then the flashes stop. After that, there's nothing.

I envision being trapped like this for hours, for days, forever. I listen to my breathing. Fast. Way too fast. I don't want to wind up screaming hysterically. Then it comes to me: I'm not on my own. I still have the skullnet. No outside input allowed, but I can still communicate with it. It's still part of me. And I think, *Calm. Be calm. Lock it all down.*

It works, just like it did yesterday. But this time, I don't even need the graph of my neurological status. My breathing slows; my fingers ease their grip on my HITR. It still feels like I've been lying dead for fucking forever, but I can handle it on my own.

I start counting out loud just so I can measure the passing of time, and at what I estimate to be three minutes and twenty-one seconds the white noise in my helmet shuts off. Captain Montrose speaks over the audio. "The exercise is over. All participants are restored. Rendezvous at the command center in ten minutes."

My overlay and my visor both wake up. Night vision kicks in. My dead sister unlocks and I can move my limbs again.

I look up to see two rigged soldiers standing over me. Not Tran, not Logan. The proportions are wrong. The enemy, then. Hired guns. My squad map affirms their anonymity, noting their positions with nameless orange dots.

The one closest, the shorter one, offers me a gloved hand half enclosed in a frame of struts. A symbolic gesture, given the assist available to me from my dead sister. A gesture of trust. I clasp the hand and, using the power of my own suit, I kick myself to my feet.

The enemy soldier speaks off-com. "Sorry about taking you down like that, Shelley. I didn't know you were playing in this game."

It's Jayne Vasquez.

Fuck me.

From day one of LCS training, the emphasis is on coordination. Our challenge is learning to work together as a fluid, adaptable unit, with each soldier utilized to his or her best capabilities within the framework of the squad and of the mission. In a high-stress combat environment, that only works if we trust each other's abilities and loyalties. We don't risk that trust by training against each other. Ever. It's not always harmony in the barracks, but in the field, we are always on the same side.

But Jaynie is not on my side anymore.

"What are you doing here?" I ask her. I'm speaking off-com, because we don't have shared communications.

She answers cautiously, "You didn't know I'd be here?"

Someone moves behind me. A reverse helmet cam shows me Logan getting up off the floor. "No. I thought you were busy with your Mars project."

"Didn't Karin tell you? We've been grounded."

"That's right. She did tell me that." One piece of good news. I eye the soldier behind Jaynie. "Roman?"

"Yes, sir."

"You came out against me?"

"We didn't know it was you, sir. We were expecting irregulars. No one else."

"Who else is here? Fadul?"

"She's outside. Escamilla and Dunahee weren't part of the exercise. They're still waiting on a medical clearance."

I am wired on the dregs of adrenaline and panic. That's not helping my temper. Neither is the growing awareness that we've all been set up.

I hit gen-com. "Kanoa."

No answer.

"Kanoa, I need you to confirm who—"

Montrose speaks again, cutting me off. "Captain Shelley, you are to report to the command center *now* by order of Colonel Abajian."

That's the confirmation I need.

"Colonel Abajian can go fuck himself, Captain. I don't play games like this. I'm done."

I turn to go. Logan steps out of my way as I head outside.

There's enough moonlight that I can see without night vision. So as I start up the stairs, I take off my helmet. That's a violation of regulations, but like I said, I'm fucking done. I'm not playing Abajian's games anymore.

Tran is waiting at the top of the stairs. "Come on, Shelley. We're ETM. You can't—"

"We're not ETM anymore," I tell him. "Not with Abajian holding the strings."

I step around him, only to be blocked by another soldier, one who's more than a foot shorter than I am. I know of only one LCS soldier of such tiny size. "*Shit*," I whisper. "Flynn?"

I don't know what I was expecting from her. Definitely not her arm hook darting out to catch my shoulder strut. Flynn is in a worse mood than I am. She uses her entire body and every bit of amplified force from her dead sister to yank me off balance. I'm about to go down when she body-slams me onto the hood of a junked car parked against the curb. I drop my helmet, but I somehow keep my head from hitting. I think my back struts leave an imprint, but I don't look. I roll away, landing on my feet. Then I backpedal into the street, still holding onto my HITR.

"Goddamn it, Flynn! What the fuck is wrong with you?"

"It's *you!*" she shouts, her voice shrill as a teenager's, though she must be twenty by now. "You fuckin' betrayed us all when you left us, LT. You let us think you were dead. Gone with all the others! You're such a piece of shit! You're just a fuckin' piece of shit."

This is not the best night I've ever had.

By this time, Jaynie is at the top of the stairs. "Flynn, stand down!"

Flynn ignores her. She starts after me again, but Tran at least is still on my side. He intercepts her, using the same technique on her that she used on me. Grabbing her arm strut, he hurls her against the building. Then Jaynie's between them, pushing Tran aside. "Flynn! You want to do this job or not?"

If Flynn answers, I don't hear it. But Jaynie lets her go.

Flynn straightens up, takes her helmet off, glares at me. She's not wearing a skullcap. Jaynie must have made her give it up. Her hair is white in the moonlight, grown out to a short cut, soaked with sweat. "You should have fuckin' taken me with you, LT."

"I did what I had to do, Flynn."

I flinch as Fadul's low voice speaks unexpectedly from just behind my ear. "She's a kid, for Christ's sake. You could at least tell her you're fucking sorry."

"I'm not sorry." Flynn might be dead now if I'd brought her into ETM.

Fadul walks past me, picks up my helmet, turns around, and shoves it in my gut. I grab it, of course. I've got no choice. "Gen-com just updated. Kanoa checked in. He says to put your helmet back on and get your ass over to the command center, wherever the fuck that is. He thinks you've got a problem with your wiring. Ask me, it runs deeper than that."

I think Fadul is probably right, but I don't put my helmet on, and I lock down my overlay to keep Kanoa out, because I am done.

I start back through the ruins, carrying my helmet in one hand, my HITR in the other. The night is clear and cold, with the countryside washed in moonlight. It's beautiful. And it's only a kilometer and half by road to the command center, with the residence just a few hundred meters beyond. That's nothing for infantry.

After a block, Logan catches up with me. He startles me by pulling his helmet off too. It's rare to see him break the rules. "We're walking back."

I glance behind us to see everyone on the move, dark shapes in the silvery light. Tran is conferring with Roman and Fadul. Jaynie is walking with Flynn. All of them have their helmets on, but now that I know who they are, it's easy for me to identify them.

"Shelley, you need to put your helmet back on. Gen-com updated. We're all one squad now."

"No, we're done. ETM is done. We cannot operate with Abajian fucking up the system."

"We're not done."

I stop and face him. "You want to stay here? That's your choice. I'm leaving. I've done too much to put up with Abajian's bullshit, abandoning us in the field, locking us up in fucking protective custody, taking half my squad away from me and running them as the enemy. You want to deal with that, Logan, it's yours. Take a field promotion. You're in charge, because I'm done." By this time the squad has caught up with us, but I ignore them. I turn and start walking again. "I'm just going to change into my civilian clothes, then I'm on my way. Shouldn't be hard to hitchhike to Berlin. I'll find the American embassy, make them issue me a passport. Then I'm going home."

"You're dreaming."

Delphi is out there somewhere. I decide I'm going to find her, even if she has moved on.

Logan is shadowing me again. "The war's not over."

"I fucking know that! But I can't operate without trust, and I don't trust Abajian. He put us up against our own people. What the fuck was that about?"

"I don't know."

I stop and look back again to where Jaynie is following just a few meters behind. "And what the fuck are Vasquez and Flynn doing here?"

"They're linked into 7-1."

"Jaynie! Does that mean you're on our side?"

She stops. "I don't know, Shelley. What side would that be?" The squad gathers behind her. They are an array of silhouettes in the moonlight, the matte-black faces of their visors revealing nothing human, and suddenly I'm not sure I can tell them apart anymore. Not even Flynn. Interchangeable parts moved around the globe by an entity whose interests only partially align with our own.

"Why are you here, Jaynie? Why are you and Flynn part of this? It's been a long time since you turned civilian."

Flynn says, "We never turned civilian."

Jaynie says, "The war got personal."

Kanoa is right that I've got a problem with my wiring. A self-induced problem, it's true, but it's a problem all the same. As soon as Jaynie says *personal,* my brain kicks into overdrive and I know, I know, I know she means Delphi, something has happened to Delphi. A flush explodes across my skin, my heart races, and I have to talk around a sucking, empty absence when I ask, "Who?"

"You know who Yana Semakova is?"

Relief washes in. She sees it on my face; she doesn't have to ask the reason. "Karin is okay. So far."

"They got Rawlings," Flynn growls.

Shit. Colonel Trevor Rawlings was a pompous old fart and we had our differences, but he wanted the best for the country and he was an integral part of missions that made a real difference in the world.

"Rawlings was first," Jaynie says. "He was killed almost three weeks ago. We didn't even know it was a hit. An allergic reaction. It happens, right? But after Yana, we knew. It's a matter of time—"

"I've seen a list of victims."

"It's a matter of time until we all wind up on that list. I thought it was the Red—"

"Is it?"

She hesitates. Then says, "Don't think so, or I wouldn't be here. Abajian's crew says they know who's behind it—or they think they know."

"That's why you're here, then? You're going after the angel of death? That's the mission's target?"

"That's the official target," Jaynie affirms.

Giving me one more reason to despise Abajian. He hasn't told me a damned thing about why I'm here, but he's briefed Jaynie.

Of course he had to, to get her on board.

Jaynie adds, "It's a mission that needs to be invisible, off-budget, done by nobody."

"Meaning us," Fadul says. "Existential Threat Management. Because dirt doesn't stick to ghosts."

"You still have the skills?" I ask Jaynie.

"I think Abajian was testing that tonight."

Maybe.

She goes on. "I took a hint from Carl Vanda. Me and Flynn and Karin, we set up our own security company. We train all the time. Think of it as Cryptic Arrow 2. So, are you in? Or are you going to be hitchhiking to Berlin?"

I shrug. "It's our mission only if the Red's behind it— and if Abajian backs off."

"Put your helmet on."

I do it. Gen-com links me in. The squad's icons line up, low in my field of view. Nine of us, because Escamilla and Dunahee are logged in too, though their status shows brown, not cleared for duty. I check the squad map. They're at the command center.

"Looks like you're our senior officer, ma'am."

Fadul's low, dangerous laugh reaches in over my helmet audio. "Shit, Shelley. Everyone knows Vasquez isn't as crazy as you. Odds are she'll live a lot longer."

"That's bullshit, Fadul. Vasquez thinks she's going to Mars. How crazy is that?"

The dead sisters encourage a long, bouncy stride that gets us to the command center in just a few minutes, even at a walk. The building looks dark and uninhabited, but as we approach, the front door buzzes and unlocks, spilling a slice of light onto the ground, green in night vision. Fadul goes in first. I follow her into the dimly lit interior, peeling off my helmet again as soon as I'm inside. A rigged MP is standing sentry in the lobby just like the first time I was here, a HITR held across his body.

Kanoa is waiting for us at the mouth of a shadowy hallway. Escamilla and Dunahee are with him, all three in combat uniforms. I cross the lobby, trade fist-bumps and *hoo-yah*'s with my soldiers, and then turn to Kanoa. "We need to get Abajian out—"

"Not here," he cuts me off. "Not now. Not even over gen-com." He raises his voice to address the squad. "Get out of your gear. Leave it—and your weapons—here. The MP will see that they're secure."

We do it, un-cinching from the dead sisters and then folding the frames into their compact-carry configuration. They go in neat formation against the lobby wall, with an armored vest draped over the frame, a helmet placed on top, and a HITR leaning against the right side. Seven sets in all.

We follow Kanoa down the hall to the lighted doorway of a briefing room. Inside, five rows of six seats face a slightly elevated table, with a podium on one side and a projection screen on the wall behind. Sitting at one end of the table is ETM 7-1's traitorous intelligence liaison, Cory

Helms. I don't think I'll be forgiving him anytime soon. A second chair, closer to the podium, is empty.

Captain Montrose is at the podium, consulting with Lieutenant Ashman, the intelligence officer who came to the house with orders to debrief our last mission. As we come in, she looks up, watching us with a skeptical gaze. "Please be seated," she says.

A seat in the fourth row is already occupied. I slide in next to Leonid Sergun.

"Where the hell have you been?" I ask him.

He's wearing a black coat, his white hair freshly buzzed to stubble. He turns to look at me, eyes stern beneath unruly eyebrows. "I have been on site for this mission, renewing old friendships and making arrangements. Not in vain, I trust? Has your god assigned this mission to you?"

I have to admit, "I don't know."

The rest of the squad moves up front, taking most of the seats in the first and second rows. Fadul is the exception. She slides into row three, one seat diagonally in front of me. Behind us, the door bangs shut and Kanoa strides past to a first-row seat.

I tell Leonid, "I took your suggestion. And I unsubscribed from direct updates."

He raises an eyebrow. He doesn't know what I mean. Not exactly. But he gives a short nod of approval before turning back to the podium. In a low voice, he says, "Captain Montrose has done most of the mission planning. He is a capable officer."

"And Abajian?"

I hear a skeptical grunt. "I am sure he is good at politics."

I smile, lean back, cross my arms over my chest. "Politics can be useful."

"Very much so."

"But so can a less-active leadership style."

Fadul turns around, making no secret that she is following the conversation, her bright eyes amused.

"He doesn't trust you, Shelley," Leonid says in the same
low voice. "He doesn't trust ETM 7-1. But these soldiers
gathered here, they have a reputation for doing impossible things, and he has been told to see that you take this
mission."

"Told by who? I thought this was a closed circle."

"Abajian serves your president. It's interesting, no? You
don't trust him. He doesn't trust you. But the president of
your country trusts you both. Who misjudges?"

Fadul smiles and turns to face front again. I scowl. I
don't have an answer for that. Up front, Captain Montrose
leaves the podium to Lieutenant Ashman, who looks
askance for a moment, as if she's listening to a message
delivered over her farsights.

Her gaze shifts back to her audience: eight of us from
ETM, plus Jaynie and Flynn, and Papa. "Colonel Abajian
has arrived and will be joining us shortly. In the mean-
time, I would like to open this briefing by emphasizing
that we *do not know* the full reach and extent of the enemy's
penetration of our own command structure—and that is
the reason for using irregular forces. This operation must
remain secret and utterly invisible to everyone—"

The latch bangs on the door behind us. I jump hard,
instinctively reaching for the pistol I'm not carrying as I
rise to my feet, turning to face what's coming.

The door swings open. Abajian strides in. We trade a
glare. He heads to the front. I start to sit down again, but
then I realize he's not alone. Delphi comes in behind him.
She catches the door, holds it open long enough to slip
through, then lets it click shut.

She's wearing a white pullover sweater and gray
slacks. A coat is draped over her arm. Her blond hair

is pulled back into a ponytail, and her transparent far-sights hardly obscure the bright blue of her eyes as they fix on me.

Up front, Lieutenant Ashman starts speaking again. "This operation," she repeats, "*must* remain secret—" And then she interrupts herself. "Captain Shelley?"

I turn around. It's like I've been staring at the sun and I need to look away.

"Yes, Lieutenant?"

"We are trying to begin this briefing, Captain. If you would join us?"

I sit down without looking behind me again. I think it was an illusion. A hallucination exploding in my wired brain.

"It is imperative," Lieutenant Ashman says, "that this operation remain utterly invisible to everyone outside of this room, right up until the moment we launch. We can trust no one else, because *anyone* could be an operative working against the current administration and the democratic future of our country."

The hallucination I'm suffering is not just visible. I hear her moving behind me as she takes a seat in the empty last row. It's a tactile hallucination too. I flinch as her hand squeezes my shoulder. "Vasquez wants me as her handler," she whispers.

I reach back and put my hand over hers, wondering how many times I can say I'm sorry.

But that's not why she's here.

She squeezes my shoulder one more time. Then she pulls away.

Calm, I tell my skullnet. *Lock it down.* And it obeys me, sending a cold, clear, analytical mood washing across my brain, a mood that reflects an ethic I've come to live by:

Mission first.

It's not the Red whispering in my head. It's just me.
Mission first.
Cerebral graffiti graven on my brain years ago.

The first bit of the presentation is a video of President Monteiro.

She is pacing back and forth in front of a gray government-issue steel desk with a windowless, unpainted concrete wall in the background. Monteiro is in her fifties, Caucasian, with short blond hair and sharp brown eyes that have begun to look a little weary. Dressed in a white blouse and gray slacks, she looks thinner than she should be.

After two turns, she stops abruptly and returns the camera's gaze. "I am recording this video in what I'm told is a secure bunker. No spies. No listening devices." She smiles. "Nothing better to inflame the suspicions of your enemies than a well-kept secret, right?"

She begins pacing again, her hands on her hips, her lips half curled. "I will state the obvious and say that in my administration, mistakes have been made. When I accepted this position, I presumed that twenty-four years of army service had taught me a sufficient cynicism, but eighteen months serving as president of the United States has shown me I was not nearly cynical enough." Again she turns to the camera.

"Wars are no longer fought just among nations. There are organizational layers enfolding the globe that have nothing to do with national borders. Some are clumsy, like the Shahin Council's attempt to carry out Broken Sky. That doesn't mean they're easy to defeat. Not when they're widespread, when their operations are as thin and fluid as smoke, when they don't give a damn about who or what gets hurt.

"James Shelley, Ray Logan, and Alex Tran, you deserve the thanks of a grateful nation for your recent actions, but those actions must remain secret, so all I can offer you is my own thanks and gratitude."

Without turning around, Fadul gives me a mocking thumbs-up. I know it's mocking, because this is Fadul.

"But there are worse enemies," Monteiro says. "There is a cabal in the world far more sophisticated than the plotters behind Broken Sky. They do not represent any specific country, creed, or philosophy. Their goal is to consolidate their own power by installing puppet governments around the world. To this end, they are waging a new style of war, a quiet war, a very careful war of disruption carried out on many fronts. The Arctic War is a symptom. So is Broken Sky. So is August-19.

"August-19 is the codename we've given to the quiet assassinations that have ravaged every large national government around the world—over two hundred sixty people dead so far in an ongoing assault against the world's leadership, at least that part of it not already in the service of the enemy. The effect of this assault is pernicious, not just because of the loss of life, but also because of the fear and the suspicion that infects the survivors. Already, members of my administration are questioning one another's loyalty simply because they remain alive. There are rumors of purges in other parts of the world. We haven't gotten to that point yet, but if this goes on, we will."

She squeezes her eyes briefly shut, shakes her head. But when she looks up again, her gaze is unwavering. "August-19 is the reason you are here today. I am entrusting this recording to Colonel Abajian so that I may personally ask all of you who are present to commit an illegal act—*another* illegal act—in the service of your country. I acknowledge this as a hypocritical request, given my own lectures to some here regarding the supremacy of the rule of law. But our Republic is under assault, as are so many other governments. Colonel Abajian will present the mission scenario. There will be no retribution, no arrests, no punishment if you choose not to accept it. I will only say that if word of what we are planning gets out before we are ready to launch, there will be hell to pay."

The video ends abruptly in a black screen.

"Wipe it," Colonel Abajian says. "And overwrite the file traces."

Lieutenant Ashman presents an overview of the threat:

"The substance deployed so effectively by August-19 is a molecular weapon. It's a kind of bioactive allergen—you may think of it as artificial pollen—tailored very specifically to induce a severe allergic reaction in a target individual, resulting in anaphylactic shock and consequent death by asphyxiation. Each attack deploys a slightly different version. To be so specifically effective, the target's genetic makeup must be known ahead of time to the designer. Deployment is through air systems. Sometimes air-conditioning, sometimes by releasing the affective dust close to the target. Though the weapon is bioactive, it is *not* a living thing. It is not contagious and it cannot reproduce or spread beyond its initial release. Unless you are specifically targeted, you do not have reason to fear it."

"Unless they modify the coding to go universal," Leonid mutters.

Fadul glances over her shoulder, meeting my gaze. More than ever, I am sure: This is the target we've been hunting on our look-and-see missions.

"Why not deploy a more generalized weapon?" Lieutenant Ashman asks. "The implication, of course, is that

August-19 could, but chooses not to, as a 'humanitarian' gesture."

The propaganda angle is clear: Unpopular leaders can be selectively removed while the people they exploited are left unharmed, perhaps even cheering—at least until the system spins apart.

"We believe the weapon is the product of self-taught bio-hackers rather than formally educated geneticists, making the involved individuals harder to identify. They appear to be hired guns, motivated by money, not by any creed or philosophy.

"We have been hunting these individuals and their base of operations for over two months. We believe we have finally established the general location of the lab where the core of the work is being performed. This breakthrough was made as a result of information recovered during Arid Crossroad, specifically, from data contained in the farsights of Issam Salib. We have no doubt Mr. Salib was targeted for assassination because of his knowledge of locally inte-grated AIs, although we do not believe he was directly involved in August-19.

"The location of the August-19 facility eluded us for so long because it was camouflaged by the activity of an L-AI. Once we understood that, we were able to modify our search algorithms to account for the effect. We now believe the primary facility to be located in the Middle East, hidden within the day-to-day chaos of an urban center afflicted by decades of conflict and destabilized by runaway population growth."

"Oh fuck," I whisper. "Is she talking about Baghdad?"

Beside me, Leonid shakes his head. "Close. But we are looking at Basra."

I query my encyclopedia. It reads me a brief: *Basra, once known as the Venice of the East, is a city in southern Iraq*

*with an estimated population of six million people, a majority
under the age of thirty . . .*

Ashman explains that intelligence-gathering is ongoing
in an attempt to confirm the precise location of the suspect
facility, but it's a difficult task in a city divided into fief-
doms, whose inhabitants have long ago learned not to see
what is not their business.

"We must give away nothing of what we know," she
warns. "Any hint that we are closing in on the location
of this lab could cause our targets to flee, or inspire other
powers to take preemptive measures—cruise missile
strikes, even nuclear intervention. Everyone is on edge: the
Russians, the Israelis, the Iranians, coalitions of dragons,
even our own armed forces. Thousands could die, and we
will still not know who is involved in August-19. And it is
imperative that we know.

"We have designed a mission designated Daylight Bridge.
It calls for a small strike force to raid the August-19 facility with the primary goal of recovering background intelligence on who is funding the work, who has supplied the
distribution network, who drew up the hit list. It is *imperative* that we extract this information. If we do not, if we
were to simply destroy the site, it's certain the conspirators
would set up again in a new location."

Of course we have already run the raid Lieutenant
Ashman has described. That was the exercise we did
tonight: Locate a suspected biowarfare lab, take control
of it, confirm its nature, collect intelligence, and transmit
all data to Command. Hold the facility until Command
authorizes us to destroy it. And of course tonight we failed
to do any of that. In the real world we will be inserted
into a city of six million people, with noncombatants on
the streets, in vehicles, in every window and doorway, with
trained fighters patrolling among them and no way to tell

the difference between a kid playing with a weapon and a
hired gun ready to slam any suspected threat.

Lieutenant Ashman steps down, yielding the podium
to Colonel Abajian. "There is an additional complication,"
he announces, scowling at the front row as if inviting a
challenge. "The L-AI which kept the target lab hidden for
so many weeks continues to operate. Known locally as
Nashira, we believe that it predates the lab and that it was
originally established to oversee security in what, histor-
ically, has been a violent district, one scarred by war and
terrorism, and that continues to be threatened by rival
militias.

"Nashira is linked into a distributed surveillance network
of cameras, minidrones, chemical sensors, and human
observers. The system distinguishes between residents and
outsiders, and evaluates activity in all public locations.
When suspicious activity is detected, it generates alerts
that are received by most of the neighborhood residents,
including the local militia.

"Nashira will certainly designate any activity associated
with Daylight Bridge as hostile, and we won't be able to
do anything about that. Our best tactic is to complete the
mission before the opposition has a chance to organize."

From my seat near the back of the room, I interrupt
to ask a question. "Do we have a physical location on
Nashira?"

Abajian looks up, finds me in the fourth row, meets my
gaze with a stonewall expression that reveals nothing. "The
physical location of Nashira is under investigation. We
believe it exists within the district. But the L-AI is not the
target of Daylight Bridge."

"But you would be interested in any data we might
gather relating to Nashira?"

"We are always interested in data, Captain Shelley."

A discussion follows. Cory is unsure if the Red is
behind us. Kanoa insists that it is, or we wouldn't be
here. Questions are asked and answered. Tactics evaluated.
Through it all, the assumption is that ETM 7-1 will take
the mission.

When have we ever said no?

As Abajian, Kanoa, and Lieutenant Ashman evaluate the
quality of the intelligence, debating the possibility that the
information we have has been corrupted by the local AI, I
get up to go. Talk won't produce an answer. That will have
to wait for boots on the ground. I touch Leonid on the
shoulder. "Send me your contact information, so I can call
if I need to." He nods, and waves me away.

I trade a look with Delphi, and when I walk out I hold
the door open for the few seconds it takes her to slip out
with me. I let it close with a soft click. The hallway is lit
only by dim lights from the lobby where the rigged MP is
on watch.

Delphi is still carrying her coat over her arm. She holds it
close against her belly, her bright eyes fixed on me. "You're
going to do the mission, aren't you?"

"Yes."

I wish I could take her in my arms, take her into one of
the empty rooms in this empty building, and destroy all
the empty days that have gathered between us. But I can't.
She's too far away, and that is my fault.

She eyes me cautiously. "I asked you before if you were
a prisoner. You're not, are you?"

"No. It was my choice."

"Okay."

She beckons me to follow. We walk together to the stairs
that lead to the basement. When I give her a questioning

look, she indicates the MP and taps her ear. With his helmet audio, he can hear anything we say. So we go downstairs. She turns lights on. We're alone in the hall, outside the door of what, just yesterday, was the medical suite.

"Tell me how you survived the wreck of *Lotus*."

So I do. In spare words, I tell her of my long fall back to Earth, and the hours that followed, alone in the water. She listens with her eyes averted, making it easier to talk.

Afterward, she says, "I looked for you. Did you know that? I didn't want to believe you were really gone." She laughs softly, mocking herself. "Technically, I'm still looking for you. I've got a facial-recognition program running, scanning public indexes for an image of you . . . anything posted after that day. You know? I thought a surveillance camera might catch you, or maybe you would show up in the background of some tourist's shot." Her shoulders rise and fall in a quiet sigh. "I never had a hit."

"I don't get out much."

"All work, all the time?"

"Something like that."

"Do you have a lover, Shelley?"

"No." My answer comes too quickly because I want her to know there's no one—though the truth is more complicated than a simple no. "Not like you mean."

"Who?" she asks.

I hold back. It's not something I ever talk about. Sex inside the squad just isn't supposed to happen. It's like admitting to incest. "It was just physical comfort. A few times. She's got no plans. No claims."

I don't ask Delphi if she has a lover. I've got no right to ask. No claim. I don't want to know.

"It's kind of a cult, isn't it?" she asks.

"Yeah. I think that's fair. But what we do is worth doing. It's not dumbass stunts. It's real."

"I believe you."

"I thought I would be dead by now."

I don't know why I say it. I regret it as soon as I do. It comes out like a confession.

Seconds pass as she studies me. I sense her shifting thoughts, imagine her revised responses reflected in her eyes as she analyzes my psychological condition, weighing the likelihood of survivor guilt, or guilt for the horrible acts I've committed, or the death wish I've always denied. But my imagination doesn't go far enough, because in the end she says the most unexpected thing: "I still love you."

Then she turns and walks away, back to the stairs, shrugging into her coat as she goes.

"Delphi . . . *Karin*."

She pauses with a foot on the first step, looking back, her expression patient. Not expectant. Not demanding.

"I think this is the last time out for me."

"That has more than one meaning, Shelley," she points out. "But at least this time, I'll know."

She disappears up the stairs. I stay for a while, sitting on the floor with my back to the wall, my wrists cocked over my knees, wondering why it never feels like I've done enough.

Kanoa only allows me a little time to brood. After a few minutes, he links in and says, "Let's go."

The program in my head is still counting down to zero assist. I thought it would be a fight at this point to hold myself together, to fend off the black mood that used to afflict me when the skullnet went down. But the skullnet hasn't gone down. It's still in my head. It's still working. And ironically, I'm in better control now than I ever was when the system was automated.

The embedded AI that operates my skullnet has had two years to figure out who I am, how I work, what I want—and it listens to me. I think, *Lock it down,* and it gives me a machinelike, cool, logical efficiency. It's a state of mind I like to be in. It's one I cherish. It's where I keep myself on that cold, dark walk back to a home that isn't mine.

The other soldiers in my squad are half-seen, fog-wreathed figures scattered in the road ahead, hauling their gear. Only Kanoa is beside me. He's silent for most of the way, but as we approach the housing area, he says, "We need to check out your skullnet. It's not functioning to standard."

"No," I tell him. "It's fine."

The women break off, going to their own residence. Escamilla and Dunahee take a path to another house.

"You'll report to medical," Kanoa says. "0800."

He doesn't stay to hear any more objections, but follows Dunahee, disappearing into a flash of white light as the door of a residence swings briefly open.

I think, *Calm. Lock it down.*

At 0800 I'm back in the basement of the command center, sitting across a desk from the physician I saw before. She's not a neurologist, so she's got a specialist present virtually, an older man, Caucasian, thick white hair neatly combed. Facial recognition informs me that he was on the team that developed the neuromodulating microbeads and the skull-caps—later the skullnets—used to control them.

He looks at me with a sentimental gaze, smiles, shakes his head like he can't quite believe I'm real. "Captain Shelley. It's good to know the rumor of your death was just a cover story."

"Thank you, sir."

"Yes. Well . . . I have good news. I've run the basic

diagnostics on your skullnet and the issue is simple enough. You've got a bad receiver. Once we correct that, we can update the software. You should be fine after that."

"I'm fine now."

I tell him about the changes I made: the program I loaded that is dialing my automatic support down to zero; the minor surgery Logan performed for me, removing the skullnet's receiver.

The local physician pops up out of her chair and comes around the desk to get a close look at the incision, half-hidden now behind a fuzz of black hair. "I thought it was a field-treated wound from your last mission."

The neurologist looks worried. "We need to replace the receiver. You're at risk for—"

"I'm doing fine."

"Of course you think you can handle it. I understand that. But every study shows that a soldier deprived of neurological support after long-term use—"

"I'm not deprived of anything. I still have the skullnet. It still works. The AI is still there and I get what I need out of it. But no one else—nothing—gets to tell me what to think anymore."

He asks questions. I answer them, admitting that I'm still figuring things out. He's impressed at how well I'm doing. "This isn't a situation we've studied. It's just too risky, because it leaves no mechanism to override the subject's obsessions except cerebral exhaustion. Any emotion could be ridden to destruction. You understand? An overwhelming pleasure, or despair, or anger. There's no system in place now to hold that back."

"There is a system," I say. "It's my will. Who I am."

He doesn't trust me to handle it. "I'm going to recommend the original system be restored."

"I'm going to decline your recommendation."

He looks puzzled. "I'm not making the recommendation to you. I'm making it to your commanding officer."

"That's a voluntary relationship," I tell him. "Legally, I'm a civilian, and that makes it my choice."

Kanoa intercepts me as I'm walking back to base housing on the weed-grown road. I expect to get chewed out, lectured on why I need to allow the Red to have its electronic fingers forever inside my head, but instead he frowns at me with his worried-dad expression and says, "Why didn't you tell me what was going on? I never would have sent you to medical if I knew."

Every indicator in his expression says he's telling the truth—which leaves me momentarily speechless, and then in desperate need of some appropriate half-truth. But before I can come up with anything, he answers his own question. "You didn't trust me."

"I guess not." And then, because I don't have any idea why he's not furious: "Are you saying you would have covered for me?"

He scans the empty fields before answering. "Let's say I wouldn't have regarded it as a problem, so I wouldn't have bothered Command with it." He comes a step closer. His voice drops. "I did the same thing over a year ago. You were so attached to your hardware, I thought it would worry you if you knew. I never guessed you'd consider doing it yourself—and I didn't think you could handle it."

I smile. "You didn't trust me?"

His frown turns into a deep scowl. "Are you sure you *can* handle it? You've been erratic. Unstable."

"I'm working it out."

A cold wind gusts past us as he asks, "What made you do it?"

"Abajian's mission only required me to reconnoiter the UGF. The Red required me to destroy it. That was a suicide mission. It was just luck we got out alive."

"I saw Leonid Sergun's report. I thought he was exaggerating."

"No. Papa was the only sane one. I am not going to take my squad on a suicide mission again."

"Understood." We start walking. "Abajian's a problem though. He got a copy of the medical report. He doesn't understand shit about how an LCS works. He wants to pull you off the mission."

"If he does, there is no mission. He doesn't get my squad."

"Agreed. We'll let him explain *that* to the president."

We run the mission at noon.

We go in as one squad with nine sets of boots on the ground. It should be enough to do the job, but it's rough. We're facing an army of irregulars. Resistance is simulated: programmed projections in our visors that look like moving figures, muzzle flash, the blast of grenades, all with appropriate audio. We need heavy weapons to get past them, but heavy weapons are considered prohibitively dangerous to civilians, so we're not carrying any. We don't reach the lab.

The mission planners decide to eliminate the helicopters, opting for stealth over speed. When we go back after nightfall, we go on foot. This time, resistance takes longer to build. In the end though, we get hit just as hard.

We try again before the sun is up—just a quiet dawn raid that leads to an all-out battle. We get another chance at noon. Same result, but at least we're getting practice working together.

We keep at it. Over the next few days, the battle AI changes the scenarios. We change our tactics. We do better when we go in as two teams, advancing on parallel blocks. That divides the defense and makes it less effective, but we still don't get inside the lab.

"They won't let us win," Tran concludes as we walk back to our housing, "because they have no fucking idea what the lab actually looks like."

I laugh, but I know it's more than that. *Civilians*, I say. I mean it as an imprecation, but it comes out weirdly flat in my synthesized voice. "They complicate everything."

Flynn turns on me. "God*damn*! *You* complicate everything. I hate that creepy synth voice. Why can't you just talk like a human being?"

What the hell can I say? It's not something I even think about anymore.

Tran is quicker on the return fire. *Silence is golden*, he says. And then jumps back fast when Flynn takes a swing at him.

Civilians *are* the problem, though. It's one thing to go all-out on an assault. It's a different game when you have to shoot around bystanders—some who might not be as innocent as they'd like you to believe. That's why we fucking hate urban combat.

We want to leave a small footprint. None of us wants to get to that lab by stepping over the bodies of noncombatants—but it's starting to look like it's going to come down to a trade, a choice of who lives and who dies. If Delphi is on August-19's list, or Jaynie, or President Monteiro, a trade will be made.

It's that simple.

A media room is set up in the basement of the command center. I'm there for hours every day, taking virtual walks through the target district, memorizing the pattern of the

streets and the placement of the buildings, circling the
block where the lab is believed to be located, studying the
setup from every angle.

The target is an old apartment building that spans the
width of the block. It has three aboveground floors and a
basement. We want to enter on the south side, where a service entrance leads directly to the basement. The alternate
entrance is the building's front door, where we'd have to
cross a small lobby to reach the interior stairs.

I walk through that lobby and then climb to the second
floor, but that's all I'm allowed. The virtual tour doesn't go
into the basement, because we've never gotten any camera
eyes down there—but I can enter some of the surrounding
buildings. I note which ones have multiple access points,
and where it's possible to enter from one street and exit
into another. I make sure I can find my way around in daylight and after dark, with and without night vision.

Leonid has operated in the area before. He has a network of associates. Those connections have let him set up
safe houses, all three of them high-walled estates. When
the mission is done, we are to pick one, proceed to it with
all haste, and then wait until an extraction can be safely
accomplished.

It's this last phase that needs to be improved.

I argued about it with Abajian as soon as he distributed
the draft mission plan. "We don't operate like this," I told
him as we met around a conference table along with Jaynie,
Kanoa, Leonid, and Captain Montrose. "The longer we
stay in one place, the more vulnerable we are. We need an
immediate airlift out."

"And you'll get one," Abajian promised. "*If* the situation
is calm."

Command is worried. If the district goes hot, helicopters will be easy targets. Captain Montrose was succinct:

"If a helicopter is shot down while evacuating you from the city, we won't be able to cover it up. The mission will be exposed and impeachment proceedings will be launched against President Monteiro."

Like me, Jaynie was suspicious. "We could be captured at any point during this operation."

"Yes, Ms. Vasquez, you are correct. But within the target district we will have more options to secure your status." Montrose didn't want to discuss those options, which tells me that while they might benefit the president, they aren't going to be good for us. "If the airlift is delayed, just get to a safe house. We'll take care of you."

I really would like to believe that.

It's evening. A few flakes of snow are falling as the squad trots to the hangar, rigged and ready for yet another trial run. The lights are out as usual. Captain Montrose is waiting for us in the dark. He's standing at the back gate of the SUV he drives, wearing a trench coat, and farsights with night vision capabilities. "I want to introduce you to a new asset," he says as we form a half circle around him. He turns and opens the SUV's gate.

It's a good thing no one is standing behind me, because I spring back two meters, powered by my dead sister. I land with my HITR braced against my shoulder and my finger on the second trigger, ready to launch a succession of grenades into the back of the truck.

Montrose scrambles out of the line of fire while Kanoa comes in over gen-com: "Stand down!"

"What the *fuck* is that doing here?"

Crouched in the back of the SUV is a robo-wolf—a four-legged, headless, gun-toting, mechanical monster— the same model that killed Colonel Kendrick on the First

Light mission. It's like a simplified wolf's skeleton, a gray titanium horror with cross-braced camera eyes where a head should be, and automatic weapons on motorized swivels mounted on its sides.

"You expect us to work with that thing?" Jaynie asks in a low, disgusted voice.

I glance at her. She's got her weapon braced, just like me, ready to blow the robot to pieces. Jaynie was there on the First Light mission. It took the two of us and Kendrick to bring the robo-wolf down. But tonight, we're armed with blanks and flash-bangs. We lower our weapons, while the squad mills uncertainly between us.

Montrose recovers himself. "Yes, Captain Vasquez," he says, stepping back to his original position. "This squad dog has been assigned to you, and you will work with it. Guidance—wake it up."

No lights come on, no burning red eyes. Its skeletal form just slides into motion, smooth as water, generating only a whisper of noise from the joints. It leaps from the back of the truck onto the concrete, landing with a slight clatter reminiscent of the sound my feet make.

A superstitious shudder runs through me as I remember the way its rounds punched holes in Kendrick's armored vest and ripped him up inside.

I don't trust the thing. I don't want it around.

But that's an irrational reaction.

It's just a weapon, a potentially effective one, but mindless, like a cruise missile. And this time it'll be on our side.

I swallow against a dry throat, suck fortified water through a tube, and try to be reasonable. "It has a human handler?" My voice is just a little unsteady.

"Yes. Human guidance in concert with an AI driver—similar to your squad's angel."

I think, *Lock it down*, and an icy, analytical mood slides

over me. When I speak again, I sound untroubled: "If nothing else, that thing should be good for propaganda value—scaring civilians out of the street."

We run the mission.

The "squad dog," as Montrose calls it, runs ahead of us, drawing a hail of simulated fire, but the battle AI doesn't tag it with any damage. Montrose speaks over gen-com. "Always keep your distance from the dog. There's a lot of ricochet off of it and you don't want to get hit by that."

As it moves, the squad dog directs dual fire at the upper floors of buildings on both sides of the street. I watch carefully placed rounds slam through the concrete. The battle AI records simultaneous hits against hidden enemy positions. We come in behind it and blow the lab door. For the first time, we make it all the way inside. Mission accomplished.

Just to make sure it wasn't a fluke, we run the assault three more times—and each time, we get through.

If the goddamned squad dog wasn't so expensive, I'd be out of a job.

It's 0200 before we're dismissed. I sleep late, not waking up until an audio signal gets piped through my overlay. I lift my head, groggy. Tran looks in the door, a grin on his face. "Kanoa says to get the fuck out of bed. We're on."

I check my messages and find an order to pack up and report to the hangar at 1400. We're going to deploy. Leonid Sergun will accompany us and coordinate local ground support.

I wish I could have seen Delphi again. Talked to her.

She's Jaynie's handler now.

It's better this way.

THE TRAGIC
FINAL SCENE

In Kuwait we acquire two battered, well-used SUVs customized with heavy armor under their faded paint, and we drive them aboard a barge bound for Iraq, parking them alongside shipping containers stacked four high. We are traveling by water because Leonid has a long-standing relationship with the custom officers at the port in Basra.

It's a short trip through the northern corner of the Persian Gulf. A tugboat hauls us past oil tankers and ships from the world's navies, to the Shatt al-Arab waterway that marks the border between Iraq and Iran. By late afternoon, we are showing false passports to an officer of the Basra port authority.

I am in disguise, wearing sunglasses, a two-day growth of beard, and a subtle, carefully applied pigment to change the apparent angles of my face. It's enough to throw off a casual observer, which is all I need, since the Red has ensured we're protected from standard facial recognition.

The officer glances at me through the clear lens of her farsights. She looks over the rest of the squad. We are strangers to her, but our nature is revealed in the way we carry ourselves, the set of our shoulders, the focus of our eyes. She's seen our kind many times before. Basra has become a market for mercenaries. We're just another squad, one she's under orders to admit into the country.

Leonid makes a performance out of presenting to her a tablet that displays our equipment manifest. They chat amicably in Arabic—it wouldn't look right to admit us too quickly—and then thumbprints and signatures get appended to electronic files and we are clear to enter the country.

Leonid takes the driver's seat in the lead truck. I ride shotgun, with Tran, Fadul, and Roman in the backseat. The electric engine engages and we roll down the ramp. Flynn drives the second truck. She follows close behind us, transporting Jaynie, Logan, Escamilla, and Dunahee.

Welcome to Iraq.

Basra is a precarious city, under siege from a rising sea level creeping up the Shatt al-Arab from the Persian Gulf, and rising temperatures that have already given it the hottest summers of any city on Earth. We've arrived in mid-January, in the late afternoon. The air temperature is barely eighty degrees American. Paradise. Unless you live here.

The other ongoing assault on the city is from its own people. The population has climbed from 900,000 in the late twentieth century to over six million now. Even though the city is veiled by a shroud of dusty brown air, I see the faint shimmer of an EXALT node. It makes me wonder: How extensive is the influence of the Red here? How does it intersect these people's lives?

We leave the port, following a narrow street that passes by modern warehouses built since the last war rolled through here. In contrast to the buildings, most of the cars and small trucks that crowd the street are worn out, dented, dusty. There is money here, but like most places, it's unevenly distributed.

We join a wider thoroughfare, packed with cars both gas and electric. It takes us briefly north until Leonid swings through a traffic circle, and then we're running south at a sedate but steady pace.

Oil facilities roll past, and the bombed-out shells of old apartment buildings. We pass a munitions factory and then a graffiti-covered wall that guards a neighborhood with bullet-scarred water towers. A decrepit slum huddles around a shining white, windowless data center. There is a massive covered stadium skirted by a vast, empty concrete parking lot tinted the same brown color as the sky.

It's said that Iraq is the cradle of civilization, the site of the Garden of Eden. Maybe so, but if this is Eden, it just goes to show that what civilization does best is fuck up beautiful things.

We leave the main road, turning off into a neighborhood with narrow streets crowded with foot traffic and lined with brick houses built with uneven masonry, making them seem old and tired. I turn to look behind us. Flynn isn't following anymore. She's been assigned a different route to make us appear less like an invasion force.

"Hey, Shelley." My gaze shifts to Tran, sitting in the backseat between Fadul and Roman. His wide lips are pursed, his eyebrows drawn in concern. "I'm starting to worry we might turn on you."

"What? What are you talking about?" Tran really does live in an alternate reality. "Why would you?"

"We wouldn't want to," he says. "But remember how

you and me and the LT all got launched into action in the
UGF? What if that happens again when we hit this lab?
But this time it happens to everybody but you, because the
Red can't get inside your head anymore to fire you up with
your skullnet?" He gets animated, gesturing with his hands.
"And then, say, you don't like the slam we're about to put
down, so you get in the way of our programmed mission.
We might have to kill you! Or you'd have to shoot us. It'd
be like this tragic final scene."

"Jesus, Tran," Fadul says, her head cocked to glare at him,
her lip curled. "We are about to commit an act of war, and
you're daydreaming about comic-book fantasies."

"You want to think it's a fantasy," he fires back. "But
you weren't part of Arid Crossroad." He looks at me
again. "You get what I mean, Shelley? You get what I'm
saying?"

I haven't known Tran all that long. Palehorse Keep was
the first mission we shared. But even in that short time I've
noticed his crazy guesses have a way of turning out to be
right. Not a comforting thought.

"If it happens, I won't shoot you," I promise him.

He nods with solemn gravity. "And I'll do my best for
you."

I face forward again, more rattled than I want to admit.
Leonid says nothing, not aloud, but words he spoke to me
on our flight out of Pakistan echo in my head: *It is possible
you are subscribed to the wrong god.*

Progress is slow. Every minute or two we stop: for people
who step out into the street in front of us; for dogs
scratching at their fleas; for cars emerging from nowhere,
wielding the toot of a horn like a magic spell to ward off
collisions.

If we were rigged in our dead sisters we could move faster than this, which is one reason we'll be withdrawing on foot.

The sun dips below the horizon, leaving the sky aglow with light the color of dusty pearls. The crowds thin as people go to sunset prayer, and we make better progress.

The streets narrow even further. I have to push back against claustrophobia as we pass through them, schooling myself to stay calm. As I do, I start to recognize where we are from all my virtual walk-throughs in the media room. The geography is the same, but the feeling in these streets is grimmer than I imagined. Loose paper, cast-off bits of cloth, and crushed cardboard boxes collect in piles in front of the two- and three-story buildings. Oblivious to the mess, or at least unwilling to notice it, are young men, all wearing shirt-sleeves and sunglasses, or opaque farsights, who stand in small groups, smoking and watching everything around them, watching the women, especially, who pass by with swift, determined steps.

All the women I see have covered their head and shoulders in a hijab, but only a few wear robes. Many more wear long-sleeved blouses over pants, or over skirts with leggings; some wear coveralls as if they've just come from a mechanic's shop or from a day spent dealing with plumbing or electrical systems. They move in groups of three or four and most groups have at least one firearm in sight. Sometimes it's a pistol. Often it's an assault rifle.

Whether the men watch them out of desire or curiosity or anger, I can't tell, but what is certain is that our battered SUV is a sight even more electric, drawing their eyes away from the passing women.

Grim faces turn to regard us as we roll past. In the evening's gathering shadows, tiny green lights blink, indicating farsights recording our presence. I think they're EXALT farsights, controlled by the Red. I hope so. I hope the Red is on our side.

As we advance, I eye the streets, the buildings, the intersections, matching them with the geography I know. At each intersection, I go over in my mind possible ways out, reviewing the complex of streets and alleys that would make a best route, and the alternate paths we can try when things go to hell.

We arrive at our staging area: a large two-story house surrounded by a high wall. The flat-black steel gate opens on remote control. We drive inside to a tiled courtyard. Sheets of brown canvas have been stretched between the walls to create a canopy to shade the yard and discourage the prying eyes of neighbors and of curious drones.

Kanoa stayed behind in Germany along with Delphi, but he's here virtually as my handler. He speaks over gencom. "There's a cat on the wall. Don't get jumpy and shoot it."

"Is it wired?"

"It's just a cat."

We get out. The evening is surprisingly cool. I can hear traffic, chattering voices, a nearby TV. I open the back of the SUV. The squad dog is stirring, its bundle of titanium bones shifting, a predatory skeleton coming to life, aligning its weaponry as it reorganizes itself into walking form. It makes my heart beat faster and my hair stand on end.

"I hate that thing. It's a fucking hellhound."

Kanoa says, "You'll be glad to have it a couple of hours from now."

It leaps out past me, landing with a soft, rattling *click* of metal on stone. I watch it retreat to a corner, thinking about the way Kendrick died. And then I make myself stop thinking about it.

"Let's move the gear inside."

Leonid gets the front door open and flips on the lights. I follow him in.

The interior has been cleaned out. No furnishings, no kitchen appliances. Doesn't matter. We'll be here for only a few hours. I check the bathroom and a small closet. It's instinct to clear all the rooms, but Kanoa issues an order to stay downstairs. "The house is secure. We've got seekers in every room making sure of that. So stay on the ground floor. Your IR profile might be visible if you go up."

He means my robot legs are easy to see in infrared, and that makes it simpler to identify me. So, instead of checking upstairs, I check on the other half of my squad. Pulling up the squad map in my overlay, I confirm their position at their assigned shelter: an old warehouse in a compound enclosed by a cinder-block wall.

I open a solo link to Logan. Jaynie is the CO of our squad, but that doesn't mean I can't do my own oversight. "Logan, report."

"Nominal. We're inside. Prepping."

"Any trouble?"

"No trouble."

"Vasquez treating you okay?"

"Yes, sir."

"Logan, I want you to keep an eye on our people."

He hesitates a few seconds, then: "Why? You know something?"

"No. I trust Vasquez. Just keep your eyes open."

We change out of our civilian clothes and into our unmarked burnt-camo, shadow-shifting uniforms. "Get your armor," I order. "And set up your bones."

The dead sisters get unfolded, but it's too early to strap in. To minimize civilian casualties, we will wait until 0130 to launch our assault. The streets should be empty then, and if we get lucky, at least a few of the guards stationed around the lab might be asleep.

Tran scowls around the room at our four dead sisters standing immobile in the corners. "Looks like a headless skeleton army."

"Someone to watch over you," Fadul says, tossing him a meal packet.

Leonid is nervous. He doesn't eat. While we sit cross-legged amid our gear, he paces. "You will need to move fast," he reminds us.

"We know our roles," Fadul says without looking up.

Leonid is not convinced. "Breaching the lab will be the easy part."

"*Papa*," Tran objects. "Didn't you hear how many times we failed to reach the lab in practice? If that's the easy part, we're fucked."

"That's why we need to move quietly," Roman says. "We want a limited engagement. Get in and get out with minimal civilian casualties."

Fadul looks up, scowling at Leonid. "Just make sure the safe-house security systems know who we are. We'll work out the rest."

It takes only a few minutes to eat. Then we stretch out

on the tiled floor to sleep while we can. I don't bother setting a watch. Guidance has a flock of seekers watching over
us, along with the hellhound out in the courtyard. That
should be enough eyes to keep us safe.

Roman checks out first, closing her eyes, turning off her
mind. Tran is asleep a few seconds later, and then Fadul.

Leonid turns off the lights—but he doesn't sleep. I listen
to him pace, wondering what's got him so worried. Every
operation is dangerous. That's just the way it is.

"You know something, Papa?" I whisper.

"*No.*" Then after a few seconds, he adds, "This time, you
will stick to the mission plan?"

"That's my intention."

"And what is the intention of your god?"

I admit the truth: "I don't know." I want to believe the
Red is behind this mission, but if it is, I can't feel it—not
anymore, not the way I used to. I made that choice. But
whether the Red is behind us or not, the L-AI known as
Nashira is here. It's the dominant AI in this district, a
night angel with an agenda of its own. I'm pretty sure that
agenda is not going to favor us.

I feel Papa's worry spreading to me, but worry doesn't do
any good. I turn it back with a thought: *Calm.*

War is never predictable. We'll do the best we can.

My alarm goes off at 0100. I kill it and get up as Tran,
Roman, and Fadul all awake. Leonid is not in the room. I
link into gen-com. "Where's Papa?"

"Waiting outside," Kanoa answers.

I wash my face at the sink, drink fortified water, and
then I rig up, pulling on my gloves, strapping into my dead
sister, shrugging on my pack, shouldering my weapon.
There's a brittle tension in my chest, in my gut. The fear

and anticipation that always precede a battle. Another battle. My first engagement without the Red's whispered warnings propagating through my brain.

"Fadul!"

"Sir?"

"Cross-check."

"Yes, sir."

She secures the last cinches on her dead sister and then we inspect each other's rig, making sure everything is in order. Roman and Tran cross-check each other. We strap on our packs. Activate our weapons. I've got my helmet under my arm.

"Listen up," I say.

They turn to me. Roman looks tense, Tran eager. Fadul has a hard, vindictive expression like she's out for payback.

"We want to move fast," I remind them. "Get in and get out. Because the longer we take, the more resistance will be in place. Once we leave the gate, we don't slow down for anything. Clear?"

Roman nods. "Yes, sir."

Tran lifts his chin and gives me a parade-ground formal "Understood, sir."

Fadul rolls her eyes. "We got it, Shelley."

I nod. "Hoo-yah."

They respond in an energized whisper, *"Hoo-yah!"*

"Helmets on."

I pull on my helmet. The fans kick in, cooling my face, while the squad icons arrange themselves across the bottom of my vision. I do an observational roll call, checking off the distant presence of Logan, Escamilla, Dunahee, Vasquez, and Flynn.

We don't have a dedicated squad drone. In a hostile urban environment, those tend to get shot down early in the game. Instead, Guidance has put together a hybrid map compiled from high-altitude surveillance, real-time observations gathered by our seekers, the location of known street cameras and their present condition—working or vandalized—and the current position of the district's security drone. The result is a representation of the district cast in shifting shadows that designate "safe" areas temporarily free from observation by machines that don't belong to us.

The district's civilians are marked too. There aren't many out on the street at this time of night, but there are a few. One is an old bearded man muttering Arabic words in a cadence that sounds like poetry as he wanders alone in the deepest surveillance shadows where only our seekers are watching. It's the route we want to use.

"Physically harmless," Kanoa concludes. "But if he has a phone, take it. You might gain an extra minute of stealth."

So our first task is to mug an old man. "Roger that." Another proud achievement for my service record. It pisses me off even more, because I know I won't hesitate to do it.

Jayme checks In over gen com. "You with me, Shelley?"

"Yes, ma'am."

"Initiate the operation."

"Roger that. Kanoa, post our route."

On my visor's display, a faint blue path appears.

"Routes are posted," I tell the squad. "Fadul, confirm yours."

"Confirmed."

"Roman?"

"Confirmed."

"Tran?"

"Confirmed, sir."

There's no way anyone can get lost.

"Move out."

In the courtyard, the squad dog leaves the corner it

occupied overnight. I watch it warily as it trots up to the closed gate. Then I turn to Leonid.

He's already in the driver's seat of the SUV. His role is to move south to one of the safe houses and wait. If things go well, we won't see him again tonight. Abajian will pull us out by helicopter, and it'll be done. If things go badly, we'll hole up in one of the safe houses, and Leonid will tap into his network of associates to try to smuggle us out of Iraq.

He looks at me as I pause beside the SUV's window. "Is it you, Shelley, behind this devil's mask?"

"It's me."

Leonid has conjured no fond insincerity to hide his feelings tonight. Night vision smoothes his wrinkles, but it doesn't disguise his worry. "Twenty minutes," he tells me. "You shouldn't need more time than that." And then he adds, "God willing."

"Open the gate, Papa."

He triggers the remote. The gate swings open. The squad dog slips through. We follow a few meters behind it, running all out. My helmet audio dampens the thud of our tread, while enhancing the sound of a television—and then it decides the TV is unimportant and slides the volume back down. I hear distant traffic, the soft buzz of seekers, my own heavy breathing—and after a block I hear the old man's voice, amplified. We can't route around him because we need to be in the same surveillance shadow he is occupying. We can't wait for him to go away because we need to be inside the target building before the district's surveillance drone makes its next pass over these streets. So we assault him.

He's walking slowly, still muttering to himself, and maybe he's a little deaf because he doesn't hear us coming. The squad dog drops back. I move up. I get to do the dirty work.

I come up fast behind him, get one gloved hand over his nose and mouth and an arm around his chest. He struggles,

clawing at my hand, at my arm struts, his heels kicking at
my shins. But his resistance lasts for only a few seconds
before oxygen deprivation makes him slump in my arms.

I lower him gently to the ground, telling myself he isn't
dead. He's just passed out. I search him, finding a phone
and a handgun.

We move on.

We meet no one else on the street, but we can't control
for eyes watching us from windows or rooftops, or for a
silent chain of alarm propagating from phone to phone or
across social media.

My helmet audio picks up and amplifies a faint flurry of
voices when we're still two blocks from the target. "Assume
you've been noticed," Kanoa warns.

And a few seconds later: "You're about to come under
enemy fire."

"Cover!"

We fall back against the brick wall of a three-story apartment, crouched, with our weapons ready. A targeting circle
appears on my visor, marking a window across the street.
I ask no questions. There's no way to know who's in that
room: a man or a woman or little kids. I just shoot. But
the neighborhood defense has rallied with shocking speed.
Muzzle flash erupts from at least three windows. A round
grazes the side of my helmet with a high-pitched *ping*,
while more bullets tear at the brick behind me. Our plan
of a quick, stealthy assault is blown.

"Move!" I order the squad, because it's a lot harder to hit
an object in motion.

We run and shoot. Even with the battle AI pulling the
trigger, I don't think we hit much, but we make it dangerous to sit in a window and for now, that's good enough.

The squad dog runs ahead, disappearing around the next
corner. In the practice assaults we did back in Germany it

behaved like a berserker, but tonight it hasn't fired a shot.
I want to ask Kanoa about it, but there's no time. More
people are waking, arming themselves, taking shots at us
despite the danger posed by our return fire. I stumble as
a round strikes my side, knocking the air out of my lungs
as it pancakes in my vest. Two more steps bring me to the
last intersection.

I crouch with my back against the wall of another
apartment building and look up, scanning the face of the
building across the street and the one diagonally across
the corner. Targeting circles pop up on my visor and I fire,
once, twice, three times.

"On the roof," Kanoa says.

I lift my gaze higher, find a targeting circle on the edge
of the roof. Three quick shots are answered by a scream.
The taste of lead bitter on my tongue. "Fadul, move! Get
across the street."

She darts across, moves sideways between parked cars,
then drops out of sight.

"Roman, go."

We do our best to discourage shooting from the windows, and one by one we get across.

We've reached the block with the target lab. We're
one building away. Someone tosses a flare into the street,
blinding me for a few seconds until my visor compensates.
Gunfire rages on all sides. Half the shooters are aiming at
shadows, but enough know where we are that the car in
front of us is perforated by bullets, the wall above us is
being chipped away. Shrapnel pings against my helmet. It
tears at the heavy camouflage fabric of my uniform.

"Grenades," I growl over gen-com.

This is my nightmare—a well-armed civilian militia—
and they're not even guarding the target lab. It's my guess
they don't know it exists, they don't know why we're here.

But they've faced rival militias before and fought off threats to their lives, their homes, their families.

I remind myself that we are here because the American government has been attacked, officials murdered, President Monteiro's life threatened. I pull the second trigger, launching a grenade at a third-floor window in the building diagonally across the intersection.

"New route," Kanoa says, his voice weirdly hoarse and mechanical as my projected route shifts, the blue path directing me down the cross street, away from the service door. It looks like Command has decided we will enter through the front door instead. *"Run."*

Kanoa's harsh tone allows for no questions. We run, sprinting in a pack for the next corner, crazy shadows cast by the flare bounding along with us in exaggerated, inhuman strides. Maybe those shadows confuse the enemy or maybe they're wondering what we're running from, I don't know, but the shooting stops before we're halfway.

"Hunker down," Kanoa says.

I dive for the ground. Roll against a brick wall and curl up beneath my pack as the wall heaves and my helmet audio locks down against a massive explosion. The pressure wave sucks the air out of my lungs, compresses my brain, leaving me dizzy, unsure which way is up as I twist around to look. My visor, still in night vision, shows me a white-out of flame boiling past the corner we just abandoned. Concrete debris tumbles from the sky, bouncing in the street. There is a roar of fire, and water spraying from broken pipes, and people screaming. A chorus of screaming. Women and men, screaming in pain, horror, despair, fury. Lights come on in the buildings around us as voices call to God.

Tran whispers over gen-com, "What the fuck? What—"

"Was that a missile?" Fadul wants to know. Her voice is

shaking. "Or a fucking car bomb? Goddamn it, Kanoa, we were not supposed to blow these people up!"

Jaynie cuts her off. "Drop the chatter! Rendezvous with team one. We have the front door open. We're going in."

For breathless seconds all is still—not silent, no—but no one moves in the street, no one emerges from the buildings, no one runs to answer their neighbors' cries of agony because bitter experience has taught them that rescuers are too often met by a second bomb.

The stillness lets us move freely. With all eyes drawn to the carnage around the corner we have become invisible in the dark cross street. It won't last. So I urge my team, *Run!*—the order repeated aloud over gen-com in my calm, synthetic voice.

Roman is closest to the corner. She takes off first. Tran gives her three seconds to establish a proper interval, and then he follows. Fadul goes next. I stay crouched in place, my HITR braced against my shoulder, ready to provide covering fire. Roman pulls up when she reaches the corner. Dropping to one knee, she raises her weapon to cover me. I sprint hard to catch up.

Fadul's questions echo in my mind. Was it a missile or a car bomb? And was it *ours*? A backup plan to knock out resistance if the mission got bogged down? None of us wanted to advance this mission by stepping over the bodies of civilians. We did not ask to do it this way. It's not the mission we planned—but it's on us anyway.

I turn the corner as gunfire erupts from a building across the street. Roman swings around, returns fire. Dunahee is farther down the block. He starts shooting, backing her up. I drop behind a parked car, my gaze sweeping the building, looking for a target. The battle AI designates two,

both in second-floor windows. I take one out with a grenade—"Roman, get moving!"—and then I nail the second
target.

The blue path points the way.

Time to finish this.

On this side of the building, there is a recessed entry
opening onto a formal lobby with slate-tile floors. The
double doors—ornate steel mesh backed with shattered
glass—have been blown open and are hanging on broken
hinges. Logan, Flynn, and Dunahee are in the entry, hunkered down, using the doors for shelter as they cover the
street. I'm stunned to see the squad dog with them, its dual
weapons sweeping from side to side as it seeks for a target
on the rooftops.

I can't hear their chatter, which means Kanoa has isolated communications so we can all focus on our own
tasks. Logan signals me to get the hell inside. I sprint past
him, pivot, and press my back against the wall while I look
around. I've already visited this little lobby on a virtual
tour, but it looks different to me now because the lights are
out and I'm seeing it in night vision.

The décor is a hundred years old: stained plaster walls
bearing tile mosaics; a threadbare carpet; on the left hand,
a bank of tiny mailboxes with little brass doors darkened
by time; on the right, a stairway with polished-wood treads
and a cast-iron handrail climbing to the second floor.
Escamilla stands guard at the top of the stair.

"Escamilla, do we have civilians up there?"

"Roger that. At least six apartments."

"No resistance so far," Jaynie adds. "They're staying out
of sight."

At first I don't see her. That's because my team—Fadul,

Roman, and Tran—are all clustered around her at the back of the lobby.

"Fire in the hole," she says. All of them scramble toward me. I turn my head away. There's a bright flash and the loud *bang!* of a det cord explosion. I look again, to see a steel door pop a few inches open, shedding smoke.

"I'll take it," I say, and move in, following the blue path. I kick the door wide and shove the muzzle of my HITR around the corner to let the battle AI get a look.

"Stairwell clear," Kanoa says. "Advance."

I pivot onto a landing above a narrow staircase that plunges into a pit. A second steel door is at the bottom. I jump down; try the bar handle. It's locked. I kick it hard with my footplate, once, twice, but it holds.

"Blow it," Jaynie says over gen-com.

I look up. She tosses me det cord. I rig it around the latch, then retreat to the top of the stairs. From out front I hear staccato gunfire. My helmet suppresses the volume, but it's clear that Logan, Flynn, and Dunahee are working hard to defend our position—and they're vulnerable.

"Kanoa, you need to get someone at an upstairs window." I flinch as Jaynie triggers the det cord. Then I pivot back into the stairwell to see the door at the bottom blown ajar. Faint light spills through, green in night vision. "If RPGs come into play—"

"We are monitoring the street fight," Kanoa snaps. "Do your part and get downstairs."

I don't argue, because he's right. I just hate the feeling that my squad is vulnerable. But the sooner we're done here, the better for everyone. So I jump. Jaynie comes down behind me.

Beyond the door is unknown territory. Surveillance of this district combined with research on the backgrounds of individuals observed here, plus analysis of surface and air

samples surreptitiously collected in and around this building, pinpointed this address as the location of the target
lab. But our intelligence team never managed to retrieve
surveillance from inside the basement. We don't know the
layout or if personnel are present around the clock. All we
can do is hit fast and hard and hope we find what we're
looking for.

I kick the door wide and pivot into the room, using my
HITR's muzzle cams to quickly scan the space beyond. The
battle AI doesn't mark any targets. I look for myself.

The basement is one big room with the stairway in the
middle of it. Left empty, it would make a great setting for
a horror movie with its rough concrete floor and unfin-
ished brick walls stabbed through with the broken stumps
of old iron fixtures whose purpose I don't want to contemplate. But it's not empty. The lab equipment we had hoped
to find is here: a sleek stainless steel counter, sink, shelves
crammed with gear, a vent hood, and a still-humming
refrigerator. I'm pretty sure power is out in the building, so
the fridge must be running on a backup battery. Modern
pipes and conduits are bracketed to the walls and ceilings,
distributing water and electricity.

I pivot to the right, wanting to get a look behind the stairwell. Jaynie moves in the opposite direction as Tran, Roman,
and Fadul come down behind us. "No targets," I say.

Jaynie responds, "Nothing here, either." Her tone shifts.
She sounds angry. "How important could this place be if
August-19 doesn't bother with overnight security?"

Good question—and it's Delphi who answers her.
"You're there to find out." Delphi is assigned to direct everyone downstairs while Kanoa handles the street fight. "Grab
any data storage device you see. Take everything you can
carry. In three minutes, you need to be back upstairs."

We do it, ransacking shelves and drawers, and pulling

chips out of the analytical equipment. Tran opens the fridge, revealing racks of neatly labeled vials. "What do we think about this?" he wants to know.

"Are those names on the labels?" Delphi asks as I move in. "Pull the racks out. We need to get a clear video record of everything."

I help Tran move the racks to the countertop. There are sixty. Each can contain up to thirty vials, but most aren't full.

I pull out one of the vials. It's the size of my little finger, half full of white powder. There's a paper label on it, printed with a tiny machine code and two lines of text, one in Arabic, one in Roman characters that spell a name, *Gunther Howe*. Not someone I've ever heard of, but as I inspect the rest of the rack, I find eight more vials bearing Gunther's name. "Kanoa, who—"

"A European industrialist. Died about two weeks ago."

"Not even encrypted," Delphi says in disgust.

Jaynie has worked it out. "They were betting on Nashira to protect them—and for four months, that was a good bet."

"It was a good bet tonight," Tran says. "I think fucking Nashira called out the neighborhood watch. We were lucky we even got here."

I put the vial back, check for other names in the same rack. I find several. Some are printed on only one vial. Some repeat two, three, four or more times. I don't recognize any of the names. "Kanoa, is this making sense to you?"

"Dragons," he says. "Politicians, journalists, bloggers, religious leaders."

The influential, the inconvenient, the uncooperative.

"You don't need to think about it now," Delphi adds. "Just get the data and get out."

But I do think about it. I think that every vial represents

a potential hit. Nine vials for Gunther, but he's already dead, so they must have gotten him the first time out. Some of the others, the ones with only one vial of white powder to their name—maybe they're still alive because they're too cautious, too careful to be hit . . . or maybe August-19's agents are out in the world trying to get close to them even now.

Tran described the enemy's strategy as a slow-motion decapitation of the world's leadership. I think he was right. The Red has been hunting this lab for months, but Nashira kept it hidden until now.

"Shelley, you need to focus," Kanoa warns.

Roger that.

I work faster, pulling out the vials, glancing at the labels. That's all I need to do, because everything I see, everything Tran sees, is recorded by our helmet cams and relayed straight to Guidance. To Abajian. To the Red.

We work our way through the racks and then shove them back in the refrigerator. Roman unpacks two thermite grenades—we'll burn the powder—while Jaynie and Fadul rig det cord and small blocks of C-4 around the lab equipment.

"We want to be done in thirty seconds," Delphi warns.

"*Shit,*" Tran whispers. At first I think he's objecting to the timeline. But then he holds out a vial for me to see. "It's got Papa's name."

"Is there only one?"

He checks the rack. "Yeah."

So, they've been after him. They've tried to hit him. "They haven't gotten him yet."

The next vial I look at is labeled *Jayne Vasquez.* I expel a slow breath and return it to the rack with exaggerated care. There are four other vials labeled with her name. "Jaynie, you need to get out of here. Go upstairs."

Each formula of white powder is tailored to affect the immune system of a specific individual. If something happens and these vials break, Jaynie is gone.

"Did you find me?" she asks, still stringing det cord. She sounds amused.

Delphi doesn't. "Finish the inventory, Shelley. Then we'll burn it all."

I hesitate a few seconds more, thinking it through. Semakova is already dead. Leonid and Jaynie are on the list. I have to ask, "Is your name here, Delphi?"

"Just finish the inventory. We need a complete list of the targets."

It's not just the targets who matter. The names that aren't here are just as important. Monteiro will need to investigate those, the absent names, the names of those not marked for death.

I shove the last rack back into the refrigerator. "We're done."

"Shelley, Tran, Fadul, upstairs," Jaynie says.

"No, you go," I tell her. "My name's not on these vials."

"He's right, Vasquez," Delphi says. "Head out."

They go, while I stay behind with Roman. We trigger the thermite grenades, shove them in with the vials, slam the fridge door shut, and bolt up the stairs as the searing hiss of a thermite fire melts the refrigerator from the inside out.

Upstairs, we find our position under heavy assault. There is a roar of continuous gunfire from the street. Rounds ping through the lobby, riddling the old plaster and generating a haze of white dust in the air.

Logan and his team have moved inside. Logan is crouched by the doorway, his HITR braced against his shoulder as he shoots rapidly at a target up the street. Flynn is belly-down across from him, squeezing the trigger of her

HITR in careful single shots, conserving ammunition. Dunahee is standing at a narrow window alongside the door. The glass has been broken out of it and, like Flynn, he's shooting methodically.

"Kanoa, sitrep," I demand as I run in a crouch to join Dunahee.

"We are under heavy fire, but enemy forces are not coordinated. They identify as irregulars—a local militia along with independent fighters. Estimated thirty or more with light arms, occupying the surrounding buildings."

Basically an angry mob, out for blood. Not that I blame them.

"Grenade," Flynn announces, just as Kanoa links everyone back into gen-com.

There's a boom and flash in the street. "Nice shot," Dunahee says quietly.

I look past him, out the window. "We getting RPG fire?"

"We've knocked two shooters down, but you can be damn sure someone picked up their equipment."

"How we doing on ammo?"

"We'll last a while."

I want to move out, but I am not CO of this squad. It's Jaynie's call.

I check for Escamilla on the squad map. He's still upstairs. "Escamilla, get down here."

"No, stay," Jaynie says.

I'm distracted from argument by a flurry of bullets whining, snapping through the window and the open doorway. I see a repeated muzzle flash across the street and return fire, even before a targeting circle comes up on my visor. I don't think I hit anything, but the shooter doesn't repeat from the same position.

"Where's the hellhound?" I ask over gen-com.

"Behind the door," Logan answers. He squeezes off

two shots. "Limited ammo, so it's being held in reserve. *Rooftop!*"

I raise my weapon in time to glimpse the head and shoulders of a shooter just visible behind a low wall surrounding the roof of the facing building. A targeting circle pops up. I cover it and fire at the same time as Dunahee. A spray of blood and brains, looking black in night vision, marks a hit as the shooter drops out of sight.

"Barriers are going up in the surrounding streets," Kanoa says. "Old cars. Tires that can be set on fire. The enemy will try to trap you inside this block."

We're rigged, and dressed in flame-retardant clothing. I don't think the barriers can stop us, but they'll slow us down, and we'll make easy targets as we clamber over them.

"Jaynie, what's going on? We need to move."

Jaynie drops in beside me. Speaks over gen-com. My helmet audio amplifies her voice over the rattle of gunfire. "It's a shooting gallery on that street. We'd have multiple wounded by the end of the block. So we're going to stay in the building. Egress on the opposite side of the block."

"Where the bomb went off?"

"Roger that. Seekers watching that side report less hostile activity."

I consider it. I consider our situation. The lobby we're defending is closed off from the rest of the first floor, which houses separate shops. "We go upstairs? Get out from the second floor?" I remember the explosion outside my dad's apartment in Manhattan. "You sure that side of the building didn't collapse?"

"It's intact except for glass blown out of the windows. It'll be easy to get out. I need you and Escamilla to go first. Clear our route. Get the doors open."

I glance over my shoulder at Logan, Dunahee, and Flynn, still holding the lobby door. "Squad follows close.

No one stays behind. Except the fucking hellhound. Let it
cover our retreat."

"That's the plan. Now *go*."

I hate leaving my soldiers under Jaynie's command. It's
not that I don't trust her. I do. But she's not their CO. She
doesn't know them like I know them. I go anyway because
it's a reasonable plan and we need to move.

"Escamilla!"

I charge the stairs, climbing them in two bounds. "We're
moving out, down the hallway."

It's a plain hall—no decoration at all—almost grim in
the green tint of night vision. The worn carpet looks black.
The doors on either side are a darker color than the walls.

Escamilla takes point. I follow five meters behind him.
Fadul comes up the stairs behind me. It takes only a few
seconds to traverse the hallway. I hear babies crying and
frantic arguments behind the apartment doors.

Escamilla reaches the last door. "Kick it in?"

"Roger that."

He hammers the door with his footplate. It's made of
flimsy wood that splinters at the point of impact. He kicks
it again, knocking out the latch just as I reach the door. I
shove the muzzle of my HITR inside to get a look and a
gun goes off. I hear a bullet punch through the broken
door and Escamilla jerks back. *Fuck!* From inside, a child
starts screaming.

I kick the door aside and drop low, ready to clear the
room.

"Don't shoot!" Kanoa orders.

I hold my fire, looking up at a young woman standing in a living room where the window has been blown
out, the tables and lamps have been overturned, books
and tablets spilled on the floor. She's dressed in a blouse
and loose pants, her thick black hair uncovered by a

hijab. She's holding a pistol in two hands, aimed at the door where my chest would be if I was standing up. A child, maybe three years old, is clinging to her leg and wailing. His shirt gleams with fresh blood; blood-stained white bandages hide wounds on his neck and the side of his head. I know without asking that he was cut by glass from the shattered window. There's another child, a little girl holding an infant in her arms. She ducks out of sight into a second room.

"Put it down," I tell the woman. I don't think she speaks English, but she understands my tone. She understands I'm serious when I shift my aim to the boy at her side. She drops the gun. Drops into a crouch. Sweeps the boy up and hugs him, hiding his face against her shoulder. She looks at me with a killing gaze. I gesture at her to follow the girl into the other room. She moves cautiously, but she moves.

"You hit, Escamilla?"

"Mule-kicked."

"Back me up." I dart after the woman, catching her by the arm just as she's passing through the doorway to the other room. She tries to wrench away, but I hold her, looking over her shoulder into a bedroom with a small bed, a closet, and a dresser covered with little vases and figurines and tiny jars of makeup and perfume all knocked over, with a shattered mirror on the floor. The little girl is crouched in a corner, surrounded by colorful pillows, hugging the wailing baby. "We're clear," I say, shoving the woman into the bedroom and closing the door. "Check the window."

Footplates crunch against broken glass as we move together to bracket the window. "Coming in," Fadul announces—a smart strategy to reduce the odds that we'll get jumpy and shoot her.

"Make sure that side door stays shut," I tell her.

"Yes, sir."

The woman's pistol is still on the floor. Fadul kicks it aside.

The street below is strewn with shattered glass reflecting shimmering light cast by the fires of two burning cars. The building behind the cars is partly collapsed, the first two floors exposed. I see bodies in the rubble. I hear people pleading. Wailing lamentations rise into the night. But I don't see anyone still alive. The battle AI finds no targets.

"Go, Escamilla. Fadul, move up."

Escamilla takes a few seconds to reload. Then he uses his footplate to sweep away shards of glass along the windowsill. Fadul moves in as he climbs through. Together we keep watch over the street as Escamilla drops to the pavement below. No one shoots at him, but in the distance I hear a shout of excitement, of discovery. Someone has seen us. Reported our position. Probably posted a photo on the locally preferred social media.

"Go, Fadul."

She scrambles outside, dropping to the ground just as Jaynie speaks over gen-com. "I'm triggering the explosives."

The concussion follows in less than a second, a low swift *boom!* The floor of the old building shudders more than I expect. Hairline cracks dart up the plaster walls. The woman in the bedroom cries out in terror; the kids wail. But the building stands. It was a measured blast, enough to destroy the lab equipment, not the building itself.

By this time, Roman is with me at the window and Tran is coming into the apartment. Outside, two gunshots echo between the buildings. Escamilla is across the street; Fadul is below me. Neither cries out, swears, goes down. We're okay. Then more shots. I think they're coming from the roof above us. Escamilla confirms it when he turns, aims his HITR high, and shoots two short bursts. Someone screams.

"Roman, go."

"Enemy knows your position," Kanoa warns as I gesture for Tran to follow Roman out the window. Flynn shows up, so I send her too. "Militia of twenty-two about to round the corner at the east end of the block."

"Cover the east end of the street!" I shout.

I lean out the window to get a line of fire.

It's not a militia that charges around the corner; it's a mob. There is no discipline, no organization to their attack. They are all men, dressed in street clothes, clutching assault rifles which go off almost on their own, spewing bullets in random directions. The leaders gesture at those behind them to seek cover, but it's too late for that. We hit them with a fusillade of gunfire.

On some higher, abstract level, I know these people should not be our enemies. Every kill we make tonight is a wasted life, gone for nothing—but nuance doesn't work in the middle of a firefight. My only goal now is to get my squad out alive, and we'll do what we have to do to achieve that.

At least three of the civilian militia fall. The rest pull back, or try to, but they run into their friends who are still coming in from behind. More go down. Some of them panic, but others stand their ground and return fire. I think Flynn is hit. She staggers and then dives for the cover of a chunk of concrete rubble. Tran and Roman keep shooting in a calm, steady rhythm, picking off the enemy or driving them behind cover.

"Coming behind you, Captain!" Dunahee calls.

I clear the window, gesturing with the muzzle of my HITR. "Climb out." I glance at Flynn's icon. It's shifted to yellow.

"Go, Shelley!" Jaynie says as she charges into the room. "Follow Dunahee."

"Where's Logan?"

He pops in through the apartment door. "Right here. *Go.*"

Dunahee is already out, so I squeeze through the window. Drop to the ground. My dead sister absorbs the shock. I turn to rejoin the fray—but the defenders have withdrawn behind the building. The battle AI gives me a targeting circle anyway, placing it over an upper-story window a block away. A live target: I see a muzzle flash as I fire. And then Jaynie and Logan drop down to the street, and we are ready to go.

"Logan, take point!" Jaynie barks.

Any hope of a quiet withdrawal ended in the first two minutes of this mission. The goal now is to get to a safe house, ditch our gear, and hope that Papa can evacuate us as anonymous civilians.

A projected path pops up in my visor. Logan moves out on it at a fast run, passing close to one of the burning cars. Escamilla follows a few steps behind him. The rest of us advance in teams, covering each other. Jaynie is paired with Fadul. Roman and Dunahee are a few meters behind. I go last, teamed up with Tran and Flynn. Bullets chase us. Not many, but they pass way too close. I hear them whizzing past my head, bouncing off concrete walls.

It's a long block. The path directs us to turn right at the end of it, onto a wide cross street. I'm happy to do it since it will get us out of the line of fire. But as Logan reaches the corner, the path changes directions, diving straight ahead.

"Barricades are going up," Kanoa says. "We've got armed defenders organizing on all sides."

Escamilla stops at the corner, covering Logan as he charges across the exposed street. Shooters are active in multistory apartments on both sides, but none seem expert. Jaynie and Fadul take over, punching rounds through windows where activity is detected. There's no way to know what's behind those windows; all we can do is shoot when the battle AI designates a target.

Escamilla crosses the street, followed by Roman and Dunahee. Then Jaynie and Fadul move.

The intersection is hot, and we've still got pressure behind us. As I send my team across I'm expecting the neighborhood militia to press their attack, but instead there's a pause in the shooting. It's like my audio has been suppressed. It's weird enough that I look back—to see the squad dog standing guard in the ruined street. It's positioned in the concrete rubble so it's not fully exposed, but it's visible to the militia at the east end of the block. It's not shooting—not yet—and neither are they.

I think it's spooked them. It's covering our retreat by intimidation alone—but that can't last. In a minute, maybe less, someone will bring an RPG to remove the threat.

We need to be long gone by then.

"Go, Shelley!" Jaynie says.

I take off after the squad, bounding across the intersection. For the scant seconds I'm in the open I glance up and down the street. In both directions, I glimpse crowds. They're a couple hundred meters away, gathered around burning barricades that are sending clouds of black smoke boiling into the night sky. I get past the intersection, but it doesn't look much better up ahead. Seventy meters away another barricade is going up, old cars being pushed into the street. Defensive fire starts buzzing through the air.

"Twenty-five meters ahead," Kanoa says. "Cut left through the alley. You'll have to go over the fence, but it'll get you to the next block."

The projected path shows the way.

This is a new neighborhood, composed of four-story housing projects, four buildings to a block, each identical to its neighbors. The blocks are divided by wide streets. Narrow alleys run between the buildings.

Logan moves out first, with the squad following at tight intervals. We are camouflaged so that to an unenhanced eye, we must appear as shadows in motion, the suggestion of a presence passing through the solid shadows cast by walls and the buildings along the streets. But that's enough to make us targets. Rounds zip through the air, but most pass over our heads or skip along the apartment walls.

Logan turns, darting into the designated alley. Escamilla follows. Dunahee is next, but he stumbles. Roman catches his arm, steadies him. They move together around the corner. Jaynie and Fadul follow, then Flynn and Tran.

I go last. That lets me keep an eye on every soldier in the squad, but I don't linger. The rate of fire is picking up. As I cut around the corner a bullet hits the masonry, sending a spray of shrapnel against my visor. Another cracks into the back of my helmet, but it's almost spent and doesn't rattle me too badly.

The alley we're in is barely two meters wide, with a chain-link fence at the back dividing it from the other buildings on the block. Logan is already over the fence. Escamilla jumps down beside him. They continue to the opposite end of the alley while the rest of us climb over.

"Straight through," Kanoa says. "Across the street and into the next alley. Don't slow down." He can see all the streets, the lanes, the alleys, the rooftops. That lets him count down the time we have to cross the street before the pursuing militia catches up. He can even see inside some of the buildings using the seekers that follow us through the street.

"Target," he tells me. "Forty degrees."

Too bad the neighborhood has its own surveillance network.

I look up, see the targeting circle, cover it, and squeeze off a burst—but I'm not fast enough. A grenade has already been lobbed. It goes off in the street with a concussion that sends Flynn diving for the next alley.

"Go!" Kanoa says, and Tran and I sprint to catch up.

The projected path takes us through the next alley, across the next street. We take intermittent fire. In the brief periods of silence between the shooting, my audio pickups feed me fragments of conversation in Arabic, grabbed from the apartments overhead. The fragments are automatically translated and echoed in English, but they don't make any sense to me. It doesn't matter. What matters is that this neighborhood is full of people. I don't have to see them to know they're looking for us, talking about us, working together to track us, using phones and farsights to report our position—to who? To the L-AI that watches over this district?

Probably not. Nashira is a security AI, trained to manipulate data. That's how it hid the existence of the lab. It's not a battle AI.

In the buildings ahead of us, lights go on as residents wake to the noise of shooting—and go off again when they get word of what's going on.

"Kanoa," I whisper, "do they have a drone? Can I take it out?"

"They're using seekers."

Just like us.

I can't shoot down a flock of seekers. They're small and fly so low that any shot I take risks injuring noncombatants, and seekers are so cheap that backups are probably being held on standby, ready to launch if the first wave gets taken down.

It's not going to be easy to shake our pursuers and just slip away.

"The only way we're going to get out of here," I whisper, relying on my audio system to boost the volume to a perceptible range, "is to convince the local militia it's not worth their lives to pursue us."

"Roger that," Kanoa says, his voice an ominous dead calm.

We reload, and then we double back through the maze of alleys as Kanoa tries to get us to the nearest safe house. From all the time spent in simulation, I know we're just a few blocks away from it, but between the barricades, the pursuing militia, and defensive fire directed at us from the neighborhood apartments, we haven't been able to get close. And I've got three wounded soldiers, their icons showing yellow.

I call a time-out.

"Jaynie! We need to stop and treat."

It's a dangerous choice. We don't want to get trapped. But Dunahee is bleeding from a thigh wound. Roman's been shot in the hand and has lost a little finger. Flynn is cut up from shrapnel.

Jaynie agrees with me. So we break into a cinderblock store and hunker down. Outside, sirens are wailing, and I hear a distant rumbling of approaching helicopters. There's shooting on at least three fronts. "What the hell is going on out there, Kanoa? All this shooting can't be directed at us."

"Peripheral fighting's erupted."

"Ah, *fuck*."

"The local militias have been slugging it out for years."

"We've started *another* war."

"We did what we had to do."

I think August-19 chose this site for their facility not

just because Nashira is here, but also because they knew that any provocation in this neighborhood would meet sudden and severe retaliation. It's a cold-blooded but effective strategy, to hide behind a hair-trigger civilian militia. No need to pay for an army and the facility stays secret, hidden in plain sight. I don't think our intelligence team understood that when they sent us in here.

A flurry of shots whizzes in. "Do not return fire," Jaynie orders in a stern undertone. "Let them wonder if we're really here."

It takes just a few minutes to get Flynn and Roman glued up and stable. Dunahee worries me more. The wound in his thigh isn't life-threatening, but he's got a couple of serious dents in his helmet. "You cross-eyed?" I ask him.

"Maybe."

If he's got a concussion, he could go down without warning. "Roman, I want you to stick close to Dunahee."

"Yes, sir."

We redistribute the remaining ammo. We're getting ready to go when Kanoa checks in with me again. "Mission update."

Our goal has changed. We're not trying to reach the safe house anymore. Out beyond this maze of housing projects is an oil storage field. Behind the tanks is a wide-open asphalt tarmac, laid out for future expansion. "Get there," Kanoa says. "You'll get picked up."

"How? By who?"

He hesitates. "A local security company. They'll be bringing in Z transports."

Chinese helicopters, flown by mercenaries. The US Navy is just off the coast with a fleet of gunships, but to preserve the anonymity of this operation, we're going to be handed over to an outfit that works for the highest bidder. Hoo-yah.

"I hope they don't get a better offer before they get us out of here."

"I hope they haven't gotten a better offer already."

That shuts me up. For Kanoa to say something like that during an active operation—he's got to be worried.

"Eyes open," he adds.

"Roger that."

Jaynie gets the news from her own handler. That would be Delphi—a thought that stirs a spike of regret. But it's better this way.

Jaynie makes the announcement to the squad. "We're heading out of this district. It's just a few more blocks. Once we're clear of the projects, we should leave the fighting behind. After that, we run an easy klick and a half to the pickup point. We're going to be okay."

She doesn't mention the private security company. Neither do I.

A new route posts on the squad map. It shows our position, and known positions of the enemy. There's a significant firefight several blocks north, but that doesn't concern us—and it hasn't distracted the militias that are hunting us. They know where we are. They're setting up barricades to contain us, and though the map doesn't show it, my guess is they're bringing in heavier weapons. We will have to get past them, out of the projects, over a canal, through a neighborhood of family compounds, and across a wider canal before we reach the pickup site. It feels like a long way.

Jaynie sketches a plan. There are forces outside, waiting for us to emerge. We intend to take them by surprise. "All right," Jaynie says as the map winks out of sight. "Let's do this."

We answer with a quiet *"Hoo-yah!"*

"Execute."

I kick open the back door. Across the street is another of the endless identical project buildings, ugly boxes to hold people with nowhere else to go.

The open door inspires shouts and wild gunshots that come nowhere near us. Flynn and Dunahee lean out long enough to fire grenades into the air above the street—a double burst intended to make everyone duck. Logan and Escamilla step outside into a rain of shrapnel, firing two more grenades, this time at a pair of black pickup trucks waiting at the end of the street with gunmen standing in the truck beds.

Fadul and I are only a step behind. We cover the opposite end of the street, working through a series of targeting circles in a determined effort to convince any would-be shooters to keep the fuck down.

"Move out!" Jaynie barks. "Go, go, go!"

Fadul stays with me. We keep shooting until everyone is out and then we turn and run like hell past the wreckage of the two pickup trucks. Bloody, burned men are strewn across the asphalt along with their weapons. Most are still alive. When one reaches for a rifle, I kick it away and keep running, chased by an escalating volume of fire.

I'm midstride when a burst stitches my pack. The force knocks me off balance. I stumble against a brick wall, which explodes in front of my face when it's hit by the next flurry of bullets.

Fadul is in front of me. She turns to shoot at whoever is shooting at me. I pivot and back her up. Tran joins us. It takes maybe twenty seconds to persuade the shooters to back off. Then we turn and run as the air vibrates with the thunder of a charging gunship.

"Get under cover!" I shout over gen-com. But there is no

cover. Not in the street. We have to shelter in a building.

"Inside, inside!" Jaynie orders, bounding for the front door of the nearest building. Logan and Escamilla meet her there, training their weapons on the door as Jaynie kicks it open. They charge in. There's no return fire.

Roman goes in next with Dunahee. Flynn is right behind them as the gunship roars in, low and fast. I'm not going to make it to the door. So I drop into a crouch against the wall, hoping my high-tech camouflage will hide me. That's how I get a good look at the gunship. It's not hunting us. It passes our position a block away, all lights off, but there is enough ambient light that night vision lets me see its insignia. "Iraqi Army," I whisper over gen-com.

I can't tell for sure, but I think it sweeps in over the bombed street beside the lab. Gunfire greets it. It answers with heavier-caliber fire.

"Holy shit," Fadul whispers. She's hunkered down a couple of meters away from me. "They're shooting their own people?"

Tran says, "Maybe Abajian sent it. Maybe he convinced the IA it's an armed revolt."

I'm thinking something else: that it wasn't Abajian who persuaded the IA.

Dunahee says it for me. "Maybe it was the Red."

"I don't care who it was," Jaynie says. "Let's move."

We hit the street again, stampeding toward the perimeter of the projects. Someone takes a couple of shots from out of a window. "Kanoa, target?"

"Let it go. It's a kid."

The route takes us right, then left, then right again, across streets and through alleys—and the gunfire directed against us quickly drops off. The streets ahead are open. It gets so quiet I can hear the faint, insect buzz of seekers scouting the street.

It's like we've stepped over some boundary, invisible to us, that marks a different neighborhood, one where people have decided their best option is to hide the children in closets and behind mattresses, and hunker down while we pass through.

It's a good choice.

Without resistance, we move fast. We only need to get past three more buildings to put the projects behind us and reach the first canal.

I start to think that maybe we're going to make it, but Escamilla kills that hope when he says, "I got a bad feeling."

And Logan: "I got it too. Let's get off this street."

Jaynie says, "Shelley, confirm?"

I can't confirm it. I took out my receiver so I don't get premonitions anymore. But I trust my squad. "We need to move."

"On it," Kanoa says. "Backtrack. Take the lane."

The route shifts, rolls back behind me, and then cuts into a lane between two buildings. "Move!" I shout, turning, stepping out of the street, taking a position at the corner of the lane that lets me watch the facing buildings.

Tran is closest. He jumps after me, taking a defensive position a few meters away and behind a parked car. The others are still scrambling when I see movement in several windows on the third floor across the street.

I should have suspected the silence. The seekers I heard were not ours.

"Take cover!" Kanoa barks. "Movement on all—"

I'm already shooting when a torrent of gunfire erupts from windows on both sides of the street. Escamilla is hit in the first volley. His icon blazes on the periphery of my vision, bright red as he goes down. Flynn gets hit too. A plume of blood flies from her shoulder. The hit leaves her staggering, but she still manages to retreat into the lane. Her icon stays yellow. Dunahee spasms, stumbles. But like Flynn, he keeps his feet, and with Roman's help, he too makes the lane.

Fadul is next, bounding past me. But as soon as she's in the lane, she turns and steps out again, firing a grenade. The concussion rattles the street and slows the assault, giving Logan a respite as he bends down, setting an arm hook around the shoulder strut of Escamilla's dead sister. Jaynie assists him, and together they drag Escamilla into the shelter of the lane while Tran and I hammer positions on the building across the street.

Fadul crouches at my feet and starts shooting too. "How the fuck," she whispers between bursts, her voice amplified by gen-com. "How the fuck did these fuckers . . . fucking know . . . our route?"

Fair question. This is the most concentrated firepower we've faced. More than we dealt with in the first block outside the lab or the fusillade as we left the shelter of the store. It's an ambush, and it had to have been in place for many minutes or our seekers would have detected the presence of gunmen assembling in the buildings. If Escamilla hadn't spoken up when he did, we might have been too far from the lane, and all of us would have been shot down in the street.

"Fadul!" Jaynie snaps. "Move out. You're on point. Kill anything that gets in your way."

"Roger that, ma'am!"

Fadul spins away. Jaynie sends the rest of the squad after her. I cover the next targeting circle, and the next, ever aware of Escamilla's red icon, willing it not to shift to black.

Jaynie says, "Tran. Shelley. Let's go."

"Right behind you."

I give them a few seconds to move out and then I turn and follow.

The apartments flanking this lane rise in windowless brick faces, but the lane is wider than the alleys we've been through. There's enough room that a line of cars is parked on one side. I've passed the first few when Kanoa speaks in a low, urgent voice. "Take cover between the cars."

Tran is a few meters ahead of me. He ducks out of sight, while I drop into a crouch between two little economy sedans.

"Seven militia, with more behind them, are gathering at the start of the lane. Shelley, you and Tran need to hold them off. Give us time to move the wounded."

"Roger that. Tran?"

"Yes, sir! They shall not pass."

I glance at the squad map. Fadul has paused in her advance, like she's waiting for the squad to catch up. They're not far behind her. Flynn, despite her injuries, is helping Logan to handle Escamilla; Jaynie and Roman are shepherding Dunahee.

I dismiss the map. "Kanoa, you got video of the street?"

He puts a feed on my visor's display. The perspective is from near the rooftop. It shows a crowd of gunmen gathering just outside the lane. Two of them ease around the corner, crouching behind the cars.

"Hold your fire, Tran," I whisper, concentrating on staying calm, cold, analytical. It's become my default state.

The two whisper together. One leans out, looks down the lane like he's trying to figure out where we are. I don't think he has night vision. I wait. I want them to take their time, think about what they're doing. The longer they take, the more time the squad has to reach the canal. Two more join the first pair. Outside the lane, another talks on a phone. He wants a report on our exact position.

"Target on the rooftop," Kanoa says, clearing the video from my visor.

I look up, cover a targeting circle, and shoot. There's a scream. The shooter drops his rifle. It almost hits me, while he falls backward, out of sight.

Tran opens fire down the lane, hitting a guy in the forehead as he peers around a corner to check out the action. Two of the men crouched behind the cars lean out to try some test shots. One of their rounds ricochets off the brick, drilling into a parked car and setting off an alarm. Another bites into pavement, kicking up grit.

I shoot under the cars, which flushes the men into the open. Tran hits one, sending him sprawling. He clips another, who ducks out of sight. The last two flee back around the corner.

"Fall back," Kanoa says.

I pivot out from between the cars, and run. Tran is ahead by several meters, moving fast, when Kanoa orders me down again. I crouch between a new set of cars while bullets fly past, zipping, pinging, cracking into the vehicles, shattering their windows and punching holes in their sides. Someone in the militia uses my trick, shooting under the vehicles. Two rounds ricochet off my robot legs, sending jolts of pain into my hips, but the legs hold out.

I wait for a lull. Then I stick my HITR out past the sheltering body of the car, letting the muzzle cams take a look at things. It's busy out there. The battle AI posts targeting circles. I cover them and let the AI pull the trigger. It squeezes off a series of single shots that put two militia on the ground and send two more diving for cover.

As soon as the last one is down, I go.

My route gleams at my feet. It's a path straight through to the end of the lane, where a wide cross street leads to the canal. "Where's Tran?" I gasp.

Kanoa answers, "Around the corner."

I can't believe Tran has reached the end of the lane already. I wish I could run that fast. I run as hard as I can, all too aware I've got no cover while I'm moving. It'll be just seconds before the shooting starts again.

I don't want to take a bullet in my back.

I want to get the fuck out of this city.

A flurry of shots erupts behind me. At least one pings off my helmet. A few slam into my pack. I don't slow down.

Then Kanoa is yelling at me, "Why aren't you on the route?"

"I am on the route!" It's glowing beneath my feet.

"You're not! You missed your turn. You should have—" He stops in midsentence, while I drop into another gap between cars. I lean out and shoot, just to let the enemy know I'm still dangerous. "This doesn't make sense," Kanoa says. "Shelley, I'm looking at a copy of your display. What you're seeing, it's not right. That's not the path you're supposed to see."

"So fucking fix it!"

"Updating."

I fire a few more rounds and then eye the squad map until it expands. It shows my soldiers nowhere near me. They left the lane earlier, turned toward the canal. They're already at the water. *"Shit."*

My shoulders heave, my hands shake, sweat is streaming down my face, but my mind is calm, machinelike. "I can't go back."

"No. You have to get to the end of the lane. There's no other way out."

Okay.

I fire a few more shots. Swap out the magazine. It's a long way to the end of the lane.

At the start of this mission we were instructed to limit

our impact, but war is not something you can control. It never goes the way the planners say it will. I shift my finger to the second trigger. A well-placed grenade could help me close up this lane, delay the pursuit for at least a few seconds.

I squeeze.

Nothing happens.

I check the grenade magazine. Still two left. I try again.

Nothing happens—and I'm taking a lot of fire. Bullets are pinging off the cars around me, bouncing along the walls, skipping on the ground. I try to return fire, just to discourage the militia, but when I squeeze the first trigger, nothing happens. It's like my HITR's been unregistered, like I'm holding another soldier's weapon.

"Kanoa!" My heart pounds about ten times in the next two seconds. "Kanoa, you there?"

No answer.

I check the icons on my visor's display. They show me still linked to gen-com, but I'm not getting through.

"Jaynie, you there? Answer me! Logan?"

Nothing, though I still see them on the map. They're already across the canal and moving in among the houses. It's like they don't even know I'm missing.

I push the HITR around the back of the car again, using the muzzle cams to get another look down the lane. There's no reason that should work, but it does. So I'm still linked to the weapon. The feed from the muzzle cams pops up on my display—it shows me figures shooting from behind the cover of parked cars—but I can't shoot back. The trigger is dead.

My system is compromised.

I'm compromised. Isolated.

And I know what's happened. The L-AI that monitors this district, the one that's called Nashira—it's not a battle

AI, but it's adaptable. It must have penetrated my electronics. Maybe it hacked the Red, or maybe it just took over the task of managing me. Isn't that what Issam told me in Budapest? That tasks tend to get transferred to a locally dominant AI?

It's compromised my communications and my primary weapon. At least my skullnet is safe. It can't reach into my head. But I need to get the fuck out of here before it hits my dead sister. I sling the HITR over my shoulder. Then I pull my pistol. It doesn't have linked electronics, so it should work.

I do not want to be taken prisoner. Just a few hours ago the people of this city were not the enemy, but our raid changed that.

I fire two quick shots down the lane, spin out, and run.

A roar of gunfire erupts behind me. Bullets slam my helmet, hammer my pack, ping off my dead sister. One bites at my thigh, another at my arm.

It's a fucking long way to the end of the lane, and it's not freedom waiting there for me. It's more militia, three or four soldiers peering out at me from behind the cover of the buildings. I slow down, wondering why they're not shooting. Then my footplate brushes the dusty surface of a deep pothole—and the ground blows up. The frame of my dead sister twists through the air, taking me with it. I'm weirdly conscious the whole time—of the dust, the explosive smell, the tumbling lights of distant apartments—and then a plunge back to earth, ending with a metal-on-metal concussion as I slam sideways across the hood of a car.

The weirdest part is the silence that follows. I don't know if I've gone deaf, if my helmet has failed, or if time has stopped, but I don't hear any shooting at all. No voices. No sirens. No helicopters. Not even my own heartbeat.

Nothing.
It's as if the war has passed me by.
Too bad it doesn't last.

Time kick-starts with the blunt heat of a gun muzzle
pressed hard under my chin. When the trigger gets pulled,
a bullet will jump into my brain case. Someone speaks an
order I can't understand. A lot of people are speaking. An
angry burr of unintelligible conversation as many hands
work to loosen the cinches that strap me to my dead sister.
I try to move, but it's already too late. My arm comes loose
from the frame. Someone grabs my wrist, wrenches it back.
The muzzle presses deeper into my chin. My helmet comes
off. The straps on my pack are released.

They pull me to my feet. I wrench my arm away from
whoever is holding it and reach for one of the grenades I
carry in my vest. But there's a problem. I don't actually
have a right foot anymore. The robot leg is gone, blown
off at the knee where a quick release was designed into it
to minimize damage to the joint. The trouser leg on that
side is shredded and soaked with blood. My left foot is still
there, but it's bloody too, looking like a human foot with
the flesh blown off.

I collapse, but arms catch me halfway. I struggle, but
there are too many hands. They strip me of my pistol holster, my armored vest, my combat jacket. They take me
down to my T-shirt, and then they cut that away, like
they want to make sure I'm human underneath. Who
can blame them, with the titanium bones of my left foot
showing? They strip my trousers off too, and then I'm
naked, bleeding from both thighs, but it doesn't hurt and
I don't ask for mercy and they don't offer it. Why should
they?

The chaos of angry voices quiets as they contemplate my artificial bones. In the lull, other sounds speak to my consciousness: a distant gun battle, the growling thunder of helicopters, and Delphi's voice—I think that part is my imagination—telling me, *"Hold on. We're coming."* The crowd recovers its outrage. There is wailing and furious denunciations. These are bereft fathers, grieving friends. A rope goes around my neck.

Who can blame them?

They could drag me by the rope, but they don't. They walk me to the end of the lane, as well as I can be walked on one foot, two strong men holding onto my arms. Odors assault me: sweat and blood and gunpowder and rot. From the end of the lane, it's a short half block to the canal and a little footbridge that crosses the stagnant water. The bridge is not very high, but if they keep the rope short that won't matter.

They want to justify themselves. It feels like an unnecessary formality to me, but they're civilians. They lecture me in Arabic. Tear-streaked faces and clenched fists. My overlay tries to translate, but the voices are too mixed, too chaotic. One man screams at me in English. "Why did you come here? *Why?*"

We came because we needed to raid the lab, to find out who was behind the assassinations, so we could target them next and prevent the collapse of President Monteiro's administration, preserving a last hope of democracy in the United States. That's why your children, your brothers, your sisters, your friends are dead.

But I don't say any of that shit out loud, because I don't understand it either.

They secure the rope to the bridge's railing. They secure

my hands behind my back. I struggle hard enough that it takes five of them to lift me up over the rail and drop me on the other side.

The drop is too short to snap my neck.

I kick and twitch above the putrid water. Everything is a blur. I can't breathe; I can't swallow. I can't scream. My heartbeat rattles my bones.

Someone transfers gen-com to my overlay. I see the icons switch on, though they're all a blur. Kanoa speaks to me. "Use your foot, Shelley. It's not tied down. Try to reach the understructure of the bridge."

I try it, but I'm hanging from my fucking neck and the rope just pulls tighter. Drool spills out between my swollen lips. Or maybe it's blood. It splashes in the water below. The splashing gets louder. For a second, I think rescue has come, that Logan must have waded out into the canal to catch me when Jaynie or Tran cuts the rope.

Then I realize the splashing is just my robot foot kicking spastically in the water . . . and I'm not sure anymore I even heard Kanoa's voice—how could I, over the roaring in my ears? A roaring that gets louder with every wild, useless beat of my heart until Hell opens up and I drop, plunging through a wall of flame—

—into water.

The transition shocks me into an animal panic. I roll, hitting debris. And then I discover the mud-covered concrete bottom of the canal. I push off, twisting into the air. I'm propped up on my robot knee and the empty joint of my other leg, in water that barely reaches my waist. The rope is still around my neck, still tight, but I can sip air past it. I arch my neck, and that loosens the rope a little more. I can't see much. Just fire, reflected in water, and dense smoke in the air. I think the bridge is burning. I hear the ratcheting thunder of a gunship making a tight turn, the beat of its blades echoing off buildings. I don't want to be here if it's coming this way.

My hands are still tied behind my back, so I shake my head to clear my eyes. That loosens the rope a little more and lets me see a body floating face down in the water beside me, illuminated in firelight. Beyond it is the concrete bank of the canal and the smoldering ruin of the bridge. I push past the body, crawling on my artificial knees. As the gunship roars in, I collapse on the bank, hoping I'll be taken for just another fresh corpse.

A machine gun hammers—multiple bursts—but they're not shooting at me. I stay down until the gunship turns back over the city. Then I wriggle out of the water and creep on my robot knees up the concrete bank.

It's surprisingly quiet. People must have run when the gunship came. I don't see anyone.

I do hear someone crying.

Farther away, there's more noise: frantic shouts, wails, helicopter engines, car horns. Shooting.

A path pops up, projected in my overlay. It's a different color than the projected paths I'm used to seeing. This one is red. The dark red of a cyber presence bleeding out of the Cloud. A blood road.

I tell myself it's just Nashira, come to fuck with me again—but I don't believe that.

Never trust the Red—but when was I any good at taking advice?

I follow the new path, stumping along on my knees, fighting to keep my balance and to breathe, all the time working my hands to loosen the rope that binds them. It's a long, exhausting journey, but I finally make it back to the lane.

The buildings are dark. I hear someone—a man— screaming his outrage on one of the upper floors. It's a one-way conversation, like he's talking on a phone. But no one's outside and thank God for that. I crawl into the lane, following the path to the crater where the IED went off. The path ends there.

I sit for a minute, hiding in the shadow of a car with a hole blasted in its door, fighting to get enough air past the restriction around my throat so that I don't pass out. Past my own constricted gasps, I listen to the percussive racket of ongoing firefights from at least two fronts, and to gunships blazing away at targets around the city. The gunships must be going after anything that looks like resistance.

They've already been through here and moved on. I hope my squad got out okay. I hope they made it to the pickup point and that they're all still alive.

Eventually I notice that the car's shattered door has a sharp metal edge. I use it to work through the rope that's binding my hands. I open up a few cuts in my palms and on my forearms, but what the hell. I get my hands free. Then I get the rope off my neck. My neck is swollen, bruised. It hurts like hell and I can barely swallow. Not sure if I can talk.

Fuck it.

Time to find my missing leg. I know it's here. Why else would the Red bother to lead me back to this place?

I crawl around the rough paving until I see it, underneath the next car in line. To reach it, I have to get belly-down, naked against the grit. I pull the leg out, blow grit off the end, and lever it into the knee joint. It locks right in. The toes flex. The knee bends. It works fine. "Joby," I whisper in a voice perfect for the wounded antagonist of some slasher flick, "you are a fucking genius . . . and holy shit it hurts to talk."

So I shut up.

I recover my ragged trousers and then my T-shirt. The shirt is filthy and shredded. I use it anyway, to mop the blood and sweat from my face and arms and chest, and then I toss it away. My jacket is gone. So is my pack with some of the electronics we confiscated from the lab. And of course there is no sign of my weapons or my rig.

I scan my overlay. I remember gen-com switching on when I was hanging from the bridge, and Kanoa's voice . . . but I'm not linked in now. I try to fix that. I send the link, but it doesn't work. The link gets rejected. I check my network icon—green—and try again, but I don't get anywhere. Before I can get seriously worried, a document pops open in my overlay:

Mission Briefing
Codename: Kingmaker Prime
Target: private Basra security and surveillance
    system designated "Nashira"
Objective: breach secure facility and destroy
    core hosting platform
Timetable: mission to be undertaken immedi-
    ately and completed before dawn.
Additional: interactive map attached. Details
    to follow.

It's a joke, isn't it?

I want to believe it's a joke.

The interactive map unfolds. It charts my position in the surrounding terrain, using a glowing red line to mark out a route to the target, three kilometers to the southwest. With no input from me, the map changes format. It expands and rolls over, superimposing itself on the terrain around me. The route begins here. It begins with me. I'm sitting at the start of the blood road, a projected path to coax me back out of the lane.

I stare at the route in exhaustion. I close my eyes, but the blood road is still there. Guess I should have known the Red didn't intervene in my execution out of gratitude for past service.

I get up. At first, I'm dizzy. Anyone can see I'm in no shape for another mission. What I need to do is get to the pickup point Kanoa designated out beyond the oil storage tanks. I try again to log in to gen-com to let them know I'm coming, but the system won't let me in.

Nothing to do but follow the blood road back to the canal. By the time I get there, my head is clearing. I look out past the canal, over a low-rise neighborhood of walled family compounds, and beyond them to the silhouettes of oil storage tanks rising against a starless sky. That's where I need to go, but the blood road turns west, paralleling the canal. Somewhere out there—I can't see exactly where—it crosses the water. I can see it again in the southwest, a fine red line projected in my overlay, leading to a low hill maybe sixty meters high. The hill is an anomaly in the flat, featureless terrain around it. My guess is it's artificial. A mansion sits on top of it, surrounded by date palms and a fortress wall studded with landscape lights that illuminate it in the night.

I'm supposed to go there—if I accept the mission.

I don't have to accept it. I cut the receiver out of my skullnet so the Red wouldn't have a direct line to my emotions, so that I'd be free to make a rational choice at a time like this, and the rational choice is to get the fuck out of Basra while I'm still alive.

I wish now I'd left the receiver in, because that would let me blame the Red for all my bad decisions.

I spit blood and phlegm and use the back of my hand to wipe drool from my swollen lips.

I've got no weapons, no rig, no angel sight, no night vision, and no squad to back me up. The setup reminds me of that Bible story about King David before he was king, when God sent him alone out to the battlefield armed with only a slingshot. I think that little adventure was supposed to be a test of faith, but I fail at tests like that. Better to know a well-connected arms dealer than to invest any faith in the Red.

I can't reach gen-com, but that doesn't mean I'm isolated, not when my network icon is green. I try calling Papa—and that works. He picks up right away. "Shelley, you made it out?"

I start to speak. Nothing comes. I try harder and manage a whisper. "Papa, things got seriously fucked. Are you still in the city?"

Silence, as he thinks this over.

"*Da*. I am still here. How many of you are alive?"

"I don't know. I got separated from the squad and locked out of gen-com. They should have been pulled out by now."

"And you?"

"I lost my gear. I need a weapon."

"Where are you?"

I capture my GPS coordinates and send them.

"Can you get across the canal?" he asks.

My hands shake at the thought of going back into that canal. "The bridge is blown out."

"The water is shallow, no?"

I think, *Lock it down.*

"Yeah. I'll wade across."

"I will come."

As soon as I step away from the blood road, it disappears. I climb down into the canal, keeping away from the debris, the floating body. Mud tugs at my robot feet, and I trip over glass and wire and old steel cans, but I manage not to fall down and of course nothing can cut me.

As I climb out of the canal, an SUV rolls up, headlights off. The passenger window glides down. The doors unlock. It's too dark to see inside, but I hear Papa say, "Get in."

I do. The window goes up as I slide into the passenger seat. "Did you bring weapons?" I ask in a hoarse whisper.

"No. This mission is over. My role in it is over." He makes a sharp turn onto a narrow residential street. "I've heard nothing from Abajian. And there is a curfew, enforced by gunship."

I twist around to check the sky and right away I see the silhouettes of two gunships over the city, but they're way off to the north. One is briefly illuminated by muzzle flash from its machine gun.

Leonid turns left at the next corner, and then right. No other vehicles are moving on the streets. "What happened to you?" he asks.

"I got hacked. And not by the Red. Mumbino breached gen-com. I think that's why I'm locked out. But I think something critical got exposed when it happened. I think the Red worked out how L-AIs like Nashira are being used against it."

The gates of a compound open ahead of us.

"I have to go out again, Papa. There's another mission."

He turns in through the gate, parks the SUV outside a house where no lights are showing, and says, "No. I've heard nothing from Abajian. It's over."

I tell him, "The target is Nashira."

Past the closed window, I hear the distant rumble of helicopters, a smattering of gunfire. And then Leonid gives in to a low, rumbling sigh. "Nashira," he says. "You know where it is?"

"Yes, I know." Maybe the Red always knew Nashira's location, or maybe that was something it had to work out through human hacking—listening to conversations, seeing through infiltrated farsights and overlays, monitoring the EXALT nodes. "Everyone visible, everyone accountable."

"That was your excuse for what happened in the cavern."

"That's the world the Red is making. L-AIs like Nashira fuck with that. Think about it, Papa. If Nashira hadn't kept the lab hidden, Semakova might still—"

"Stop! You want to persuade me? You want to remind me of what is lost? Stop first and think of your own life. Do you remember what happened in the UGF, Shelley? How close we came to dying in that tunnel?"

"*Yes*, I remember it." My voice is almost gone. "I don't know why I'm still alive, except for this. If we find Nashira, figure out who's behind it, maybe we find the Arctic AI too. Maybe we can stop that war before things get worse."

"You're a madman, Shelley."

"No. It's just I've seen behind the curtain. And I need your help, Papa. You know and I know there are a thousand ways this world could die—but not on my watch."

"Go inside," he growls. "And then you can tell me a madman's plan."

Leonid gets his first good look at me when the lights come on in the house. "You look like a man who just crawled up from Hell."

"It's really fucked down there, Papa. I'm not looking forward to eternity."

"*Da*. I'm not either."

It's a Western-style house, the layout and furnishings

generic and familiar. Leonid orders me into the shower. I wash off the blood and the stink under a lukewarm trickle of water, and clean out my wounds—gouges and cuts and lacerations. I'm dizzy, and I don't think I've got a square inch of skin that isn't bruised. For sure, everything hurts like hell. Leonid helps me treat the shallow wounds and glue the bigger ones shut. "What happened to you?" he asks me.

I tell him about the hack, and the hanging, and the attack on the bridge.

"I think a missile hit it. Thought I was in Hell, but it saved my life." He thinks about all this as I dress in civilian clothes—brown slacks and a short-sleeved beige shirt. "Abajian must have seen the missile strike," he concludes as we return to the living room. "He believes you are lost, dead. He would say to your squad it was too late to rescue you. Priority, to get the electronic intelligence out."

"And the wounded," I remind him, collapsing into a chair beside the table. Leonid has gathered equipment there: a folded med-kit, plastic-wrapped camouflage shirts, two digital night-vision glasses, two armored vests, a pair of Lasher 762 assault rifles. I gesture at the gear. "All this." I look up at him. "You're going to help?"

He's glaring, his eyebrows knit in a fierce scowl. "Do not ever doubt the existence of God, Shelley. I asked that I be allowed to serve Him in some small way. And what did He do?" He raises his eyebrows. "He sent me you. But as you reminded me, this Nashira helped those who murdered Yana. So yes, let's go. And see what can be done."

"Okay." Leonid's reasons are no crazier than mine. "But I need to link up with Logan. I need to know the squad got out."

"You want Logan to know you're alive?"

"Why wouldn't I?"

He opens the med-kit and sorts through the blister packs of pills. "Because this mission was given to you, and only you. If it was given to Logan too, and Tran, why cut you off from gen-com?"

"Because my security was compromised." I think about it. "Or maybe it was to keep Abajian out?"

He looks up from the med-kit, eyeing me from beneath his heavy brows.

"I trust my squad," I insist. "It's the Red I don't trust. And Abajian. So yeah, let's find out where they are. If they're still here, maybe we can bring them in. Do the mission, but do it our way."

"Tonight?"

"Tonight."

He hands me three blister packs. "A stimulant, an antibiotic, a pain killer."

I get a bottle of water from the fridge. Swallowing those pills is one more torment added to the evening, but I do it.

Then I sit for a few minutes and think. *Should I do this by myself?* The way the Red intended? In the Bible, David went alone to the battlefield, but I'm not David. I want my squad around me.

I dictate a text to Logan: "Need a sitrep. NOT on gen-com. Did you get pulled out?" The text-to-voice handles my hoarse whispering without a problem.

Send.

It takes twenty-two seconds for Logan to get back to me. *Who the fuck is this?*

"Who do you think? Sitrep! Where are you?" *Send.*

You asshole. We are out here looking for your fucking body.

They're still here. Part of me is happy to hear it. Relieved. But they're not supposed to be here. "You were supposed to get pulled out." *Send.*

*Abajian wasn't joking about your fucking messiah complex.
You figured we'd just leave you behind?*

"Escamilla was almost dead. You damn well better be able to tell me he's out." *Send.*

He's evac'd. Dunahee, Roman, and Flynn too. There's your sitrep. Now where the fuck are you?

"Safe house. With Papa. We've got another mission." *Send.*

I look at Leonid. He's buckling on an armored vest over a long-sleeve black-camo shirt. "I might have handled that wrong," I admit. "Those pills work pretty well, though."

"Keep a man going until he drops." He shoves two more blister packs in my direction. "Another round to keep in your pocket."

I check the labels. Just the pain med and the stimulant this time. "Thanks."

"If you're really going, than get out of the dress shirt. Put on some camouflage, and the vest too. Do it before Logan gets here. That way, if he shoots you, you might live."

Good advice.

I'm pretty battered though. My shoulders are messed up and the camo shirt is a pullover, not button-up. I need Leonid's help to get it on. The vest is easier. I'm standing by the table, adjusting the buckles, when Leonid's phone beeps.

He glances at it and presses a code. "They're at the gate."

It takes Logan twelve seconds to clear the courtyard. Hell, maybe he came over the wall. The door bursts open. He stomps in, fully rigged, carrying his HITR in two hands. I can't see his face behind the black shield of his visor, but I know it's him. Jaynie comes in behind him. Then Fadul and Tran.

"Close the door," Leonid says.

Tran closes it.

They all take off their helmets.

Logan's face is flushed and sweat-streaked. He's staring at me like I'm a ghost—a shockingly messed-up one. "*Jesus*, Shelley. Gen-com thinks you're dead. It's showing you as dead."

I tell him what I know, in the hoarse voice he couldn't hear by text message. "I got hacked, and then I couldn't log in anymore."

"Kanoa said they hanged you . . . from a bridge. And it's true, isn't it? You look like it. How the fuck are you still alive?"

"I think the bridge got blown up."

"Yeah. He said that too."

Tran is looking at me with an incredulous grin, like I've just been revealed as the secret civilian identity behind Bounce-back Man. "You're a fucking walk-on-water superstar!"

"Papa gave me magic pills. But we did not win this one. We fucked it up bad. How's Escamilla?"

"The navy's taking care of him," Fadul says, eyeing me cautiously, like she's not sure it's me. "That's all we know. Roman and Dunahee will be okay."

"And Flynn?" I ask, turning to Jaynie.

She's standing there, strapped into her dead sister, her helmet under her arm, studying me like maybe I'm a trick, an illusion, an anomaly that doesn't belong in the world. "Flynn will be okay. But I'm starting to think you can't ever die."

"Matter of time," I assure her.

Fadul puts her helmet on the table, walks up to me with her HITR slung on her shoulder. Walks right up to me. I'm getting ready to duck, because I'm sure she's going to throw a punch, but I'm wrong. She cups my face gently in her gloved hands and says, "You were supposed to keep up with us, Captain."

"I took a wrong turn."

"Didn't we all. Glad you're here, though." She steps back. "What are we after now?"

"Nashira."

"I didn't get a briefing on that."

"Neither did I," Logan says, stepping forward. "What the hell, Shelley?"

"Papa thinks I was supposed to go by myself, but that's not how we do things, and I don't think I could have made it there anyway."

"Where?"

I forward the briefing with the attached map to their overlays, saying, "Don't share this with gen-com." Abajian gets to see everything that goes through gen-com and I'm not ready to bring him all the way in on this yet.

They all get glazed looks as they scan the briefing. "I've seen that place," Fadul says.

Logan has too. "It's not far."

Tran eyes Jaynie. "You going to link Vasquez in on this?"

Jaynie looks at me, one eyebrow raised.

"Can't," I tell her. "You don't have an overlay."

Her voice is taut, expectant, when she asks, "So this is a rogue mission? To hit Nashira?"

"We don't do rogue missions," Fadul says. "This is straight from the boss. Right, Shelley?"

"Roger that."

Jaynie doesn't protest. She doesn't argue that we're overstepping our mission. Instead, she says, "You don't have to go dark. Abajian will back you on this."

It's not the response I expect, but it tells me a lot. It tells me that her sudden return to service is not all patriotism; that Jaynie is after something beyond the original target of our mission. It makes me uneasy, but I just tell myself, *Lock it down.*

"We need to do this before Abajian can fuck it up," I say. "Get your gear ready. We move in five."

"What is the plan?" Jaynie asks.

Logan says, "The plan is still being written. We'll get more information going forward—enough to successfully engage the target when we get there."

"Get where?"

"The vault that houses Nashira's core."

"So we have a target," Jaynie says, "but no plan. That makes me worry."

"There is a plan," Logan insists. "It just hasn't been issued yet."

"Need to know," Fadul says. She shrugs out of her pack and thumps it down on the table. "We'll know when we need to." She starts pulling out fresh ammo to load into her HITR. I pick up one of the Lashers to get it out of her way. It's new. The key is still hanging from the trigger guard. Fadul scowls at me as I use the key to reset the weapon's electronics. Then she turns to Logan. "Hey, LT."

He looks up from his own reloading operation while I register the Lasher to my biometrics. "What's up?"

"Why aren't we telling this idiot he has to sit this one out?"

Logan shakes his head. "Go ahead. Try it."

And Leonid snorts. "You will be wasting your time. He has his orders."

Fadul eyes me. "We don't need you. You are going to be a liability on this mission."

Fadul is no better at diplomacy than I am.

"I'm fine," I whisper. I toss the key into the corner of the room. I don't want it with me, because I don't want anyone else to be able to use the weapon. "Maybe not fine, but functional. Papa, do you have hand grenades?"

"No."

"Here." Fadul tosses me one. "If you're going to be stupid, have one on me."

I drop it in my pocket.

"Jaynie?"

She's getting her pack in order. "Yeah, Shelley?"

"Did Abajian talk to you about going after Nashira?"

She looks up, that eyebrow raised, an expression suggesting there is more, much more, than either of us is willing to say. "It's a target of interest."

Maybe it's the hurt I've taken, maybe it's the pills, but when she says that, doubt grabs me and I ask myself, *Was tonight's mission even real?* What if Abajian ran the whole bloody exercise as a setup—a way of exposing the presence and the influence of Nashira? And the people who died tonight? Were they just collateral damage on the way to cracking the cyber-camouflage of an L-AI?

Is Abajian that ruthless?

Have we been played?

I pull out a chair and sit, thinking, *Be calm. Lock it down.*

I look up at Jaynie to find her regarding me with a worried frown.

"What does Abajian want with Nashira?" I ask her.

"He wants to take it down. And then he wants to take down the Arctic AI."

FaceValue doesn't tag a lie, but there is more that she's not saying.

"Isn't that *your* goal, Shelley?"

"Yes."

ETM 7-1 has made a lot of mistakes lately—maybe because we were operating on faulty intelligence. We have to do better. Going after the L-AIs should help with that, help us get back on the right road, help us unwind the damage we've done.

"We are on the same side," I say.

"In most things."

"Mars is a mistake."

"We'll fight about that later."

I nod. "Who's still got explosives?"

Jaynie, Fadul, and Tran are all out of det cord. They used up their supply at the lab. But Logan digs into his pack and pulls out a couple meters of cord and a packet of C-4. "Might not be enough."

I turn to Leonid. He shakes his head. "No. No explosives. I was to help you get out of Basra, not help you to level the city."

"Give it to me," I tell Logan. "We'll make it work."

He hands over the packet. I put it in a deep pocket of my vest.

"We need to hook you back into gen-com," he says. "We need to be linked, and I can't stand looking at your dead black icon anymore."

He's right. It's an issue I would have addressed right away if I was thinking clearly. "Ask Kanoa—"

"Yeah, Kanoa says he's going to reinstall gen-com on your system—and he wants to see the order."

"Send it to him."

A tag slides open in my overlay, alerting me to the install.

"Are you really going in like that?" Tran wants to know. "No dead sister? No helmet? You're going to go down as soon as the shooting starts."

"Let's see what happens when we get there."

"How are you going to keep up?"

"I'm not. I'm going to split the squad, ride with Papa. Everyone else goes on foot." That will give me more flexibility in our approach, and time to consider what the hell we need to do. I look at Leonid to make sure he's okay with this, and get a confirming nod. It's Jaynie who objects.

"No, that's not going to work. We need to stay together. Either that or you come behind us, Shelley."

"This isn't going to be like the lab," I tell her. "I think the Red has isolated Nashira and taken control of the district. It's not going to be hard to get inside."

"What makes you so sure?"

"Because the Red wanted me to go there alone, with no weapons. How hard could it be?"

We just need to get in, find the vault, and blow it.

Easy.

"And if we move in two squads, one mounted and one on foot, odds go up that at least some of us will get there."

The update to gen-com completes and Kanoa checks in. "I thought we'd lost you this time, Shelley."

"Not quite. Did you get the mission briefing?"

"Roger that. It's confirmed—but Fadul is right. You need to sit this one out."

"You know I can't. The mission was given to me. That might not mean anything, but if it does, I need to be there."

He's quiet for several seconds. "I don't like the setup, Shelley. Feels like another look-and-see mission. Too many unknowns."

"We're supposed to do it," I remind him. "We got the order."

The Red issued this mission, but it's a mission that's being written as it's executed and that means it's going to be weakest in the last stage, the step where we get pulled out—the step that got missed during Arid Crossroad.

"You need to get us an extraction plan."

Kanoa tells me, "It's taken care of. Abajian has Black Hawks standing by."

I think I'd rather have the mercenaries. Abajian worries me. Jaynie agreed we're on the same side, but I'm not sure.

Still, by the time his helicopters reach us, we should be done.

I am officially given command of mission Kingmaker Prime in light of my "superior knowledge of the mission plan." In other words, Abajian doesn't want to risk getting cut out of this operation, so he'll do what he can to make me feel I'm in control. Jaynie goes along with it as if it was all a prearranged deal.

Leonid doesn't have grenades or explosives, but he has an angel, and that makes up for a lot. He gets it out of the back of the SUV, unfolds its meter-wide crescent wing, and launches it over the wall. He texts me the address. I share it with gen-com, and we all link in.

I check the time on my overlay. *0404.* Dawn is still two hours away. The dusty night sky is faintly luminous with the reflected glow of lights still on in distant quarters of the city.

Jaynie, Logan, Fadul, and Tran are all fully rigged, helmets on, HITRs in hand, waiting at the gate. Leonid gets behind the wheel of the SUV. In his right ear he's wearing an audio loop with a tiny mic that links him to gen-com, and he's got a map of where we're going on the dashboard navigation screen. I take the passenger seat, the Lasher 762 at my side.

"Okay," I say over gen-com. "The mission is to destroy Nashira. We want to collect as much intelligence as we can, but let's get the job done, fast and clean."

I get a whispered "*Hoo-yah!*"

Leonid triggers the gate to open. My squad slips out, bearing right. We roll out behind them, without headlights, turning left onto the dark deserted street. I look for my squad but I can't see them. They've vanished into the night. I shift to angel sight.

This is the way I'm used to operating, with a clear vision of the terrain around me. I look down on the neighborhood streets and inside the walled compounds. No one is in sight, and our SUV is the only vehicle moving on the residential streets. It surprises me. I didn't think a curfew could be this well respected.

Farther out, on a main avenue, I spot police cars, one stationed at every major intersection. I warn Leonid. He says, "We will stay on the small roads."

I look for the gunships that were hunting in the city earlier in the night, but the angel doesn't pick up any. Stranger than that, the angel fails to map any other aerial surveillance devices in the immediate area—no other drones and no seekers.

"Kanoa."

Several seconds of silence follow and I start to get concerned, but then he answers, "Here."

"Did Abajian pull his seekers?"

More seconds of silence, and then, "We've lost contact with them."

I look again at the streets around us. "Hey, the police cars are pulling out." It's an exodus, as if they've all been called back to the station at once. I count twelve cars crossing the canal, leaving this corner of the city unprotected—and just in time, because we've gone as far as we can on the neighborhood streets.

We enter a main road, swing around a traffic circle, and head south toward the low hill with the fortress mansion on top. It's an artificial hill, I'm sure of it, built to elevate a dragon's home. The angel flies over it.

"Anything?" Leonid asks.

"No. No one on the walls or in the courtyard. Maybe security is all electronic."

"Bad decision."

Delphi startles me by linking in. "Shelley."

Guilt hits. As my handler, Delphi saw me maimed and seemingly killed again and again and it tore her apart. That gave me one more reason to leave, because I knew it was inevitable that it would happen again, and I was right. I close the feed from the angel. The blood road is visible again, a faint red shimmer against the asphalt.

"Shelley, are you there?"

"I'm here." I want to ask her if she's doing okay, but a question like that has too many layers; now is not the time.

"Major Kanoa has cleared me to talk to you." She's using her stern handler's voice. "Back at Dassari when you would tell me you had a bad feeling, I learned to believe you. We know now that was the Red, warning you, but sometimes a feeling is just a feeling—and I've got a bad feeling about this mission."

I've never heard her talk like this before. I check the link. It's her, me, Kanoa. No one else. Not even Jaynie. "Tell me what you're thinking," I say.

Leonid looks at me, a questioning eyebrow raised. I tap my finger beside my eye. He nods, returning his gaze to the road.

"You said the Red assigned you this mission, assigned it only to you. You were alone, with no weapons and no explosives—and you weren't in any condition to fight and you still aren't. How were you supposed to carry it out, Shelley? How were you supposed to take down Nashira under those conditions?"

Power of God. That's what I'm thinking. *The Red will deliver this victory into my hands.* But that's bullshit.

"I don't know how it's going to work, Delphi. I'll know when I get there."

"You're too trusting, Shelley. There is something wrong with this setup. Critically wrong."

"Maybe. But even if there is, we have to do it. If Nashira is run by the same group behind the Arctic AI—"

"I understand your sense of responsibility for the Arctic War. And the potential intelligence gains are undeniable—but something is off. Don't assume anything going in—and don't trust the Red to keep you safe."

"I promise you that, at least."

"Okay. I'll be watching."

She closes the link. I lean back and close my eyes.

"Talk," Papa says.

I relay Delphi's suspicions. I have to assume Kanoa shares them, because he was linked in and listening. "I think you were right, Papa. This mission was given to me. Only to me. So let's skip the rendezvous. I want to reach the target ahead of the squad."

A dead sister helps a soldier on foot move quickly, but a vehicle on an open road is always going to be a lot faster. Leonid pushes us over sixty. We close rapidly on the target hill. Jaynie notices and tries to intercede. "Shelley, you are ahead of schedule—"

Kanoa comes in on my side, cutting her off. "Driveway on the right, one hundred sixty meters."

Leonid gets the update over his audio loop. "I see it."

"Ten meters in," Kanoa adds, "it's secured with a steel gate."

"The gate will open," I promise them.

Leonid keeps his eyes on the road. "You sure, King David?"

"Pretty sure." The place has been hacked. How else is this going to work? I trigger my window to go down, then I lean out with the Lasher, bracing myself with an elbow against the door.

Leonid steps on the brake, preparing to make the turn. The tires scream and smoke.

"The gate is opening," Kanoa says. "No other sign of activity."

We make a hard right onto a concrete driveway. The gate has rolled back, out of the way. There are no other defenses.

"Punch it," I tell Leonid.

The driveway climbs around the hill. He sends the SUV rocketing up its steep grade, the electric engine quiet, but the tire noise loud in the predawn hush. The house at the top is protected by its fortress wall, but on the way up, Kanoa says, "Now the next gate is opening. No other sign of activity."

I knew this would be easy.

The angel red-alerts. It's picked up suspicious movement to the southeast, in the direction of the Persian Gulf. I glimpse a text report indicating three gunships in the air— but the report gets wiped from my overlay. Delphi cuts in. "No threat. Supporting forces coming in."

"We don't need supporting forces. We just need to be extracted when this is done."

She doesn't answer.

We pass the second gate and enter a wide, tiled court-yard surrounding a mansion three stories high. To the right of the mansion's front door is a window wall of one-way black glass that wraps around the corner of the house and reaches all the way to the roof.

There are still no defenses; no enemy is present; not a shot is fired at us.

In the Bible, when David got called out alone to the bat-tlefield, he stood in front of a warrior of giant reputation, but I'm not required to do even that. I could have walked here alone and still triumphed. The Red planned it that way, it prepared the way for me, but I refused to take it on faith—not for the first time.

James Shelley: nonbeliever.

It's because I refused to do what I was told to do that I'm walking on artificial legs.

We drive across the courtyard and stop fifteen meters from the house. I open the car door just as Abajian breaks into gen-com. "Captain Shelley, this has gone far enough. You will stay where you are. Do *not* enter the building."

Leonid hears the order over his audio loop and pauses, his own door partly open. He gives me a questioning look.

Off-com, I tell him, "You should stay here."

This gets me an annoyed *tsk*. "I have made my bet. Let's go."

He slides out. I do too.

Colonel Abajian is not my commanding officer. It's tempting to tell him to get the fuck away from my mission—but I'm not a jacked-up lieutenant anymore and I'm relying on him to extract us. So I go for the diplomatic approach. "The mission is clear, sir." The blood road glimmers beneath my feet, crossing the tiled courtyard to the mansion's front doors. "I am required to enter the building."

"Captain, you have no idea what's at stake. Do *not* approach. A team of specialists is on the way and will be taking over."

I don't have time to argue. My soldiers are moving fast. The squad map shows them less than five minutes away— and I need to know what we're walking into before they get here. Delphi thinks something is off in this mission, that it's not as straightforward as it seems. If that's true, I can back out. I took the receiver out of my head so the Red can't compel me to complete the mission. But Logan, Fadul, and Tran are all still vulnerable. They will get here before Abajian's team. So I need to know.

Lasher in hand, I follow the gleam of the blood road toward the mansion's front doors—big copper double doors with a raised abstract design. Leonid parallels me a few meters to my left, his weapon held in two hands, ready to use.

"Captain Shelley, you will stand down! It was your rogue action that ignited the Arctic War. What we recover inside that building could neutralize that mistake. It could expose our hidden enemies. But not if you destroy Nashira. Destroy it and we have nothing."

"Sir, I will gather what intelligence I can, but the goal of this mission *is* to destroy Nashira."

"I am revising that goal. For our own national security, we must recover the L-AI. Your orders are to hold the site, allow no one to enter pending the arrival—"

I drop out of gen-com.

Back in the hospital in Budapest, Issam tried to explain to me about the L-AIs. *They're like the microbeads in your brain. They can change the personality and affect the goals of the Red.*

Of course Abajian wants to capture Nashira and take control of that technology, because if you can manipulate the Red, eventually you'll own the world.

Leonid was right. I should have done the mission myself.

Another mistake, but it's not too late. I grasp the grandly exaggerated rectangle of the door handle.

"Be cautious, Shelley," Leonid growls.

There is no time for caution. Already I hear the background growl of a small fleet of helicopters flying in from the gulf. I wonder if the Iraqi Army will object to this incursion . . . but Abajian would have taken care of that contingency. He will have already cut a deal.

I pull the door open. It's not locked. I knew it wouldn't be.

Inside, it's dark. I can see out through the window wall to the courtyard, but inside, the only thing I can see is the glimmering of the blood road. I can't hear anything either, not even the hum of appliances, and there's a stale

smell to the air the way a closed room gets when the
air-conditioning is off.

I get out the digital night vision glasses Leonid gave
me and put them on. They reveal a dragon's living room:
couches and chairs, side tables and flower arrangements.
"Whoever was here, I think they pulled out as soon as they
got word of our raid."

Leonid looks around through his own D-NVGs. "Yes.
It feels empty."

Standard procedure would be to clear this floor before
doing anything else, but there's no time. So I go where I'm
directed, across the living room to a wide flight of stairs,
open on both sides, that climbs to the second floor. Leonid
can't see the blood road, so he follows me.

We're ascending the stairs when I get a link request.
"*Karin Larsen*," my overlay's voice announces.

"Papa, I'm going to pick up an outside link."

"Who?"

"Delphi." I link in, "Is Abajian standing over your shoulder?"

She sounds frightened: "No. I'm outside. Let me see
what you see."

I trust Delphi. So I link her my video feed.

She doesn't say anything as she studies the terrain,
though I can hear her nervous breathing. There is a sitting
room at the top of the stairs, and doors that probably open
onto bedrooms and playrooms, but the air here is as stale
as it is downstairs; the house is silent.

I turn to climb the next flight of stairs, which rises in
the opposite direction, with the window wall on one side.
Leonid follows, several steps behind.

"How do you know where to go?" Delphi asks.

"It's a projected path."

"Do you have a seeker?"

"No."

"*Shit.*"

Delphi rarely uses profanity.

"I need more data," she whispers. "I feel like I've lost half my senses."

"Yeah."

An LCS helmet can detect EM fields and filter faint audio signals. A seeker can detect the chemical signature of explosives, and of course we could send it ahead to collect an advance view of what we're facing—but we have to get by without any of that. There aren't even muzzle cams on the Lasher I'm carrying.

"I want you to slow down," she says.

"We don't have time. I need to know what's here."

The third floor is different from the other two because it's only a partial floor. The curved window wall is met by a wall of flat glass with a sliding door that opens onto a rooftop deck painted with lines that mark it as a helipad. There are no furnishings, just a smooth marble floor. I cross the floor to the window wall. Look three stories down to the courtyard where the gate stands open to the driveway. I can't see the squad from here, but I know they're just a few minutes away.

"Turn around," Delphi says. "Let me see what's behind you."

I do.

A rail encloses the stairwell. Beyond the rail is a concrete wall with a steel door. The blood road leads right up to that door. I sure as fuck hope it's got an electronic lock and that the Red has hacked it, because otherwise it's going to take all of the C-4 I'm carrying just to blow that door open.

"That's where I'm going," I tell Delphi. And to Leonid I say, "Through that door."

He moves toward it, but I put a hand out to stop him. "Let me go first."

"*Wait*," Delphi says. "Both of you. Let's think about this for a minute—"

"We don't have a minute."

"—because something else is going on."

Leonid moves to the glass wall that looks out on the helipad. "Black Hawks are four minutes away, no more."

"Delphi, we need to move now. I know the setup feels wrong, but that's because it's easy. And it's easy because the mission was set up for me: get in, set the charges, check for any obvious intelligence assets, and then get out. I need to get it done before those Black Hawks get here."

"But that was *not* your assignment," she argues. "You were supposed to come here alone. No weapons, no explosives. Let's say it happened that way. What could you have done?"

"I was probably supposed to pick up explosives on the way."

"That's tenuous. You can't assume it. I've seen the order. Major Kanoa showed it to me. You were to destroy Nashira. Not locate it, or document it, or collect intelligence. Simply destroy it. How? How, if you were here alone? What would you do? What *could* you do?"

I glance at angel sight. It shows me the squad already at the lower gate. They're not even maintaining interval, while the rumble of the Black Hawks has grown audible even past the heavy glass. What could I have done? I put myself in that alternate timeline and the answer is easy: *Only what I am doing.*

"I have to go in that room to find out," I tell her. "All I know is that the Red would not have sent me here unless . . ."

I catch myself as I recognize the fallacy in my own thinking. "Ah, *shit*, Delphi—unless a means to accomplish the mission was already in place. Papa!" He's eyeing me with a tense expression. "We need to get the fuck out of here."

"What have you found?"

"This place is booby-trapped. It has to be."

We *always* assume booby traps when we find sites abandoned by the enemy, but I didn't think about it at all this time because I knew the Red had prepared the way; it saved my life at the canal so it could lead me here; the blood road gleamed under my feet; I am a soldier of the Red and we are on the same fucking side.

But in the calculations of the Red, the success of this mission must count for more than my survival.

Never trust the Red.

"Get *out*," Delphi says.

But Leonid wants to know more. "Do you see a wire?"

"No. It'll be on the other side of that door. Or the trigger could be a motion sensor."

"If it was a motion sensor, we would have set it off." He walks toward the steel door.

"Goddamn it, Papa!" I can't help myself. I back away until I'm against the window wall. I bump up against it and motion catches my eye. I glance down to see Abajian's hellhound, trotting in past the gate. "Delphi, can that thing get in here?"

"No. It can't pull the front door open."

Leonid has reached the steel door. He crouches to study the latch. Then he looks over his shoulder at me. "You are right. Come. Record this. And the next time you trust the will of your god, remember this moment."

"Don't do it," Delphi says. "Just get downstairs and get out."

I want to get out. My heart is hammering. I'm breathing hard. But I tell myself, *Lock it down*, and I do what Leonid says. I cross the room to the steel door and record the glint of a freshly cut wire just visible twelve inches below the latch, light green in night vision. "Delphi, send that to Abajian." His people will be here soon. They need to know the risk.

"Roger that. Now *get out!*"

It's like Leonid hears her. He's made his point. Now we move together back toward the front of the room. But while Leonid turns to head down the stairs, I detour to the window, worried about the hellhound, which Abajian's people control.

"What are you doing, Shelley?" Delphi pleads. "Get downstairs."

"Where's the hellhound?"

While I wait for her to answer, I fish out the second round of pills Leonid gave me. I got a feeling, a bad feeling, so I dry-swallow them, just in case.

Delphi comes back after half a minute, sounding puzzled. "I don't know where it is. Just go."

Out past the open courtyard gate, I see Jaynie coming up the driveway, with Logan fifteen meters behind her. I log back into gen-com. The squad map confirms Fadul and Tran close behind.

Logan sees my icon and pulls up. "Shelley, sitrep!" he demands as Fadul, and then Tran, bunch up behind him. "Where the hell did you go?"

"Stay where you are," I tell them in my whispery voice. "Everyone, stay put. Do not proceed." Jaynie is well ahead of them now, but she stops just outside the gate. I say, "There's a tripwire set to go off when the vault door is opened. Destroy Nashira, right? That was the order. I was supposed to open that door."

"Ah, *shit*," Logan says.

"Abajian can have whatever is in there," I tell them, "because we are not suicide jihadi."

I turn to follow Leonid down the stairs—but Fadul's voice stops me: "Find another way to get it done, Shelley." It's a soft-spoken threat that makes me look outside again. She's still holding her position behind Logan, but Jaynie has started to advance.

"Jaynie! Stay where you are. That is an order."

Jaynie ignores me. She slips past the gate, while Fadul argues. "We have a mission, Captain."

"The mission is bullshit."

"That's not your call." She tries to step past Logan. He gets in her way.

"Stand down, Fadul," he warns.

Fadul says, "Looks like Vasquez has her own mission."

It does look that way. Jaynie is moving swiftly across the courtyard, passing the SUV, heading for the front door.

"Shit, get down!" Fadul shouts. Tran dives for the ground, while Fadul drops to one knee, bringing her HITR to her shoulder.

"Fadul, no!" I plead, sure that she's targeting Jaynie. But I'm wrong.

Fadul fires her HITR simultaneously with a muzzle flash that blazes from beneath the SUV. The fucking hellhound must be under there. It has to be. Lying in wait beneath the vehicle, out of angel sight because Abajian has decided we are the enemy and he's launched an ambush of my squad.

Jaynie breaks her silence. "Who is running that thing?" she yells over gen-com. "Shut it down! Shut it down!"

It's Fadul who shuts it down. Abajian's hellhound gets off only six rounds before she sends two grenades rocketing in under the SUV. The double blast bucks the vehicle and shoots a 360-degree circle of flame out from under it.

I check Jaynie's icon. She must have found cover from the shrapnel, because she's still green. But Logan is hit. I see him on the ground, while in my overlay, his icon goes yellow, then red. Tran scrambles to his side, his pack already halfway off so he can get to his first aid kit.

The rumble of the Black Hawks jumps to a higher decibel as someone opens the front door. At first, I think Jaynie has come inside. But then I see Leonid leaving the house. He circles wide around the burning SUV and then takes off across the courtyard in his fast, lumbering stride, heading for the gate, shouting at Tran to get the first aid kit ready.

"Kanoa!" With my ruined voice, it's just an urgent whisper. "Who gave the order for the hellhound to shoot? Was it Abajian?"

Kanoa doesn't answer.

Delphi says, "Abajian must have locked him out. What you need to do is get out of that house."

"No. I need to know if Abajian is planning to gun us down when those Black Hawks get here."

Her voice is trembling when she answers. "I'm going back inside. See what I can do."

Our link closes.

Outside, Tran starts working on Logan, while Fadul heads alone for the courtyard.

"Fadul," I tell her, "stay with Tran. Don't make yourself a target by coming in here."

"Can't do it, Shelley."

Leonid has made it across the courtyard. He intercepts her at the gate, grabs her arm strut, says something to her off-com. She jerks her arm away, but she half turns to watch him as he moves on to crouch beside Logan, lending what help he can while Tran tries to staunch the bleeding.

For a few seconds, I let myself hope that she'll go back to help—but that's not in the program. She passes the gate.

"Fadul!" Jaynie barks over gen-com. "You will stand down. Go back outside the gate and stay there."

Fadul hesitates, taking a cautious look around the courtyard. "Abajian give you special orders, Vasquez?" she asks.
"You supposed to gun me down next?"

"That wasn't my call," Jaynie answers. "And I don't want
to hurt you."

"I don't want to hurt you either, sister. I respect you. But
you need to stay out of my way."

I hear in these words the same hell-bound determination that was in my own voice when I asked Leonid,
Who said I'm not willing? I can't doubt it anymore. Fadul
is operating and she will do what it takes to carry out
the mission.

I turn and bolt for the stairs. I've got no plan in mind,
but the pills are kicking in and I tell myself there has to be a
way to keep Fadul from killing herself or killing Jaynie—but
then Fadul shouts a warning that freezes me at the top of
the stairs. "Heads up, Shelley! Vasquez is coming after you."

No real allies, I think. No fixed enemies.

The rumble of the Black Hawks is mixed with a roar of
fire from the burning SUV, white noise that doesn't quite
cover the urgent footfalls of a dead sister racing up the
stairs.

I bring up my Lasher, ready to defend myself as Jaynie
bounds to a stop on the landing below me. The black shield
of her visor looks up at me, but she keeps the muzzle of her
HITR trained on the floor. She says off-com, "I don't want
to play this game, Shelley. Let's go outside before one of us
gets hurt."

I go off-com too. "Goddamn it, Jaynie! Is Fadul right?
Are you working for Abajian? Because Logan is dying out
there and fucking Abajian ordered that!"

I'm talking fast, holding down the trigger on my words,
determined to have it out. Last chance.

"That shouldn't have happened," Jaynie says. "But don't

make it worse. I've got orders to protect the vault, and if you can't rein in Fadul—"

"Why are you here, Jaynie? What did Abajian promise you? Did he promise you he'd get control of the Red?"

"Isn't that what the L-AIs are for? But it wasn't Abajian. This is Monteiro's operation. She wanted you on this mission because she wanted you to bring the Red. Let it find Nashira for us. You did that. Now you need to step aside."

Yeah, I thought it might be that way. And Monteiro got all the data from the lab too. I have to admit, it was a master play. "What did you get out of the deal?" I ask again.

"She said if I recruit you for this mission, she lifts the restrictions on the Mars project."

Mars again?

"*Fuck* Mars! Why are you so goddamned eager to leave us, anyway?"

"You got no right to ask me that."

"Tell me anyway."

"I just want it. I want to be the first. Come from nowhere. Claim a new world. That so hard to understand?"

"There's no coming back from it, Jaynie. Never."

"There's no coming back from anything, Shelley. That's how life is. We got only one way to go."

That's not an answer—at least, it's not the one I want to hear. But it's all I'm going to get in these seconds given to us, borrowed time.

I lower the muzzle of my weapon and trot down the stairs. "All right. Let's go. But you need to help me with Fadul. I don't want her hurt, but she's operating."

"What does that mean?"

"She's been given the mission that was meant for me—and she's willing to do whatever it takes to get it done."

"You mean the Red is running her like a puppet."

"Yes."

I reach the landing just in time for a flash-bang to go off at my feet.

I'm down on my back, looking up the stairs to the third floor. Not sure I ever want to get up again. My ears are ringing, my chest aching—hell, everything hurts all over again—my eyes are dazzled, my D-NVGs are askew on my face, and those pills have got my heart racing so fast I think I'm going to have a heart attack.

"You're supposed to wear your helmet," Fadul says as she bounds up from the first floor. She's speaking on gen-com, so her voice reaches me through my earbuds. I couldn't hear her otherwise, not with the roar of the Black Hawks. Even so, her voice is muffled and reverberant. I wonder if my ears are bleeding.

I turn my head. Jaynie's nowhere in sight. I reach for my Lasher. Fadul kicks it away. "You talked yourself out of the mission, Shelley. I'm not sure whose side you're on."

She pauses just long enough to reach into my vest pocket and retrieve the fragmentation grenade she gave me. "Just in case," she says. As she pockets it, she fires her HITR one-handed, launching a grenade straight into the window wall. The shock wave blasts past us as glass sprays out across the courtyard.

I cringe, sure that a bigger explosion will follow. But it doesn't.

"Vasquez," Fadul warns over gen-com, "that's to let you know I'm serious. I reloaded on the way in. I've got two more rounds. And you do not want to be up there, ground zero, when those charges go off. You got five seconds to clear out."

"Goddamn it, Fadul," I rasp. I grab her leg strut to help me sit up. Looking up at her from the floor, she's fucking intimidating, rigged out when I'm not. "You don't think this whole building is going to come down when you set those charges off?"

"Maybe," she concedes. "But I'm not leaving this for Abajian's crew. Our job is to make sure everyone is visible, everyone accountable. And Monteiro is not going to be visible or accountable when she sets up her own L-AIs. So get the fuck out of here, and I'll be—"

She twists around, bringing her HITR up to shoot at something overhead. I don't bother to look. There's only one thing up there that could threaten the mission. The bullshit mission.

I throw all my weight against the strut I'm holding and yank Fadul's foot out from under her. I don't want her hurt. I don't want Jaynie hurt either. I just want this to fucking stop.

Fadul goes down on her back as incoming rounds stitch the air. They plow into her shoulder and chew through the stairs above her head while her HITR punches a similar line of holes in the ceiling. The hammering crack of her weapon is about to split my skull open, but I move anyway I throw myself over her, hoping Jaynie won't shoot through me. As I do it, I grab for Fadul's HITR—one hand on the stock, one on the burning barrel. The weapon is slick with blood.

Jaynie doesn't shoot. She drops over the stairwell railing, bouncing hard on her shocks as she comes down with one foot on the landing, the other on the bottom step.

I try to twist the HITR out of Fadul's grip. She's hurting, but she holds on. Her synthetic voice speaks in my head. *Don't make me kill you.* She could kill me easily if she let go of her HITR. One blow with her arm strut and she could break my skull.

Jaynie intercedes. Calm and determined, she shoves the muzzle of her own HITR past my head, jamming it into Fadul's throat. "Drop it."

I flinch as gunfire erupts. But Fadul's life doesn't blow up in my face. It's Jaynie who's hit. Her HITR tumbles. Her icon shifts from green to yellow. I turn my head, and in disbelief, I see her crumpled on the floor.

I wrench the HITR out of Fadul's weakening grip and pitch it down the stairwell, almost hitting Tran, who's charging to the rescue with his own HITR in hand.

"You shot her!" I yell at him. "Goddamn it, we promised not to shoot each other."

"I had to do it, Shelley! Fadul needed help!"

We both turn to see Fadul with an arm hook on the railing. She heaves herself up. She's not in good shape. Her icon is past yellow, on its way to red. Blood soaks her sleeve, drips from her fingers, bubbles pale green in night vision from her nose—but she's operating. She is not thinking about her life bleeding away, only about the mission: *destroy Nashira.*

I'm thinking I don't want her to die.

I lunge for her again, but this time I get a footplate in the chest. It's a gentle shove that knocks the wind out of me and sends me hurtling back against Tran. I waste seconds trying to breathe, while Fadul turns to look up the stairway.

The dirty air over the city has been set aglow by a fiery light that shimmers in the facets of the shattered window wall as they tremble in a storm front of roaring engines.

I don't want anyone else to die. But the Black Hawks are here.

Fadul, it's too late. They'll kill you before you reach that door.

Her synthetic voice comes back to me. *Don't need to reach it.*

She's right. She doesn't have her HITR anymore, but she's got my fragmentation grenade.

She starts up the stairs, slowly. I don't think she could make it on her own, but she's powered by her dead sister.

I turn to Tran. "Take care of Vasquez. Get her out of here. And don't come back inside."

"But Fadul needs help!"

"I'll help Fadul. You get Vasquez out of here. And shut down your overlay. Keep the Red out of your head before you kill us all. That is an order!"

I leave Tran and sprint after Fadul, propelled by the tireless gray bones of my artificial legs.

It really is too late.

On the third floor, chunks of glass are tumbling in a hurricane breeze as the first of the Black Hawks roars in to circle the building. All lights are off on the craft, but night vision reveals the gunner in his window, sitting behind the machine gun. His orders will be the same as Jaynie's: protect the vault, don't let anyone near it. Because Abajian has a duty to deliver this site intact to the intelligence team.

Fadul knows this. At the top of the stairs, she reaches for the pin on the fragmentation grenade. If she can heave the grenade across the room, get it close to the steel door, the concussion should set off the rigged explosives—and it's my bet that will bring the whole house down, along with the circling Black Hawk.

But that's not going to happen. The rocket-fuel stimulant Leonid gave me has got me cranked up to a giddy superhero optimism and I am determined that this bullshit mission is not going to take anyone else's life.

I kick off the last stair, jumping to tackle Fadul, to get her down under the sweep of the machine gun. I hit her high and hard, all my weight on her shoulders. She's not expecting it. Her weakened grip can't hold the grenade. It's gone from her hand, bouncing out the shattered window wall. Her knees bend under my weight. The rig enhances the motion, and we are falling to the floor.

It's a fucking long way down.

On the way, the machine gun lights up in a storm of muzzle flash and thunder. The last remains of the glass wall transform into a fall of hard rain. And we hit.

I lose my grip on Fadul. Cubes of glass grind under my shoulder. I must have lost my D-NVGs because it's fucking dark. I can taste blood. I can hear someone breathing in short, sharp gasps. I think it's me.

Fadul is close beside me. I feel her stir.

Stay down, I tell her. A Black Hawk is on the helipad. *It's over.*

She gives up, goes quiet—and that's not like her.

I scan the squad icons in my overlay. Tran is our superhero: He's the only one still green. And he's not operating. I know, because the map shows him safe outside with Jaynie. I have to believe he listened to me, that he shut his overlay down.

Jaynie's icon is yellow. I tell myself she'll be okay and maybe someday she really will get to go to Mars.

The red icons worry me. I know Papa is with Logan, getting him stabilized. But shadows are creeping across Fadul's icon; I think she's bleeding out. And there's a third red icon. That one is mine.

Over gen-com I hear Tran pleading, "Kanoa! Abajian! Whoever's monitoring this network—we need medics upstairs! *Now!*"

I appreciate Tran's concern, but he needs to understand that Abajian has a bomb to disarm.

Fadul was right, though. I talked myself out of the mission. It *was* a bullshit mission. But there would have been a lot less trouble all around if I had just opened that door.

Shadows move in the night, vaguely human-shaped. There's a roar of wind or engines.

That's all I've got.

INVOLUNTARY
SEPARATION

EVERYONE VISIBLE, EVERYONE ACCOUNTABLE.

That's what I'm thinking as I wake up, and it's like despair is eating me from the inside out because I know after the disaster in Basra we are farther than ever from the goal. I was assigned to destroy Nashira, but Abajian was out to capture it, and I let Abajian win. Who knows what atrocities he'll be hiding behind the screen of a well taught I-AI?

And then, for just a few seconds, I'm mad as hell. *Why the fuck am I still alive?*

How many lives do I have to burn through?

"Shelley," Delphi says, "can you hear me?"

I blink my eyes, feeling hollowed out and dark inside. What the fuck is wrong with me?

Lock it down!

That's what I think. It's an instruction to my skullnet, but the calm and the control that I expect don't come.

"Shelley," Delphi whispers, "look at me."

I do. I have to blink a few times to bring her eyes into focus. She's leaning over the side of my hospital bed, a worry crease in her pretty forehead. "Welcome back," she whispers.

My mouth is dry, but I'm close to panic, so I make myself talk. "My skullnet's not working."

It's not Delphi who answers me. It's my dad. "I had the surgeons take it out."

I turn my head, stunned to see him standing on the other side of the bed. He looks different than I remember. Older, grayer, but more determined, if that's possible. And then anger hits. He had no right to make that decision for me; that's what I'm thinking. He must have used an old power of attorney to have it done. He puts his hand on my shoulder. "You'll be okay," he assures me.

Delphi backs him up. "Vasquez learned to go without the hardware," she says. "You can too."

I'm in no position to fight it. Not now. And there are other things I need to know. "Is Jaynie okay?"

"Yes. She's back in San Antonio. She'll be fine."

"And Fadul?" I whisper. "Escamilla? Logan? Are they alive?"

"They were medevac'd," Delphi tells me. "That's all I know. Abajian locked me out of the operation."

"I need to see Kanoa!"

I try to sit up, but my dad squeezes my shoulder, just hard enough to let me know I'm not going anywhere. "It's over, Jimmy. It's not your battle anymore. You're retired."

Time goes by and my injuries heal. I get my head straight. More or less.

I'm seeing a shrink, who prescribes measured doses of crude medications. I keep telling him that a skullnet would fix all my issues. He tells me I'm a civilian now and a skullnet would be illegal.

It's a selective appreciation of the law. Despite everything I've done, the FBI leaves me alone. No one accuses

me of murder or insurrection or illegal weapons posses-
sion.

It's good to be a war hero.

Or maybe this is just Monteiro's way of saying thank
you for delivering Nashira into her hands.

It's been four months since Basra, but I've never had
a word or a message from Kanoa and I still don't know if
Logan and Fadul got out alive. Delphi warns me I might
never know. Leonid has disappeared too. I used to call him
every few days, but he never picked up, and around the
end of March, I stopped trying.

I'm not alone, though—not yet.

"Hey," Delphi says, coming into the living room of the
apartment we share. It's a beautiful afternoon in mid-May
and I'm waiting for her by the window, gazing down on
the street from twenty-eight stories up. She studies me for
a few seconds, a little furrow of concern in her forehead.
Then she remembers herself and smiles. "Vasquez is going
to want to know why you didn't come."

She's got a small suitcase in her hand. I take it from her,
give her a kiss, and say, "You're a beautiful liar."

She's flying to San Antonio. It's a regular thing. She goes
at least once a month on company business. A few weeks
ago, I went with her. Jaynie had decided to marry one of
her rocket scientists, so we went for the ceremony. He's a
nice enough guy, I guess.

It was the first time Jaynie and I had spoken since Basra.
Neither of us wanted to talk about the past and we'll have
nothing between us in the future, so that didn't leave us
much to say. I think we were both relieved when I got back
on the plane to New York.

I walk Delphi to the door. I put my arm around her
shoulder while we ride down together in the elevator. I
know it's irrational, but every time she goes I worry she

won't be back. She senses my disquiet, but Delphi is a stern woman and instead of offering reassurance, she drops into handler mode. "Don't forget, you're having dinner with your dad tonight."

She likes to hand me off to my dad when she goes out of town. I tell her, "My phone will remind me."

"Assuming you remember to carry your phone."

I frown and reach into my pocket to make sure it's there. "I've got it."

A phone is such fucking primitive technology, but that's what I use these days. No overlay for me, no farsights. My dad wasn't satisfied with stripping out my hardware. I was still high on pain meds when he coerced me into an idiot promise to go without augmentation for a year. I'm already counting the days until that's over.

Just before we reach the lobby, I lean over and kiss Delphi again. "Come back," I tell her.

She rolls her eyes. "You know I'm coming back."

I kiss her again. I don't know what she sees in me, except we're veterans together. We understand each other. But her name is still on the Mars crew list for a scheduled launch that's only fifteen months away.

We don't talk much about that. She needs to make her own decision, but I'm hoping she gives up her slot. Whatever she decides, I won't be going. I can't, even if I wanted to, even if there was room. I took a psych test to prove it to her. My shrink can't fix all the scars knotted in my brain. But I'm okay with it. I've fought too hard for this world to abandon it now.

Delphi has a car scheduled to pick her up. It arrives as we reach the sidewalk. I put her suitcase in the trunk, then open the door for her. She looks up at me, concern in those bright blue eyes. "Are you going to be okay, Shelley?"

I fake a smile. "Roger that."

After she's gone, I go for a walk. My celebrity is faded, my image is still scrubbed from most public databases, and I've gotten in the habit of wearing shoes when I go out, to camouflage who I am, so I'm rarely stopped—and walking gives me something to do. The sun is warm this afternoon, the air is cool, the trees are green, and flowers are blooming in the concrete barricades that guard the buildings. This is a resilient city, slowly regaining the energy it lost after Coma Day.

I walk until I wind up at my usual haunt: an open-air table in a café close to Battery Park, where I sit with a glass of fortified water and puzzle over the question of what the fuck the rest of my life is for.

It's my habit to watch everything around me. I've been in too many hostile situations to ever completely relax when I'm out in the world. So I notice him as soon as he presents himself to the maître d'. Granted, Leonid Sergun is a big man and hard to miss.

He looks across the patio, right at me. It's the first time I've seen him wearing farsights. As soon as he spots me, he slips them off, stashing them in an inner pocket of his coat. He smiles a charming smile at the maître d' and then weaves his way through the tables.

Leonid comes dressed like the wealthy man he is, in designer casuals topped with a charcoal-colored coat made of a burnished fabric intended to discourage passive scanning. His hair is freshly cut, his fingernails manicured.

"Where the hell have you been?" I ask him as he pulls out a chair.

"Business, my friend," he says, sitting down. "There is always business."

"You couldn't answer the goddamn phone?"

The café chair creaks as he leans back. He crosses his arms over his chest. "You must know Abajian has people watching you."

I shrug. How could it be otherwise?

"The colonel wasn't so confident he could keep eyes on me once I left his guest quarters."

"You're saying it took time to persuade him?"

Leonid nods. I imagine him talking his way out of a dark-site detention facility—and I can't help but smile in admiration. "You're a wizard of the dark arts, Papa."

"I debated coming to see you," he tells me. "But I was certain you would want to know."

I look away as my heart quickens; heat flushes from my pores. I think I know what he's going to say. "Fadul?" I ask tentatively, remembering her icon stained with black shadows.

Against all expectation, he tells me, "Fadul will be fine. You saved her life, Shelley. Her life, and Tran's, and Captain Vasquez's, and, I suspect, mine. No part of that house would have been left standing if the explosives had gone off."

So there's that. I'm stunned. Pleased. I ask him, "Is she still with ETM 7-1?"

"This is what I am told. And your friend Escamilla, as well."

I'm relieved to know Escamilla survived, but there is one other name Leonid hasn't mentioned. I steel myself and ask, "What about Logan?"

"I am sorry. It was a long struggle for Logan, one that he lost just a few days ago."

Shit.

I've got no words.

A waitress stops by the table to deliver a tall iced coffee and a sugary pastry to Leonid.

If I had accepted the mission I was given and opened that door, Logan would still be alive.

"You cannot blame yourself," Leonid says, reading my mind.

I shrug. "We lost the war."

"It could have been worse," he tells me. "At least your President Monteiro won."

It's true. Things could have been worse.

I don't know how much of the credit belongs to Monteiro, but peace has been breaking out all over. The Arctic War faded before spring. Tempers cooled in the nascent conflict between India and Pakistan. The city of Basra has been quiet since the anomalous incident in January. And while the fallout from Broken Sky continues to threaten a host of LEO satellites, at least there is now a well-funded global consortium tasked with developing a means to confront the problem of orbital debris.

History suggests this is only a respite. Monteiro captured the technology behind L-AIs, but how long before she oversteps? How long before the Red sees through it and sends someone to unbalance her plans? It's not easy to tie down a Titan. That should scare me, but it doesn't. Like an enemy once said, we've always lived with the Devil. So what?

We'll adapt.

I take a few moments to regroup, to gather my courage, and then we go on to talk of other things. Leonid tells me of his nephews and his hopes for their futures. I tell him of Delphi. I have hopes too. Maybe neither of us has the right to hope for anything, but hell, we're only human.

So do I regret what I've done?

I regret the need for it. Is that enough?

I wanted to serve. I wanted to be the good guy, to do the right thing. But how do you know if the sacrifices you're asked to make are worthwhile? If the blood on your hands means something? You don't know. You can't. That's the soldier's dilemma. What it comes down to is trust. Do you trust those who send you into battle?

In the end, Leonid lifts a fresh glass of iced coffee. "To those we have lost," he says.

I touch my glass to his. "Never forgotten."

He uses his phone to settle the bill, adding a generous tip, and we walk out together.

ACKNOWLEDGMENTS

Thanks go first to my agent, Howard Morhaim, for encouraging me to take the Red Trilogy to the next level, to Michael Prevett who saw the potential, and to Joe Monti at Saga Press for daring to take these books on.

I also want to acknowledge and thank those who helped specifically with *Going Dark*. People kind enough to answer random questions that appeared in their inboxes include Ilona Andrews, Amy Sterling Casil, Wil McCarthy, Jesse Reyna, Deborah J. Ross, and Edward A. White. Judith Tarr helped me to get an early version of this novel into shape, Edward A. White and Jeffrey A. Carver provided additional feedback as beta readers, while Joe Monti furnished essential editorial insights. And as always, I want to thank my husband, Ronald J. Nagata, Sr., for putting up with me and making my writing possible.

Last but certainly not least, I'm grateful to everyone who's taken the time to read my books and stories. This series exists because of your support and encouragement. Thank you all for coming along for the ride!

If you enjoyed the Red Trilogy, please consider reviewing the books at a blog or an online bookseller, or mention them on your favorite social media. To be notified of my latest books and stories, please visit my website at MythicIsland.com and sign up to receive my occasional newsletter.

Linda Nagata, June 2015

ABOUT THE AUTHOR

Linda Nagata is the author of many novels and short stories, including The Bohr Maker, winner of the Locus Award for best first novel, and the novella "Goddesses," the first online publication to receive a Nebula Award. The Red: First Light was a finalist for best novel for both the Nebula and John W. Campbell Awards. She lives with her husband in their longtime home on the island of Maui. Visit her at MythicIsland.com.